TOUCHED BY THE WILD

BY

LAZETTE GIFFORD

Copyright © 2020 Lazette Gifford
ISBN: 978-1-936507-90-0
An ACOA Publication
www.aconspiracyofauthors.com

Touched by the Wild
A Conspiracy of Authors Publication
www.aconspiracyofauthors.com
Copyright © 2020, Lazette Gifford
ISBN: 978-1-936507-90-0
Cover Art Design: Copyright © 2020, Lazette Gifford
Starling: Design Cuts/Eclectic Anthology (Birds of a Feather Watercolors)
Flower Alphabet: Design Cuts/Eclectic Anthology (Enchanted Florals)
Interior Art:
Flowers -- Design Cuts/Vector Hut (The Handcrafted Florals Collection-Part 1)
Birds -- Design Cuts/Feingold (Sky Builder for Photoshop)

First Print Edition, January 2020

I dedicate this book to everyone hoping for good luck in 2020 and beyond -- and especially to all my writer friends who give us such joy with their imaginations.

TABLE OF CONTENTS

Chapter One

P ale mist held tenaciously to the ancient gnarled limbs and bright autumn leaves of chestnut oak and sugar maples along the trail. The dampness occasionally collected into small pools on the leaves, and then dropped an icy cascade of water, splashing down on the weary men and horses. The small party rode on, traversing the quiet woods through the damp morning and into the sodden afternoon.

The inclement autumn weather won quiet curses from the three guards, though Derry SanOsen accepted, and silently delighted, in the ride in the growing fog. This wasn't the first time he'd been wet, and he'd spent far more uncomfortable days since the last time he'd traversed these trails. The quiet ride through the mist-haunted hills of Lynashin was nothing less than a wonder to him.

Derry had never expected to come home again.

Home.

The single word made any hardship bearable today. Derry hadn't minded sleeping on the hard ground the last few days, eating trail food, or even riding in sodden cloaks. In one more day they would reach the golden halls of Tyleen Castle and

Derry's four-year nightmare would be over. He'd been lucky to leave the muck-covered stinking cell where he'd been held on the Isles. King Robert, who had mistrusted everyone, had been assassinated by a servant. The new Regent, Olivia, had released Derry and several others, sending them back home as soon as they could travel.

The change had come too quickly. Twenty days ago -- or maybe more since he'd lost track -- Derry had still been a prisoner and expected King Robert to order him killed, as he had ordered the deaths of so many who had shared that cell with him. Instead, he now rode where he could breathe clean air and watch raindrops collect on the edge of leaves, mirroring the world upside down in their reflections.

A symbol of his life, Derry supposed: upside down and backward. Nothing had gone right the last few years.

"Damn weather," Captain Killough growled as he brushed water off the back of his hand as though that particular drop offended him. Derry's horse shook his head, scattering more water through the mist. The older man gave Derry a quick glance and a bow of his head. "Begging your pardon for the language, your lordship, sir."

Derry shifted uncomfortably and hoped Killough took it as a dislike of the weather. The truth, though, was that he didn't feel much like a Lord of Lynashin. King Robert had stripped him of any such pretentions when he threw Derry into a prison cell with thieves, murderers, and more than a few who had done nothing wrong at all.

Like him.

"Lord Derry?"

"My apologies," he replied with a quick bow of his head. Dark hair fell across his eyes; he brushed it aside with a swift, nervous swipe of his fingers. "The weather doesn't bother me much, Captain Killough. I've always loved the wild places, almost as much as I loved Tyleen Castle."

Those were the most words he'd said at any given time since the Captain and his two men collected him at the docks, five days ago. Killough gave him a quick, startled look. Then the older man bit at his lower lip and gave an odd shrug. "Well, Tyleen hasn't changed much in the last four years, my lord."

A warning came in those polite words, but Derry didn't want to hear it. He purposely shoved the sudden surge of anxiety aside. *I am going home!* He'd dreamed of returning to Tyleen from the day Queen Alisia had sent him to the northern islands as her envoy. The Queen had known she was sending him to a hostile court. She had known he was going to face trouble --

Derry leaned forward on his horse, huddled into the cloak, and fighting tremors that came at so clear a memory of being thrown in a cell. Captain Killough pulled his mount back, riding with Casey and Bay, the other two guards. Derry hadn't spoken much to any of them and suspected they thought him just another snobbish young lord. He didn't care ... much.

Derry's companions did give him the peace he craved and didn't push him into traveling faster, despite the miserable weather. Derry had peace and quiet, though he knew this wouldn't last for long. They were closer to Tyleen, both the city and the castle of his dreams. He thought he might even recognize this area and the brook. They hadn't stopped at any villages for the four nights, and they had seen very few people. He had washed in books, shaved with water heated in a pot and had Casey trim back his hair to a reasonable length. He wanted to be civilized when he came home, not some animal released from a cage.

Still, Killough hadn't taken him near any settlement. Derry now suspected that had been for a reason, just as Captain Killough had tried to give him some warning about Tyleen.

Damn. Derry didn't want trouble.

They took the stone-lined Old Road, a well-kept path this close to the capital. Soon Derry and his guards would pass through a few small villages and skirt the edges of farmlands closest to the city. His little party went unnoticed across the brook on an ancient stone bridge and then went down the other side past the woodcutter's cottage. The place was closed tight, despite it still being quite sunset. Derry hoped the old man was all right and wished to see that familiar gray-bearded face. He did not ask to stop, though, in case the news there might be unpleasant. He wanted no sorrow to mark these last miles home.

They reached the edge of a village not long afterward. The neat little cottages were locked up tight and the windows barred, even though the sun had barely touched the tips of the trees. A single man rushed towards a stockade, trying to herd a half dozen sheep ahead of him with frantic haste.

One scrawny and ragged young boy darted past Derry's group, startling the horses and winning a quick curse from Bay. Derry watched the boy disappear into the shadows between two buildings. He'd had the look of one of the homeless children who frequented the towns and villages, but they usually came begging of anyone on horseback. Only people of wealth rode, and especially beautiful horses like their mounts. Derry would have given the boy his cloak on such a cold, miserable day as this. He had no coin.

Derry had always hated to hear the tales of beggar children who died of the cold and hunger, abandoned on the streets. If he hadn't been the King's nephew, he would have been one of those children after his parents died.

Captain Killough rode up beside him, a hand on the knife at his belt and a scowl on his face. He carefully kept watch to both sides and clearly didn't like what he saw.

"Isn't this Glendalow?" Derry asked, feeling uncertain

now because the town had never been this quiet and the mist hid the details of the place.

The question startled Captain Killough, but he gave a quick nod, focusing on Derry for a heartbeat, and then gave a cottage a glare as someone inside laughed. When the Captain looked back at Derry, he gave a nervous nod. "Yes, we've reached Glendalow," he said.

"This used to be a pleasant place." Derry felt a shiver retake him, and it had nothing to do with the mist and the cold. He wanted nothing good to have changed. "My friends and I used to ride here some days; a pleasant trip to a lovely and friendly village. What's happened?"

"Superstition, sir," Killough said with a sneer, though he seemed to relax a little. "A couple children went missing and maybe a few sheep as well, though I doubt for the same reasons. The locals seem to count the loss of the animals as important as the homeless children what disappeared. King Nevin believes there are bandits about in the woods, though his guards can't seem to track them. The locals insist there is a band of fae wandering about the area."

"Fae?" Derry felt the corners of his mouth pull upward in a brief smile. It felt odd and uncomfortable, making him wonder how long it had been since he last smiled. "I wouldn't think anyone would bring those old tales back out again."

"Maybe they just be looking for a little magic," Killough replied with a sigh. "These be hard times, after all."

"Have things gone that badly?" Derry asked. He immediately regretted the words. He didn't want to hear any tales of woe that might overlay the bright dreams that had kept him alive.

Maybe Killough even understood how Derry felt. Killough looked at Derry with a slight tilt of his head before he spoke. "Not so much as you'd see, your Lordship. There have been peculiar things here and there, like fields failing for no reason, especially in the south. Animals dying in the north as well -- I heard of an entire herd of deer dead in a field. There's been an odd quality to the air, though maybe that's just all this damned mist."

Derry felt another small smile come to him, and he accepted the touch of humor this time. He couldn't say he felt better for it, but he was glad for the slight change in attitude. What would they do now? They'd be camping soon and have another damp cold night unless they rode on to Tyleen and reached the city about midnight. No, not a good idea. That would leave his group sitting at the gates or taking refuge in a traveler's inn outside the castle walls. Those places were not often safe or quiet. Besides, he wanted to see the High Castle in the light of day when he rode home. He was tired of shadows.

Maybe the time had come to quit acting like an animal hunted through the woods, too. "There is an inn here in town -- or there was," Derry said, looking down the rock-laid road. The mist hid buildings even a few feet away. Derry thought the fog came too quickly, gathering up in the shadows and spreading outward like a veil. He wanted out of the weather for the first time in days. "Do you think we might get rooms there tonight? I'd like a good rest and to cleaned up before I ride into Tyleen tomorrow."

Killough glanced his way and then did another quick check to the right and left. The man hadn't been this nervous before they entered this village. Was it the people who worried him or was it the idea of the fae gathering about in the nearby trees? Why hadn't they avoided Glendalow like all the other places they'd bypassed?

Because the King's guards were in the woods looking for bandits and it might not be wise to be slinking around in the trees? Someone might make a mistake, and this was not the time to take such a chance.

Having that thought and connection to what was happening felt like waking up. Derry wasn't entirely confident he wanted to be so aware, but he couldn't hide in his own gray and misty world forever. He had to prepare to go home to Tyleen, and stop huddling in the cloak, hoping not to be seen. That realization was like a slap in the face. He did not want to bring that cell home with him, so he had better start working at a change.

Derry sat up straighter and glanced around the little village again, wishing for signs of the good people he had known. "Is there a problem with staying here, Captain Killough?"

They rode a couple more paces before the older man spoke. The horses even seemed uneasy now. "Sir, I'm going to bold. We've stayed clear of places where you might be spotted. No use taking chances while getting you back home. Besides, you've disdained even the covering of a tent, your Lordship. Why the change now, to go to some local inn?"

"We'll be in Tyleen tomorrow," Derry said and stared down the Old Road where it went past the village. He remembered the curves, the streams, the sounds of the trees and the call of the birds. "I had better get used to being inside again before I set foot in Tyleen, don't you think?"

"Ah now, there's a bit of truth I hadn't considered. I won't complain of a warm meal and a dry bed for the night."

"And some of the local honeyed mead, I imagine." They were moving slowly forward, and Derry could just pick out the swaying sign, moving enticingly in the breeze. The Glendalow Inn had always been a friendly place, and Derry felt as though this was the first true link back to his former life. "Thank you for your escort, Captain Killough. I suspect that I might have simply wandered off, the state I was in."

"We haven't gotten you home yet, your lordship," Killough said with another nervous look around the area. Was he worried about something specific?

Derry didn't ask. He wanted peace, and he'd leave the worries to the Captain and his men for now. Then he looked around the mist-shrouded village and admitted a different truth aloud. "I seem to be having trouble simply connecting with where I am. Nothing seems real yet."

"I'm sure everything will come back to you, Lord Derry," Killough said with a worried glance his way. "I suspect you have not forgotten ... everything about Tyleen."

"You don't need to walk so carefully around what you are trying to say, Captain," Derry replied. "I understand your hints. I grew up in Tyleen castle, and we breathed politics from our first moment. I know enough to be careful of whom I annoy. I truly just hope to retire to some rooms and rest for a long, quiet time."

Killough looked oddly relieved. They'd reached the inn, and the older man swept off his horse and took hold of Derry's bridle. "You've been naught but polite to us, your Lordship. Even when it was plain you weren't clearheaded, you never put on airs nor complained about being uncomfortable."

"I was never as uncomfortable on this journey as I had been in that cell in the Isles," Derry replied and felt a shiver pass through him. He dismounted and let Bay take hold of his horse, listening to a few voices within the building, both a welcome and a frightening sound. Strangers.

"Too many Lords moan and groan if they have to ride out before the sun is halfway up the sky, or if there is dew on the ground to dampen their pretty boots," Killough said with a hardly concealed snarl of disgust. "I feared you were one of them."

Well, that certainly wasn't a very politic thing to say on Killough's part, though Derry appreciated the acceptance that went with those words. Killough's words had kindled a rush of memories about those people and brought a grimace of distaste. The worst of the bunch had been led by his cousin, Prince Egan. He and his friends had made games of escaping from the Prince's view...

"Boys' games," he mumbled aloud. He didn't feel much like a boy anymore.

"Lord Derry, sir?"

Derry had been staring at the door, unmoving while his mind tried to sort through uncomfortable reflections. He could feel all the aches and pains he'd tried to ignore on the horse. The wet cloak seemed little protection against the cold, damp breeze -- but even so, he couldn't make himself walk forward to the door and take that step back into a world he had left behind.

"I have no coin," Derry remembered again.

"The King sent us with plenty to cover far more expenses than we've had, your lordship. Casey and Bay will take care of the horses," Killough said and signaled for the two to take the mounts away to the stable behind the building. "Let's go in and see if we can arrange for some hot food and soft beds."

Derry nodded, but he still didn't move forward. His heart pounded too hard. The door itself, with the old wooden pull and the half-rusting hinges, seemed a pattern of memory to him. This wasn't what he had dreamed about, though, in that cell. The Inn was neither part of the dreams of Tyleen, nor the nightmare of the cell ... and for a few heartbeats he felt lost.

Derry thought he heard odd, pretty bells, but Killough nudged him forward and up the two steps. Killough even reached past and pushed the heavy door open, and Derry stepped inside rather than be pushed forward again. He still had some control over his life.

The common room felt warm and welcoming after the cold, wet days they'd spent riding. Derry found the interior little changed with the haphazard arrangement of tables and benches. Yes, there on the wall was his own pennant, which he'd given to the owner years ago, a proclamation that put this little place under his care, for all the good that did when he'd been gone. A pot with rabbit stew, by the smell of it, hung over the central pit and the fire gave off the welcome sweet scent of cherry wood.

Derry found more people inside than he had expected since they were relatively quiet. Nervous, worried men, he thought. They didn't all believe the tales about the fae, did they? The patrons gave the two strangers looks of worry, then went back to their own meals and drink. Conversations rose a little, bringing a dull hum of noise to the room.

Derry glanced quickly around, his eyes adjusting to the shadows and smoke-filled light. The table he and his friends had usually taken remained empty, there in the corner under the pennant. Derry didn't cross to sit there. Instead, he hurried to a smaller table in a darker corner, pulling the cloak around him as he moved and wishing he could simply hide. He sat with his back to the corner of the wall, there in the darkest shadow he could find.

Killough settled on the opposite bench and turned slightly so he kept a view of the door, and he eyed the innkeeper with some trepidation as the man neared. Finil stood over six feet tall; a big man with wild gray hair and a matching beard, and a no-nonsense attitude that had kept the place free from most brawls. He allowed no trouble from the commoners, and since Derry and his friends were the only nobility to favor the Inn, he didn't need to worry about their manners. Derry had brought no one here who wasn't a friend. He'd been on a first-name basis with Finil, and his wife Cara, for years.

The man crossed to the table, nervously wiping his hands on the cloth in his belt and giving a polite bow of his head. "What can I serve you, gentlemen?" he asked, cautious as he always had been around strangers.

The words struck Derry like the stab of a knife into his

heart. This was a sure sign that he couldn't go back to his old life. Derry had held tightly to the hope of return for all those years in the cell, but now as he faced someone who had known so well, and didn't even recognize him, Derry knew the truth.

"I think we'd like to start with some honeyed mead," Killough said, filling the silence. "And dinner for four. The other two will join us after they've seen to the horses."

Finil nodded ... and kept nodding as though his head had come loose from a spring. He took a sudden deep breath and placed both of his large, scarred hands on the equally disfigured table, bending down to stare straight into Derry's face. His hazel eyes brightened, and he grinned with such delight that a mirroring smile played at the corners of Derry's mouth.

"Holy Gods All!" Finil's gasp drew the attention of people nearby. Finil's sudden laugh put everyone at ease as the big man stood straighter, and the patrons paid no more attention than the occasional glance they gave to all the others. The ambient noise covered most of what anyone said, even at Derry's table. "Not a word of it, just showing up without a bit of warning!"

"I haven't even been back to Tyleen yet, Finil," Derry answered softly, surprised by the emotional outburst which proved more healing than he could have imagined. "But how could I pass by my favorite inn and not stop for some of your fine mead and food?"

"You honor me, Prince Derry." The man rubbed the back of his hand across his eyes. "Not even home yet, but you thought to stop here."

"It's Lord Derry, Finil. You know better," he said softly and with a bit of warning.

"You were born a prince," the man replied with an unexpected conviction and a bit more fire in his dark eyes. "No decree to please the queen can change that --"

"I am Lord Derry SanOsen," Derry said and reached out to put a hand on the man's arm. "That's title enough for me. Don't anger the Queen on my account."

"Yes, of course," the man said, though some old anger lingered in his face for a moment. Then he grinned again. "A fine meal for you, Lord Derry. Will you spend the night?"

"If you have room," Derry replied with a glance around at the crowd.

"Not to worry. These are common room people, most who would ha' spent the night outside in the fields at other times." He shook his shaggy head but said nothing of the trouble they had here in town. "You'll have the best room, Lord Derry. And a fine meal."

Finil spun on his heel, and Derry swore the man all but danced across the room as he headed back into the kitchen.

"I was right," Killough said, leaning back and looking Derry over as though they'd just met. "You are not like any of the other young lords of Tyleen, who wouldn't have a kind word for a commoner to save their lives."

"You must not know any of my friends then," Derry replied. He felt more at ease. "I know four years won't have changed the likes of Shannon SanSota. We are very much alike."

"It isn't time that changes a man, your lordship," Killough said. He must have seen the worry in Derry's face, and he spread his hand in a gesture Derry couldn't quite read. "I haven't had much contact with Lord Shannon, though. Still, hear me out on this: I came to serve at Tyleen barely ten days after you had sailed. The castle was in an uproar still, with your friends angry long before King Robert sent word that he had locked up the *spy*. Your friends could do nothing, though, and many left the King's court soon afterwards to avoid trouble with ... to avoid trouble. You were the lynchpin for your group at the court with your high rank, whether Prince or Lord -- but mostly because people liked you."

This was not what Derry had wanted to hear, but the news might have been worse, considering the situation he'd left behind. "I hadn't considered any changes that might happen," he admitted and finally put off his wet cloak and settled it on the seat beside him. No reason to stay covered now, though he wasn't certain the others had heard Finil. "I had imagined life went on much the same without me. I -- I imagined a great deal while in the Fairfall prison, waiting through those damned long days."

"I'm sure that now you're back, your friends will be more themselves again."

"I do look forward to seeing them," he said and frowned. "I would have expected Shannon to meet us --"

"King Nevin hasn't announced your return to court yet," Killough said softly. "When he sent the three of us, the King said he wasn't sure he trusted the note that you were going to be sent home on the next ship. He didn't want to create a stir if it weren't true. And besides, he didn't want Queen Alisia to know you were heading back to court."

"Oh, and won't that be a wonderful surprise for her," Derry replied with a sigh. A new worry worked up through his thoughts. "Queen Alisia never cared much for me. Is that why we've kept off the Old Road?"

"Mostly," Killough admitted and appeared pleased that he'd picked up that idea. "By the time I'd first come to serve at court, the Queen was under a great deal of displeasure, shall we say, since she sent you on that ill-fated journey to a place where everyone knew you would not be welcome. Lord Shannon was even blatant about you being sent away because you outshined her boys."

"Gods, Shannon --" The words caught in his throat. Shannon couldn't have been such a fool!

Killough nodded at the unspoken words. "Not a wise

thing to say, no. The Queen exiled him, but don't worry. King Nevin and the troops, including me, came ridin' back, having settled the trouble in the south, and saved the young sir. Then the King raised hell over you being sent off to the Isles on the Queen's orders. That was before the news even came of you being locked away. When the King learned your fate, well Queen Alisia retired to the Daria Temple up in the far north for her exile. She's only been back to court for a few months. I can't say living with the acolytes did anything to improve her temper, and she's certainly no humbler for her religious sojourn. Egan chose to go with her. Roe did not."

Derry stared at Killough in shocked dismay as the room seemed to swirl, voices melding into a rush of sound. He took several deeper breaths. Maybe the man joked. Maybe. "You can't seriously mean the queen was exiled from court because of me."

Killough gave him another of those odd looks, his eyes narrowed as though they might not be speaking the same language -- or that Derry was too dense to understand. "You are the only child of the King's late, and much beloved, brother. People call you Lord to appease the Queen, but we all know you are a Prince of the Blood, your Lordship, sir. King Nevin favored you, as well --"

"Favored me?" Derry asked. He began to think he didn't understand anything.

"I heard a great deal about you in the last few years," Killough admitted and drew Derry's startled attention again. "You weren't forgotten, you know. And this is what I realized: The King never let his own sons run wild with their friends, nor come and go as they pleased from court. I heard tales about wild races where you won even against the King -- and when he wouldn't let his own boys join in. I gathered Prince Tevin didn't care much, being Heir and knowing you couldn't steal his glory. Prince Egan and Prince Roe, though, listened too much to their mother, and she told them you were stealing their rightful place before the people. You stole their glory."

Derry stared at the older man and felt utterly dumbfounded. Though he had been nearly twenty when the Queen sent him to assess the state of affairs in the Isles, he had been young in many ways. Derry had been trained for such work and handled a few diplomatic assignments for King Nevin, though those had been within Lynashin where he'd been well known. Protected -- and that protection disappeared when he had sailed away.

Shannon had advised him to take a ship to anywhere but the Isles and wait this trouble out. The King would be back soon from the trouble in the south, after all. Derry, perhaps unwisely, had refused to be a party to anything that might dishonor his family name, which had been left to him when his parents died.

"Lord Derry, sir?" Killough said softly and looked worried once more.

"I was too happy," Derry said with a rueful shake of his head. How could he have been so blind? "I knew Egan never liked me, but then he was snide to everyone, even those who followed him like puppies behind a cook. I knew the Queen didn't like me, but she didn't much care for the King either, so I didn't take it personally."

"But it was personal," Killough said softly, his head bowed a bit as he leaned closer. "Any time you stood beside Egan people would think you the better choice."

"That would hardly matter, even if it were true. Egan isn't the crown prince --"

"Not yet," Killough replied. Derry didn't like the ominous sound of those words. "The Heir has had an uncommon run of bad luck the last half year, but he's survived it all so far. However, we look to Egan with more worry now."

"Ah. I never saw Egan and Roe as anything but foppish

young princes, aping the styles of their foreign mother. She always thought Lynashin backward, you know. She's hated everything about our lovely island from the day she arrived. She instilled that disdain in Egan and Roe, but at least the King took Tevin from her hands."

"She won't be glad to see you back, Lord Derry. Just so you are warned. Until you are in the King's company again, you are in some danger from her."

"Should we worry about someone heading for Tyleen and giving her word?"

"Not from here," Killough replied with a wave of his hand toward the others in the crowded room, and more coming in, a rush from near darkness beyond. "I made certain we arrived at sunset for that reason. Remember that they worry about their fear of the fae, so most everyone has already taken to cover for the night. Besides, the King will be careful these last few days of anyone riding in to see the Queen, her servants, or her sons. We're safe enough still."

"We'll leave early in the morning," Derry added and almost regretted that decision. This would have been a nice place to hide and rest for a while, though he still longed for Tyleen. "With only a day left on our journey, I'm betting we'll be safe enough for the night."

"Good." Killough looked at his rough hands for a moment, staring as though they held answers that he couldn't find anywhere else.

"Egan and Roe really had no choice in how they acted. Their mother always controlled them and got more covetous after Tevin officially went to be his father's son and heir at ten. She had power over the other two, and they had no choice in what they did."

"Well, and neither did you have a choice, except if you had chosen to shun the good King's friendship. That wouldn't ha' been wise, even if you had it in you."

"True." Derry took a deep breath and sat back, letting some of the tension ease from his shoulders. Whispers spread all around them and heads turned their way, but no one appeared hostile. "So, is there anything else blatantly obvious that you want to point out to me before I walk back into Tyleen with all my youthful innocence and lack of tact?"

Killough gave a little laugh but fell silent as Finil and his daughter Mina arrived with plates and platters of food and drink. The table was soon covered in bread, cheeses, thinly sliced venison, bowls of rabbit stew, and cups of honeyed mead. Mina gave him a tentative little bow of her head and scurried away. She'd still been hanging at her mother's skirts the last time Derry had seen her.

The smell of so many foods startled him, and he stared at the food for a moment too long, trying to remember the last time he'd seen such a feast. Then he looked up with a start. "Thank you, Finil. This looks very fine, indeed."

"Lord Derry, sir --" Finil began, then bit at his lip for a moment before he continued, his hands mangling the cleaning cloth he kept at his waist. "I can see you ha' been ill-kept these last years. You're too thin and pale, and I can see scars that were not there the last time you dined here. There will be prayers of thanks in the Temple next Holy Day. Now eat a bit and get some rest. You look weary to the bone, you do."

Finil spun and hurried away before Derry could reply.

"Well, I'd say he's covered the matter pretty well, your lordship," Killough said as he began ladling out food like a servant. "Except for one thing: don't change now. I gave you the warning because the Queen has only been back at the court since late summer, and she's not going to be happy to see you returned already to step on her glory again."

"I was never a threat to Queen Alisia or her sons." Derry felt a flicker of anger try to take him, but he'd learned to tame that emotion in the first weeks in a cell where he kept company with men older and tougher than him. He could feel the chill of those damp, stone walls. He focused back on Killough and buried that memory, though the chill remained. "She was petty to send me away, Killough -- and she sent me to the Isles knowing I wasn't going to return."

"But you have."

Derry blinked.

Killough pushed one of the cups toward him and Derry caught the heady scent of fine mead. "Sip this. Just a bit, since you've had little to eat the last few days." The Captain paused while Derry obeyed, picking up the cup with trembling hands. The mead tasted sweet and warm. He thought it might help spread some warmth through him. "I'll tell you some truths. The Queen is a jealous woman, Lord Derry. People liked you, so she was bound to take notice and turn Egan and Roe against you. Roe has slipped the leash a bit of late. Prince Egan never did. I can't say the time of rough beds, and dawn prayers at the Temple helped the young sir. He's still an ill-mannered braggart with absolutely no good sense of style."

Those words came close to winning a laugh from Derry, an unexpected surge of humor. Egan had always been a pretentious fop. He'd remained in his mother's care, while everyone else at court grew up around him -- and she expected him to be a good king?

No. Queen Alisia expected him to be her puppet. There was a sobering thought. Queen Alisia was a foreigner, and she couldn't rule in her own name. She had always favored her second and Derry had thought she was only being petty. Now, a little older and far wiser, he could see the Queen's manipulations and worried move about Tevin than for himself.

"So, there are two people who are not going to be happy to see me returned to court." Derry played with the soft bread, tearing off pieces, but eating none of it yet. Old memories and new worries bounded through his aching head, but he began to sort them out. He especially remembered Egan who had dressed in velvets and lace, though the style didn't suit the pudgy young man. He'd have grown older in the last four years. Wiser? From Killough's observations that was not the case.

Casey and Bay entered the room and headed toward them. Their moment of privacy was over. "Thank you for the discussion, Captain Killough. I don't like to think I would have been blind to the trouble when we reached home, but my mind simply has not been making the proper connections. Being here at Glendalow Inn has helped. This was a place I enjoyed."

"With good cause. The food is excellent," Killough replied, sopping up some stew with a bit of bread. His brown eyes narrowed. "You'd do well to try at least some of it, your lordship."

"I will. I'm working up to it." Derry still toyed with the bread that never reached his mouth. "I am glad we had this discussion, Captain. You likely saved me from a rude and rather uncomfortable, awakening at court."

"From all I've heard, you were as fine and kind of a young gentleman as was ever at court," Killough said and grinned at the snort of amusement those words won from Derry. "It would be a shame if ... if some people ruined your homecoming. Forewarned may shield you from falling into a trap."

"Yes, thank you," Derry replied. He finally ate the bit of bread and cheese, chewing slowly as the thought about going home in this new light. It did not dim the joy he felt at returning. If anything, it made arriving home seem more real.

He'd be careful, though Derry wasn't certain taking care would help much.

Two

Captain Killough, carrying Derry's travel bag, escorted Derry up the old creaking stairs to the room at the end of the hall, moving as though he feared that Derry might get lost somewhere between one stair and the next. Killough had gone down the hall and opened the door and gone in, waving him back -- he supposed that was wise. Killough was quick with the work and came back out.

"Rest well, your lordship. We'll leave at first light if that suits you."

"That will be fine. Thank you, Captain Killough."

Killough gave a slight bow of his head and walked away to join Casey and Bay in the common room and left Derry to walk into the room and close the door behind him. He looked at the wooden bar leaning against the wall that could be slipped into place -- and shuddered at the thought of having a door locked behind him -- even from his side.

He stood there with the candle flickering by the window. Alone. This was the first time he'd been alone in years. He'd shared a cabin on the ship with two ranking crew, and they had made sure he was never alone, but mostly because he'd been so ill and feverish on the first part of the trip. He thought he'd even thanked them for their care when Killough collected him. Old manners came back to him as he tried to believe he was going home.

Derry pulled off his tunic, wincing at sore muscles. The bruises he'd had when he left The Isles had mostly faded, but the scars remained. Derry traced a cut from his left shoulder and down his chest, remembering how he had thought he'd die from that one. He'd still been strong then, though, those first weeks in the cell. The later wounds, although not as severe, had proved to be more dangerous.

This was not the cell. Derry sat down on the bed and let his fingers brush over the wonderful quilt made of blue and green triangles. Cara's work. Derry remembered her sitting in the common room one morning, working away on one much like this. The memory drew him back to here again.

This room, though, still felt odd. Derry had been glad to avoid walled buildings on the journey from the sea-edged port of Queton and inland to Tyleen. The feel of the soft bed sent a shiver of fear through him, and he stood again, stepping away from it in haste. Derry feared he no longer belong in a world of even simple comforts.

Captain Killough's discussion should have unsettled Derry, but instead, the warnings made him feel closer to home. He had awoken from the numbing stupor he'd felt from the moment the Fairfall Guards had taken him from the cell, but not to his execution, as he'd expected.

Every time Derry had closed his eyes since then, he had expected to wake up and find himself still in the cell, still waiting for his impending death. He had seen others go crazy after a few months ... or years. He had feared it more than he wanted to admit and felt terrified at the possibility more now. This might not be real.

Would he have imagined Captain Killough? No, he would have called up the memory of someone he'd known. He would have brought Shannon here to escort him home, not a stranger.

Everything Killough had told him about Tyleen rang true. Derry remembered life in the castle clearly tonight, rather than the imagined paradise he had made in his dreams. He sat on the edge of the bed again and carefully sifted the real from the unreal.

Tyleen was a castle foremost, but around it also stretched a few lesser clan-held castles, and around that a city. Every building was filled with people who held power, and many who reached for more -- like the Queen herself. Derry's life had always been filled with intrigues, but Derry had lived by one crucial personal rule: he would never betray the King or his own friends. People had quickly learned not to approach him in hopes of offering him a chance at the throne. Exiles or executions had followed such discussions, and that had not made him popular with some groups.

He'd had many friends at court besides Shannon, and not all of them in the nobility. He'd had one or two enemies, not counting Egan whom he had never taken seriously. Egan's mother was a different matter. The Queen had been ambitious from the day she arrived at court from mainland Talia, and Derry had been very wise not to cross her in such a way that she could use a mistake against him.

Instead, she had waited patiently like a spider in a web, and when King Nevin and Prince Tevin had gone to do battle in the southern reaches of their large island nation, she had leapt at her chance to get Derry out of the castle.

Derry could have gone with the King into battle. He had before. However, he'd been away from court playing envoy to a northern lord when the trouble sprang up, and by the time he made it back home, word had come that most of the crisis was over. Shannon had been with Derry, his usual companion. The two of them often went on such assignments together, the King saying they had an excellent touch for such refinements that kept others happy.

The King never sent Egan anywhere.

Queen Alisia and Prince Egan hated Derry, but he'd had the protection of the King and simply did his best to avoid them. The battle in the south and his ill-timed return home had given the Queen a chance to do more than be rude to him. He had always counted himself lucky that she hadn't sent Shannon with him. Even if Shannon had gone into exile, he would have been safer than going to The Isles.

Shannon wasn't an orphan, though. Derry knew the SanSota family would have backed not only Shannon but also Derry against the Queen if he had asked for their help. Derry would not start that kind of war, dragging the SanSota's into a bloody conflict with the Queen and her followers. He hadn't sullied his own family name by refusing her commission either, which had left him no choice but to go to The Isles.

Derry SanOsen had never regretted the decision, only the results of what King Robert had done.

Now he was going to return home with the Queen still hanging under a cloud of displeasure and enraged by her years of disgrace and exile. King Nevin would make much of Derry's return. The man had a great heart and a boisterous personality, and he had never considered tact to be a kingly virtue. That left Derry with two choices. He could try to avoid all public notice until the surprise of his return died down or he could face the Queen and her anger, knowing he had King Nevin to guard his back this time.

Part of him -- the more significant part, Derry admitted to himself -- wanted to hide. He wanted no trouble and didn't want to draw attention --

Did he want to remain a prisoner?

The candlelight flickered, and he let his fingers brush against the quilt again. Clean. Soft. A hint of home. Outside the still open window -- he couldn't stand the thought of shuttering it -- he could hear the whisper of the wind in the trees and a soft patter of rain against the leaves. He'd heard no such sounds in the cell beneath King Robert's castle.

Derry had dreamed of coming home, though after a few weeks he had stopped believing it would happen. Now he sat within a day of reaching that impossible goal, and part of him kept trying to throw it all away. He could have left here tonight and gone into exile. He could disappear into the woods --

Had he survived the last four years so he could simply come home to die in some hovel away from friends and enemies? What would Shannon think? Shannon had come close to throwing away his own future because of Derry's troubles. Didn't he owe his friend to at least try returning home and not running away now?

Besides, what good would that do? He could hide for years, and it wouldn't matter: The Queen wouldn't forget -- and *forgive* was not a word in her vocabulary. If he even retired from court, it would only give her more chances to torment him. If he showed any sign of weakness, she would strike at him and the peace he craved the most would be lost.

The reality struck him like a knife in his heart. Derry couldn't have what he most longed for, to go home to the world he'd left behind four years ago. That world had disappeared before he even took ship at the port. He didn't want to hold on to the memory of the dark, dank cell -- but if he couldn't have the dream that had kept him alive, then what was left?

He felt quite lost.

And he heard bells.

These were not the loud, pealing bells of the temple or even the softer bells that hung inside a shopkeeper's door to warn of someone coming inside. These bells sang with a whisper of gold and silver, and the tune they played wove through the air, intricate and lovely. The sound drew him to the window, and he leaned out, looking into the fog before he realized this might be something he honestly didn't want to see.

Fae bells.

He'd grown up on the legends of the fae and the sound of the bells where they passed, but he had never believed such a thing could be real. Tonight, the world lay wrapped in the thick fog below his window, so impenetrable that clouds might have come to the ground. On such a night, the fae might have stolen all of Glendalow, and no one would have seen.

The air tingled as the bells drew closer and each breath tasted of spring rather than late autumn. He caught a hint of movement along the mist-covered road, and the bells sounded so lovely that he wanted to follow them and know there truly was such beauty, and even magic, in the world.

He crossed the room and grabbed the tunic from the edge of the bed, pulling it on.

A shiver passed over him, and he turned back to the window.

A woman sat on the sill like some careless child daring the window's ledge and the drop below. Her wild hair looked like spun sunlight, and her dress seemed to be nothing more than leaves and vines, all of them shifting slightly in the breeze. A lovely bell rang close by as she stared at him with spring-green eyes in a sweet face that seemed young, and yet was not. *Fae.* He stood in the company of a fae.

Derry stood with his tunic unlaced and his heart pounding too hard. A myth had come through the window into his room. Had he gone mad after all? He had expected it, which now made him mistrust everything, including the idea that he was going home.

The fae woman tilted her head and watched him with a slight frown and a touch of what appeared to be curiosity. Her skin seemed tanned, or the color of twine -- a pale brown, shadowed here in the uncertain light. He would have thought it an unnatural shade -- but no, it seemed more natural than his own pale skin.

He took a step back. Stopped.

"You are a curious thing." Her voice sounded like a sweet-toned flute.

"Me? Curious?" he asked, his voice uncommonly steady given the situation. If this wasn't reality, what did he have to fear except to awaken in the cell again?

"You are not a child," she replied and swung her other leg over the sill and into the room as she stood. Her hair fell in waves of golden light across her shoulders, glittering where the candlelight brushed against the strands. Her pale brown legs were bare halfway below her knees, a scandalous appearance in human terms. She wore no shoes, and she made no sound as her feet touched the floor. Derry thought the room glowed brighter for her presence. "Human adults rarely sense the magic we bring into the world. But you head the bells."

"Yes," he said. He took a quick, gasping breath, trying to pull his scattered thoughts together in the face of this wondrous intrusion in an already troubling night. "You are fae."

"Yes, I am." She smiled, and he thought the room brightened even more. "I am from one of the lesser clans who roam the borderlands, tying humans and the older race together still --"

"And you steal children?"

Not a very politic thing to say, Derry realized as her green eyes flashed. He was out of practice. The breeze at the window blew harder, and her scowl made his mouth go dry. Then she frowned and gave a deceptively uncaring shrug.

"The lost ones come to us, Derry. Oh, yes, I know who you are."

He thought this must simply be another sign that nothing was real. How would a fae know him? If this was not real, how could anything matter? The thought inexplicably calmed his mind. He could play games with this fae because none of it mattered.

"The lost ones?" he asked, his voice steady.

"The children who have been abandoned and mistreated," she replied and leaned against the sill, at ease as well. "Sometimes, if the children are truly lost and have nowhere else to go, they hear the bells and follow after us. Once they live with the clan, they learn the joy of life again."

"I wish --" But he said no more.

She stepped away from the window and came closer to him, a vision of golden light and green life. The soft sound of a bell and a hint of the mist came with her. He thought he could smell lilacs and he watched her golden hair swirling about her in a mesmerizing dance of light and breeze.

Derry thought he ought to back away. He ought to run, but as she neared, he felt a whisper of peace and hope that had been lost to him for so long.

"You can hear the bells," she said with a wave of her hand that started a lovely melody. "Are you truly one of the lost, Derry? Would you come away with me now and walk paths where spring blooms eternally and where every creature is your friend? Would you come away to the wild?"

Go to a place without prison walls? Go to a place of peace without the vindictive games of nobility? Could he walk away from everything that had happened in the last four years?

He wanted to go to such a place ... with *half* his heart.

Tyleen still called him -- Shannon and his other friends, and the King who had treated him so well --

"Ah," the fae woman said and smiled with a look a friend

might give another at a painful parting. He'd seen that same look on Shannon's face four years ago when he rode away from home. The fae's hand brushed against his arm, a warm touch of delicate fingers. "I think I understand. Of late we have noticed something dark moving in the world, something we don't welcome here. Trouble inches closer and scurries through the shadows, Prince Derry --"

"Lord Derry," he corrected out of habit.

"*Prince* Derry," she repeated, as stubborn as Finil. "You are what you were born to be -- but listen to me. The heart of the trouble lurks in human places where the fae cannot easily find it. We who are of the wild have sensed something wrong, and humans will see the trouble soon. Until now, I hadn't realized we would ally with the humans."

"Lady?" he said, surprised by her words.

"I am Leanora," she said with a slight bow of her head, a show of acceptance. "You are not ready to come with us yet, Derry. I think you will still find your way to us, but not yet."

"I don't understand." He couldn't decide between worry and relief.

"You have your place still." Leanora stepped towards the window, her hair still moving in the breeze. "And that place is not with us, though we have made a needed connection."

"I could go with you --"

"Not yet," she replied and stopped by the window, looking back at him. "We shall meet again. You are the link."

She turned, slipped over the edge of the window, and was gone.

He stood there in shocked dismay for a half dozen heartbeats before he rushed to the window. Leanora had reached the street below, the fog starting to flow in around her. She reached out, and a ragged young boy darted from between the buildings and took her hand. The mist covered them both.

Derry feared he had lost something very precious.

"Wait for me!"

Derry nearly threw himself out the window before a small tendril of sanity caught hold. He backed away and spun, racing to the door and threw it open with a bang loud enough to wake the dead. He didn't hear another sound until he took the creaking stairs, nearly stumbling and falling down the steps. The tables had been pushed aside in the common room, and men slept everywhere, their ragged snores ending as Derry rushed through, leaping over bodies both prone and supine, and rushing toward the door.

Captain Killough sat up, spotted Derry, and groggily surged to his feet. "Lord Derry, sir. What's wrong?"

"I have to --" Derry gasped, darting past men starting to wake up. "I have to stop her!"

"Sir?" Killough said, still half asleep. The captain nearly tripped over the legs of someone only now starting to wake. "What --"

"Don't let him open the door!" a man shouted, his voice slurred with liquor and growing hysteria. "Stop 'im!"

Other men began to scramble about in haste, but Derry had no intention of being stopped. Captain Killough might have reached him, but the guard was more concerned with stopping the angry men who were trying to take hold of Derry. Derry reached the door and had no trouble pulling aside the bar and pushing the door open to the foggy night.

Men screamed in panic as the thick fog rolled into the room like a wave brushing up over a shore. Derry could barely hear the bells over their yells, a whisper of lovely music moving away along the mostly hidden road. Derry followed, ignoring the feel of mud beneath his bare feet and the cold breeze that rushed over him.

"Lady!" he shouted.

"Lord Derry!" Killough yelled from somewhere behind

him. He hadn't expected Killough to come out into such a dire night to follow him, but Derry didn't slow. He ran faster, hearing the music louder again, but still not seeing any of the fae. His bare feet hit a stone, bruising his right heel, and he limped but hardly slowed.

"Derry," she said softly.

Leanora caught his arm, and he came to a stumbling stop, nearly going to his knees as he gasped and shivered. He could feel warmth in her touch, though, and the impression of spring spread out around her once more. A warm breeze feathered her golden hair and touched his face like a soft caress. A child, his thin face pinched with hunger and his clothing ragged, held desperately to her other hand.

"Lady," Derry gasped. "I --"

"Go back, Derry," Leanora said, her voice soft but the order firm. "You are not ready. Go to Tyleen, Prince Derry SanOsen. Something human calls to you there, and you must still answer."

"I want peace," he said, his voice just as soft. He could hear Killough coming closer, cursing the night and probably cursing Derry as well, though he did that silently. "I want away from the nightmares --"

"Ah, but if the humans still call to you, how could you find peace among us?" she asked, her fingers tightening on his arm. "You have heard the bells, Derry. You are linked to us in a way that I don't fully understand. We were meant to meet this night, Prince. I think you needed to know that you are not alone when you face the trouble ahead."

"Trouble?" he asked, testing the word. He didn't like the sound of what she'd said and didn't want to think the trouble might be aimed at him.

"Something is stirring in the land, moving at the command of one we cannot see or find. The trouble has been manifesting in a few places but leaves no path we can trace back to the source." She sounded bothered and annoyed ... and troubled. "Changes are coming, Derry SanOsen. I think you could not abandon your friends in such a time of danger."

Her words reached Derry on a level he had not expected. She had his attention as he felt a surge of worry that did not center on himself. "Are you saying the others are in danger? The King? Shannon?"

"*Everyone* is in danger," she replied and pulled the child closer, as though to protect him from some danger that lurked close by. "Both humanity and the fae face trouble from this problem. What moves out there in the world is no friend to any of us, Prince Derry."

Leanora had been hinting at some trouble they shared before this. Now he started to see the depth of the problem, though he couldn't begin to understand what they might face. Magic? He suspected it must be so for the fae to be involved. What could humans do against such a problem? They could become allies with the fae, but that was going to be no easy --

Captain Killough surged out of the fog, nearly colliding with all three of them. He stopped short by grabbing hold of Derry's shoulder and as he tried to yank his ward back away from the fae woman. Derry went down to his knees and Killough, his face pale white, stepped up beside him.

"Let the child go, creature," Killough warned with a hand on his belt knife.

"Don't let him take me!" The boy took hold of her with both hands and Derry could hear other bells coming closer, the sounds not as melodious this time. Anger and worry played the tunes now, and none of it good.

"Go back to your own kind, man," Leanora ordered, her voice quite unearthly with the command. A wind blew around them, sharp and cold, dispelling any hint of spring. "Go back and take Prince Derry with you -- or stay and become one of the lost. You will not get another chance."

"Give me the child," Killough repeated, taking another step closer.

"The child is ours now, human. Your kind abandoned him, and he came to us of his own free will. Take your Prince away and go back to your own people and live to tell this tale to your grandchildren. *But go now.*"

A few fae had come close enough to become shapes in the fog, their bells almost discordant, and the feel of danger nearly overwhelming Derry. Killough, though clearly panicked, still reached for the child and Leanora lifted her hand to fend him off. He must have thought she intended to attack --

Derry surged back to his feet and threw himself between the two, heedless of any danger. At that moment, Derry had seen the entire village, if not all of Lynashin itself, at risk of destruction because of his ill-advised rush to escape personal fears.

The fae woman, caught off balance with the child pulling at her, took a small cut across her fingers before Derry slapped the blade aside, taking a deeper cut across the palm of his hand.

And that, finally, shocked Killough into dropping the weapon as he realized he had injured the favored nephew of the King, which apparently bothered him more than his attack on a fae. Derry took a quick step backward, shaking his head as though to deny everything that had happened. The child cried out, and Leanora soothed him. She made a gesture that stopped the other fae from coming any closer. Their bells fell silent. The night felt dark, cold, and dangerous.

"Go, Lady," Derry said softly, holding his wounded hand in the other, although he didn't feel the pain as panic continued to surge through him. "Take this poor, lost child, and go before any other madness comes to try and take us."

Leanora nodded though she glanced at Killough who backed away as sanity and panic waged war in his face. Derry had not expected her to reach out and take his own hand, but maybe she considered it safe enough with the knife still on the ground. Derry gave a sign to Killough to hold back much as she had signaled her fae to do the same.

"Blood of my blood," Leanora whispered, wrapping her wounded fingers around his bleeding hand. She bent closer, her words barely a whisper of breath against his ear. "I give you a gift, my friend. You will know when we are near, and you will come to us when you are ready. You are touched by the wild."

The fae woman drew her hand away, and he felt an odd tingle move through his hand, up his arm, and then spread through his entire body. Derry gasped as the world changed around him. Everything came alive with lights, sounds ... the essence of life he had never seen or felt before. He could even hear the whisper of animals, almost loud enough that he thought he could understand them. The wind itself felt alive, and the moon shed warmth as strong and bright as any sunlight.

The change had come too quickly, and it felt like a blow. Leanora released his arm, and Derry staggered back, catching hold of Killough to stay to his feet and to keep the guard from doing anything else rash. Leanora took a step away as well, but then she stopped and smiled when she looked back at him. The look took him by surprise amid so much else that seemed dire. "I think I shall love you, Derry SanOsen."

Leanora spun in a whirl of light and bells and walked into the mist. Derry stared, more shocked by her words than he had been by anything else that had happened on this odd night.

Killough looked equally shocked, but he shook his head as though to clear away a dream and then focused on Derry again. "Lord Derry, sir. I think we best return to the inn or they're likely to lock us out for the night and there's no other door will open for us. I'd rather have the warmth and companionship -- human companionship -- tonight."

Derry wanted to walk through the village and the woods, feeling everything alive around him. He wanted to run wild and escape -- but he wouldn't. Derry looked back at Killough and saw the worry in his companion's face. He could, in fact, almost feel the emotion. Besides, his hand still ached, and the night had started to feel cold again. A brisk wind picked up, and he could hear the trees creaking ominously around them.

"Yes, let's get inside," Derry agreed, pleasing the older man.

Killough picked up his knife from the ground and stared at it for a moment before he wiped away the blood and turned back to Derry. "Sir -- what happened --"

"This was an accident," Derry said, lifting his still-bleeding hand. Killough quickly tore cloth from the edge of his tunic, and Derry gratefully wrapped the wound. Whatever Leanora had done, the magic hadn't healed the injury, which seemed unfortunate. His feet still ached at the feel of hard stone as they walked slowly back towards the inn. He hadn't realized he'd run so far, nearly all the way to the end of the village. "An accident, and that's all we need to say regarding the matter."

"Yes. Good." Killough took a deeper breath but didn't move any faster. "I'm sorry, though, Lord Derry. The truth is that I simply felt as though I'd gone mad with fear. I never thought such things existed, you know. At least not in places where a plain man like me might see them."

"There was certainly enough madness in the air," Derry agreed. He tried to pull his tunic closed for what little warmth that would provide. The sounds distracted him, though -- sounds he had never heard before in the world, even though he knew they had always been there. Trees seemed to sigh, and owls laughed while crickets sang their last songs before winter came. Derry slowed, overwhelmed by everything he heard and felt, and not wanting to let go of ... of the magic.

Killough, however, started at the sound of leaves rattling in the breeze and looked back over his shoulder with apprehension. He had shoved the knife back into place, but his rough fingers brushed against the hilt. Derry suspected the captain wouldn't trust the night again for a long time.

Killough, though, was the one who held up a hand and signaled a stop, surprising Derry. The older man met his look with obvious trepidation before he dared speak. "She'll come for you again, won't she, your lordship?"

"No, she won't come for me," Derry replied and smiled, surprising the man. "But I will go to her someday, and of my own free will. Not yet, though. Not for a long time still."

Killough nodded with relief and said no more as they once again headed down the muddy street. They neared the Glendalow Inn and Derry could see the door still open, light pouring out in a welcome glow, though the voices sounded troubled. When they neared, he found two burly men standing in the doorway with swords in hand, and they clearly were not ready to hear a tale of wonder about the fae. Killough stepped forward, visibly pale but prepared to take the men on.

"I fear we lost the child," Derry said, hoping to stop any trouble from happening. The two men, still mostly drunk and bleary-eyed, didn't move out of the way. "Come on, friends. It's cold out here."

The one on the right brought up his sword and his ruddy face showed the kind of unreasoning rage that Derry had gotten used to seeing the cell he'd shared with others. He muttered some words, too drunk to make any sense.

"Let his lordship inside, you fool," Finil said, nudging the swordsmen aside. Bay and Casey followed close behind Finil, and it was probably the swords in their hands that got the men to back down. "Come in and let us get the door bolted closed again. A shame about the child, but praise the gods that you are all right, Prince Derry."

The name, clearly used for the effect, got their attention; the two stepped away so quickly that Derry feared they would skewer themselves on Bay and Casey's swords. Everyone watched Derry and Killough carefully, but they apparently both still *looked* human enough. The door closed behind Derry with a loud bang and the men quickly put the old oaken beam in place.

Finil brought out pitchers of ale and Killough paid for a round for everyone, putting the entire group in a much better mood. Derry drank a few sips with the men and then took his cup to his room, limping slowly up the stairs and waving Killough away when he tried to follow. He needed some time alone.

Derry sipped a little more ale as he stared out the window, heedless of the cool breeze. The world sang, even in the dark and cold. He could hear the fae still, but he couldn't see them. He wasn't sure what he wanted --

Which meant Leanora had been right, and Derry was not ready to go to the fae. More than the dreams about the castle and home still had hold of him. The thought of disappearing now, and not returning to even talk to Shannon, left him almost ill. He didn't pull the shutters closed, but he did finally cross to the bed. Derry carefully brushed off all the mud he could from his feet, and finally settled amid the blankets and excellent pillows. He'd been a long time from such comforts.

He could still hear the silver and gold bells, but they soon lulled him to sleep.

Chapter Three

D erry rested better than he had in years. The nightmares missed him for the rest of the night, and he awoke to find bright light streaming through the window, highlighting a scattering of dust motes in the air.

The new day held far better promise than the one before. A sense of worry still lingered in his thoughts, but the sunlight was bright, the air fresh, and the world alive around him. Derry still felt a chill when he thought about the years that he had spent in King Robert's cell, but for the first time since his release, Derry felt as though he could see a future that would be better.

He tried not to consider the implications of what Leanora had told him about trouble lurking in the world, which he had no way to understand. Derry pushed those thoughts away. A moment of peace was not too much to expect without rushing off into other troubles.

Derry could hear people outside; laughing voices and birds singing in counterpoint. Killough had not awakened him to ride at dawn, and he appreciated having the time to sleep so well. Sitting up did not make his head pound as it had all the other days. His hand, still wrapped in cloth, felt stiff, but not very sore. He sat on the edge of the bed and stared at the windowsill, remembering Leanora there. Oddly, she seemed more real now than she had the night before. Maybe that came from the feel of magic he now held within him. He wondered, still, if he shouldn't have gone with her -- though nothing seemed as dire in the bright light of day as it had the night before.

Derry washed, pouring cold water into the bowl on the stand and splashing it on his face. His travel bag yielded his shaving kit and soap, so he made quick work of that job. The beard he'd been forced to grow in that cell was long gone, and he disliked even stubble now.

His feet were sore and bruised, and he limped over to the window with a softly muttered curse. Putting his boots on was not going to be pleasant.

He held his hand out to the sunlight, which felt like something soft caressing him.

Three sparrows landed on his hand, and Derry found he could almost understand their little chirps. Bright day, they said. Good sun. Food before winter.

Cautiously, and then with more daring, he reached out with his other hand and gently petted each one, winning bright whistles each time while they preened and danced on his hand and arm. A half dozen more came to the windowsill, all of them singing about the lovely bright day and the pretty trees.

A soft knock on the door sent the birds all flying to the nearby tree. Derry smiled, thankful for this gift from a friend.

Another knock, louder this time. "Lord Derry, sir?" Killough asked softly.

"Come in, Captain. I'm up."

Killough pushed open the door and peeked inside, appearing very much relieved not to find any new insanity. Derry didn't know what Killough had expected, although, considering the madness of the night before, he supposed the caution was reasonable.

"I have the boys getting the horses ready, your lordship," he said. His voice steadied. "I thought it best we all get a little extra rest."

"I feel better," Derry admitted. He didn't say if was the touch of the fae or not. The sleep hadn't hurt him any.

"If the weather holds, we'll have a fine day of it and reach Tyleen about sunset. I've gotten food from the Inn, too."

"Well done." Derry limped back to the bed and reached for the bag Killough had hung over the nearby chair. He was not going to return to Tyleen looking like a tramp. Regent Olivia had gifted him with some fine clothing, and he'd saved them until now. He also found some coins he hadn't realized were in with travel bag. He tossed a couple pieces of silver to Killough who caught them easily. "Take this down to Finil, if you would, and tell him it's to buy breakfast for those here, along with a round or two of ale tonight on me."

"That's bound to bring some worried men around to thinking well of you," Killough said, tossing the coins in the air and catching them again.

"My thoughts exactly."

Killough left. Derry decided not to change the pants since he was going to be riding a horse for several hours, and the clothing Olivia had sent with him wouldn't stand up to such wear. They were court clothing; well-made and lovely, but not the kind of apparel one wore for a few hours on the road.

Of all the clothing, he chose one sturdy looking green shirt with delicate embroidery and a nice vest to go over it. The cloak he'd been wearing was a good weave and fine enough for a Lord. He sat on the bed and pulled on the boots, wincing at cuts and bruises on his feet. He'd suffered with worse, but he was glad to be able to keep his pride somewhat intact and not have Killough there hovering over him while he dressed. By the time Killough returned, he was brushing out his hair and tying it back, anxious to be on their way.

"Is your hand all right then, sir? No need to have it looked at? We don't want an infection now."

"It's fine," he said. He flexed the fingers. "A bit stiff, but no trouble. We'll leave the bandages in place, so the reins don't bother it, but I should be fine."

"That relieves me a great deal, sir," Killough admitted. His voice dropped as he stepped away from the open door. "They're tellin' mighty tales in the common room this morning, and they don't know the half of it. We stayed a bit late so I could spread lesser tales of fog and fae. We never saw them, I said. And the wound came from startling each other, there in the fog. I'll own up to that part, which is mostly true."

"Well, we'll simply leave them to those tales, shall we?" Derry said with an unexpected grin. He might have been half-drunk considering the giddiness he felt this morning.

"Fine by me, your lordship," Killough agreed with a decisive nod of his head. "I must say that ridin' with you has been more of an adventure than I looked for in me old age."

"We're almost to Tyleen, but who knows what adventures we might still have along the way."

"Oh, well, that's wonderful then," Killough said but laughed this time. "And here I was lookin' forward to a nice quiet few days by the hearth with my wife and young ones."

"You are married then?" Derry asked as he glanced back out the window. Time to go.

"Very much married," Killough said with a happier nod of his head. Killough grabbed up Derry's bag, acting like a good servant rather than a guard. "Nearly twenty years married to a fine woman. Her father was a blacksmith clear up in Banlien on the northern coast. I met her while I was stationed there."

"Twenty years?" Derry said, hoping to keep the discussion going and light-hearted as they went down the old stairs again.

He did not want to encourage conversations with anyone else on the way out.

"Aye. We've been happy, Sarah an' me," Killough said with a smile. Both he and Derry gave nods to Finil as they passed. The man still looked happy to see Derry, which seemed inexplicable after the night before. "Our eldest son is married to a lovely girl, her a servant in Tyleen itself. She'll gift us with our first grand babe any day now."

"And you didn't ask to be relieved of this duty? I can't imagine King Nevin would have denied you the leave."

They went to the door with little more than a few nods from the people in the room which was mostly empty now. He did wave farewell to Finil who still grinned brightly, despite all the trouble of the night before. Cara even came out of the kitchen to wave to him as well. She'd always been shy.

Killough said nothing more until they were outside, the door shut, and they'd walked out into the street where Casey and Bay stood with the horses.

"The King came to me, quiet like, and asked if I would take the trip to escort you home. He asked me to pick my own men," he replied finally, his voice soft. "He knew I didn't have any ... entanglements at court."

He wasn't one of the Queen's men that meant.

Derry gave a nod of thanks as he glanced around the street. Both fog and fae were gone in the full light of day, except Derry could hear the distant sound of bells, and he suspected that his companions could not. The world seemed more alive to him again this morning, and when he crossed to the horse that he had ridden the last few days, even the animal felt different. The horse was anxious to get moving, to be back on the trail, and heading for home and all the comforts of a well-tended barn. Derry supposed he ought to take the same attitude. He rubbed the nose of the black and white gelding and mounted. Soon they had turned and started down the road, and one he knew well.

Derry did note that the locals seemed happy to see them go. He wondered if word had already been sent to Tyleen, but Killough didn't appear to be worried about it. The man seemed cautious as they left town, but soon they went past the last of the cottages and into the fields. By then Killough had relaxed, which confirmed Derry's feelings about the bells that he hard and they did not. He didn't mention the lovely sounds to his traveling companions.

"Your lordship, sir -- I'm going to be bold, if I may," Killough said after a few miles on the road, and giving him a sidelong look that Derry couldn't quite interpret.

"Of course," Derry said, wondering what bothered the man now. "I appreciate the candor you've shown me the last two days." Their horses matched pace, both equally glad for the beautiful day. The feeling proved both a distraction and infectious; Derry wanted to run and finally shook his head to dislodge the thoughts and focused on the still worried Killough. "I don't know why I was so willing to walk blindly into Tyleen. I know better. I grew up there. No one who had lived at the castle as long as I did could be naïve about how to survive there."

"Sir, if I may --" he began and looked uneasy.

"Speak freely, Killough. I'm not easy to offend and very hard to shock."

Killough gave an unexpected laugh. "Yes sir, I have learned that much! I was going to say, Lord Derry, that from the moment you came off the ship I could tell you'd had a hard time of it. The Captain had feared to lose you on the voyage and pushed to get here, so something unfortunate wasn't on his hands. You looked half dead and starved."

Derry shivered at the unexpected memory of a dark cell, filthy floors and rough companions, both the men and the rats. He had survived simply because some of the wiser people realized King Robert wanted him dead, and they were not going to oblige the hated man by doing the work for him. That had left Derry waiting for the executioner to come for him instead.

A long, long wait.

"Lord Derry, sir?" Killough said softly.

He took a deeper breath and pulled himself back to this far more pleasant place with the fresh air and singing birds. "It's all right," he said to the grim-faced man beside him. "It wasn't a pleasant experience, but I don't intend to let it rule the rest of my life."

"Well, you're wise in that at least," Killough replied, implying that in some things Derry was not wise. Derry laughed, and Killough reddened slightly. "This is what I meant to say, sir. You seem clear-headed now, but I think there's a fever upon you still. Many is the man who survived an ordeal only to fail at home. Take care, sir."

"Yes, I will. Thank you for your concern." He gave the man a nod of thanks and tried to take the words to heart. He found it difficult to consider something so serious, though, on such a wonderful day. He delighted in the laughter of the birds and watching the rabbits and squirrels peek out to watch them pass. The world had changed --

No. Derry was the one who had changed. Leanora's blood had mixed with his and opened a view of the world that he'd never expected. The breeze through the trees created music, and the robins sang with it. Somewhere not far away, a hunting fox yapped in frustration, and a retreating mouse laughed in return.

Every sound tried to draw Derry away, but Killough talked to him through the day, which helped keep him grounded when his mind wanted to wander off. He would have headed into the woods and lost himself in the new wonders, and probably not even regretted it -- at least at first.

No village of any size stood along this path that wound up and down through the rolling hills surrounding the great Tyleen Valley. They passed a few small cottages, mostly kept by foresters and other King's men. Geese and chickens ran wild through the forest edges and were apt to turn up unexpectedly, watching where he passed. A few people had homes in the occasional open dells and they often had sheep and maybe a cow or two. Those animals seemed placid and content, and not nearly as lively as the horses.

One farmer was smoking meat over a great fire, preparing for winter storage. The scent nearly made Derry ill, and they passed on quickly, Killough giving him another worried look. He'd probably turned pale.

"I think we're going to be in for a cold winter," Killough said, glancing up at the sky. Clouds moved across the expanse of blue, and the wind had gone colder. At least the ride was almost over. Derry shivered at the thought of reaching Tyleen, and not at the feel of the colder weather. Before the sun was down, he'd be back home. "We've had some cold weather early on, but it warmed a bit again."

"Lucky for me," Derry said, trying to focus again. The wind sounded, and felt, odd. Was this what winter would be like? Darkness and an underlying rage? "I didn't mind the rain so much, but ice and snow -- no, that would not have been welcome on this journey."

"So true. We probably would ha' stayed at the port, truth be told. Once I had a look at you, I wouldn't ha' trusted you to survive to Tyleen in winter weather. There were times enough I thought we ought to find some village as stay put as it was."

"I'm glad to be here," Derry admitted, ignoring all the aches and pains. "And the faster we reached Tyleen, the less chance the queen could send someone against me."

"Yes," Killough agreed and looked glum. "She's not going to be happy."

"Has she ever been happy?" he asked and then felt an odd truth in those words. "I honestly don't remember her ever being pleased. It's not as though the King mistreats her. She has whatever she wants within reason."

"The woman knows no reason," Killough said softly. Bay and Casey were not riding very close now, and it seemed Killough didn't want even them to hear his words. "That woman has plans, your lordship. I wouldn't be a person to stand between her and what she wants."

"I wouldn't want to," Derry agreed, but he tilted his head and met Killough's wary look. "But I don't think I would want the Queen to get everything she wants, so it may be that I'll be one of those who stops her. I wouldn't be alone."

Killough pursed his lips and nodded. Derry wondered if he had just passed some sort of initiation. If so, Derry was glad for the company. Killough knew where Derry stood with Queen Alisia, as though there could be a question after what the Queen had done to him.

Despite that Derry wanted to rush the last few miles home, he didn't urge Killough to hurry. By mid-afternoon, exhaustion unexpectedly set in and they took a short rest beside a sheep pen in mid-afternoon. Derry found he was glad to be off the horse. He didn't want to go to Tyleen stumbling over his own feet and too groggy to answer questions.

Was that his pride or wisdom? Maybe some of both, Derry decided. He ate some bread and cheese, drank a little ale -- and held out his hand when a butterfly swept close to him. The pretty thing landed on his fingertips and seemed to study him. Derry smiled and wished it away again, watching as the bright wings fluttered towards some late-blooming flowers at the edge of the trail.

Killough watched him much as he had studied the butterfly. Did the guard understand the implications that came with the butterfly? *Touched by the wild*: Derry had a link to nature, and he didn't think it would disappear.

Complications. The gift from Leanora would soon create a new set of problems for Derry. Would they be worse than facing the Queen? The connection with nature complicated his reactions, and he feared they could cause a misstep when he needed his wits. So, for the rest of the ride to Tyleen, he decided to do his best to block the feelings rather than seek them out.

Even so, the wind, with the whisper of hidden rage, distracted him. Maybe this was the feel of all winter winds, coming from the cold north and driving away the warmth. He didn't know. He wished he might have asked Leanora about what more to expect.

Derry didn't realize how close they were to Tyleen until they came up the last rise and the land slipped away below them into the vast, green valley. The sun stood hardly above the horizon, though not by much. The Faerena River wandered in a thread of silver in the light and filled with ships coming from the west. The Faerena didn't have a port on the ocean since the river ended in a series of falls right up against the sea. They could have caught one of the ships somewhere inland -- they moved along the river in an extended network of trade. That, however, would have risked him being recognized.

No matter. Derry pulled the horse to a stop. He stared across the massive city to where Tyleen Castle rested on higher ground. A half dozen other, smaller castles circled her like goslings beside a goose. There sat the power of his family -- all the power that ruled Lynashin. He could feel it from here with an odd surge of warmth that spread around him -- though he thought he felt a touch of darkness, too. Derry wondered what those feelings meant and wished there was a fae close to ask. He didn't dare say anything to the others. Killough still looked worried enough.

The last golden light of day caught the battlements of

Tyleen, and the castle appeared to glow. He held the horseback to watch while a wagon passed on the way back up the hill -- a farmer finished with his trade for the day and looking happy to be heading home. Derry stared at lovely Tyleen, and he watched with delight as the torches were lit on the four towers, looking like stars brought to ground. The lesser castles that stood on the lower flanks were the official homes of the heads of the clans, and they looked like gems tonight, set in a crown around Tyleen.

Lights went up here and there in the castle windows and in the city's buildings in the foreground. Unlike the villages and the farms, life went on after dark here.

"Here, pull up your cloak, Lord Derry," Killough said and reached back to pull the hood up. "It's getting a bit cool. Besides, you're more likely to be recognized here, and we've come this far with little enough notice. We shouldn't take chances here at the last. I can't say word hasn't spread before us or what the Queen might have waiting for you, so we're going to go roundabout and not straight up the Royal Road to the castle gate."

"Wise," he agreed and pulled the cloak up.

They started down the wider road that passed cottages first and then inns for those who couldn't afford to stay in the city. Rough places; the guards moved in closer to Derry as they went by. He started to feel less at ease as well as feeling the weight of all the journey again. His new fae senses had kept him intrigued during the long ride today, but they had not given him more strength.

Derry would be glad to be home. Pleased on very many levels, although he felt his heart pound harder as they passed through the outer gate, and they were finally within the city of Tyleen. Tall buildings rose up along the Royal Way, the road that led toward the castle. They had a long ride still, and Killough almost immediately moved off the main road. No straight approach then -- probably wise with the worry of what Queen Alisia might have prepared if she had word of his return.

The city felt alive tonight, the feel of human life everywhere, though now and then something wild hidden nearby. They passed by rows of taverns and inns; a wise way to go since they weren't likely to draw attention here with all the other people out and about. They were not the only ones on horseback, either. Derry kept his head bowed out of the flickering light whenever they came close to any other riders. Only people of wealth kept horses in the city -- well those and some of the guard. He looked, he hoped, like one more of the soldiers with Killough. Unlike back at Glendalow, he didn't think anyone here he would really want to recognize him, though.

Killough's discussion about being favored by the King had wakened Derry's sense of preservation again, though. He'd been careful in the past. He and Shannon had spent a lot of time in this somewhat rowdy district when they were younger and had learned it wasn't safe for young lords who might have fewer friends then they thought. He and Shannon had always done well standing up with each other in a fight, but neither of them sought out that sort of trouble. They'd moved off to places like Glendalow, well away from anywhere the local boys were likely to ride to torment them.

Beyond the noisy inns and taverns, they took a side road and headed into the temple district. Here, for the first time, Derry wondered if there wasn't going to be a real backlash about his connection to the fae. Of the four main temples, at least two held strong anti-fae sentiments. He felt a chill as they rode past those two buildings, and he was glad enough to be out of the district. That was a problem to face in the future, if word about his link to the fae became known.

Then they entered the nearly empty streets of estates that

stood closer to the castle. They'd been moving up the hill a little at a time on the switchback road. Tyleen Castle stood tall over the city, and every time he looked in that direction, he could see the lights there, beckoning him home.

"We're going faster now, your lordship. Bay, Casey -- you both hang back a bit and make certain no one comes upon us now. You know the work."

"Yes sir," they said, almost in unison.

They pulled back and let the two push on ahead. People nearby shouted and laughed, and creatures raced across the road -- rats, cats, dogs, mice. Many of them paused to look at him and then hurried on as they looked for warm places before winter set in. They startled him, though. Derry tried to control the trembling in his hands. He simply wanted in and this madness done.

"They'll be at a feast by the time we arrive," Killough said, looking up the hillside to the towering walls. "I can't say if that's good or bad."

"Good," Derry replied and shifted slightly in the saddle. His body ached, and the growing cold of night had started to hit him. "If the Queen is in residence, she'll be at the feast. It will be harder for her to stop me before I get that far."

"Oh, excellent point. She and the boy. Prince Egan, I mean."

Killough clearly didn't think much of Egan, and Derry supposed a lot of people had to feel that way. Derry shifted again, feeling a growing worry as they drew closer to the place where he had so longed to be. "Are there any changes I need to know about?"

"The old Lord Nigollan died last winter."

"He held out longer than I expected, poor old man. Blind, deaf, and senile -- I don't remember a time when he wasn't. All my life, people waited for Lord Nigollan to die. Paric succeeded then?"

"Yes," Killough said and slowed, no doubt to let the small group ahead of them go in first. "The change of power came with hardly even any formality to it, since he'd already held clan for so long. I think, for the most part, people were relieved to find the business done at last."

"I imagine so." His mouth had gone dry. Home? He had dreamed of returning for so long, and now they neared the large, arched gate that led to his place of dreams. They rode in silence as the buildings began to crowd in closer together -- and then disappeared entirely near the curtain wall dotted with towers where lights flickered. The castles of the lords spread to the right and left, but straight ahead stood Tyleen. He could see the guards at the gate. If they had arrived any later, there would be questions, but right now they were not the only ones riding up to the portal.

Derry dared not ask any more questions. He didn't dare turn and ride fast away, either. Not that he truly wanted. Something still called him to Tyleen.

Derry's hand tingled when he thought of other things calling to him as well. The silver and gold bells began to sound closer as the night descended around them. Others might have feared that sound, but Derry welcomed the distraction and the promise of companionship of a different type that he would not find in the woods.

Even so, he went willingly up the road and to the gate of Tyleen Castle ... and home.

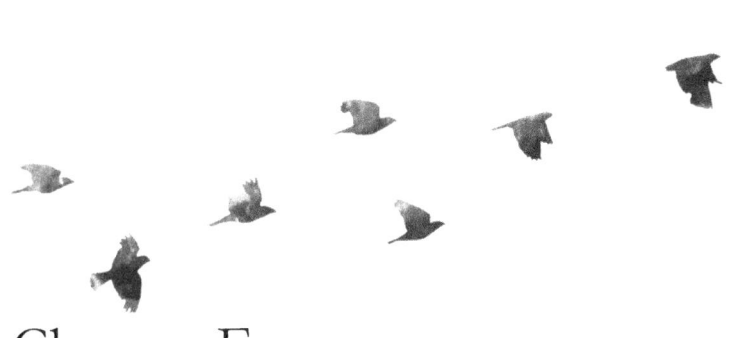

Chapter Four

The guard at the main gate greeted Killough with a friendly shout and let the two through without any fuss. Killough was clearly a trusted man in the castle proper, or else the King made certain the guards would not question Killough when he returned. Derry supposed both to be likely.

How odd. Once Derry and Killough rode past the gate and into the barbican, he could no longer hear the fae bells. Even past the inner gatehouse and into the courtyard, and he still could hear nothing but human sounds.

Maybe that was good. Derry didn't need fae distractions now that they were inside. *Home.* He had to repeat that to himself as he glanced left and right, marveling at how little things had changed. He recognized guards and servants moving with their usual haste at the end of the day. The scents from the kitchen ... oh, there was a problem. The smell of cooked meat threatened to make him ill, but he could also catch the scent of fresh bread and cheese.

Everything confused him.

Bay and Casey caught up with them near the stables, both

looking relieved. "No one, Captain Killough," Bay said softly. "We did fine, I think."

"Off you go then. Not a word of it yet."

"No, sir," Casey agreed with a quick nod.

"Thank you," Derry offered. "I won't forget that you helped get me home."

That won bright smiles as they hurried away.

Derry stayed wrapped in his cloak, thankful for the anonymity and the shadows of nightfall. He let Killough lead him away from the stables and towards the steps to the keep. The guard there let them pass as well, and this time Derry thought he saw a bit of recognition that held both pleasure and worry. Derry said nothing still.

Inside the walls...

His legs wanted to give way. Killough caught him by the arm and hurried him off to the right into a little alcove in the hall where he could stand with the wall at his back. Servants looked their way and hurried on to where the Lords and Ladies were feasting.

"Your Lordship?" Killough said softly.

"A moment. I thought I was ready for this, but I was wrong."

"No surprise, sir. I don't think you ever really accepted that you would be here."

"You're very observant."

"Part of why I am so good at my work, I suppose. Are you ready? The longer we stand here, the more attention you'll draw, and I don't think you want word to go on ahead of you now."

"True." He stood up straighter and forced calm this time.

"I'll take you to the entrance to the Grand Hall, but you'll have to go on in without me," Killough said, reminding Derry that no guards were allowed inside the room during the feasting. The High Lords had insisted on that rule after a bloody massacre more than two centuries ago. Granted, the King could surround the room with guards and simply wait for people to come out, but at least they didn't have to fear their meal being interrupted.

"Let's do it," Derry said. He took a deeper breath. "This isn't going to get easier."

Killough agreed and looked worried again. The Captain had gotten him this far, though, and they both needed to see the journey through to the end. Killough escorted Derry the last few steps across the marble floor and to the large stone archway from which both light and sound escaped. The servants had mostly finished bringing in the food for this course of the dinner. They'd start with the next part soon, but for the moment, the area stood empty.

The Lords and Ladies were a loud group, but the King's rich voice rose over them sometimes. Whatever King Nevin had said brought a round of laughter to the room, and that helped Derry feel better. Killough got him to the alcove, the servants barely glancing their way, too busy to take much notice. Guests came this far with guards all the time, so they didn't draw too much attention even still.

Killough stood there for a moment, patted his arm, and walked away without another word. Derry watched him go with a bit of trepidation, but it was what he needed. Derry had to move forward on his own now.

The smoky light of the torches nearly blinded him, and the scent of half-cooked meat threatened to make him ill yet again. Derry took a step forward and hovered at the edge of the room. The King and his family sat at the High Table on the dais just to the right, and the rest of the court spread out across the room. A quick glance proved that Shannon was not at the SanSota table which was unfortunate. Seeing Shannon would have given him strength. In fact, only one of Shannon's brothers and a few cousins sat there tonight.

A harper sat below the King, playing some bright tune that most of the others probably didn't hear at all. Derry found the song delightful, and it helped to calm him again. Derry blinked away the tears from the light and smoke, trying to decide if he should retreat after all. Surely there would be a better time to see the King and let him know his nephew had returned. The Queen and her three sons sat at the High Table as well. He would rather avoid a scene with her --

Just then, the King looked his way, froze for a moment, and then left the table so quickly that a worried silence spread throughout the room. Derry hadn't expected the rush to him, the sudden embrace that wrapped him in his uncle's strong arms, reminding him of the day his parents had died. He could still find peace and contentment in that embrace.

"Well then," King Nevin said, his voice loud as he pulled back, though he kept one arm across Derry's shoulder. "Let's not keep the surprise to ourselves. Take off the cloak, boy, and come join the feast."

Derry supposed he couldn't have asked for a more dramatic return. He undid the clasp and let the cloak slide away as voices throughout the room took up the call of his name with surprise and pleasure.

King Nevin embraced him again, giving Derry a chance for a somewhat furtive glance at the High Table.

Queen Alisia's face had gone stark white except for two spots of bright red on her cheeks. Egan, still looking like a stuffed toad in his ridiculous bright green clothing, stood and put a hand on his mother's shoulder, as though to protect her from some horrible danger. Tevin and Roe, on the other hand, both appeared pleased. Derry couldn't remember the last time he'd seen his cousin, the Crown Prince, smile so brightly. Roe, who had always been Egan's shadow, didn't even bother to look at Egan or the Queen. He clapped his hands with obvious delight and shouted Derry's name along with the others.

"Let me look at you, boy!" King Nevin abruptly pushed Derry away, and he almost lost his balance. No one laughed as he put a hand to the wall to keep from going down. King Nevin's face grew somber. "What in the name of the Gods have they done to you, Derry SanOsen? You look a decade older!"

"Ah, but you often told me I wanted for maturity," Derry replied with a bright smile. Being with King Nevin gave him strength.

The King gave a grunt of amusement, then carefully took him by the arm and led him through the myriad of tables. He surely wouldn't have gone so quickly without his kingly escort. Derry saw worried faces watch him and glances to the Queen, but those were mostly discreet. Some of the people dared pat his arm as he passed and welcomed him home. Here, in the heart of the human stronghold, Derry felt less fae suddenly. Derry knew coming back had been the proper decision because he thought he might put a few things to right by being here and not be a thorn between the King and Queen.

Granted, the Queen looked likely to sharpen that thorn into a deadly dagger and use it against him. Derry would have to move carefully there.

Derry accepted Roe's hand when the boy came to help him up to the top of the dais, another sure sign of his defection from the Queen who glared at both of them.

"Welcome back, cousin," Roe said, and not softly. He'd gotten daring when he abandoned Egan and his mother. Derry wondered what had driven him away. Maybe it was because the Queen had always kept her attention on her darling Egan, and Roe had been on the outside even there. The Queen and her prince had been gone for a while, giving him a chance to be himself. He seemed genuinely happy, and that was nice to see.

Derry forgave Roe for any trouble they'd had in the past.

If Queen Alisia herself had so much as given him a nod of greeting, he would have forgiven even her. He had come back home looking for a place of peace, and he'd gladly spend a little of his pride to get it. Unfortunately, a glance at the woman showed there was no chance of reconciliation there.

Servants hurriedly brought another chair and wisely put him beside Roe and at the far end of the table, and well away from the Queen and Egan. Derry moved to the chair and waited, remembering his manners. One did not sit before the King, who was still on his feet. Egan and thrown himself into a chair, though. Tevin did not, and those who had stood in surprise remained there, though many had been too shocked to even get to their feet.

"Sit, sit," King Nevin ordered, though he did not take his chair yet. Derry found himself caught between protocols and obeying the King. Obeying won out, especially when Roe gave him a nudge. He was starting to tremble and decided sitting was better to falling over. "My friends," the King said, his voice booming out over the room. He had never been a quiet man. "I had word Derry would be coming home soon, though I admit I little trusted this woman, so I kept quiet."

Derry lifted his head and chanced to see several people look to their Queen, and quite obviously, she was the one they would not have trusted. Derry dared not make that glance to her as well and see her reaction. This could get out of hand very quickly and without any help from him.

"Derry later -- no, tomorrow -- we will discuss what acts of retribution we need to make against these people who imprisoned you for no reason." King Nevin watched him, anger in his eyes this time.

"Sire, if I may?" Derry said, getting a nod from the man. "Thank you. I can tell you things have changed drastically in The Isles since Regent Olivia took over. The land is far different than when I went to Fairfall under King Robert's rule. If I had any quarrel, it was with him and those who backed that madman. However, King Robert is dead, his people killed or exiled. Regent Olivia is not our enemy."

"That's a bold statement to make." Queen Alisia leaned forward and faced him with her grey eyes sparkling with anger, and her voice shrill. He felt a whisper of dread spear him in the heart, and he hoped it didn't show in his face. He dared not appear weak before the Queen. The blush of color in her cheeks had spread across her narrow face as she leaned towards him, a hawk ready for the strike. "What gives you the right to make such a statement, boy?"

"I do believe you gave me the right," Derry answered and marveled that he found the nerve to answer her at all, let alone with so much daring. His voice stayed calm, and he felt a flicker of warmth, the touch of fae blood, as it swirled through him. "That was the mission you sent me on. Your orders were to ascertain the state of affairs in the Isles and report my opinion."

Derry had shocked her with the answer, and probably everyone else as well, considering how silent the room had gone. He'd caught her off guard, but it must have been madness that made him so bold. Or maybe this was the lesson he'd learned during those hard years in that cell. Derry knew now that he never dared back away from an enemy or show weakness. That only led to more, and worse, trouble.

The young lord she'd sent to the Isle's had never shown his claws before. He did now and didn't back down. Egan had gone white, he noticed, but the boy's eyes blazed. Boy? He had to be nearing twenty.

No one except for the King seemed to dare breathe or move. King Nevin dropped into his seat. "Good point, lad. We'll talk on that matter later."

Derry nodded, grateful for the easy way out of the discussion. The King looked relieved not to have to deal with the Queen either. She said nothing, but her glare remained on Derry for longer than need be.

"You've hurt your hand," Tevin said suddenly with a nod his way. Derry glanced at the cloth wrapped palm, having forgotten about that trouble. "And recently, I'd say. It's bleeding."

"Ah." He fiddled a little with the bandage. "That was last night at Glendalow when I chased after some fae --"

Oh, wrong thing to say. He was far too scattered. Everyone went still and silent. The Queen blinked. The King stared at him.

"Fae," King Nevin said. His eyes widened this time, and he held to his golden goblet as though he had forgotten he'd picked it up. "Fae. Truly."

"Yes, sire," Derry said and wished he'd had better control.

"Well, I guess I will have to re-evaluate the trouble there then, won't I?" he still looked startled. "Not bandits after all."

Derry gave a bow of his head and said nothing more. He had come close to telling the King that he need not worry about the fae, but this was not the place to make that statement and be forced to explain more. Better to talk to the King later, and in private -- and when his head didn't spin so much.

The King still stared for a moment and then gave a quick nod. "This is not the time for such a discussion, with you barely through the door and in need of rest. Welcome home, lad. Truly, welcome home."

He hadn't expected those words to sound so heartfelt, and they brought unexpected tears to his eyes. He blinked them away and offered his uncle a smile. "Thank you, sire."

"Now eat and celebrate with us. We have a fine reason for a feast tonight."

"I am afraid I won't be able to eat much, sire -- but I am glad to be here. You cannot know how much."

King Nevin gave a quick nod, his face troubled. "I know you'll have a hard time of it for a while but make your old uncle happy and let me see you eat a bit, lad."

The servants had brought him food. He nibbled at the bread and cheese and ignored the rest for now. No one would consider why. He didn't need any other questions, and no reason to mention the fae again. There was a problem that might even win a few people over to the Queen.

Derry hadn't expected the King to make so much show of his homecoming and he wondered if King Nevin didn't use this to make a jab at his wife...

No. The King had never been duplicitous in the past, and he'd never hidden or faked his emotions, no matter what the occasion. His uncle was clearly pleased to have Derry home again. That welcome had healed wounds Derry hadn't even known he held, and he sat back on the chair feeling better than he had expected, given the show. He didn't dare even glance at the Queen, though he was sure he could feel her attention on him far too often.

The harper started up the music again. Voices rose in the room, and a feeling of happiness filled the air. He wondered if that feeling was his imagination or one of the fae senses he had somehow gained from the magical Leanora.

Best not to think about that trouble right now.

Tevin had sent for clean cloth, and he came to the end of the table and insisted on treating Derry's hand himself. The Crown Prince had been going to battle with his father for years now and had early decided that he would learn everything he could to help soldiers survive. The people loved him for it, though his mother declared the work unfit for nobility.

"It's good to have you back, Derry," Tevin said with another bright smile. "Things were dull, if not outright maudlin after you were gone. No one was happy about it in the end."

"I heard," Derry said with a quick glance towards the Queen.

Tevin leaned closer. "Don't let her win now. Be careful."

Everyone worried that he might not be safe, and all because of one person. Derry didn't look at the Queen this time. "I don't intend to do anything that would cause trouble for some time, Prince Tevin. I'm simply not up to it."

"I do hope you enjoy yourself, though." Tevin glanced at Roe, who was watching the two and staying silent. "I think my youngest brother could use a responsible role model these days."

"Me? Responsible?" He laughed and drew smiles from everywhere in the room, though they couldn't hear the conversation. "That wasn't what people said of me four years ago."

"No, they didn't," Tevin agreed and tied off the new bandage. "People learn to appreciate something when it is lost."

He appeared to mean those words with a sincerity that Derry found just as surprising as the King's boisterous welcome.

"Tevin," Roe said, leaning closer and tugging at his brother's shirt sleeve as though he had no other way to gain his attention. "See if father will send for Shannon."

"Now, there's a good idea!" Tevin patted Roe on the shoulder as he went back past. Roe smiled as though the Gods had taken notice of him. Derry had never considered how difficult it must be for the youngest of three princes. Tevin had the King and Egan had the Queen. That left Roe very much on his own now that he'd stopped tagging behind Egan. He'd been too young to go to his father's side before this. Maybe that was changing.

"Send for Shannon?" Derry asked softly, watching as the

Crown Prince crossed to lean close to his father and speak. The Queen viewed her eldest son with such open mistrust that it bothered Derry.

"Shannon and mother had a falling out over what she did to you. Since she returned, he's been excused from the feasts, except on the High Holidays," Roe explained with a glance at his mother and a shake of his head. He'd lost his baby fat in the last few years and now looked more like Tevin rather than Egan. He dressed better, too. Roe also didn't try to cover his words with any form of politeness towards his mother, which surprised Derry, though that was the way the King would have said it. Maybe Roe simply had a new, and better, role model. "Shannon had a shouting match with mother after you'd gone, and she exiled him, but father and Tevin came back before he even reached the port and sent people to bring him back to court. Father tried to buy your freedom, Derry. Offered a fortune, but King Robert wanted none of it."

He'd not thought about what King Nevin would do, and he felt another surge of gratitude for the attempt to get him back -- and glad it hadn't gone to anything worse.

"Rory SanSota!" the King suddenly shouted, startling Derry and everyone else. "Go fetch that rogue brother of yours -- you know the one. Tell him I want to see him here *immediately*. And don't you dare to whisper Derry is back. I want to see Shannon's surprise."

Rory gave a bright laugh of his own as he stood --

"You cannot bring that rude boy into my presence!" Queen Alisia shouted, banging her golden goblet down on the table.

No one appeared surprised by her reaction, though Rory paused with a worried glance at the King.

"Go," he said with a nod, and Rory retreated in haste. "Alisia, either you forget your own petty pride, or you are welcome to leave. Derry has made little of the trouble you caused him, which is far, far worse than the few bad words you had with Shannon. You can stay and be quiet, if not polite, or you may leave. In fact, you are free to take Shannon's choice and take your dinners elsewhere if you do not like the company here."

Oh, now that was more than anyone present wanted to hear. Derry had not expected such a reply, and neither did Queen Alisia from the look of shock on her face. Derry had the feeling she must have pushed the line a few too many times for King Nevin to say something so blunt.

"You can't prefer --"

"I have given you your choice," King Nevin replied, cutting her short. She didn't like to be interrupted, but she held her tongue at the lift of his hand. "You are welcome to stay, but only if you can manage to hold your tongue, and act with some decorum."

The Queen stared at him, her face going red again. The rest of the room had gone quiet except for a few whispers. Roe and Tevin didn't watch the Queen. Egan held her hand, as though to comfort her after some vicious attack. Derry found Egan's actions far less understandable than the Queen's reactions. Egan acted as though he had no thoughts of his own at all, but simply mirrored what his mother felt or what she expected from him.

Still, when Egan looked at him, he saw fires burning deep in those dull gray eyes. He could almost feel the hatred until Egan blinked and looked away again.

Derry didn't trust either of them -- far less than he had before he left. All the warnings from others were starting to add up. The Queen had never been his friend, but now he had to consciously consider her an enemy. He would rather not have been forced to do so, but this was no new problem between them. He'd never considered how serious the trouble was, though.

"You do not look well, Derry," King Nevin said, drawing his wandering attention again -- and moving past the discussion with his wife. "How is he, son?"

Tevin frowned. "The cut on his hand isn't bad. It should heal well, but he has a fever, and he's half-starved. You need rest, cousin."

"And I hope to have it," Derry admitted. "Rest for a good long time. It has been a difficult few years, but that's past now."

Roe shook his head, and his face darkened. "You can't forgive that easily."

Oh, not good words from the way the Queen looked at her son. Roe needed to be more careful.

"King Robert is dead," Derry reminded him. "I see no reason to hold anger toward someone who has already gone to his own reward from the Gods. I would like peace. I'll do what I can to avoid any trouble."

He looked past Roe to the Queen, but the glare she gave him showed there would be no peace there. He'd simply have to avoid her, which he hoped wouldn't be too difficult. Derry wondered if she could hear all the whispers through the crowd thought -- forty or more of the High Lords and their families had watched this show, and Queen Alisia had not come off better for her act.

"Derry," the King said and drew his attention again. "I gave your estates over to Shannon to care for them while you were gone. I knew I could trust the boy never to cheat you."

"Thank you, sire," he said, glad to have a reason not to study the Queen any longer. "In truth, I hadn't thought about it."

"No surprise there," Nevin replied with a definite laugh. "They were *never* high up on your thoughts as far as I could tell."

Derry didn't argue. The King and his people had usually

handled his estates since he'd come into ownership so young. Nevin had been right. He had rarely asked about the lands, but that was because he had trusted the King and his chosen men to take care of them. Derry had enjoyed visiting the estates, though, and he thought that it would be good to go there and winter away from the castle, so he and the Queen were not locked up in the same location.

That seemed very wise.

He played with his food for a while longer. The smell didn't make him as ill, but he couldn't eat the meat. He wanted to rest --

Movement came at the archway, and Derry looked up to see a harried Shannon SanSota still straightening his tunic as he crossed to the high table. His golden hair wasn't even tied back. Clearly, he had not been ready for a call from the King. His brother Rory kept behind him, looking somber until they came into the room. Then he grinned with delight though, he stayed at his brother's back where Shannon couldn't see.

"Sire," Shannon said and gave a very proper bow when he neared. "Rory says there is something..."

He stopped and stared.

"Well now, there's something I never thought to see," King Nevin said with a bright smile. "Shannon SanSota himself at a loss for words!"

Laughter spread through the room and then as quickly stopped when Shannon swayed, and his brother caught hold of him.

"Gods all," Shannon whispered, but the words were clearly heard. "Derry? Is that really you?"

"Oh yes." He leaned awkwardly to the side of the table so that Shannon could reach up and take his hand. Derry wasn't certain what others were whispering and didn't care. Shannon looked very little changed, which relieved Derry after all he'd heard. "It is good to see you, Shannon."

"You --" Shannon caught Derry's hand in both of his and didn't look likely to let go. "You look terrible, Derry! What the hell have they done to you?"

"Well, they let me go," Derry said with a smile and hoped that Shannon stayed calm. His friend was already glancing at the Queen with narrowed eyes, and she clearly was ready to start a battle. Derry didn't want to be in the middle such trouble. "I admit that I am tired, though."

"You do look worn to the bone," King Nevin admitted with a frown of his own and another dark glance at his wife. "I hadn't thought of what to do with you once you arrived, boy. So, it might be best if you go off with Shannon and let him and the SanSota's take you in for the night."

As though the King couldn't order a dozen suites readied with merely a wave of his hand. The King did him a kindness by letting him go off with his friend tonight. Derry had begun to think he wouldn't last much longer in this tension. This also got him away from the Queen, which he appreciated.

"Thank you, sire," Derry said with a bow of his head, and had trouble recovering his balance. "If you don't mind, I'll go now before I fall asleep at the table."

"Off with you then," he said with a wave of his hand. "We'll talk tomorrow. Or perhaps in a day or two. I trust Shannon will see you well cared for."

"I will, sire," Shannon said with a deep bow. He didn't even look at the Queen.

Roe helped Derry stand and then handed him down to Shannon, who whisked him away so quickly he couldn't get his breath. At the archway, a servant handed Derry back his cloak and Shannon wrapped him in it and started out again, but this time with a worried glance back at the room. Laughter had started to spread there again and a sound of people eating.

"The King -- he will watch her and Egan," Derry said softly as they began to move again. "For the love of the Gods, slow down before I pass out."

"Derry," Shannon said. He stopped and held Derry to his feet, but there was such an odd look on his friend's face that Derry couldn't begin to understand. "Praise the Gods, you finally came back. I'd been planning a raid, you know. My father and I talked about it most nights -- even tonight, at dinner. What we would need to hire a ship, mercenaries, how difficult it might be to fight our way in --"

Derry caught hold of both of Shannon's shoulders and looked him in the face. "Have you gone insane?"

"Yes," he replied and sounded entirely too serious. Then he grinned and took hold of Derry to help keep him moving. "Though I do think father just let me make those plans to keep me from doing anything equally stupid without his knowing about it. You're back, though. *You are back.*"

Spoken as though he mistrusted this moment almost as much as Derry did. They headed out the door into the darkness of the baily. Lights flickered along the walls, and people still moved everywhere. Derry could see them well enough, but he wasn't confident he trusted them. That mistrust came entirely from the confrontation with Queen Alisia

"I'll get you somewhere safe and warm," Shannon promised as his arm tightened around Derry's waist. "Gods, you feel as though you are nothing but skin and bone, my friend."

"A bit more than that," he said, although he had trouble keeping the pace. "I am tired, Shannon. I fear I won't be outstanding company tonight."

"Company, you fool? What do I care if you don't hold a conversation? I feared you would never come home again, Derry."

"There were times enough when I wondered if I would return," Derry admitted with another quick glance at the courtyard, the stables, and the vegetable garden in the corner. "I'm not certain I believe it's real yet."

"We'll get you back on your feet," Shannon said and looked him over again. "As long as we can keep you out of fair Alisia's path, you'll be fine."

"And away from Egan, from what Captain Killough told me. He made certain I was aware enough not to walk off with them and think myself safe. Roe and Nevin warned me as well."

"Good. Can we go on now? I don't think you should be standing here in the cold night."

"I am not an invalid."

"Prove it."

"Well, you might have me there," he admitted with a laugh. He let Shannon take hold of his arm this time, his friend's fingers a little too tight, but Derry didn't protest. They went to the postern door on the north side of the wall rather than out the main gate. The SanSota Gate, this one was called, and the path outside lead straight to the SanSota castle. The soldier bowed once and must have thought it was Shannon and Rory going back out at first, but then he paused and gave a hiss of surprise.

"Gods be blessed. Prince Derry!"

"Lord Derry," he reminded the man with a tap on the arm. "Good to see you, Tad."

"By the Gods. I never thought to see --" The older man stopped and ran his hand over his face. Did he brush aside tears? Derry had never expected such a reaction, especially from the guards. "Go on then, you and Shannon, sir. Do be careful."

"We will be. Thank you."

The guard opened the door and let them out, then stood there to watch them head away, which might not have been wise if his commander saw the gate left open. Derry was glad to have a guard at their back until they were well away from the wall. Then he finally closed the gate again, and the two seemed alone in the world.

Derry found much needed quiet out here on the path between the castles. Shannon slowed again. He must have remembered how much Derry always loved this walk, especially in the dark of night, when the stars hung around them with all their sparkling beauty. He glanced up once, but he wasn't steady enough to walk and look to the skies. Besides, there was still a bit of a mist in the air.

And the ring of fae bells called to him, though Derry said nothing when they called.

This was a familiar walk, and a place filled with good memories, drawing him back to better times. Derry had spent many nights with Shannon's family, sometimes too drunk to go home to Tyleen. Oh, the King knew, of course, and never said anything about it.

Derry had led a blessed life, but he'd not realized it until he lost everything.

"You're quiet."

"I've not had much use for conversation lately," Derry admitted. He almost stumbled and caught himself. Shannon took hold of his arm again. "And I am truly exhausted. I can hardly keep my thoughts straight, let alone speak them. So, talk to me. What's happened since I left."

"The first few days were hell," he admitted. "The Queen and I had a row --"

"I heard. You were a fool to take her on, Shannon."

"Not a fool," he denied, and his hand tightened again. "That angry and lost, though. I had hoped, to be honest, that the Queen would order me to follow you. I thought I could catch up, and when she exiled me, I hoped to find you -- but King Nevin came back and ordered her and that little toad Egan out of the castle instead. He called me back. I almost

didn't return, but Captain Killough -- you don't know him --
convinced me it was wiser. He was right. I never would have
caught up with you by then."

"Killough is a wise man. He brought me home from
Queton."

"Matters are still touchy between the Queen and me, so I
avoid her as much as possible."

"Well, I suspect I'll have much the same trouble."

"Then we can avoid her together," Shannon said and
smiled brightly.

They began walking again, and Derry could hear bells
following somewhere behind, added protection, he suspected,
on a night when he was likely in considerable of danger.
Anyone who wanted the Queen's favor -- or who knew their
lives depended on her good will.

Shannon stopped suddenly, and looked back over his
shoulder, frowning.

"What's wrong?"

"I thought I heard bells," Shannon said and shook his
head as he turned and started hurrying Derry along again.
"Lovely bells, really."

Derry was not at all surprised to find that Shannon might
be lost as well. He said nothing, though. Shannon clearly had
enough on his mind tonight. Besides, he felt breathless again,
hurrying down the long stone-paved path that led through the
narrow stretch of grasslands to the SanSota castle. Sheep
grazed here during the day, but they were long gone to the
sheepfold. They startled a fox who gave a yip and ran away in
haste, annoyed by the intrusion into his grounds. The fox
thought they had an agreement, he and the humans, of when
the two legs could walk the land and when not.

He smiled a little, listening to the complaint as the fox
retreated.

Safe. Safe with Shannon, safe with the fae, and for the

moment, safely out of Queen Alisia's reach.

Chapter Five

The lesser castles had no high walls, of course. The Lords had elegant courtyards and towers, but the places were small compared to Tyleen. The elder High Kings had been wise enough to order the most powerful lords to rule from Tyleen. They also made sure they couldn't build a stronghold to rival the castle that stood over them. The SanSota Castle had a single gate into the courtyard and walls topped by a walk, but only half as high as Tyleen's. They provided just enough protection to keep livestock in and raiders out if need be until the King could bring in the troops and save them.

If he wanted to.

A lot of bloody history stood between Tyleen and the lesser castles. They'd had their wars, but peace had held for the last two generations, and the single guard at the gate didn't even have it closed. He must also have thought Shannon and Rory had come back, which helped. Derry kept his head down this time. He didn't want anything to stop them as they headed towards the Keep.

Odd, but he could still hear the bells inside these walls.

The courtyard was smaller than Tyleen's and more crowded with small buildings. Few people moved along here, none of them as hurried as the servants at Tyleen. Shannon urged him on and into the main building, a tall, sturdy tower without even a wing off the side. The ten stairs seemed too high, but he reached the top, and Shannon got them inside. The door closed loudly behind them, and the sound of the bells diminished but still did not entirely disappear.

Safe.

Lord Arlis came rushing down the curving stairs, clearly prepared to go out with a cloak over his shoulders. He stopped most of the way down and gave a nod of relief.

"Shannon, good. Your mother just told me you had been called before the King. What -- Sweet Good Gods!" The man rushed the rest of the way so quickly, Derry almost stepped back in shock and fear. Lord Arlis took Derry by the shoulders, staring at him as though he didn't believe what he held. He was a large man with wild, graying hair and piercing blue eyes, known for both his temper and his kindness. "Gods all! Prince Derry SanOsen himself!"

"Lord Derry," he corrected yet again and felt a surge of surprise that Lord Arlis would make that mistake, and that he appeared so pleased to find Derry in his home. "It's good to see you again, sir. I hope you don't mind a guest --"

"I can't believe you're here," he said and smiled, a flash of teeth behind his beard.

Derry swayed a little, feeling his legs start to tremble as the tapestry-hung walls around him blurred. He caught hold of Shannon's arm before he went down.

"Gods. Get him up to your room, Shannon. I'll send some food --"

"Please, no," Derry protested. "Not food. I just came from the feast. Some tea would be nice, though, if you don't mind."

"Tea. Yes, we can manage that, Lord Derry. Go."

Shannon started him up the long stairs. Derry sighed and forced his legs to keep moving. At least they were heading for somewhere he could get some rest at last.

Or maybe not. Shannon took him straight to the bed and laid him out, boots and all, before he could protest. The door remained open, and Lady Pera appeared -- gave a cry of dismay and covered her face in both her hands before she rushed off.

"What was that about?" Shannon said with a shake of his head.

"I fear she thought I was dead," Derry admitted. "Do go tell the servants to reassure her."

Shannon nodded and quickly went to the doorway, calling to a servant. Derry simply laid still, savoring the stillness and the quiet. By the time Shannon returned, he'd even managed to get an elbow under him and sit up a little. Shannon shoved pillows at his back, saying nothing still.

Lord Arlis arrived with a pot and three teacups. "You've given us quite a start, my lad," he said and sounded far more himself this time. "How long have you been back?"

"I rode it at sunset after three days on the trail from Queton Port, sir." He frowned. "At least I think it was three days. And before that ... I can't say how long it has been since the Regent Olivia released me and sent me home. I wasn't well. Almost everything is a blur."

"You don't look well, Derry," Shannon said with a shake of his head. "Not well at all. I think it's going to take more than rest to get you back on your feet."

"Rest to start with," Derry replied and gratefully took the cup Lord Arlis held out. "Thank you. And at least I've saved you a fortune in mercenaries."

"Oh, told you of that, did he?" Lord Arlis said with a bit of a laugh. Derry suspected he had been serious in his plans with Shannon after all. "King Robert was in for a shock, he was. But we're all safe from that madness now. Sip the tea."

Derry lifted the cup from his lap, though his hands shook. He tasted wild berries and fresh honey; the flavors washed through him and brought contentment in their wake. He thought he answered a few more questions, but his eyes blinked several times, and Derry fell asleep before he finished the tea.

Sounds around him, voices ... Derry drifted away again and then awoke with a start, fearing --

"It's okay. I'm here."

Shannon sat in the chair by the bed. A candle had nearly gutted itself, the flames wavering as shadows danced around the room. Derry found himself gasping, and he wasn't certain why. Something had seemed to grab hold of him in his sleep and tried to drag him away. Back to the cell? Was that the truth of it -- that he was dreaming this homecoming --

"Derry?"

"I don't want to go back," he said, which probably made no sense to Shannon. He took a breath or two to settle himself. "Is there another candle? I would -- I would like it not to go dark tonight."

"I can arrange it," Shannon said. He looked worried as he stood and crossed to a cupboard across the room. Yes, where the candles were kept. Derry knew that. He'd spent time enough in this room. Shannon brought one back and lit the candle, the light brighter then, and not given to so many fluctuations. The room seemed to settle into familiar patterns as Shannon sat down, leaning forward. Worry furrowed his brow, and his hand, warm and welcome, took hold of the fingers of Derry's right hand. He had a gentle grasp as though he feared to break something.

"We'll see you through this, Derry," Shannon promised, his voice steady. "You know I won't give up on you. I didn't. I wanted to find you --"

"I didn't need you to be a fool," Derry said. He put his other hand over Shannon's and began to realize what an ordeal these last years had been for his companion. "I shouldn't have let her push me into the journey, you know. I couldn't sully my family name. It was all I had left of my parents. I had not expected the kind of trouble I faced when I got there, though. I thought I would deliver her letter, have him say a few rude things, and leave again, annoyed but nothing worse. A useless journey. But he opened the letter and..."

Shannon sat up straighter. "You don't know what she wrote."

"No. I didn't break the seal, of course."

"Damn her."

"I can't be certain -- but given the way he reacted -- I didn't expect it, Shannon. I wouldn't have put either of us through this if I had expected something that treacherous from her. We dare not hint at such a thing, my friend. We've no way to prove it, but I thought you ought to know."

Shannon nodded and sat back again, obviously doing his best to calm once more. "Thank you for telling me. It made no sense, you know. We all had heard Robert was a problem, but no one expected anything so drastic. Except maybe the Queen did expect it. She didn't seem much surprised at all when you were kept there -- well not until the King sent her off to do penance."

Derry winced at that reminder. He realized that his boots were off now and the blankets over him. He felt better for it, though everything ached.

"Come to bed, Shannon -- just come to bed and rest, nothing more. I don't want to wake up alone. I'm having trouble. I keep thinking this isn't real. I'm dreaming of home."

Shannon stood and stripped off his shirt but not his trousers. "Slide over. I need to be here so I can get up and get another candle if we need it. I've lost track of time. It might be dawn before this one is done. And I don't want you slipping out of bed without me knowing it."

Derry didn't argue as he slid over towards the wall, and Shannon climbed into the bed, pulling the blankets back up over the two of them. Derry felt his body relax, and his eyes close again. He was safe here, with Shannon to protect him.

Peace. The feeling swept over him, and he fell back to sleep before Shannon was even fully settled. This was not the cell and a dream; he could not have dreamed this much contentment.

The rest helped, but not enough. By dawn, the fever he'd been holding off came upon him like a fire, and though he tried to fight the illness off and stay here, in this place he loved, his mind slipped away too often. He had visions of King Robert with a bloody sword, coming to kill him. Or to kill Shannon or King Nevin -- or all of them, and Queen Alisia by the evil King's side and laughing.

Derry sometimes found himself back in the cell with glaring faces close to him, strangers all of them, and thinking he would be easy prey. There had been fights, but he'd held his own well enough until the others began to realize they didn't want to do King Robert's work for him. The guards had taken others away and beheaded them in the yard by the window, tossing severed heads to land and block the view.

Derry shoved that gruesome memory aside and tried to pull back the remembrance of Shannon's suite. Chess games. Maids flirting with them. His father throwing up his hands and laughing at a prank that got Egan dumped in a pond, and if anyone else had ever known --

Derry couldn't hold to those better times long enough to escape the nightmares. The fire drove them away, and the Queen always stood there, laughing as she won --

"Drink a little more tea, Derry," Shannon said. Derry

focused on his friend for a moment, trying to believe he was here and not lost somewhere. A cup touched his lips, and Derry sipped without argument. He would do that for Shannon. "He doesn't appear to get ill from tea or water, Tevin, but I feared even the little taste of broth we gave him last night was going to kill him."

"As long as we can get anything into him, it should help," the Prince answered. "Lots of honey -- that will give him strength."

The crown prince sounded worried, but Derry slipped away again before he could speak.

He came awake a little later, aware that he was alone in the bed and that bright light filled the room. Shannon had the door to the room partly open and spoke softly. "Yes, you can come inside, Roe. I fear he's still asleep, though --"

"Not asleep," Derry said and drew Shannon's startled attention. He lifted his head from the pillows and let it fall again. "I feel like a rock. A very much abused and aching rock."

Shannon and Roe crossed from the door, both looking very pleased. Derry felt a wave of embarrassment since he didn't even have the strength to lift his hand when Shannon settled in the chair beside him. Roe stood at Shannon's back, looking troubled.

"How long did I sleep?" Derry asked, running a hand over his rough chin and grimacing.

"Two days, though sleep is not the word I would use," Shannon replied. He poured a cup of water and helped Derry sip. Shannon helped Derry sit with pillows at his back again. "You were unconscious for most of the two days. Prince Tevin came to check on you every few hours. The King has ordered you to remain here until Tev says you are well."

"There were things he wanted to ask me," Derry recalled with some worry. He felt more clear-headed than he had been

this entire journey. "I do need to make certain he understands
--"

"King Nevin says he trust your judgment about Regent
Olivia and the trouble with the Isles. He's sent her a thank you
note saying you have arrived. However, he did say he was
troubled by the tale he heard from Captain Killough about
your encounter with the fae."

Derry knew that tone, and he winced, putting aside the
cup. His hands trembled with weakness, and Roe looked
worried. The look on Shannon's face and the knowledge of the
upcoming discussion was not going to settle the boy's nerves.
Derry might have delayed the conversation with a somewhat
valid claim of weakness so that it was only he and Shannon.
However, Derry had the distinct feeling the young Prince
needed to hear what was going on. Maybe he had the ear of his
father. Maybe Derry only needed him there so that he could
judge the reaction. Shannon was going to be unsettled no
matter how he told the tale. He wouldn't lie.

It wasn't as though he could hide things from Shannon.
He had changed, after all. That part wasn't merely a dream. He
could feel the brush of fae blood through his body and the call
of things beyond the walls that mankind made to keep the wild
out. He stared at the window for a long moment, listening to
distant animals and the gentle breeze -- and what might have
been an underlying sound of something out of place and
dangerous. He wished he understood --

"Derry?" Shannon began, reaching forward to put a hand
on his arm.

"It started when I looked out the window at the
Glendalow Inn," he said, forgoing the original discussion with
Leonora for now. No reason to complicate the story. "I saw
the fae take a child. I left the inn and ran after them --"

"Because you wanted to go as well," Shannon said, his
voice forced to calm, though his face paled and his fee hand

tight to the arm of the chair.

"Who told you that?" Derry asked, surprised.

"The servants have been whispering the tale, and I suspect they got it from the guards, though not Killough. He's been closed-mouthed about the entire affair except what he might have told to the King. Tell me it isn't true, you fool. Tell me that you didn't want to go with them."

He saw fear in Shannon's face just then. Shannon had lost him once to the cell in the north, and now he dreaded something he couldn't entirely understand. Derry didn't understand either, but he gave a little lift of his hand, a sign to be calm.

"I was lost, Shannon. If you had been there, everything would have been different -- but somewhere between the cell and Glendalow, I stopped believing in reality. I didn't want to awaken in the cell again. So, yes, I would have gone with them to a better dream. However, the fae women, Leanora, said this wasn't the time. She spoke of trouble coming and that we would need each other's help."

"I hadn't heard that part," Shannon said, worried again.

"Killough is the only one who might have heard, and he's saying nothing."

"I never thought the fae were real," Roe admitted softly. He glanced at the window, but he didn't look as bothered as Derry had expected.

"Neither did I, Prince Roe --" Derry began belatedly. He was not tracking well.

"Just Roe," the Prince said with a nervous shrug. "Prince doesn't mean much in a third son. I'll leave all that glorified nonsense to Egan since he craves it so much. And to Tev, though it doesn't seem to mean as much to him. Would you go willingly to the fae, Derry?"

"I might someday," he answered truthfully. "There was a draw to the wild places and the peace away from human trouble."

"Are we going to have to keep a watch on you, then?" Shannon asked, leaning forward and staring into Derry's eyes.

What did he see there? Something changed he could not fully understand. Was the change from the fae, or was more of it still shadows of that damned cell?

"If I ever go, it will be because I want to, Shannon. You need not worry, though. I won't leave any time soon."

Shannon would worry, of course. "It's a wonder you made it all the way home, Derry, the shape you were in." Anger showed in his eyes, and Shannon leaned back in the chair, clearly fighting to get control of his own emotions.

"Shannon --"

"I'm all right." Shannon stood, giving a wane smile as Roe glanced from one to the other. "For the last few years, I've harbored incredible anger and fear. I never expected to find you returning home again, Derry. I think I'm having a hard time adjusting to reality. I desperately want you to be the person you were before you left. Is there any hope for it?"

"I'm going to give it a try," Derry replied with a brighter smile and felt a lifting of his heart when Shannon and Roe both returned it. "I need to readjust, that's all. I need to believe that I'm free. I need *calm*."

Even as he said those words, Derry felt as though something moved around him, dark and troubling. The fae had warned him. Derry knew they were going to have problems before too long.

Chapter Six

The days passed slowly for Derry. He barely had the energy to walk to the privy and back, and he slept more than stayed awake. His nightmares woke him too often, though. Sometimes he feared the cell still drained the strength from him, as though some sort of chain still held him tied to the place. Derry remembered Captain Killough's warning about failing in health now that he was home, but he wasn't certain how to fight such an insidious invasion of his body and thoughts.

Sitting by the window in the sunlight delighted Derry, though he stayed wrapped in blankets. He felt as though he'd aged decades in the north. At least the birds came often, and even some mice now and then, much to Shannon's dismay. Derry and his friend talked, mostly of old times, and read books on fae ... but the days passed slowly, and he made small progress in recovery.

However, he did get better, at least in body. The cut on his hand became nothing more than a thin line across his palm and fingers; such an insubstantial mark to indicate such a considerable change in his life.

Derry took his meals in Shannon's room, often with Shannon there as well, though sometimes his friend ate with his family. Derry appreciated the company and the time alone. He hadn't thought he would have so much trouble returning to his old life. Many of the problems he faced had nothing to do with the fae blood he held now, either. He often woke in the middle of the night from nightmares of that other place, and then the room seemed too small and the darkness too close. Derry did notice that as the winter drew closer, he awoke more often with a cry of anger than fear. He accepted that as an improvement. Ghosts with the faces of people who had died in the cell or had been beheaded outside the window tormented him in those dreams. He feared he would never put those memories to rest.

Only Shannon's presence returned him to calm, but because of it, neither of them got much sleep some nights.

One change from the inclusion of fae blood became evident the first day. Derry could not eat meat. He could barely stand the scent of it, and Shannon quickly made it clear that even his food was not to contain any when he dined with Derry.

"I talked to Captain Killough myself this morning," Shannon told him over a noon meal on a cool autumn day. Trees were going bare along the hills, and wood smoke filled the air. They'd put the desk by the window and ate there. "He's back on duty now. Said to tell you he has a fine, bonny granddaughter."

Derry smiled, glad that the man thought to tell Shannon such a thing. Derry nibbled on some late autumn berries. "You talked to him about something you didn't think you could ask me?"

"Quite honestly -- no. Not until I had things confirmed. How is your hand?"

Derry glanced at the scar and looked up as he smiled

brightly, startling Shannon. "That wound was never a real problem. Yes, she gave me a touch of her blood, and yes, it did change me."

Shannon gave a sudden laugh and pushed aside his plate. "Well, that was easier than I expected."

"I do hope you will keep quiet about it, though."

"Too late, my friend. I went to Killough because I heard part of the tale from our fine Prince Tevin as well as from servants who were worried about serving you."

"That's going to be more trouble than I need." Derry pushed his plate aside, the tasty berries and cheese forgotten. He glanced out the window where bright blue sky outlined Tyleen not far away. "The Queen --"

"Oh yes, the Queen," Shannon said with the same snarl he got every time he spoke of her. "I asked. She's heard, and she's raising all kinds of hells over it. King Nevin, however, is not."

"I hadn't considered that word would get out. I should have realized." Derry felt a new welling of panic. "I can't blame Killough, and Bay and Casey didn't know the full story. I suspect the Queen heard from spies who probably listened to whatever Killough told the King and Prince Tevin."

"Very likely. Alisia has been more than interested in anything concerning you since you got back. If I didn't know better, I'd say your return worried her. That doesn't make a lot of sense, Derry. You are no more powerful now than you were before you left. Less so since you aren't even at Tyleen Castle. Maybe she expects you to ask the King to send her away. That's all I can think."

"I wouldn't," Derry replied with a frantic shake of his head. "And King Nevin wouldn't do it for me anyway. Gods. I may have to leave court entirely."

The realization almost made Derry ill. He'd spent four years dreaming of coming back home, and the thought that he might have to leave again, and because of her --

"Calm, Derry. You are going nowhere until the King says you should, and he's said nothing so far. It's not as though he hasn't heard everything, you know. Roe says King Nevin has forbidden the Queen to speak of you to him or at court. She attempted to get the temples to back her, but even they're staying clear of this one. She has no friends, you know. She only has Egan."

"There must be others who want me gone because of the fae trouble."

"No doubt there are, but here is the problem they face, my friend: none of them want to be grouped with the Queen. They distrust and dislike her more than they do the thought of someone with fae blood being at court. The fact that you are doing nothing at all has helped. Once they get over the shock of the idea, they'll have less trouble dealing with you."

"I didn't think things could get worse," Derry admitted. He slumped in the chair, feeling the weight of everything starting to add up again. "I need to leave, Shannon --"

"No," Shannon replied and with more force than Derry had expected. "And that, my friend, is Prince Tevin's orders, which he hinted came from his father. You are to stay here and rest for as long as need be."

"Not just for as long as I need -- but until the King can figure something out with the court?" Derry asked with a shake of his head. "That's a lot to ask of the SanSota's."

"Do you really think so?" Shannon leaned forward over the desk and looked him squarely in the face this time. "You may have forgotten this, my friend, but the SanSota's have been rebels for quite a while. We've not always gotten along even with King Nevin. I have spoken with my parents, my brothers, and my sisters and they've all agreed. You are going to stay here until it's safe for you to leave."

Derry wanted to say something, and to take charge of his

own future -- but the enormity of what the SanSotas were doing overcame him. They didn't merely side with the King, which was easy enough to do. However, they also kept him here, and by doing so, they made an active enemy of the Queen.

He felt a shiver. "If somehow either Alisia or Egan comes to power --"

"Then we're damned anyway," Shannon replied. He broke off some cheese and nibbled it, glancing out the window and shaking his head. "Alisia will come after us, Derry. She would have before this because we were all vocal about what she'd done to you. We are not friends with the Queen, and she will never forgive us for what we did long before you came home. So, if she somehow wins, we're going down anyway. Tell me, knowing that truth, that we should be careful of her now and give her what she wants."

Derry took a deeper breath and nodded. "You're right."

"I knew you could see reason. You are staying here until we see how matters shake out. You are to get rest. That's Tevin's orders. It may be that you will leave the entire city, and suddenly, if things get out of hand. You need to be ready for the journey. You will not be going alone, of course."

The idea of riding anywhere didn't appeal to him. Derry didn't mind the quiet. The SanSota castle was far less frantic than Tyleen, and even the servants who cleaned and changed the bedding were quieter and more polite.

More days passed, and the fear of Queen Alisia eased somewhat in the quiet, warm room with the window that looked at Tyleen -- but also at the bright skies and birds that passed.

"My father wants to come and see you," Tevin reported one evening after he'd again told Derry to eat more. "I've talked him out of it so far, but I think that won't last for long. I've told him I fear the fever might be contagious, which was true at first. Obviously, there's been no problem."

Derry glanced at Shannon --

"Don't even say it," Shannon said with a wave of his hand.

Tevin smiled. He'd gotten more at ease with the two of them over the last few days. Derry wondered if Tevin came here just for the peace. They had interesting discussions about anything *except* the Queen. Derry's lack of knowledge about the fae amused Tevon and Shannon.

"I was raised just like the two of you," Derry reminded them when they laughed. "How am I supposed to know anything more than you do?"

"Well, you have to admit that under the circumstances, it is a bit funny," Tevin said as he moved toward the door. "But I think there are some manuscripts in the archives at Tyleen. I'll see if I can smuggle them out for you."

"I would be grateful," Derry replied.

Derry slowly started to regain his strength. He kept to Shannon's room for the most part. Lord Arlis would have given him a place of his own, but Derry had the feeling Shannon wouldn't trust him out of his sight anyway. Besides, he was more comfortable in this familiar room with the old tapestries and the warm fire. Waking up somewhere he didn't recognize would not have helped.

Derry awoke one chilly autumn afternoon to find Shannon seated by the window and playing his lyre. He hadn't heard his friend perform for years, and the sound was both welcome and startling. Shannon must have sensed his attention.

"I shouldn't have wakened you --"

"It was nice," Derry replied, cutting him short. He sat up, feeling better and more connected with the world again. For a moment he thought he even heard the fae bells outside. That helped; he'd started to feel abandoned by the fae, and that would not help. Derry sensed a bit of change in himself almost every day. Magic, he guessed, though he had no way to do anything with it. He would need the fae to help him.

Derry wasn't confident he wanted to learn magic yet, in fact. Once he started using magic that would forever put a wall between him and the humans. Leanora had been right about the most important thing -- he was not ready to leave the human world yet.

"How are you doing?" Shannon asked as he put aside the instrument. He frowned. "You look better. Should I trust that?"

"I feel better," Derry admitted. He stood and crossed to the desk by the window. He didn't feel as unsteady as he had for all the previous days. "You don't have to lecture me. I'll still take it easy since I want to get well enough to take care of myself again. That's no reflection on you and your family, though. I appreciate everything the SanSotas have done for me. I've been afraid to ask ... but how are your parents taking all of this?"

"Mother acts as though there is nothing unusual going on," Shannon replied with a smile and a wave of his hand. "That's the way she always acts, no matter what the situation. Father? I get the distinct feeling father is rather happy to be doing something that is annoying the Queen and helping the King. They haven't always gotten along, King Nevin and my father, but the King knows he can trust the SanSotas. And that, my friend, is why he sent you home with us, even more than the fact you and I are companions."

"I can't have helped the SanSota reputation any," Derry said with a shake of his head. Odd how such thoughts were starting to come to him again, as though they came from the walls themselves.

Shannon gave a snort of a laugh, an unexpected sound. "You know better. My clan has always had a reputation for doing whatever we wanted -- and not what might be politically wise. We've survived it so far. In fact, father said we're simply carrying on a time-honored family tradition of annoying someone in power. Mother laughed."

"I really don't know if that should make me feel better or not," Derry admitted. He finally settled in the chair and glanced out the window. The world looked stark and gray today, but he found a harsh beauty to the land, and it called to him. He had to force himself to look away. "This is a mess, Shannon. More so than I had considered, you know."

"Oh, I've no doubt about that," Shannon replied. He took the lyre from the desk and put it on the larger bed. Derry almost asked him to play again, but Shannon looked ready for a serious discussion. "You have always had a habit of doing things and considering the complications later. It's what made me think you are mostly yourself, after all."

Derry laughed. They'd had that discussion in the past, and the link back to those days made him feel far better again. "I can't hide here forever, though, Shannon."

"For a while yet," Shannon replied. He looked bothered as he ran his fingers though his hair. "The Queen is enraged about your return, Derry. Many people think she's enraged because of your connection to the fae, but I think it is simply because you are back home -- and that, my friend, makes me very worried. I want to keep you out of her sight for as long as possible."

Derry couldn't argue, especially since he had no wish to face her either. He worried about the trouble he caused the SanSotas, though. When Lord Arlis stopped to see him later that night, he wondered if Shannon might be blind to his father's worries.

Derry started out carefully because he didn't want to annoy either of them.

"Thank you for your hospitality, Lord Arlis," Derry said

with a bow of his head when the man entered. He knew better than to try to stand and give a proper bow.

"Hospitality?" the older man said with a shake of his head. "And here I thought that we'd worked that out years ago, and this was your home whenever you needed it."

"Yes." Derry took a deeper breath and felt that unconditional welcome wash over him again as he looked up. "Yes, this is home. Thank you."

Lord Arlis nodded and sat on the edge of the bed, waving Shannon to the other chair at the desk. The Lord of the SanSota clan had often done just the same in the past when Derry had come here, often in trouble with the Queen-- even back then. Alisia had been a problem for him from the day his parents died, though he hadn't ever wondered why until Killough told him the obvious. He had usurped the attention that she felt should have gone to Egan and Roe.

Even so, the Queen's actions seemed excessive. Derry supposed she was simply bored, and he provided an easy outlet for her frustrations, as well as Egan's annoyance at the world. Derry could almost feel sorry for the prince since he was raised by such a woman -- except that Egan was such a pain in the ass that Derry couldn't mentally side with him for more than a heartbeat.

"You need to rest, my boy," Lord Arlis said, his eyes narrowed in worry. He'd been staring at Derry, who hadn't noticed while his mind wandered. "It is good to see you up and moving again, but I'd guess a stray breeze would blow you over. Right now, we simply need to keep you out of fair Alisia's notice for a while."

"I don't think she forgets about me," Derry admitted and felt an odd little shudder almost take him. Was that part of his fae powers? Did he *know* the Queen harbored anger that never really died away, despite the best attempts of others to keep Derry away from her?

"You are probably right," Shannon agreed. "But we can still keep you here and safe for a while. We can hope that once winter sets in, she'll be less troublesome. She doesn't like the cold."

Derry nodded. "I don't want trouble. I just want peace, Lord Arlis."

"Yes," Lord Arlis said and looked as though he thought Derry very wise for those words. Derry supposed some would want to face the Queen and prove themselves. He had never been that stupid. "We'll keep you safe and at peace here, my boy. You have my word on it."

Derry didn't like to think that he needed that much protection, but they were right. He began to believe he had survived his childhood merely by chance, and probably because he had friends who were smarter than him when it came to dealing with the Queen.

Lord Arlis left when dinner arrived. Derry almost suggested they go down and eat with the rest of the family, just to show he was not a rude guest. However, he felt worn simply from the conversation and the emotional overload.

Besides, several books arrived along with dinner. Prince Tevon had managed to get the works out of the archives and to him.

"This might help," Derry said as he carefully turned the pages of one of the ancient books. "If I can read it. The text is very old, faded and --"

Shannon reached over and took the book. "Eat first. Then you can read for a while as long as you don't tire."

"What would happen if I pointed out that I am of a higher rank in court than you, and you really can't order me to do anything?"

Shannon looked him straight in the face. "I would laugh."

"Yes, that's what I thought."

Derry did win a laugh from Shannon. The meal tasted

wonderful. There was never any meat in the food he and Shannon shared. Eating in the main hall would have been far more difficult, he realized, since the scent of cooked meat still made him ill.

Derry glanced at the books on the corner of the desk and hoped he found a solution there to some of his troubles. He suspected he would not locate a lot of information friendly towards the fae. Even so, there might be some hints that would help him sort out what he was feeling.

Derry appreciated the quiet meal with Shannon tonight. He had become complacent in some ways. He accepted that the SanSotas would take him in because they always had, even though he wasn't a child any longer. There were aspects of the battle with Queen Alisia that could be dangerous.

It didn't help that the terrifying nightmares about the cell still haunted him. Derry could not sleep for more than a couple hours at a time. His fears were winning, and he feared what he needed to learn would not be in the books.

Chapter Seven

The slowness of Derry's recovery began to wear on him as autumn moved closer to winter. Frost formed around the shutters, and they kept the fire going throughout the day. Reading was the best way to spend the daylight hours. Derry regained his strength, and after that, Shannon escorted him down to the courtyard each afternoon so that he could walk around in the fresh air despite the cold.

The walks tired him, though. Shannon worried too much when he barely made it to the chair and settled with a sigh of relief. Shannon frowned and put a kettle on the cob, warming it up for a bit of tea. He sighed when he looked back at Derry again.

"Will you please stop looking as though you expect me to fall over dead at any moment?" Derry finally said and won an unexpected laugh. "Sit down and tell me about your luncheon with Lady Clara."

"Worse than I expected," Shannon admitted with a grimace of distaste. He took the chair across from Derry. "I don't think I'll ever find a compatible woman. They all want me to change, Derry. It is almost the first thing out of their pretty little mouths. Little Lady Clara had some definite ideas on that one. She's very religious."

"I've never seen you break a temple law," Derry replied. He leaned back and frowned, but he was pretty sure where this was going. "She's a SanKella, so half of her family has served in one temple or another. What does she want from you?"

"Well, first is that I immediately disassociate myself from you."

"I am not at all surprised."

"I didn't think you would be. The problem is that Clara is not stupid, you know. She knew that was not going to be an answer. What do you think the point was in this farce?"

Derry didn't have to consider the situation for long. "Clara is a Lady in Waiting and working directly for the Queen. There's no other reason why a SanKella would suddenly approach your family for a marital tie. She was doing a test of some sort."

"Right. We can't figure out what it might have been. Did the Queen expect me to suddenly kick you out of the keep simply because pretty Clara threw herself at me?"

Shannon seemed genuinely confused, but Derry thought he could see the situation. "She was testing to see if the SanSota's are perhaps tired of having me as an unpopular guest. The Queen doesn't really understand friendship, you know -- and loyalty only applies to her."

Shannon blinked several times and leaned forward. "You're more awake again, aren't you? I didn't see those links. Clara did straight out ask if Lord Arlis wasn't tired of having to deal with you, but I took it to be no more than small talk."

"There is likely the entire answer for this charade, Shan. I wonder what kind of reaction you would have won if you'd leapt at the chance to seal a marriage with the SanKellas. I imagine she would have left quite suddenly."

"I wish I had thought of it, except even as a joke makes

me ill," Shannon admitted. He stood still for a moment and Derry imagined he played the conversation with Clara over in his mind. "She was such a pretentious little doll, all made up in her fine silks. I suspect Clara would have been far more worried than me if I had shown any interest. She's aiming far higher; Egan would be my guess. She must know Tevin would never have her. You're right; this was a show. I don't know why I didn't see it."

"And she learned that you aren't ready to turn me out in the winter cold, so to speak." Derry smiled as Shannon prepared the tea. Lots of honey tonight; the scent filled the room with a reminder of spring. He caught the scent of chamomile as well. Derry relaxed. "The Queen is trying to feel things out -- more to find if I am losing allies rather than if she is gaining them."

"There have been some very wild rumors at the court," Shannon said as he stirred the tea.

"Yes?"

"Mostly wild tales about you and the fae and all the trouble you've created with them. Impossible tales, really, and most of the people know it. However, there is one that is causing some trouble. Rumor says that the King will not have you back in Tyleen because of your connection to the fae."

Derry considered that for a moment. "I need to go back, at least if King Nevin will actually have me there."

"We're both going," Shannon replied, surprising him. "Tomorrow afternoon unless the weather is bad. The King expects me to come with you. He was very relieved when I said I wasn't sending you back to the castle alone."

"This is dangerous, Shannon. We'll be where she can more easily get to the two of us."

"Better if we are both together to fight her, then. Think it through, Derry. She'd have to come after me if she did anything to you. I wouldn't be safe anyway."

"True. Okay, I'll be glad to have you with me," Derry admitted. He looked around the room. "I'll miss this place, though. I've felt at ease here."

"You needed to be here." Shannon put a cup before Derry as he sat down and sipped his tea. "We'll stay in Tyleen for a while. Once everything calms down, we might come back. Next spring, if you are feeling well enough, we can go to one of the estates -- yours or mine, it doesn't matter. We just have to get through the winter here."

"Is that supposed to be some sort of bribe for me to take care of myself?" Derry asked with a bright smile.

"Yes, actually. Will it work?"

"It might. You realize that the longer you associate with me, the less likely you are ever going to find a wife, right?"

"I am a younger son. I don't need to marry. We'll see what happens in the next few years. I'm in no hurry."

Derry didn't say the one thing neither of them discussed: Derry was the last of his line. If he wanted the family to continue, he'd have to marry, and that suddenly appeared far less likely. Derry hated the thought that he might have disappointed his parents and perhaps even the King. He pushed the thought away. Derry would have to talk to King Nevin about the dispensation of his lands and wealth. He would want everything to go to Shannon first and the SanSota family second if Shannon didn't survive him. Derry would not think of both he and Shannon dead. If he did, he'd have to start ordering Shannon away, and that would never work.

If the King worried about the SanSota's with so much power, Derry would suggest everything go to Roe instead.

He didn't sleep well that night.

They spent most of the next day resting but were both packed and ready to go long before Lord Arlis came to escort them downstairs. The older man looked worried, and when they got to the keep's door, he took Derry's bag from the servant and sent the man on his way.

"I'm walking you over myself," Lord Arlis declared and lifted a hand before either of them could protest. "There are guards on the wall to keep watch, and yes, we are being obvious in protecting you. There's no reason to take any chances. It's not as though the Queen is going to gain any points by pretending to be shocked by our actions to keep you safe."

"What about the King?"

"I had a note from him this morning. He said to take all precautions I could to see you safely to Tyleen."

Derry sighed. He knew better than to argue the point. Lord Arlis and his youngest son were both too stubborn to listen to him. He'd learned that down through the years. "You'd think we were in the middle of a war zone rather than taking a walk from one friendly castle to the next. I appreciate the care, though. I would hate to make anything easy for her."

Lord Arlis nodded grim-faced. "I am trusting that the two of you will be careful. You've both grown wiser over the last few years. Don't take any chances. And Derry, don't bait her. The Queen is starting to worry everyone, even those who think they ought to side with her. I am trusting that the King still rules in Tyleen, you know. If things go wrong, both of you -- or either of you -- get back here as fast as you can. There will always be someone on the wall, watching for you."

"Thank you, sir. I trust we'll be fine, or else I wouldn't take Shannon with me."

"Like you could have stopped him," Lord Arlis said with a snort of amusement.

"I like to think that I have some control over my life."

They both laughed as they went out of the building and headed for the gate that led to Tyleen. The guard there looked bothered. Derry wasn't at all surprised when Rory caught up with them just a few yards away from the Montrose walls.

"Nice day for a walk," Rory said, daring his father's glare.

Derry simply laughed. He wanted to argue, but it would be a waste of time and breath. He thought the path to Tyleen looked very long, though. His legs felt weak, but he was determined not to be more of a problem for his companions.

About halfway to the castle, he heard the whisper of bells, and he felt stronger for the lovely sound. The fae hadn't been around much of late, and the echo of the bells gave Derry hope that he and his friends would be safe.

Shannon had heard the bells as well. He looked to the right with a frown but said nothing. Clearly, Lord Arlis and Rory had not heard them, for which Derry was quite happy. They didn't need complications.

Derry's legs ached by the time they reached the postern gate at Tyleen. Killough was the one who stood there and let them in.

"Your Lordships, sirs," Killough said and smiled at Derry. "Good to see you again and on your feet. The King is waiting. I'm to take you straight in and allow no one to stop you along the way, by the King's order."

Lord Arlis nodded. Killough led the way, Arlis and Shannon flanking Derry, and Rory a guard behind.

"Congratulations on your granddaughter, Killough," Derry offered and won a bright smile. "Does the Queen know I'm coming?" he dared to ask and tried not to sound breathless from the walk.

"Not a word of it, as far as I know, sir." Killough looked around and slowed as they neared the castle's steps. "Careful now. It was a bit icy here this morning." And then his voice lowered. "She's been in a ripe bad mood. You be careful. We'll watch out for you as best we can, but she has her own ways."

Derry nodded, feeling less safe as they entered the building. Servants, a few nobles, and guards all watched them pass, and word would spread quickly. Killough took them to one of the waiting rooms, and the King waited there to greet them.

"Good then," King Nevin said with a nod when they entered. "Off you go, Killough. Thank you."

"An honor, sir," he said. He gave one last nod to Derry and left again.

"Thank you for delivering the boys, Lord Arlis. I'll do my best to keep them both safe."

Lord Arlis nodded, grabbed Rory by the arm, and they both left. The SanSota Lord clearly didn't trust himself to say anything, and King Nevin appeared to understand.

"The dinner is less than an hour away, Derry." He leaned against the wall and looked them both over. "I need you to get cleaned up and make a proper appearance at the High Table."

"I'm going to surprise the Queen by appearing at dinner, again? You think this is wise?"

"There is no wisdom in any of this, just necessity. We're going to put you in front of the Queen at a time when she can least react the way she might if she found you alone in your room. I don't know how far she'll go, Derry. If she pushes, then I want it to be in public where she can't deny her own actions."

"Yes, sire." Derry hadn't thought he'd be thrown right into the midst of battle. "I better get ready."

"You can't sit with him at the high table, Shannon. I'm sorry. Do make certain you're ready at the SanSota table if you're needed."

"I will sire," Shannon said. He didn't look happy, but he wouldn't argue the point.

They followed the King out into the hall. Startled servants took the two bags, and they headed off to Derry's suite while he and Shannon followed. At least it felt like home once they were inside that familiar door. The room was far fancier than the place they shared at Montrose and reminded Derry that he really was a prince. He sat on the edge of the bed and let Shannon wander around and check things out. They'd not shared this room before. Derry had always gone to Shannon; that had been his escape from the start.

"This is going to be troubling," Shannon admitted as he settled into a high-backed chair by the fire. "Whom do we trust in the servants?"

"I'll let you know which ones I knew before I left," Derry replied. "We'll have to be careful of the others. I better dress well for tonight. And you need to play your part, too. We *should* be happy to be here. I need to show no reason why I wouldn't be glad to be home."

"Yes. Games. Politics."

Someone knocked on the door. Shannon went and let the servant in, scowling at the back of the man's head.

"Petric," Derry said and smiled. He gave a quick nod to Shannon. "Good. I need to dress for tonight. Nothing too gaudy. I don't want to stand out like a peacock at a mud bath."

Petric immediately relaxed, which was what he'd hoped. Shannon didn't look quite as assured. It occurred to Derry that while he had shared a great deal of Shannon's life and family, Shannon had not shared much of Derry's other world. He'd gone to Shannon to escape, and it had not occurred to him to bring his friend here.

Petric went to the cabinets and brought back clothing. "We've been keeping them up since you got back," he said, pulling out a few things. "Most are going to be too big for you, Lord Derry. But we can make do for tonight, and I'll have my cousin in here to start taking things in tomorrow if it suits you."

"That would be nice," Derry agreed. He'd have to get used to dressing for the part again. "Shannon will need some court clothing too -- don't argue with me."

Shannon had barely opened his mouth. Petric gave the

two of them a quick glance and then grinned, looking far less worried. "Oh yes, don't argue with him, Lord Shannon, sir. He's apt to turn you into a rat, sir. That's what I've heard."

"Oh, have you?" Derry said. Petric had always been a good source for castle information. He gathered it from all his cousins who worked in various posts, and Derry had been more than happy to give him a coin or two now and then to spread out to the others.

"That and worse," he said. He looked serious. "The Queen's not happy about you having come home, though we aren't certain why, sir. I doubt it's about the fae, though she's quick to use that as a reason for her distrust. It's made many of us wonder why she was always so apt to speak badly of you if she got a chance."

"I've heard it might be because I was more popular than Prince Egan."

"Well, that's no good reason, sir. The garden snail is more popular than Egan."

Shannon gave a delighted laugh and was more at ease from that time onward. They got Derry cleaned up and dressed, and he didn't even fight over the fussing like he usually would. Derry hated the pretense, but if they were going to put on a show, he was going to do it well.

"I suspect she will have heard I'm on my way by now. Servants do talk," Derry said as he and Shannon headed for the main hall. Derry had rubbed a little vanilla on his wrist so he could take a sniff of that if he needed to during the dinner and counteract the other scents that would make him ill. "I hope so, in fact. I don't want to surprise her again. You be careful, Shannon."

"I will be."

"Don't eat much, just in case," Derry said and hated to be that paranoid. "We can get food later, straight from the kitchen. If anything seems even a little off, avoid it."

"I think she's too subtle to poison the SanSotas at dinner," he said. He lifted a hand before Derry could say anything. "But I won't take any chances, and neither will father and Rory. They've had reason to worry for a long time, you know. They've been careful of the food for years now. We won't fail this time."

"Yes. Good." Derry pulled at the vest, not uncomfortable in the clothing but rather with the show. They reached the archway, and people looked their way in surprise. "Go on in. I can make it the rest of the way."

Shannon's hand tightened on his arm before he nodded and walked away.

Odd. Derry had not been alone for a long time. He certainly had not stood by himself and prepared to face some danger. The Queen was, beyond a doubt, a serious problem for him, and he had to be able to deal with her. Derry did have the King, Tevin, and Roe on his side. He was glad to see Roe already at the table and looking annoyed -- right until he spotted Derry.

Roe stood and crossed to escort Derry to the table, despite the glare from Queen Alisia and the snarl of anger from Egan, who sat between the Queen and Roe. Derry took the endmost chair and had hardly settled when the King arrived so that they all stood again.

"Derry! Good to see you made it down," he said, going past and slapping Derry on the shoulder. He had wisely braced himself to keep from falling. The King reached his spot and lifted his hands. "In the name of the Gods, all be at peace!"

"Let there be peace!" the others replied, and Derry didn't think he was the only one who said it rather fervently.

For all of that, the dinner went very calmly. Derry tried his best not to look to the Queen too often, and she seemed to take no notice of him at all. The game played at his nerves; without doing anything at all, the Queen won the night. He was very much relieved when the meal finished, and they were dismissed to their suites.

Shannon already waited at the archway by the time Derry made his way to the edge of the room. They said nothing; too many people lingered close by, including Clara SanKella who made a great show of not paying attention to them. Derry simply managed nods of greetings to people who were not always his friends and wondered how many of them sided with the Queen as well.

The meals went that way for the next three days. Derry found the shows exhausting and barely made it back to his room before he collapsed. Tevin, who checked on him each day, wanted to order Derry not to attend, but he disagreed.

"It's a problem, but one I can manage," Derry explained. "I'll get better at it. I need to be out in the open, Tevin. People are already looking at me less often."

"All except for the Queen," Shannon added. "I don't like the looks she gives you sometimes, Derry. She's waiting for her chance to do something."

"And she has never been known for her patience," Tevin added. "Don't relax your guard."

Two more days passed. Then in the early afternoon of a cold, rainy day, the door to the suite opened without even a knock. Derry and Shannon both stood from the desk where they'd been reading and gave Egan and the Queen bare nods of courtesy. Derry's heart pounded as three guards came in behind her, and Derry made a grab at Shannon before he did anything rash against such numbers.

"I knew if I made enough trouble, he'd have you home again and within my reach," the Queen said. "Sit down. I have something for you."

A servant carrying a tray followed the guards. Derry caught the scent of cooked meat and backed up a step.

"You can't get away, you know. You are going to sit down

and eat a meal like a human. Don't move, Shannon. My guards have specific orders about you."

"Sit down, Shan," Derry said, his voice unexpectedly calm. "Just do it. Let's not make this worse."

The smell of meat made him ill. Derry sat as well, without the Queen's leave, but she didn't really care. She knew she had won this round. He met her look, and when the bowl of stew was placed before him, he didn't even flinch.

"You will eat the food --"

"No, I will not."

That finally drew a look that bordered on pleasure. Queen Alisia nodded to a guard who moved quickly without any orders, pulling Derry's arms back and tying him to the chair. Shannon started to stand, but another guard shoved him down as well. Derry met his look, shook his head, and fervently wished him to stay calm. Shannon took one wild-eyed breath and then bowed his head.

"Feed him, Egan. Guard, get his mouth open."

Derry fought them, not only because he couldn't stand the thought of eating the meat, but also in hopes that someone would get help. Tevin said they had people watching over her. Had they gotten lax? Had --

The guard yanked Derry's head back by the hair and another pried his mouth open. Derry saw no emotion in the man's face. Egan, on the other hand, laughed with a maniacal sound and with a brightness in his eyes that showed too well how much he enjoyed causing someone else pain. Egan shoved a massive piece of meat into Derry's mouth, and the guard not only pushed his mouth shut but also pinched his nose closed.

Derry immediately began to choke, and even though he tried to chew and swallow the food, his body reacted against him. He couldn't breathe, even when the guard let go of his mouth. The food had lodged somewhere in his throat. He heard voices, heard the Queen's laughter, but the world started going dark and --

"Derry!" Shannon frantically shook him. He was no longer tied to the chair. "Breathe, damn you! Breathe!"

"Shan --" He choked and coughed, and then came close to fainting.

Voices rose all around him, and eventually he picked out the King's voice, loud over the Queen's protests.

"Perhaps the court life is too much for you," King Nevin snarled, a roar of anger barely held at bay, his hands in fists at his side. Derry turned away as he trembled in Shannon's hold. "I think it might be time to send you back to the Temple, wife. Clearly, you didn't stay long enough the last time. You and your perfidious son."

"He refused to eat meat --"

"I don't recall that ever being a requirement for living in *my* castle. Shall we ask the priestess of Arin Temple, since I do seem to recall they and their followers eat only food grown from the soil."

Derry dared a glance to the side where King and Queen faced each other, and everyone else stayed very quiet and still, including Egan, who huddled behind his mother.

"They tell stories about that boy --" Her eyes flashed as she glanced Derry's way, and he felt a new chill. The hatred filled the air like something alive and ready to claw him apart.

"They tell stories about you too, mother," Tevin said, moving to his father's side. Queen Alisia gave him a sharp look. "I would be far more worried about those tales if I were you."

Queen Alisia snarled something under her breath and turned, leaving the room with Egan scurrying at her back. Her three guards left as well, but they looked nervously at the King this time.

"She's gone," Shannon told him. "Let's get you back to

the chair. Are you alright now?"

"Better," he said as Shannon helped him sit in the high-backed, ornate chair by the desk. The taste of meat still clung to his mouth. "Some water would help."

Tevin got him a cup of water and helped hold it while Derry sipped. The water washed some of the taste out of his mouth but did nothing to settle his stomach. Shannon told the King all that happened while Petric arrived and cleared away the food -- praise the gods. Tevin opened the window despite the cold.

"Roe, smart boy, kept an eye on the two." King Nevin nodded to the younger prince who still stood by the door. "The guards only knew she went down to the kitchens and didn't think much of it. Roe realized she'd gone out again by the servant's entrance. He came and got Tevin and me, knowing no one else would be able to stop her."

"Thank you, Roe," Shannon said. "Even if I had dared do anything, she came with enough guards to stop me."

King Nevin looked to the door and shook his head. "I hope she takes my threat seriously this time. I don't want you to be in danger from her, Derry lad. I would have thought she tried to poison you, as pale as you look now. It isn't poisoned, is it? Tevin --"

"Meat is like poison to me now," Derry admitted softly. The King frowned but nodded. They really hadn't discussed the change in him, but he had to believe that Prince Tevin had told his father everything. "I don't wish to be a problem for you, sire. It might be best if I leave -- not just the castle, but the area --"

"Well, here's a problem, boy," King Nevin said with a shake of his head and a different frown. "This is not simply about you and the Queen. Now she's brought it into the realm of *my* politics, and I can't let her openly defy me without any reaction. Besides, Tevin says you are still not well, so how far could you go? I think, boy, you may be safer here where there is more than just Shannon to watch over you. I hope that we'll do better. She won't surprise the guards again; I can guarantee that much -- at least after I have words with them."

"Roe did well," Derry said. "Thank you, Roe."

Derry rose unsteadily and walked to the window, even though Shannon started to protest. He heard frantic bells somewhere in the far distance beyond the castle walls, but they calmed as though the fae realized he was better. Derry liked to think they were out there watching over him as well, though he suspected they couldn't have acted quickly enough to save him.

The fresh air helped, though. After a couple deep breaths, Derry turned back to find the others still waiting.

"You look better," Shannon admitted and dropped into a chair, clearly too shaken to still stay on his feet. "I was helpless --"

"If it comes to it again, I give you my permission to force your way past the Queen, and even to strike Egan if you need to," King Nevin said which was no small concession. Shannon looked appalled but nodded. "I'll tell the two as much and all the guards as well. I am going to have a latch put on the inside of your door, Derry. She won't come in unannounced. I'll order her not to bother you at all, but I wouldn't be surprised if she got around it somehow."

"I don't understand what is provoking her into these actions," Roe admitted and looked more bothered than Derry had seen before. "What would she have done if you had died, Derry?"

"She would have put on a good show of being quite remorseful -- oh and religious too, to use it as an excuse for her actions," Derry replied and with a touch more sarcasm than he usually showed. That shocked Shannon, but the others nodded. Shannon at least seemed to be getting some of his own control back. "But she would have won this battle, for whatever good that would get her. I still can't see what she hopes to gain, sire. If anything, my powers here at court are far less than before I left."

King Nevin nodded and then gave a little smile. "What is this? Trained birds?"

Derry glanced back at the partly open window, not at all surprised to see a half dozen sparrows on the window ledge. He crossed to them and tapped each bird on the head, winning a little song from each in turn before he pulled a bit of bread from his pocket; he'd taken to carrying it for the little creatures who came to him. The tiny birds were not the only ones, and this was a continuing show of his link to the fae.

"Not trained," Shannon explained as Derry fed the sparrows. "They come to him now. Mice and even the damned rats, though he's convinced those creatures to find homes somewhere else. Cats, dogs -- a walk near the chickens is only for the fleet of foot."

The humor broke the tenseness of the situation, though when Derry looked back, he found the King watching him intently. He had feared to see distrust in the man's face, but there was none. Derry thought he saw acceptance and perhaps even a bit of hope. Derry believed the King still trusted him, despite the changes the last few years had brought.

"What do these fae want, Derry?" King Nevin finally asked. "What should I know about them?"

"Mostly, I think they want ... the lost ones," Derry replied but frowned at his own answer. It explained nothing and sounded worse.

Derry sent the sparrows off with a wave of his hand and closed the window and shutters against the colder wind, though it didn't bother him. He had to think of the others, though. He also had to be careful about how he explained what little he knew. Derry took the half dozen steps back to the desk, and by then, he had his thoughts in order again.

Derry felt calmer and ready to deal with something that had been a long time unsaid. He'd had to wait for the King to breach the subject, though. He couldn't have gone to the man with information about the fae if King Nevin wasn't ready to hear it

"They are not dark and evil, sire," Derry said, daring much in those words. He found he was rubbing the scar on his hand and forced himself to stop. "I think if you studied the situations about the missing children, you might find there was a reason for them to want to go with the fae."

"I don't think --" King Nevin began.

"He's right, father," Tevin interrupted, surprising them all. "Even before this matter with Derry, I had looked into the disappearance of the children."

"Did you?" The King gave his son a surprised but relieved look, which showed how much he trusted the Crown Prince.

"I soon realized that someone did, indeed, take the children. I quickly learned that the children were all beggars or children in quite dire situations. Glendalow is only the latest of places where the fae -- or whoever was taking the children -- had passed. We simply hear more about the incidents now because it struck so close to Tyleen. At the other villages, people were mostly relieved to have the unwanted children gone."

"Were they?" King Nevin said, his eyes narrowed in anger. "And what if these children are going to worse lives?"

"I have been trying to find where the children go at all, father, since none have been seen again, either alive or dead. We've had soldiers in the woods, you know. Many soldiers. Nothing has shown up which made it seem as though they just disappeared, sometimes within yards between village and woods where soldiers were waiting. Yes, I began to consider fae and magic then. And quite honestly, father, it would be impossible for these children to go to worse lives. I started out thinking someone used the myth of the fae to cover bad deeds -- but the more I studied the situation, the more I thought this must be something different. Also, the earliest reports of fae taking children came from backcountry areas, the places where they still believed in fae and held to the old tales of when humans and fae still worked together."

"And now we trust the fae?" Roe asked. He glanced at Derry, troubled.

The fire cackled in the silence of the room. Petric cleaned everything without a sound, a quiet presence that even Derry hardly noticed. The man didn't waste time and he left again, with hardly a glance back at Derry. The moment had given Derry time to consider his words, though.

"My link to the fae could be a ploy to get the humans to trust the fae," Derry admitted. He felt better just for the chance to talk about the matter. Tevin's work had paved the way for him so that he didn't have to make them believe not only that the fae existed, but also that they were not evil. "I don't believe this is true, but my contact with the fae themselves was very short. Honestly, if they were going to work some odd sort of magic on us, I believe they would have chosen better than me for the first step. Still, it won't hurt to take extra care in all that happens. We almost had a major incident already when Captain Killough tried to save the child and me."

"Yes, he told me so," King Nevin admitted, calm and accepting of everything for the moment. "What can you tell us, Derry?"

"I'm still too muddled," Derry admitted. He didn't add that the recent battle with the Queen hadn't helped. His mind wanted to wander. "I remember that Leanora claimed her clan wandered the borderlands and brought the humans and fae together in peace. They find the lost ones, which I think meant both human and animal. I heard them because somewhere between the prison cell and reaching Tyleen, I simply lost myself and couldn't believe anything was real." Derry shook his head when Shannon started to speak, and the others remained silent. "Leanora told me trouble was coming; she thought I was a sign of the link that would be needed between her people and humans."

"And she said she thought she might love you," Tevin added a bit softly.

"Oh, Killough told you that part too, did he?" Derry laughed, mostly at the shocked look on Shannon's face.

"And will she come for you someday?" Tevin asked.

"More likely that I'll go to her and willingly join the fae someday," he answered and did his best not to sound wistful. That came only from this latest trouble with the Queen. "But not now. Not for a long time, I think. She said I had ties still to the human world and wasn't ready to go. She's right. If there is trouble coming, I might be able to help somehow."

"Going to the fae always sounded like such a fearful thing," Tevin admitted, surprising him. "I had nightmares when I was a child -- yes, I admit it now, father. I still wouldn't want them to come for me."

"They wouldn't," Derry said. "You know your place, and you will never be lost."

"Yes. True." Tevin stood straighter again. "I have work to get back to before the evening feast."

"Yes, that," King Nevin said as he started to the door. He stopped and looked back. "You need no longer make an appearance at the evening feast, Derry. Neither you nor Shannon. We're through with that pretense now that the Queen made her move. She'll worry more about you not being in sight, I think, so be careful."

"I might like to join you two if you don't mind?" Roe asked, his voice almost unsteady. "I don't exactly like sitting with Egan every night. He's a little pig. He grabs half of my food before I can get it. Maybe if I'm not there, he'll lose some weight."

King Nevin gave a startled little laugh but glanced at Derry and Shannon.

"I'd be happy to have you here," Derry replied and pleased the boy and apparently his father, too.

"Excellent. Not every night, Roe, but good for you to get out of that mess, too," the King said. Then he and Tevin left, their conversation already turning to the fall harvest in the area. Roe hovered at the doorway, but Derry waved him inside to join them.

"Did I thank you, Roe?" Derry asked when Roe settled on a chair by the fireplace, looking young again. Had he just turned fifteen the summer before? He looked younger just now, but Derry had the feeling that came more from uncertainty.

"I knew they would do something," Roe said with a shrug and looked ill at ease now. "I don't think the guards took her very seriously. Father's bound to strip her of her personal guards and make her use his own now. I think he was simply waiting for a reason. She lost this power play. She and Egan are going to be sorry they tried to play this game."

"I never much liked those palace games," Derry admitted. Shannon only nodded and still looked worried.

They would have a lock on the inside of the door before the day was out. The King would not forget. Derry didn't mention how much that idea bothered him. He'd have to get used to it because he wouldn't put Shannon in that kind of danger again. Derry considered asking the King to order Shannon out of Tyleen, but he didn't let that thought come to his lips. He knew what Shannon's reply would be (and he'd hate to shock Roe with that kind of language). Besides, they guarded each other, and Shannon would be in a more vulnerable position alone. She wouldn't be slow to take advantage of such stupidity.

"What are all the books?" Roe asked, a tentative question, as though testing the water to see how far he might go.

"Books about the fae," Derry replied with a wave of his hand toward the tomes. "I really don't know much about them, but I am learning."

"And this is a far more interesting subject than crop rotation, which is my father's latest interest," Shannon added. "I just read a short, and relatively even-handed essay, if you'd like to read something."

"Yes, I would." Roe crossed to the table. He accepted the little booklet from Shannon with a nod of thanks, but then he glanced at the closed window, his head tilted a little. "That's odd. I thought I heard bells."

Derry wasn't surprised to find that Roe might also be one of the lost.

Chapter Eight

Winter struck with fierce winds and bitter cold. Snow piled up around Tyleen in high drifts, and few people went beyond the walls of the castle if they had no reason to be out. Shannon and Derry spent most of the time in his rooms, reading and talking about the future. The fire, sprinkled with pine, gave a pleasant scent, and the light dispersed the gray days and darker shadows.

During those calm and quiet days, Derry finally began to grow stronger again. His mind cleared of the fog that had held him. He also began to sense the difference between being wholly human and the changes the fae blood brought to him, both in body and in mind. Derry could feel magic within him, although he had no idea how to access it. In fact, he did his best to make sure all but the most benign aspects of his connection to the fae remained inactive. He wanted no accident that might hurt others or draw attention to himself.

The birds came to him more often in the winter, and partly because Roe had started bringing all the leftover bread from the kitchen. Mice showed now and then, but the rats had seemed to take his suggestion that they no longer congregate in his room and scare the servants. An occasional squirrel and a few raccoons even dared the icy walls to reach him, though. Petric had stopped being startled when he found them resting by the fire.

The fire kept them all warm. Derry and Shannon had moved from reading about the fae to books on history, searching out tales about interaction between the two peoples in those as well. They were not many such references, but they were always at times of danger, and the fae might have been mistrusted, but they had never been the enemy.

For hundreds of years, there had been only occasional tales of a child gone missing or an unexpected meeting with fae in the woods. People had simply stopped believing in what they no longer saw, and the rumors became myths and tales to tell their recalcitrant children at bedtime.

As Derry grew stronger, the rooms sometimes felt too small and cell-like. Shannon understood once he explained with a shaky wave of his arms toward the walls. Walks to the archives helped. They even took an occasional dinner in the main hall with the King and others. The Queen said nothing. The Queen did nothing, though there was a question about some tainted cheese that showed up for their breakfast.

Snow flew on the colder days, plastering against the shutters. Derry didn't mind it so much. Along with the growing strength of his body, his mind focused better as well. Shannon took note of it and was clearly relieved when he no longer had to direct Derry out of obvious trouble. The Queen wasn't the only one who had questions about him now, and Derry had been apt to simply greet everyone as though nothing had changed.

Those greetings were more purposeful than Shannon seemed to realize at first. Derry didn't go out of his way to find people in the halls, but if someone turned up, Derry wanted to see their reactions to his greeting. He thought he could feel the emotions sometimes. He still treated them all the same, whether they trusted him or not.

Spring came in an unexpected rush of warmth. The snow melted into a frenzy of small streams and mud holes. Plants began to bloom, and the scent of life kept Derry by the window for most of the day, even when it might still be a bit chilly outside. When the rains eased Derry, Shannon and Roe even took morning rides out into the fields nearby. Derry suspected Roe had never had such freedom. It did their young friend as much good as it did Derry to get of the shadowed, cold stone of the castle.

On the warmer days, they'd hobble the horses and sit in the growing grass. Rabbits and squirrels always came to Derry, and sometimes deer and foxes, rats and snakes. Shannon and Roe tried very hard to act as though this were all normal.

Sometimes they saw fae at the edge of the nearby woods. A small colorfully clad troop, bells ringing brightly, would show themselves for a moment, nod in Derry's direction, and then they'd disappear again. Derry was glad to know they were so close. Seeing the fae settled a worry, though, he had heard the bells often enough. The sounds were intangible, though. He didn't know what the music even meant.

Once the fae came out to the edge of a field and watched Shannon and Roe try to catch a couple sheep, which they apparently found as amusing as Derry. He gave them a wave of greeting, and they returned it with bright laughter and ringing bells.

Two children went missing that spring, and rumors began almost immediately that Derry had been responsible. For the first time since he returned, he sought out the King. Tevin and Roe went with him, and Shannon came along. King Nevin, as chance would have it, was waiting for two of his Lords to arrive, and no one else was in the room where the King did most of his work. King Nevin sat at his desk, a scattering of parchments everywhere, seals and a wax jack ready to make things official. King Nevin had clerks, but he always wrote the first copy of any proclamation in his own hand before it went off to be copied for others.

"Sir, about the missing children --" Derry began as soon as he received a nod from the man.

"I don't suspect you," King Nevin said. He tossed down a parchment and frowned. "You need not worry."

"I appreciate your faith in me, even at this unusual time and circumstance. However, there was something else that worried me. I believe the children went to the fae. If another should disappear now and not by the hand of the fae, and I was somehow implicated --"

The King gave a quick nod. "Yes, I see your point. I'll keep an eye on the matter."

Neither of them named the Queen.

"With your leave, Shannon and I are going to head to the SanSota estate in a few days. I think getting me out of Tyleen for a while will help all of us."

"And you'll be careful, won't you? The two of you off without protection might be dangerous."

"Yes, sire, that's true. I've had a feeling, though, that I need to go."

King Nevin looked him hard in the face, scowling. "A fae feeling?"

"I think so, but it's not as though I'm used to such things. I can't be certain. I might simply need to get out and ride and feel that I am truly free."

"Ah, now that I can understand -- and more than understanding, I can say the same to others who are bound to ask."

"Good," Derry replied and felt a new wave of relief. He didn't want to make matters worse at Tyleen. "We'll leave in two days. We will not be making any sign of it."

King Nevin nodded and said no more since the guard knocked and let Lord SanKella into the room. The older Lord scowled to see Derry and Shannon, but they left with polite bows and hurried back to Derry's room. Roe went with them; people were used to seeing the three together. He wondered if Roe ought to go with them on this journey.

Once in the room, Roe settled that question.

"I'm going to keep an eye on mother." Roe sprawled on the bed, having lost worries about being proper with these two. "I'll play the poor little kid, abandoned by people I thought were my friends. Egan might fall for that act, though he is far more secretive since he came back from exile. I don't think mother will care one way or the other."

"I'll miss you," Shannon said even before Derry could. "You be careful around here."

"Let's all three of us ride to the forest this afternoon," Derry said. They didn't usually go late in the afternoon, but he didn't think it would draw much notice. "We can speak more freely out there."

Shannon gave him an odd look. Maybe he'd picked up on Derry's unease. Shannon went ahead and got horses, the three of them heading out towards the forest edge as usual. Derry felt better as soon as they were out of the castle and wondered if he had just begun to feel trapped there. Trapped was not a good reaction for him these days.

They had a pleasant ride and stopped well into the woods by a favorite brook, letting the horses drink while they sat on boulders and talked about the upcoming trip. The woods were alive with birds, deer, and small animals. The chatter of sound hardly paused as they rode through, and the breeze softened to a whisper of warmth. Shannon tossed stones into the water and looked more relaxed than he had since Derry returned to Tyleen. Derry found himself looking forward to the journey now that they were committed to going. Getting supplies, even quietly, wasn't going to be a lot of trouble since neither needed much these days.

"Remember that word is out about you, Derry," Roe warned and gave a nervous glance around as though he expected someone nearby. "It's gone well beyond Tyleen. So, if you can go without notice, that would be good."

Roe glanced his way and looked as though he didn't believe Derry could be discreet.

"That's a good point to remember," Derry said. "I'm sure your mother sent out word --"

"Actually, father did first," Roe replied.

"He did?" Derry replied, startled by that answer.

"Oh, yes. He wanted to make certain everyone knew that he sided with you before mother made any show of her own feelings. I hope it helped. The Lords from the outer estates are starting to wander in now, and they're nervous about you. Father said there was no outright hostility. I guess I should have mentioned this before, right?"

"Now is a good time," Shannon replied. "I --"

Bells rang and quite close by this time. Derry spun and blinked in surprise as a very young boy stepped out from the trees. He couldn't have been more than eight. Though thin, he was browned by the sun, and his hair had grown long and wild. Two rabbits and a squirrel followed him from the covering of the bushes, and he waved them back with an exaggerated sigh. The creatures retreated a little way but held their place with the boy in sight.

The bells sang out in wild abandon as the fae stopped at the other side of the brook and dropped on his heels, his head tilted as he looked at the three. After a moment, the music, which seemed like the song of nature itself, quieted to a soft murmur of pretty bells.

Fae beyond a doubt, though this one could have been a human boy -- probably had been at one time. The wild clung to him now. The sound of silver bells that came with him grew louder when the boy smiled, and he laughed when a rabbit charged back out of the brush to sit at his side.

"You don't recognize me, do you Prince Derry?" he asked with another tilt of his head and a bright smile. "Not a surprise since we only met briefly in Glendalow."

"You're the boy who went with the fae that night," Derry said, surprised. He had changed and very much for the better with his tanned skin, and sun-bleached hair. He wore clothing woven of leaves and flowers, and the scent of spring came with him. This was not the haunted, nearly starved boy he'd seen in Leanora's care that night. "You are happy now, aren't you?"

"Oh, yes, my Lord!" He held out his hand, and a bright red and yellow butterfly landed on his palm. "Everything is so wondrous and bright! My lady Queen Leanora sent me to give you a message, sir."

Queen? Derry hadn't known her station, and he tried not to show his surprise as he gave the boy a nod. "What is her message?"

"She says that you and Shannon should be careful when you go north and you should go soon," the boy said and won a little sound of surprise from Shannon. "Something happening there, happening to the land itself. She hopes you can go and see. There is trouble coming, my Lords. Unrest moves among the humans, and it feels as though darkness lingers at the edge of spring."

"Magic?" Derry asked since he knew nothing of magic. He couldn't help there.

"Of some sort, but not fae-made magic." The boy shrugged and looked towards the north as though he could see whatever waited out there. Derry glanced that way as well, and for a moment, he might have felt something darker as well. "We can sense something, but we don't understand what creates the darkness. Not natural, we think. Not of the world as we know it."

Those quiet words sounded ominous and portended something more than Derry thought he could handle, but he would not refuse to go. "I'll do what I can," he said and hoped he sounded more assured than he felt.

"Go north, she said," the boy answered, looking back at him again. He looked more somber now. "Some of us will remain near Tyleen in case anything moves against this place of human power. Leonora says that we will report any trouble to Prince Roe if he agrees to come here to the brook some days."

Derry glanced at Roe, not at all surprised to see him delighted with the idea. Roe had spent far too much time with Derry if he thought nothing of being a messenger for the fae.

"Is there anything else you can tell us?" Derry asked.

The fae boy gave a slight shrug, looking more human again. He stood, and it seemed the breeze itself moved as he did. "Let yourself feel what is happening around you, Prince Derry. You have fae blood now, and you are touched by the wild. You have gifts that no other human possesses, and you must learn to use them to help us all."

With a quick little bow, the boy headed back into the woods with bells sounding bright, and a half dozen butterflies following him. Derry could hear the bells long after he had disappeared.

"Well, I guess that settles it," Shannon replied. He dropped one last stone into the water and then stood, brushing the dirt from his hands and clothing.

"There's trouble out there." Derry closed his eyes, and he thought he felt something wrong brush against him. He shivered as the others gathered the horses. "What do you think about all of this, Roe?"

"That you should do what the fae say," he replied and

handed over Derry's reins.

"You trust them without question?" Shannon asked and sounded as though he didn't trust much at all.

Roe frowned as he looked at the shadowed woods and then back at them. "Maybe I do trust them, but I trust the two of you more. You know I've heard the bells as well, and I suspect I know what that means, though you two have been careful not to say anything. Oh, don't worry. I won't tell anyone about our little encounter here or about what I hear late at night beyond the walls of Tyleen. I don't want mother bothering me any more than she already does."

"Oh yes, very wise," Derry agreed as he mounted, the other two quick to follow as though they expected him to rush off without them.

"I'll go to Tevin later tonight, and, if he thinks it wise, we'll go to father," Roe said with a steady nod of his head. Then he grinned. "A year ago, I wouldn't have thought to go to the King with anything so outrageous. He was never one who dealt well with any time-wasting fancies. Until you showed up with your tie to the fae, I doubt he'd ever thought twice of them in the same year. Tevin is different. He was already making the study of the missing children. I can talk to him. But it is you that brought father around, Derry."

"So maybe that's reason enough for the fae to have sent me back among humans," Derry said with a slight shrug. They were already clearing the woods and he wanted to turn back -- he still felt the longing he had that night when he chased after Leonora. "I fear there has been a great deal going on the last few months while we sat snug and warm in Tyleen."

"We would have heard about any trouble," Shannon protested as they headed toward the city and the castles. He looked back at the woods as though he expected to see the boy there again.

"No one would send messages about small problems,"

Derry replied and held out his hand to a little sparrow chattering at him. "However, small things have a way of adding up to bigger problems."

"True enough," Shannon agreed. "Until a few minutes ago, your link to the fae seemed nothing more than a hint of odd magic that brought birds to you. I guess it's time that I accept the full truth of it -- and no, I am not upset, Derry. I can see there is work for us."

"Then let's get to it," Roe said.

Prince Roe didn't sound much like a boy now. Derry supposed they had all three changed over the long, cold winter. Despite the situation, Derry could see no doubt in either of his companions. He supposed that meant it was time for him to give up his own doubts as well.

Chapter Nine

Two anxious horses stood in the gray predawn light, both saddled by the sleepy stable boys who were glad to retire back to their warm blankets as soon as Derry and Shannon took charge. Mist clung to the equipment and walls around them, drops of water sparkling in the flickering light of a half-dozen torches. Derry patted the nose Kirwan, the bay he usually rode, and found her quite pleased to be heading out for a ride. Shannon's chestnut, Asten, seemed even more excited, and hardly able to stand still. The horses were ready to go.

Derry wasn't quite so ready. The idea of leaving behind the safety of Tyleen -- and the King's watchful eye -- bothered him. However, the more he thought about those worries, the less he wanted to feel as though he couldn't leave and be safe. He didn't want to make a new prison for himself.

Derry wasn't surprised to find Roe arrive to see them off, though he looked half asleep, blinking at the torchlight, his cape haphazardly pulled up to his ears against the cold. What did surprise Derry was King Nevin and Prince Tevin arriving as well. They looked more alert, and Derry had the feeling they were used to working before dawn.

"Roe told me all that happened out there by the brook," King Nevin said and with a frown. He hadn't even put on a cloak, though Tevin had. The man looked oblivious to the weather. "I don't know what to make of it." He glanced around, ensuring that one lingered too near. Guards paced the high curtain walls, and a couple servants scurried past with baskets laden with food. Once they were gone, the courtyard appeared to be empty except for the horses and the five of them. Nonetheless, the King kept his voice quiet. "It worries me, this attention from the fae. I admit. I don't know what I should believe and who I can trust."

"Trust your instincts," Derry replied. "You have always had a good head for trouble, sire. This may be unusual trouble, but it will be real and cause problems you will be able to see. I suspect when the time comes, you might not even need the fae to warn you. However, if they do, I think you shouldn't ignore them. That's my best advice, sire."

Nevin gave a brief nod, somehow looking less kingly out here in the mist and cold, and more akin to some force of nature. Derry wouldn't have been surprised to see the weather change at his frown. Even without magic, this was a man of power.

Derry and Shannon bade farewell to all three and mounted their horses. Shannon looked almost as anxious as the horses to be away, and Derry tried to gather some of that feeling for himself.

"I have a problem with the idea that I should trust the fae." King Nevin admitted. No real surprise there. "Should I?"

"Yes," Shannon said, surprising them both. "I've spent nearly all my time with Derry since he returned. I have a good feel for what has changed in him. I've also studied more about the fae than anyone but him. They were never our enemies, sire. They only had different interests."

"We fear what is different," Derry said, shifting in the saddle. The day would get warmer, and he thought he might enjoy a nice ride, though the idea of days of travel worried him. He had gotten used to his soft bed and warm food. "And we fear powers we can't have."

The King nodded, but he didn't appear to be any more assured. After a moment, he gave a shrug over things that couldn't be changed. Derry had come to feel the same way, and he realized he and the King had often seen things the same way in the past. The King frowned, looking up at the two. "I still think I ought to send a couple guards with you."

"We'll be fine, sire," Derry said and hoped the words would be true. King Nevin didn't look placated by the answer. "Besides, if you sent a guard with us, you would have to do the same for anyone of rank who traveled away from Tyleen. You can't send them off with Shannon and me and ignore everyone else. You don't dare show that much favoritism."

"I can damned well do as I please."

Derry hadn't expected any other answer, and when he laughed, the King finally gave a grudging smile as well. Things felt very much as they had before Derry taken his dark journey to the Isles, and even the shadows around them now seemed to lessen. Roe had looked worried and then surprised and pleased at his father's laughter. Tevin simply nodded as though he approved of what Derry had said and done.

"Well, maybe you are right," King Nevin agreed. "I don't need to annoy everyone, and I don't need to strip the castle of the guards they would demand. It's like herding children some days, with their constant shouts that I'm favoring over one of them. You two just be careful. There are dangers aimed only at you, Derry, and you know it."

"I'll be careful," he promised.

"And here I thought we were going to have a wild ride through Lynashin," Shannon said with his own little laugh.

"I suspect we will. I doubt we'll enjoy ourselves much, though."

"I really don't need this kind of pessimism."

The King laughed again, which was probably a good show for the soldiers on the walls and even for the Queen's spies who doubtlessly lingered nearby. They'd always been close by, and Derry had been aware of them all his life. She certainly kept a closer watch on him now. He could feel them watching, but he didn't let it bother him.

"Hurry back, both of you," Tevin said, slapping Shannon on the knee. "I think things will be terribly dull with the two of you gone."

"And you think the kind of excitement I bring is good?" Derry asked, pulling the horse backward and preparing to turn.

"You keep the court in gossip, and not about me. And besides, you keep mother busy and out of our hair."

A daring thing to say. Derry grinned but dared not laugh aloud, reminding himself of those spies close by. The Crown Prince could get away with that statement, but his orphan cousin would not be so lucky.

The King, though ... he laughed.

The two gave bows from the saddle and rode across the quiet courtyard, startling sleepy chickens and annoying a couple cats. The guards at the gate had orders to let them through and gave nods that didn't seem too unfriendly. Perhaps they were just glad to see the two go.

Shannon had said goodbye to his family the night before, but a servant waited on the trail when they went past. She handed over travel bags with cakes and cider, saying they came from Shannon's mother. Derry could tell his friend didn't trust the gift, but Derry could feel the truth of the statement and knew the food was safe. It might even be more reliable than what they brought from Tyleen. He hadn't had a chance to feel out the supplies in their packs since hadn't wanted to be noticeable back at the castle.

The first pale light caressed the taller city buildings by the time they reached the outskirts of town. The mist had begun to lift as well. Though this wasn't a market day, a few merchants already set up stands for food and other necessities for those passing through town. The King and the various Lords in the castles overlooking the city would have visitors. Tyleen was busiest in the spring since few people traveled far during the latter part of winter when the weather often turned bitterly cold and dangerous.

People glanced their way, but they wore their hoods pulled low over their brows, and they didn't ride with banners, so they could have been practically any of the younger nobility. They didn't stop, and they said little, riding down the main road. There was only one gate into Tyleen, and right now, Derry could have wished for a faster way out and away.

As though he was trying to escape from something?

Derry thought the feeling swept over him, like a wide-winged bird that cast a shadow across the land. He tried to shake the mood, but it wasn't until they were out the city gate that he felt as though they were even marginally safer.

Derry shook his head, trying to convince himself that this was his overactive imagination, but he still didn't have any idea of how the fae magic worked. When he glanced at Shannon, he was surprised to find his friend glancing back and looking relieved as well.

That made Derry reconsider what he felt and why.

"You know, I suddenly suspect it's really you who wanted out of Tyleen," Derry said, startling him.

"That's true in some ways," Shannon agreed. His friend already appeared more relaxed, and Derry could feel the change, much as he could feel how the horses wanted to go faster with the feel of the breeze against their faces. He found it difficult to concentrate on human things, except his tie to

Shannon always called him back. "I didn't like being in the same building as the Queen and the Toad. Egan."

"Toad is fine by me."

Shannon laughed and glanced to the left as they headed down the first trail leading to the northeast. There were many riders and wagons along the way, but these people were not likely to recognize the two. They did have to be careful of their conversation, though, because word could get back to the Queen if they were at all indiscreet about her or the fae. They didn't ride fast, giving themselves breaks between groups.

"Derry, the truth is that I don't trust the humans right now, and that makes me uneasy," Shannon admitted. "I don't know where I stand."

"I understand." Derry dared a glance back toward Tyleen which stood down in the valley as they climbed the hills. Then he turned and smiled to see how much closer the woods were already. They didn't intend to take the main trails once they got out of sight of Tyleen, and Derry hoped that would help keep them from danger. "All those dark years I spent in Fairfall, I constantly dreamed of coming home to Tyleen. You know I'm uncomfortable inside the castle, even though I love it. And now, the contrary person that I am, I fear to leave the place again. I couldn't stand to be locked away somewhere else, Shannon."

Derry hadn't expected the sudden shiver that took hold of him just then. He unsettled the horse and took a deep breath to call back his controls. Birds had cried out in dismay for a moment, and he hated to upset them -- and Shannon.

"It won't happen," Shannon promised, his emotions so strong that they startled Derry. Shannon reached across and tapped Derry on the arm as though to make certain he paid attention. "That's why you are not going to ride off anywhere without me. Besides, we have other allies now."

Derry heard bells in the woods not far away. Shannon

laughed and didn't show a moment's pause as they continued towards the fae sound. His friend had accepted this change in the world more quickly than he had, and Derry wasn't sure why. Or maybe he did -- Derry suspected Shannon would have accepted any difference, as long as Derry came back from Fairfall. Shannon's wait had been different from his own, but it had been just as long.

"I suppose we will go north and do what we can," Derry said. "Besides, if Lynashin is in danger, I can't simply walk away."

That reminded him of what Leanora had said to him about the ties that still held Prince Derry to the humans. She had been right; he couldn't simply abandon everything he had loved to and head off with the fae. Besides, it was apparent the fae weren't ignoring this problem either.

"Derry?"

He smiled at Shannon. "Just realizing that we are doing the right thing, Shannon. There is a good reason why the fae left me in the human world, even though I have a tie to the world of magic now. I need to go among the humans where the other fae can't go. I can see things they might not be able to understand. Besides, it is good to get out. I am worried about leaving Roe behind, though. His mother will hound him."

"He'll manage. She's not very subtle, you know, and if Roe plays at pouting the way Egan does, she'll probably not think much about him. Her fixation on Egan has grown since they returned to court, and it was easy enough for Roe to avoid her anyway. Tevin and the King will make sure he is safe. Tevin even mentioned it to me yesterday when we passed in the halls."

"Good." That settled one last worry. Derry relaxed, and this time let the peace of the world slip in around him. They might find trouble somewhere ahead, but right now he decided to enjoy the lovely spring day.

Bells rang, not far off in the darker woods. They had traveling companions, he guessed, and was happy for that too. Derry breathed in the fresh air. Had the castle seemed so dank? He hadn't thought so while he was there, but out here he felt far better. Trouble might not be far away, but for now, he would enjoy the ride. He needn't even worry about Roe, left behind.

But he should have thought of all the others who were also still in the reach of the Queen.

Chapter Ten

Four days of pleasant riding and camping each night in the open had done wonders for Derry. He felt truly felt free and being in Shannon's company had helped call him back to the world he loved. They'd had a rebellious youth, fighting the chains of conformity. They'd been wild boys --

Now Derry was wild in another way. By the second day, birds and butterflies rode on his shoulders, and their camps were often overrun with squirrels and rabbits. The fae bells kept close for the first two days, but they moved off on the morning of the third. Derry and Shannon rode mostly through newly planted fields and small villages on the third and fourth day, and Derry suspected there was not enough wild here to draw the fae closer.

Shannon certainly looked better after a few days away from Tyleen. Derry hadn't considered the pressure his friend must have been under, standing with his odd friend -- not only against the Queen but also in the face of anyone else unhappy with Derry's new fae connection. They didn't speak much about it because Shannon simply waved it off.

"What else would you expect me to do?" he demanded

and the laughed before Derry could answer.

"I'm just saying, Shannon --"

"That you wouldn't have done the same if I was the one who had come back home with a touch of strangeness?"

There was no arguing the point. The two sat around a small fire, sipping cider and preparing to sleep. There hadn't been as many rabbits and such tonight, so Derry thought he might get rest for a change. He didn't have many nightmares out here in the open. He hoped that carried over when they returned to Tyleen.

"Time to sleep," Derry finally said and abandoned the argument. "I'm tired."

Shannon spread out their blankets and stretched out beside Derry and fell almost instantly into a deep sleep. Derry had always envied Shannon that ability. His own mind constantly leapt and danced and made pretty pictures -- or dark nightmares -- as soon as he attempted to turn it off. He tried not to toss and turn since that would wake Shannon, and one of them should get a good rest --

Only Shannon wasn't sleeping well tonight. He almost came awake several times and grumbled sleepily. Derry stayed still in hopes that he wouldn't bother his friend, and in that silence, he heard things in the world that bothered him. There were no bells; he would have welcomed those pretty sounds very much right now. Instead, he sensed worry that swept through the trees and grass like a malignant wind. A night owl gave a startled cry and fled to her nest and young ones. Field mice and rabbits who should have been safe in their burrows were fleeing from ... from something dark that moved in the night. Something unnatural disturbed the rightness in the world.

"Derry?"

He had sat up and didn't remember doing so. Derry blinked, but he looked past Shannon into the night, watching for something he couldn't really see.

"Derry friend, you are being peculiar, even for you." Shannon sat up as well and looked around with growing worry.

"It's all right. I just feel something wrong out there, I think. Go back to sleep."

"Like hell, I will," he said, a hand on Derry's arm as though to make certain his friend didn't do anything rash. "You've been fine for the last few days. Now you look nearly as pale and shaken as the day you came back to Tyleen. I haven't been asleep for long. What the hell happened?"

"I'm not sure."

Shannon threw more wood on the fire as though he understood about the dark and wanted to push the shadows away. The feeling did recede somewhat as the brighter light lit their area. So maybe it had only been his imagination.

The trees whispered differently.

"Talk to me, my friend. Tell me what it is you sense out there."

"Sorry," Derry replied and took a deeper breath. He lifted his hand and thought he could feel all sorts of things in the world around them. "It's as though everything is suddenly anxious. I think something moves in the darkness, Shannon -- or it is the darkness itself that moves. Maybe this is what the fae have been talking about."

"You can feel it now because we are closer to the area?" Shannon asked. He watched the trees around them, alert for any sign of trouble. Shannon had also pulled his sword closer, though Derry feared that weapon would do little good against whatever he felt, although he didn't say so.

"The fae felt the trouble in the north at Tyleen, but I didn't feel anything there --"

"But you, my friend, are not full fae, are you? I've seen your fae gifts becoming more apparent this trip. It may be that you are finally accepting enough of your connection to understand what bothers them. And not to put too fine a point on it, but I am rather bothered that they're not around tonight."

Shannon looked towards the woods as though he expected one of the fae to show up. Derry hoped for one as well, but only the slight breeze moved, and he couldn't hear even distant bells.

"Why do I get the feeling that we shouldn't be here?" Derry asked.

"Time to go." Shannon instantly took to his feet, grabbing up their blankets.

Derry stood and started putting out the fire, though he hated to lose the light. The shadows seemed to move oddly as the flames died, like tendrils circling around the nearby bushes, inching their way forward.

"We can ride on to Keirkell," Shannon continued as he saddled the horses. He glanced up at the sky. "We'll get there about midnight. I know a good inn. We can get some sleep and face this in the light of day."

"The Greenwood Inn," Derry said with overly anxious cheerfulness. He moved quickly to help gather up their few supplies. Time to go, time to go.

Their mounts were clearly uneasy, as well. The wind had picked up, though fitfully with a gust and then such stillness fell that Derry thought the world held her breath.

Derry had been ready to mount when a fox dashed into the area and straight to him. Derry leaned down, and she stood with her paws on his knees and whimpered softly, her head twitching back the way she had come.

"Her young are in danger," Derry said and didn't find it odd that he knew this was the truth. "She can't reach her den and -- Gods all -- I am the only fae she can find to help her."

Shannon looked at him, eyes blinking twice. Then he

pulled his sword and gave Derry a nod. "She can lead us there?"

He could not have asked for a better friend.

They took only long enough to kick more dirt over the embers. Shannon mounted, but Derry took hold of his horse's bridle. "I need to stay close to the fox," he said and started out, the fox giving a yip that held both hope and anxiousness.

The wind grew stronger almost immediately, and the fox crept close to the ground. Dark clouds scuttled across the nearly full moon, and he heard the echoes of thunder, but they seemed odd and unreal. No lightning lit the sky.

A knot of panic grew in Derry's chest as the fox danced away in front of him, her frantic yips drawing him on. An enemy moved out there ... an enemy of both the fae and the humans. Derry could feel the movement of evil darkness drawing too close -- but he saw nothing.

The fox yipped again, and then with a cry of anxiety, she darted into the brush to the right. Derry forced his way through the twigs and thorns, breaking a path for the horses to follow. He took only little breaths because something felt like a knife jabbing at his heart.

As they stepped into a small clearing, he could see darkness moving like a swirling cloud brought to ground.

"What the hell is that?" Shannon asked, his voice soft.

"You can see it?" Derry asked, the words forced out between gasps he could no longer hide.

"I can see *something*," Shannon replied, his voice soft as he leaned down from the horse, clearly ready to grab Derry and ride fast. "Like a shadow moving between the trees. I think you had better get back, Derry."

"No. There's the den."

The vixen had rushed off to the left side, and Derry could hear the frantic cries of the younger foxes now. Derry couldn't tell what the shadow creature did, but the trees lost life as it passed them, and creatures that could not move fast enough fell dead in the path it had taken.

The horses protested going any closer. When the creature moved their way, they went mad with fear. Derry tried to hold on and to calm his mount, but it dragged him back and down, and before he could get clear, an iron-shod hoof struck his right shoulder. The world went red as he hissed in pain and the horse raced away.

Shannon shouted a curse and leapt from his own horse. The animals careened away from the danger, taking everything but Shannon's sword, which he had somehow gotten into his hand.

"Derry, my friend, get your feet under you. We have to move!"

Derry had been nearly senseless, aware only that the fox growled as though to fight back the dark. When he sat up, Derry could see the fox kits heads pop up out of the den. He suspected the mother had been hunting, and the young ones were too frightened to run.

Derry got to his feet, even though his shoulder and arm felt as though they were on fire. He shoved the pain behind a wall; he'd learned that trick in Fairfall, though it seemed easier this time.

The shadow shifted slightly as though to follow the horses. Drawn to life? However, the moment Derry moved towards the kits, he could feel it shift awareness again. There might not be full intelligence there, but it did have attention trained on them.

No, on *him*. Fae, he thought -- more filled with life than anything else here, even if he was not really one of the fae people. Derry could use that link, though he suspected Shannon would protest. Best not to tell him the plan.

"Shan," he said softly. He tried to sound steady. "Move to the kits and grab them."

"What are you --?"

Derry didn't wait for the question. He moved in the opposite direction from the kits. Not far, but enough that the thing, which seemed at least horse size if not larger, shifted with him.

"Son of a bitch," Shannon whispered, but he moved quickly. The vixen went with him and didn't protest when Shannon scooped up the two little fox kits, which couldn't have been more than four weeks old. "Now, what do we do?"

"Retreat," Derry said. He saw Shannon place the kits inside his vest and take up his sword again. "Retreat as fast as we can."

"I don't think we can fight this thing," Shannon admitted, even though he held the sword out as though to duel with someone from court. "I think we're lucky that it seems to move slowly."

"Very lucky since I can't move very fast, either."

"What is it?"

"I don't know. I just hope it's the only one we face."

"Oh, there's a fine thought." Shannon moved slowly until he reached Derry. The horses were long gone and there was no hope of calling them back. Shannon handed one of the kits to Derry and helped get it settled inside his friend's shirt. Then he took hold of Derry's left arm with one hand and kept the sword in the other. "Let's go."

They moved backward for the first few yards. The shadow creature followed carefully, and Derry wondered why it didn't attack. Maybe it could sense the little magic Derry held. Derry wished he knew how to use the power.

"You need to lead the way, Shannon. We aren't going to get away like this," Derry finally said. He nudged Shannon to turn. "Go. We need to make better time."

Shannon looked apt to argue, but he finally turned and started away, though not much faster until he was certain

Derry could stay with him. The vixen yipped at their feet and urged them on.

By now, Derry knew his shoulder was not broken, but it hurt like hell to move anyway. He kept up with Shannon determined that none of them would fall to this creature because of him. They hurried through the woods that were silent except for the odd wind and distant thunder. Derry sensed an unnaturalness in the air that came from more than the shadow creature, though he didn't say so to Shannon. He suspected his companion had figured many things were wrong anyway.

They stumbled into a larger glade, and Derry gave a little sigh of relief between gasps. He wouldn't have been up to this prolonged hike before the horse stepped on him. The meadow would be easier to cross, at least. Shannon had used his sword to hack a path for them, but even so, the branches and bushes had torn at his clothing and skin.

They were over halfway across the glade, pausing for a moment to catch their breath when the shadow creature cleared the trees.

And as quickly retreated.

"What --" Shannon said, but stopped and shook his head.

They watched as the creature moved to another spot and stepped out. Clouds rushed across the sky, and for a moment, Derry couldn't clearly see it. But the clouds cleared, and the creature retreated in haste --

"Shadow creature," Derry said. "It can't stand to be in light -- even the moonlight."

"Then we're safe here -- no, we aren't," Shannon said before Derry could speak. "The clouds might cover the sky, and besides, the moon will go down before the sun comes up. We have to keep going."

Derry didn't argue. They tried to map out the farthest area the shadow would have to go to reach them and then headed back into the trees again. They passed through an area where the shadow had already passed some time before, leaving dead animals and plants in its wake. Even the older trees still shuddered and wept leaves.

They had too far to go to Keirkell. Derry couldn't imagine who they'd manage to stay ahead of a creature that never appeared to tire. He tried to remember the area better, but he'd rarely ridden this far. Were there more open areas? As they got closer to the village, they should find fields and maybe if they made a large enough fire --

He stopped.

"Derry?" Shannon asked, gasping for breath. He took hold of Derry's arm to urge him on. "We have to go."

"We can't. We can't lead this creature to the village."

"We don't have -- oh hell. Of course. All those people." Shannon looked frantically around. "What do we do now?"

"I don't know. Keep heading for glades if we can find them. I would hope we'd have time to make a big fire, but a chance of the clouds would ruin that hope. Or rain, which feels like it might start at any moment. I will try to think of something --"

The fox had been keeping pace with them and now gave a few nervous yips again. She started in one direction and looked back.

"Follow her," Derry said. "I think she knows a safe place."

"Why not? Of course."

Derry suspected Shannon would have plenty to say about this once they found safety, providing he was right about the fox knowing where to go. He wanted to order Shannon away, but he knew better than to waste his breath on something so useless. Was this how his life was going to be from here out? Following foxes and listening to trees? Pursued by shadow creatures?

They cleared the woods, and a hill stood before them,

round and topped with ancient standing stones of the type that legend said were fae built. Derry suddenly knew that was no legend; he could feel the power even at the foot of the steep hill.

"Safe up there?" Shannon asked, gasping as they paused.

"Fae," he said. "I think this should be powerful enough to keep it out."

"Best chance we have. Can't keep wandering around the woods all night."

Derry gave a grunt of agreement and started upward, awkward with his injured arm and still holding to a now squirming fox kit. He wished the little one quiet, and it did settle, but he couldn't be sure if that reaction came from fae power or not.

Shannon stayed behind him while the vixen yipped and urged them both upward faster than they could go. Derry knew why; the darkness had come much closer. If this proved not to be as safe as he hoped, then they would not survive.

He tried to hurry, went down on his knees once, and scrambled back up with Shannon's help. He could feel the trees not far away shuddering as the creature drew life from them. Too close --

They were halfway up the hill when he glanced back and saw the shadow moving at the edge of the trees.

"Get into the moonlight," Derry warned and pushed Shannon slightly to the right where the light traced paths through younger trees. "And move faster."

"I'm not -- leaving you behind."

Derry tried to move faster. He could feel the creature coming up the hillside behind them; the darkness slowed and moved one way or another to avoid the light, but shadows fell almost everywhere, and it wasn't much slowed.

The shadow creature didn't rush forward, though. Derry thought that it didn't like the circle of stones, but neither did he. The magic emanating from that spot felt like little needles tracing paths across his body. It wasn't until they were within a few steps of the stones that he realized the full danger. These were not just fae stones; they were guardian stones --- he'd read that term and never understood it until now. The stones held the essence of fae lives. The standing stones were haunted, and the ghosts of this place were not happy with a human that held fae powers.

No choice. Derry didn't know what the guardians could do, but he was aware the shadow creature had come closer and was going to kill them all.

"Derry -- something is wrong with these stones --"

"Go!" He shoved his friend forward and leapt in after him.

Pain shot through his body, and he was unconscious before he hit the ground, though not for long. A gasp of breath and his eyes opened. Light flashed all around them, and he thought it was a storm until he realized illumination was not in the sky.

The glow came from the stones. The fox kit in his shirt didn't seem injured by the fall, and he wiggled out to join his sibling and mother where they cowered at Derry's side. Shannon was on his knees, his face pale as he glanced at the stones and back to Derry.

"Is the darkness still coming?" Derry whispered. He could still feel the needles on his body, though perhaps they lessened in intensity.

Shannon's eyes narrowed. "Hard to see past the light, but I would guess that light would keep the creature back if nothing else. Are you all right?"

"Better," he said, which was true, although his shoulder throbbed, and his body tingled. "If the lights last through the night, we'll be safe. If they don't -- well, I hope we're recovered enough to run by then."

"What is going on here?" Shannon asked with a wave of his hand toward the swirling colors.

"Ghosts. Powerful fae ghosts from all I can tell. I'm not sure why they are here, Shannon. I don't know what triggered them to show themselves-- me or the shadow creature -- since normally they clearly don't behave this way. They're not very happy with me, but right now, I think they're less happy with the shadow creature."

"So, once the light comes, we'd be wise to move on as quickly as possible."

"We'd want to anyway. We're a long way from any village, especially on foot. We don't want to be caught out in the open tomorrow. If we can keep light around us, we'll be safe, and so will anyone with us in the village."

"You'll take that chance?" Shannon said, surprised.

He sat up, rubbing at his shoulder. "I don't think this thing is here just for us, Shannon. The people are in danger anyway, and we might be able to help them stay safe if they understand about the light. This is going to come back to give us trouble, though, Shannon. Someone is going to say that I brought the shadow creature."

"The queen will say it," Shannon replied. He appeared to be calming despite the bizarre situation. "And if she says such things enough time, eventually people will believe her."

"Yes," Derry agreed. He felt weary of that battle already, and he knew this war with the queen had barely begun.

"At least we get some rest while we're here," Shannon said and even stretched a little. "Though I wish we were in a warm, bright inn tonight."

"We will be in one every night after this," Derry promised. He rubbed at his shoulder and drew Shannon's attention again. "Just bruised and hurts like hell, but it is not broken."

"Good that something isn't worse." He looked drained.

"Well, at least it is an adventure being with you again. We always did tend to be a bit wild. I don't suppose this is much different when you think about it."

"I suppose not," Derry agreed as he petted one of the fox kits. The lights brightened, and he could see the shadow creature retreated in haste. "Or maybe this is a bit more than either of us want to admit."

Shannon nodded. "Get some sleep if you can. You first, then I'll wake you in a few hours. I will. Don't give me that look. I'm tired, too. I want you awake at dawn to decide when to wake me to go."

He supposed that made sense. "The creature might linger in the woods, even in daylight."

"Maybe, but he'll be restricted. If even moonlight is too much for him, then the brighter daylight that sifts through into woods, and there will be fewer spots for him. If we can keep to brighter areas, we should be able to make it to the main trail, and that will be wide enough for more sunlight."

"Yes. Good." Derry settled back on the hard ground and tried not to wince as he moved his arm. "It's a good thing I'm so damned tired. This would be miserable."

Shannon gave a nod of agreement. He glanced around at the stones. They were not flashing as brightly now, and the feel of needles had eased, so Derry assumed they were starting to accept him. Good. He didn't need another problem.

Derry forced himself to sleep as best he could, though he awoke too often at odd sounds. He finally convinced Shannon to sleep, which gave Derry a chance to study the standing stones without feeling as though Shannon studied him.

The circle was haunted. Derry could see the ghosts of fae braiding in and out around the tall, beige stones. They moved in circles around the stones and around each other. Bright, colorful lights flared in the night in a succession of rainbow colors. Derry could almost hear their ghostly voices.

But fae were immortal.

That didn't mean they couldn't be killed. Derry had read many tales about the confrontations between fae and human, and there had been myths about wars between different groups of fae as well. How did so many of the dead fae end up here in the standing stones? Were all standing stones like this? He'd have to ask one of the fae what it meant and how he could better deal with such a problem in the future.

The fae ghosts were aware of his interest, and he could sense their distrust. He thought it might be because he was still too human, but they knew he had some fae blood. They took more interest in him once Shannon went to sleep. One came close and hovered an arm's reach away. They stared at each other. Derry saw the face as a hazy film slid over the air. He couldn't tell if he looked at a man or a woman; the eyes seemed green, the face thin, the hair long and fair. The apparition clearly had a connection to the world. When the fox moved, the fae looked that way for a moment, and then back to Derry before finally drifting away. Over the rest of the night, several of the fae came to look him over, and he felt a gradual acceptance so that by dawn, he didn't feel troubled by the guardians.

He stood as the dawn sun crested the edge of the world and sent tendrils of light through the woods. The shadow creature had stayed at the edge of the trees until the sunlight came within inches of it. Derry could see the unnatural beast more clearly now. What had seemed featureless black at night had now developed ridges on a small head with deep-set eyes, black lips, and a flat nose. The beast growled in anger and retreated in haste. Did it have a burrow for during the day? Perhaps they could hunt it out -- later.

He woke Shannon. They had far to go to find shelter for the night.

Chapter Eleven

The day turned grey and cloudy not long after they reluctantly left the standing stones. The ghosts had calmed. Derry bade farewell with a bow of his head, trying to show both politeness and respect for their help. They had kept him and his companions safe, and Derry had no doubt they could have done them harm instead.

Even so, Derry hoped to take refuge with humans tonight. He might have felt safe enough with the fae, but fae ghosts? That was something he hoped never to have to do again. Maybe it was a very human feeling that he shouldn't disturb the dead.

Derry and Shannon worked their way quickly through the silent woods and on to the main path. So far, Derry had no sense that the shadow creature lurked anywhere near, but he was still glad for the open road and fewer shadows. Since the vixen showed no hurry to leave them, Derry carried one fox kit and Shannon the other. The trail stayed remarkably quiet for the first few hours, which Derry appreciated, though he suspected it meant they would find more trouble.

They stopped to rest at about noon. Clouds had obscured

the sky leaving the day in a uniform gray illumination, devoid of much bright light, but lacking in shadows as well. The food had disappeared with the horses. Even so, Derry hoped both the animals found safety somewhere and didn't get a saddle snagged on a tree and become trapped. He didn't say it, but he attempted to find a feel of the horses, just in case. Shannon probably thought he was resting with his eyes closed. The horses, Derry thought, might be moving in the opposite direction, and even on a trail. Maybe someone had found them. He hoped so.

The vixen nursed her young, cleaned them up somewhat, and let them play, though she kept them close. Derry had expected her to take off with her young, but when he and Shannon stood, she yipped and made it apparent that they should carry the fox kits again. Shannon didn't seem to mind.

Derry had a hard time judging distance since his mind wandered, but he thought they were doing well. Then the rain started. The deluge came quickly and hard, drenching the woods and making the road into a quagmire of treacherous mud holes. They were both soaked, and a layer of mud covered them to their knees by the time they saw the first of the outer cottages. Neither had said much for the last few miles as they outraced the sunset, though Shannon often muttered about the northern weather and the reason he preferred to live at Tyleen. The fox had wisely stayed off the central part of the road. She danced through the weeds along the right side, but now her coat was covered in burrs. She only came back to join them when they reached the edge of the stone-paved main street of Keirkell.

Startled people looked their way. The village streets were busy, and the place didn't have the feel of Glendalow, the last village he'd visited, though Derry sensed some dread in the air. Many of the people gave hasty bows, thought Derry couldn't decide if the villagers recognized him or Shannon, or if they noted the fine clothing under the mud and bowed to avoid any trouble. The locals did look bothered, but that might have been because of the fox who kept at their feet.

The rain had lessened, but the breeze felt colder now. Derry had to fight not to shiver. Were they going to have more trouble tonight? He hadn't the ability or the energy left to deal with anything out of the ordinary. Right now, all he wanted was somewhere inside a wall, warm and safe. A human place, he realized. He didn't feel safe in the wilds just now.

Derry glanced at the sky and back to the village. He started moving faster, catching Shannon by surprise. His friend had to rush to catch up.

"What brought on this sudden show of energy?" Shannon asked.

"I can see the sign to the Glenwood Inn." Derry waved toward the place that sat almost to the other end of the town. A half dozen geese darted out into the road, looked them over, and probably would have stayed to follow them if the fox hadn't been at their feet. A dog lifted his head from where he'd been sleeping in a doorway, gave a slight woof of sound, and went back to sleep. The animals, at least, appeared calm enough. "I want to get inside, Shannon. We can get cleaned up and maybe even sleep for a couple hours before full nightfall. Perhaps I could sleep through the night and pretend there isn't a problem in the world, as long as others put some lights up to keep the shadows at bay."

Shannon gave a grunt of agreement, though he cast a worried look at the people they passed. The strangers watched the fox more than either of the men, though, so Derry didn't worry too much.

"Food," Shannon suddenly said. "You didn't have food on that list."

"I'll eat later. I just want clean and sleep right now."

"There might not be time later." They took a couple more

steps. "You'll eat first, then clean up and rest. And I can make certain you won't even get a room, Derry. We are on my family lands now, you know."

"And you think you could pull rank?" Derry said, laughing a little. "I am a Lord in my own right, you know."

"And I'm just a lowly Lord's son," Shannon said with a laugh of his own. "But I know these people better than you do, and even our fine Prince Derry would have a hard time getting cooperation if I put some blocks in the way."

"Prince Derry? Don't try that one --"

Shannon lifted a hand and silenced him. "We're well away from Tyleen now. You know people here have always been pleased to call you *prince*, so far from the ear of our fine queen. You are the highest-ranking person they are likely to see most of the time. I think the King has been through here once in my lifetime. They like you, Derry. And we have had this conversation every time we've come up here since you lost your title. So, get used to it. And you'll still eat first."

Derry wanted to argue, simply because he was tired and wanted clean before he touched food. They trudged down the road and drew nearer to the building. Could he pull rank on his companion, since Shannon insisted on his title?

However, before he could say anything, someone shouted. "Shannon! A moment of your time!"

They both gave a grunt of annoyance and turned. An older, stocky man made his way towards them at a prodigious speed considering his size and age. Derry found himself smiling despite the situation. Silas, who was the village leader, had always been a favorite to visit while they were in Glenwood. Derry hadn't seen him in years, but the man had only lost a little more of his scraggly, white hair.

"Shannon, glad to see you, lad," he said when he neared and slapped Shannon on the shoulder with enough force that he almost knocked him sideways. "And Gods all, if it isn't our fine, fair wild Prince Derry himself. I didn't recognize you under all that muck and mud, boy. Well, let's get inside and have a dram or two, shall we? Careful now; don't trip over the wee fox."

The greeting lightened Derry's mood, and he laughed as they reached Glenwood Inn. They weren't the only patrons covered in mud, and the benches did look like a nice place to rest. While the interior held the scent of cooked meat, Derry merely grimaced and nodded towards the corner with an open window. The vixen, however, lifted her head and let out a plaintive little whine. He'd be sure she got her fill of food.

The innkeeper looked up in surprise as they settled at the table. Derry suspected the locals' reactions came because of the state of their clothing rather than fear of what Derry had become. The place had a scattering of patrons already as sunset neared, and none of them looked angry to see Derry. While Evan, the innkeeper, wasn't as friendly as Finil in Glendalow, he did give a quick smile of greeting. Mulled cider came quickly to the table, and the servant boy began to light the lamps, dispelling shadows, for which Derry was happy. The fox laid down at Derry's feet and they settled the fox kits with her, all of them glad to be safely inside.

"Now, my lads," Silas said with a sigh of contentment as he leaned back, warm mug in hands. "Let's not waste time on trivialities since we all know there are problems. I have a tale or two to tell you. There have been odd things going on about here already, and now here comes our young man and a very prince of the line, both on foot and looking as though they've brought a tale of their own. We missed you both, you know. Glad to have you back with us, Derry, even if you do bring some oddness with you."

"I have the feeling you are going to tell us a tale of oddness that began long before I arrived," Derry replied and sipped his drink. "You can't lay it all at my feet."

"So true, so true." Silas sipped the cider, but his eyes narrowed slightly. Despite his carefree manner, Derry could tell this tale would be one of serious trouble. "There's been a problem here since last spring, boys. At first, we didn't take account of what was going on. We had a part of a field fail here, another there, but such things happen. Brother Callen said he felt an oddness to it, but he couldn't find the cause. The plants withered as though something sucked the life from them. Something made a jagged path through the fields at night. Later, towards the start of winter, we found dead animals as well. However, the winter came, and all went quiet. We thought the evil had gone elsewhere. I sent reports to your father, Shannon."

"That's likely why he sent us," Derry replied and wished they'd known more of the tale before they arrived. He didn't say so aloud. Shannon's father, despite accepting Derry into his home, had never been one to chase after magic tales. He probably just hadn't believed any of the warnings and hadn't wanted to sway Shannon and Derry. "But he dared not say anything at all in court since everyone is uneasy there already -- and yes, some of that is my fault." Derry lifted a hand to stop Shannon from protesting. "I'll make a guess that the evil came back with the spring thaw."

"Yes, it did, and it's struck more than a few fields and animals this time." Silas paused and looked from Shannon to Derry. "You've seen it."

"We barely escaped," Derry confirmed. He cast a quick glance around the room and noted the faces turned their way, people straining to hear what they said. "The people blame the fae --"

"No," Silas replied and startled him. "Even those who mistrust the fae would never accuse them of killing animals and destroying nature. Besides, a few have seen it --"

"A dark, shadowy thing that only comes out at night,"

Shannon said. His voice sounded steady, but Derry could sense the surge of fear his friend had held at bay during the flight from the creature. "A thing of at least some intelligence since it senses others and follows them."

"Yes," Silas said and gave a slight shiver before he took another sip of cider. "A dozen have claimed to see it and fled to safety, but three were not fast enough two nights ago, and they're dead."

Derry bowed his head, feeling as though he had somehow failed those people, though he didn't think they could have gotten here any faster. "They know enough to be inside, in a lighted area at night?" he asked at last.

"Yes."

"If anyone is caught away from town, tell them to stay in the moonlight as much as they can. Carry torches -- that might help. Don't go out alone. And if you are in the area to the south, try heading for the standing stones. That's where we spent the night, safe even in the dark," Derry explained. "I didn't have the feeling it was safe only because I was there."

"The people stay clear of that place," Silas said. "They don't like it much."

"They wouldn't like being dead any better," Shannon pointed out. "Best if they make certain people are someplace lighted but spread the word that they might find safety there. You are right about one important fact: the fae are the enemy of this darkness. The standing stones are theirs, and they seemed to give protection."

"I've heard an odd sort of question," Silas said. He put his cider down and looked at Derry with a frown. "Where are the fae? Why are they letting this happen?"

Now there was a thought that had played along the edges of Derry's mind. There hadn't been fae around in the last day, and he would have expected their help. He frowned, staring out the window and realizing he had a sense of where the shadow creature might be, but none of the fae.

Why would they run away and leave the others?

Not their choice?

"I think --" Derry stopped and considered the situation. "I think this is such the opposite of them that it is painful to be even near it. They've had to flee the area --"

"Painful for you?" Shannon asked and then nodded without Derry speaking. "That wasn't just your bruised shoulder that gave you so much trouble."

"Painful," he agreed. "But not to the degree it would be for the fae. And I think, Shannon, that might be why I'm here. I can help, and we might be able to find a way to destroy this creature if we work together."

Shannon nodded agreement. Good. He didn't want his friend fussing. They ate a quick meal with Silas and discussed the situation, though Derry needed some time to consider the trouble. They even gave some meat to the fox and she didn't mind finding it seasoned and cooked.

Derry finally had a chance to clean up and change into clothing Silas sent them. He rested for a bit, but he awoke too soon with the last light of day still lingering at the window. He felt the weight of something evil out in the world. It grew as the night came, and Derry couldn't sleep through it. He had to do something.

Shannon had slept for a bit as well. He'd been more restless, though, and up before Derry. Shannon took the foxes out for a walk before it got dark and brought them back again, quietly shooing them in through the open door before heading back downstairs. Derry had thought the creatures might run off given a chance, but he was glad to see them return. Derry spent a little time petting them, basking in the feel of their soft emotions. The foxes were happy to be here. They were safe inside the human's building.

Then Derry went downstairs and spotted Shannon sitting

by the window with Silas, as though they'd never left the spot. The inn was very busy with more people coming in, including families.

"Farmers mostly," Silas explained with a wave of his hand at the crowd. "People who feel safer in town and in groups. Evan provides them with haven during the night, but this can't continue for long."

Derry agreed as he slid onto the bench beside Shannon. Meat cooked over the hearth fire, but he was having better luck ignoring it this time. Maybe that came from the need to help these people, or perhaps it was more the panic of having no idea what to do. He gave polite nods to everyone, but the people were clearly uneasy with his presence, and he didn't think that came from his rank. Not tonight.

"It might be better if we go to the room to talk," Shannon suggested. "The conversation we're going to have isn't going to settle well here."

"I'll go have a word with a few people," Silas said and stood. "And I'll see you upstairs."

"I'll find us a bit of food," Shannon added.

They deserted the table as quickly as Derry had arrived. He turned around and headed back towards the stairs, trying to consider what they could possibly do. Derry tried not to look at the people as he passed and the harsh stares. At better times, these people had welcomed him as though he were Shannon's own. He couldn't blame them, but the glares still brought a new sort of pain.

Derry had almost made it to the stairs when he heard something that gave him hope for the first time in days. The sound of fae bells sounded nearby, which meant he wasn't alone in this madness after all.

Derry had taken a half dozen steps towards the bolted door before a large hand caught tight hold of his arm, and a rough-looking man pulled him to an abrupt stop. The room felt odd suddenly, with danger inside rather than beyond the door. The fae had moved so close that magic seemed to fill the air, and Derry had a hard time thinking clearly. He turned to the man who still had his hand on his arm, his own glare almost matching the one he saw behind a stand of wild, bushy beard and hair.

"You try an' unbolt that door, boy, an' I'll slit yer throat. Don't care who you be --"

"*Let go of my arm.*"

The man released him in haste, though his face darkened with a new threat of anger. Derry stood too close to him and could feel rage growing in the man and in those all around him, like a spark leaping from place to place to start a new fire. People started to press in, their mumbles becoming louder and all their faces showing the anger that moved through the room like something alive.

Derry had to get control of himself; there was no chance of dealing with these people. He glanced towards the door but didn't try to go that way again. He needed to get to his room and a window; that would be good enough if the fae had come to talk to him. He'd been a fool to try and walk out of the inn, especially remembering the reaction at Glendalow. He had to work at getting clear of these people. Shannon and Silas would be somewhere near, too. He didn't want them caught up in his mess.

"I am Prince Derry SanOsen," he said aloud, his voice carrying through the noise. There. The old rank did count for something because people stopped and blinked, as though they'd forgotten even who he was. "You need not worry. I am going back to my room. If the fae have something to tell me about these troubles, they'll find a way."

"We do not deal with devils here."

He sighed and turned, and then bit back the words he had begun to say. A priest of the Daria Temple, dressed in his simple gray robes, stood before Derry. An older man, going as gray as his robes, but with piercing blue eyes that held the power of a believer in them. Derry even gave the man a polite enough nod, which apparently surprised him. He'd grown up in the Tyleen Court where one learned to curb initial reactions, even if you were the favored nephew of the King. He was not going to get into a shouting match with a village priest. Those things had a way of getting out of hand.

"The fae are not devils, sir," he said and kept his voice steady and calm. "I don't expect you to believe me, but I do expect you to realize there is something truly evil out there. I suspect the fae have come to help us deal with it."

"We must stay true to the gods if we want their help --"

"I am not here to argue with you. I happen to believe you are right. But I don't remember that the gods were ever against the fae, their other children --"

"Don't speak of such things to me, young man --"

Derry bowed his head, ready to back away and leave this useless digression behind. He could feel the rush of emotions growing around him again like a wave crashing upon a shore. He looked frantically around for Shannon, who surely couldn't have missed the unfriendly sounds. Where was Silas?

The people started to shout, but he couldn't make out their words. Derry tried to retreat towards the stairway again, though he wasn't sure that was any safer, although he might reach the higher ground. He gave the priest another bow of his head. That man looked around with a bit of worry now as well. Derry saw sanity, at least, and maybe the priest could get the people in hand if Derry simply got out of the way.

For a moment, the crowd pressed in again -- and Derry sensed danger. He moved to the left and felt a sharp, sudden pain in his side. Derry looked down in shock to see a gloved hand pulling back, a bloody knife gripped in the fingers. He tried to turn to see the enemy, but between the shock and the crowd pressing in so close, he couldn't see anything but a blur of bodies and equally angry faces.

His hand had gone to his side, and he probably paled, but no one seemed aware that he'd been stabbed. Derry thought that might be good; he didn't want to appear weak before this mob. *Get to the room,* he told himself. Just get somewhere out of sight. They were still shouting, though the priest had lifted his hands and tried to call for calm. Derry took another step away, fearing that his legs would give way, though that was more from the emotional turmoil in the room than from the wound.

"What the hell is this madness?" Shannon bellowed from the stairs.

The words shocked people who moved aside in haste, looking as though they didn't realize what they'd been doing. Derry scanned the faces near him, trying to find the one who had stabbed him. Unfortunately, they all looked -- and felt -- equally guilty now.

Shannon had pushed his way through the crowd and arrived at Derry's side, his eyes blazing with the kind of anger Derry had rarely seen in his friend. He was so angry, in fact, that he didn't even look to Derry. Derry carefully pulled his vest a little to the side, hoping to hide the blood he could feel trickling down his side.

The priest backed up with a bow of his head, which was more apology than Derry had expected. He looked bothered as his eyes swept over the crowd. Even the fae bells had quieted to a softer sound that didn't seem quite so intrusive.

The priest glanced at the door and shook his head. "He is not going to open that door, Shannon."

"I'll let the King know that was *your* decision. And since you don't need Derry's help, we'll be on our way in the morning."

The priest had to rethink that one. "We don't want the kind of help that waits on the other side of that door," he said, but he didn't sound quite as assured as he had been.

"You need some help," Shannon replied. His face had lost the semblance of anger, but a fire still lurked in his eyes. Silas had finally come to stand with him, too. Derry felt better for having at least a couple people near whom he could trust. "Nothing you've done so far has helped, has it?"

The priest gave a sigh of frustration, which was almost as good as an agreement. Despite how nicely Shannon handled the group, Derry feared to stay any longer. He had a ringing in his ears that grew louder than the bells, and he braced his legs to keep from going down. He didn't hear the next part of the exchange between the priest and Shannon, but he finally reached out and tugged Shannon's sleeve, feeling like a child trying to get the attention of adults.

"Shannon. Let's go to the room."

"Gods, you're white as a ghost!"

"Shan --"

His legs gave way, and Shannon caught hold of him before he went down. "Derry -- Oh, hell!" He drew his hand back, the fingers covered in blood.

Derry heard cries of dismay throughout the room as Shannon and Silas caught hold of him.

"Who did this?" the priest demanded, looking at the people with a different kind of anger. "Who did this, Prince Derry?"

"Didn't see," he said, glad that they were moving out of the crowd, the priest keeping pace with them. "Gloved hand, knife. The crowd was too close."

"I've got him, Silas. I'll need bandages." Shannon's voice trembled with emotions. They were going up the stairs, Derry trying to walk, but so lightheaded that he wasn't sure his body obeyed him at all. "You should have said something, you fool!"

"Hoped -- get clear first. I didn't want to be weak. Not with an enemy there and not sure whom it might be."

"You truly didn't see who did this?"

They reached the top of the stairs, and just a few steps down the hall would take them to the room. He felt better already, though that might simply have been from getting clear of all those emotions. "I didn't see, Shannon. You can trust me. I don't make it a habit of protecting people who try to kill me."

"I wasn't sure. You have been odd of late." Shannon kicked the door open with a bit more force than it deserved and took him to the bed, settling him on the mattress.

The fox and her kits leapt from the bed and scrambled under it, which seemed wise. A candle flickered on the table, casting odd shadows all around them. Derry looked away, his heart pounding.

"You have got to put on some weight, my friend. I've gotten more winded carrying firewood at camp."

Derry gave a quick smile, but it passed as Silas and the priest arrived at the door. They both ordered the gawkers away, and the little rush of emotions that had been coming his way retreated again as they closed the door behind them. A slight knock opened it again, but only long enough for Silas to take bandages from Evan. Then it closed and the bar went down.

"Is the wound bad?" the priest asked.

"No, it isn't," Derry answered while Shannon began to fuss with the clothing. "I suspect the knife grazed a rib."

"Praise Daria," the priest said and kissed the round pendant he wore. "I don't approve of murder, Prince Derry. In fact, I don't like what happened down there much at all. The emotions were too raw, and everyone too quick to anger."

"Magic?" Shannon asked, his hands still for a moment.

"I don't know," Derry replied. "I really don't."

"I felt as though madness had come upon us all," the priest said. He leaned back against the door, drained and probably nearly as pale as Derry. "I don't think it could have been natural."

"Something to keep everyone worked up and give the assassin a chance at Derry," Silas suggested. "I assume it was no secret you were coming here?"

"Not much of one," Shannon agreed. He was already nearly done with the bandages. The cut couldn't have been too severe, or else his companion would have been more upset. Derry gave a sigh of relief as everyone calmed. "Better, is it? If you'd had a little flesh between your skin and that bone, it probably wouldn't have been more than a scratch. You need to put on weight, Derry. I'm serious."

"Easier for me to avoid being knifed," he replied.

"How about a unique answer, and you do both?" Shannon suggested.

Silas grinned first, and a small smile played at the edge of the priest's lips. Good. Better --

And then they all froze at the sound of fae bells quite close and the tap of fingers on the shuttered window, even though they were on the second floor.

"Derry?" an unfamiliar voice whispered. "Let me in."

"Sweet Gods," the priest whispered and took tight hold of his pendant. The man had gone white again, and his lips moved in prayers. Derry couldn't blame him for that part.

"You had best go, Brother," Derry said softly and without rancor as he started to stand. Shannon pushed Derry back down and started to the window himself. "Go now or be witness to something you don't want to know or understand."

The priest stood there, biting at his lip, but making no move to leave. Silas looked intrigued, rather than upset. Shannon crossed to the window and pulled open the shutters without even a pause. The young man -- young fae -- who quickly came through was no one Derry had ever met before. He landed lightly on the floor, pushing back long black hair as he gave a nod to Derry. Although they were mostly hidden by his green vest, Derry could see the pattern of old scars on his chest, and suspected he knew very well why this one had gone to the fae. The bells had come to the window with him and quieted as he came inside. He brought the scent of spring with him, a slight warm breeze that danced through the room.

"Prince Derry," he said with a quick bow of his head. "She sent me because I know the area --"

"Gods. Brian."

The priest took an abortive step forward and then fell back against the door, so pale and shocked that Silas crossed to the man and took hold of his arm. The fae turned, and Derry saw a surprisingly bright smile cross his face.

"Brother Callen, sir!" Brian sounded surprised but not displeased. "I am surprised to find you here, given the talks we sometimes had about the fae and all!"

The look on the priest's face changed from shock to delight, and not at all what Derry had expected. There was a story here and some unexpected connection between the fae boy and the priest whom Derry never would have expected to smile in the proximity of one of the wild ones.

The priest was clearly pleased, though still confused. "We thought your father had finally killed you," Brother Callen said with a desperate shake of his head. "He told us you'd run off, but I never thought you would go without saying goodbye to me. We searched, but we never found your body."

"He left me for dead in the woods," Brian replied, and his voice had lost all animation. His finger traced a scar on his chest, and unhappy thoughts chased through his face, there and gone. His smile came back in the next breath. "The fae found me, healed my body, and showed me how to love life again. I have missed our talks these last few years, though. You were the one who gave me the strength to survive. And though you never realized, I've often been close to hear your

Holy Day sermons."

"Gods all."

Silas led the stunned man to a chair and pushed him into it. The priest watched Brian for a moment, his hand on the emblem he wore around his neck, but then he shook his head as though he was having some sort of disagreement with himself. As fascinating as it was to watch, Derry knew they had to get back to the trouble at hand. Brian must have realized so himself. The fae turned back to Derry and gave a slight nod that might have been an apology.

"Prince Derry," he began than shook his head and lifted a hand, as though to feel out the air. "You're wounded. Let me help. I'm not much of a healer, but this will give you some strength. You'll need it to face this trouble."

Not very encouraging words, Derry realized. Shannon frowned but took a step away as Brian came closer. The fae's fingers lightly traced a pattern over the wound. For a moment, Derry thought he heard distant music and caught the scent of flowers blooming. In the next breath, the pain eased, and his body began to relax. Derry must have looked better because even Shannon smiled.

They'd given Brother Callen and Silas a few moments to get used to the idea of a fae in the room, and they both looked better. Good. Derry wanted calm, which he was finding hard enough to hold on to himself without dealing with the emotions of the others.

"There. That will help," Brian said, a little breathless. He looked around the room, and Derry wondered how long it had been since he'd last been inside walls. Was this himself in a few years? He couldn't imagine it.

"Thank you. That's better." Derry sat up straighter, and every breath didn't hurt. The wound was still there in his side, and his shoulder held a distant ache, but both felt far better. "Tell me what you can about this enemy we face."

"The Shadow you fight is an old, old creature, called back to the world by some magic we have not been able to trace. The anger that passed through this inn was not entirely natural either."

"I knew it," Brother Callen mumbled. "I could feel something moving us."

"Are they connected?" Derry asked.

"The magic feels much the same, but we can't find a direct link," Brian explained. He shook his head and looked bothered by what he told them. "The worst part is that the fae can't get close enough to learn anything helpful. We lost one already, and that death gave the Shadow far too much power. Only those of us who were human once have any chance of getting very close. A true fae dies when too close to the Shadow, without being touched. This creature is the opposite of the fae, you see. The Shadow is all dark and death, destroying everything the fae are born to protect."

"So, what can I do?" Derry asked, feeling powerless in the face of this news. He'd hoped for help from the fae; had counted on it since he had no idea of how to face this trouble. If they could not even get near, how could he hope to do the work for them?

"Queen Lenora told me to say you are the only hope to contain this evil. You have no training, but you have abilities."

"That is not really any help, you know."

"I know," he admitted with a slight frown. "The fae, though -- they can do nothing. They can't get close, but you can. You are still human enough to withstand being near the Shadow, and fae enough to feel his presence. He's coming closer."

"I know."

"There are myths so old that even the fae can't say where they came from or what they mean," Brian continued, though he glanced at the window with some worry. "We found was a single quote that seemed to resonate with the trouble: *Use light to banish the heart of darkness.* I know, that's rather obvious, but there must be something helpful in it. I'm sorry because that's all we've found so far, although others are still trying to search out lost and forgotten information. The Shadows haven't walked the land since long before the time of humans."

"Why have they come back now?" Shannon asked with a glance toward the window and the darkness beyond. "What brought them out?"

"Not them -- so far, praise the gods, there is only the one. Someone pulled it into the world."

"Magic," Brother Callen said with a snarl of anger.

"Dark sorcery," Brian replied with a look at his old friend. The priest bowed his head as though in apology. "This is not the same as the powers the fae use. We would never do anything that would harm the land or kill innocents."

Brother Callen clearly began to glare, but then he stopped and gave a nod of agreement. A person simply could not change so quickly, no matter what the circumstances. Derry also suspected Brother Callen wanted to hold on to his old ways and things he at least thought he understood.

"Why has it struck here?" Shannon asked. "Why in my family land?"

"I don't think it is aimed specifically at your family, sir. While this is the only Shadow we've found in the world, there are other problems throughout Lynashin, here in the north but also in the west, east, and south. The symbolism of attacking at four quarters is obvious."

"Only Lynashin?" Silas asked.

"So far." Brian looked bothered and he moved closer to the window, clearly anxious to go. "That may have some connection to the fact there are still active fae in Lynashin. There are not many other places where we still interact with humans."

"This enemy might be targeting the fae as much as humans," Shannon said and looked at Derry with new worry. "As though you need more enemies right now."

"The creature is no friend to anyone," Brian reminded them. He began to look more uncomfortable, and Derry knew why. That knife-like feeling was starting to press against his own heart again.

"The creature is coming closer, isn't it?" Derry asked.

"Closer," Brian agreed with a slight gasp and a wave of his hand when Shannon went to steady him. "I'm fine. You did well to hide in the standing stones, Derry. Those are the best protection outside of light itself. Unfortunately, there are not many such places."

"It was filled --" He stopped and looked at Silas and Brother Callen, but he thought he might as well go on. "Filled with the ghosts of the fae. They were not happy to have me there, at least not at first. I don't think they had a problem with Shannon, though."

"Oh, them," Brian said with a sigh. "Yes, they can be troublesome to those of us who were not born fae. They are the essence of fae who lived a long, long time before humans came to this land. Apparently, they could not move on with the other first fae, and their dislike for humans finally destroyed them. There was a change of sorts then; they became guardians for the sacred places. They have lost their mistrust of humans, but they still don't think humans who become fae are a good idea. You don't have to worry about them unless you do something they don't like."

"I had guessed -- or felt -- the part about being guardians," Derry said.

"I think I've told you all I can about the Shadow. We have reason to think the assassin might have come from the Tyleen Court, Prince Derry. Someone came skulking into town not long before you arrived. We sensed him, but there was magic involved, and all we could ken was that he had come from the same area as you. The magic controlling the crowd might have simply been a chance opportunity for him."

"Thank you for telling me." Derry glanced at the window. "You had better go. I can feel it, you know."

"Yes," Brian stood. "I'll see you again."

He started to the window.

"Brian," Brother Callen said. "Stop by and see me when -- if you can."

"I will, sir. I will!" Brian smiled brightly. Outside they could hear somewhat frantic bells, and Derry wished Brian quickly on his way. Brian slipped out the window, and Shannon crossed to close it again. He looked back with a frown.

"An assassin from home. Why am I not even a little surprised?"

"Have you gone mad?" Silas asked and waved his arm in a frantic sort of movement. "A fae comes to your window, and that's all that draws your attention?"

"Oh, you get used to fae meeting with Derry," Shannon replied with a dismissive wave of his hand. "And while Brian gave us a bit of news there, it wasn't much more than we already knew. But an assassin from the -- from court? That's something to worry about."

"But not now," Derry added. "We have a different problem to deal with tonight."

"The sun is down," Shannon said with a glare at the window as if it were at fault for the passage of time. "I don't think we have much time, Derry."

"It is closer," Derry said. He fought to keep his breathing steady against the growing stab of pain. "I fear it might be coming to the village. Silas, Brother Callen -- can you warn everyone to stay inside with as many lights as they can manage?"

"Yes, that seems wise," Brother Callen said and was the first to stand. The change in his attitude helped, though Derry could see there was still doubt in his eyes when he looked towards the window. Then he looked back at Derry. "Stay safe, Prince Derry."

He left the room.

Silas gave a slight snort of amusement as he stood. "Oh, there's a man who will be praying to Daria tonight, won't he? But then I suppose most of us will when it comes to it. I'm going downstairs and having words with the patrons. They're going to have to realize they can't stop you if they want this business handled."

"Thank you," Derry said. "Though I have no idea what to do."

"I'll leave that part out of the conversation," Silas said.

Shannon laughed and crossed to the door as the man went out, putting the bar in place after he'd gone. Derry didn't like it much, but he supposed it would be stupid to take a chance with an assassin in the building. Besides, they wouldn't be staying here long.

"Don't ask me what to do now," Derry said before Shannon could speak.

"Maybe you have done all you can for the night," Shannon offered. "A little more rest wouldn't hurt."

"I can't. I feel better, anyway. Brian's magic has helped. Besides, every night we let this monster roam free, the more power it will gain. I won't be any stronger than I am now."

"That's not a good thing to hear," Shannon said and dropped into the chair where the priest had sat only moments before. "This is a mess."

"I'm sorry, Shannon. I don't like that I've drawn you into such trouble, and don't tell me this isn't my fault. If I hadn't gone after the fae that night in Glendalow --"

"Then you wouldn't be linked to the fae now -- but we'd

still be here, you know, and we would still have to face this problem. Tell me it would be better without the likes of Brian coming to the window to help us."

"Ah." Derry hadn't considered what a difference not having the fae on their side would have made. "I wouldn't have known about the fox, and she couldn't have led us to safety, either."

The fox came out from under the bed just then, her kits following her. Derry smiled to see them. There was a good deed he'd done. Maybe saving the foxes wasn't much to weigh against the rest of the trouble, but it was a fae thing and another step along the path understanding his fae side.

But how could it help them now?

"There has to be an answer," Derry said. He stood and walked to the window but didn't open it this time. There and back to the bed. The foxes watched him. Shannon watched him.

"I have no idea what to do," he admitted as though Shannon didn't realize. "*Use light to banish the heart of darkness.* It's what we've been doing already, and although it keeps the Shadow away, it doesn't banish it."

"I know. I had hoped for a little more help," Shannon admitted. He settled on the bed and leaned back, relaxing slightly. That wouldn't last for long. "You can feel this creature. It causes you pain --"

"Discomfort for now. Pain if it comes too close. I hope to avoid that from now on." He stood by the window for a long time, his hand against the shutter. Then he nodded. "The fae appear to be leading it off. I don't think that will last for long since they don't dare let it get too close to them. It will be coming back this way, Shannon. Right now, the best we can do is keep the people locked up at night. How long until someone's candles run out and they're alone in the dark? Or until a stranger happens along the trail and runs out of time, not knowing the danger?"

"And besides, it grows stronger with every tree and creature it kills, right?" Shannon added. "Maybe it will grow strong enough to stand in the light of day."

"We don't dare take a chance to find out. I can't sit here in this room, though I'm not sure what to do." Derry reached for his cloak. Shannon didn't argue as he stood and took up his own. "Shannon, I would rather --"

"Don't even waste your breath."

They went down the stairs, Derry worried about appearing in the room again. The place sounded subdued, though. People looked his way with worry and then with relief. Brian's magic had done more than help him. Coming down here had reassured the locals, too.

"I've had a few words with them," Silas said as he crossed to intersect them at the bottom of the stairs. "And we removed five strangers to another house. I don't think any of the locals were involved in trying to kill you, Prince Derry."

"Neither do I," he said and meant those words. "I understand that they are upset about what is happening, and I was not wise, heading straight to talk to my fae friends. However, they're gone now, so no one needs to worry about them."

Silas gave a grim nod. Derry doubted anyone knew there had been a fae in the room upstairs. Let them think a barred door would keep that supposed problem outside. They needn't consider the fae any longer. Right now, Derry could feel the Shadow coming closer, though the fae had given them some time, at least. He could hope for the entire night without an attack, but the Shadow was moving quickly.

"Where is Brother Callen?" Shannon asked as he glanced around the room.

"Taken the five to some other safe place. Brother Callen said he'd be back," Silas said with a touch of worry in his voice.

"The Shadow is nowhere near," Derry assured him. "I want to get a feel --"

A knock on the door, polite and calm, won startled responses from everyone. One of the men nearby muttered something and heard an answer before he lifted the heavy bar. The old oak door opened an inch and then wider to let the priest back in. Derry was glad to see him again and especially when he gave a nod of greeting. The man carried a book that looked old and cumbersome.

"Good to see you up and moving, Prince Derry," he said and won a few surprised looks. "I've brought this for you. It's from the archives at the local temple. We used to be the main temple of Daria, you know, until the larger and more remote place was built in the mountains."

"I remember reading about that change," Derry said and reached to take the book. Shannon intercepted and gathered the book into his hands. "I am not helpless."

"I'm saving your dignity, my prince," Shannon said with an almost hidden grin. "The book is heavy, and you might have toppled."

"Give the damned book -- begging your pardon, Brother Callen -- give the book to me, Shannon."

Shannon shoved it into Derry's arms with no warning and a little too much force. He did almost fall, and the priest let out an unexpected laugh which was echoed through the room. Derry only sighed, but he grinned at Shannon. They took the book to the table by the window, which was shuttered closed but still let in a leak of fresh air.

The book proved to be ancient but well kept. Derry opened the ornate, gold-encrusted cover and read the title with a nod of appreciation. *The Book of the Ancient Days* -- he'd seen a newer copy, much shorter. This might have answers --

"You can read this?" the priest asked.

"Oh, yes. I learned to read older scripts many years ago. My father had collected antique books, and I was always fascinated by anything that he found interesting. Trying to make a connection to him again, I suppose."

The priest nodded. Derry went to work reading the book. Sometime later, Shannon arrived with food and drew his attention away from the pages. He blinked and shook his head. The night was late, but not many people slept. Derry was too aware of how they watched him.

"Cheese and some bread just out of the oven and a very nice sweet wine. Don't drink much of it. Given how little food you've had lately, I suspect it will go straight to your head."

"You are neither my keeper nor my servant," Derry pointed out. He worried, suddenly, about what the locals would think about their lord's son spending so much time taking care of him.

"You don't think you need a keeper?" Shannon asked. He dropped down on the bench beside him and tore off a piece of bread. It did smell good. "Just eat, Derry. You need strength, and we need you. This is no time to start thinking about personal status and pride of place. We never have before."

"True enough." He even took up some of the bread and cheese, though not because he was particularly hungry. He simply didn't want to argue with Shannon over the meal. Besides, he was right. Derry realized his hand trembled slightly, and that came from simple weakness of the body.

"Have you found anything helpful?" Brother Callen asked. He came and sat down again. Derry hadn't really noticed what the others were doing while he read, which pointed out how right Shannon was about him needing a keeper.

"Bits and pieces," Derry replied. He took a little sip of the wine and thought Shannon was right to warn him against drinking too much. "I would like to think everything will add up into a clear picture. I only fear I won't have the time to make any sense of it."

"Closer?" Shannon asked softly.

Derry nodded and ran a hand through his hair. He had hoped for something helpful in this book, but maybe it had been enough simply to pass the time. This had been close to rest, after all. He'd learned more about the fae themselves. Even back in those days, they'd had a queen named Leanora. He absolutely refused to believe it might be the same woman.

Immortal fae...

They had other problems now. Derry could feel the Shadow getting closer.

"How long until the dawn?" he asked.

"Maybe three more hours," Shannon replied. Everyone should have been exhausted, but the worries of the night kept the patrons awake, along with Derry and Shannon.

"Too long," Derry said and felt the Shadow move closer still. "It's going to be here before the first light."

"Everyone is inside and safe behind locked doors and with whatever light they can find," Silas said. "You can stay within the walls tonight --"

"No," he said and felt something unsettling, besides the Shadow coming closer. "We have to destroy it. Tonight, if we can manage it --"

"Manage what?" Shannon asked. "If you have an idea, my friend, now is the time to mention it."

"Ideas? No. But --" He stopped and tilted his head. Then, with a jolt, he realized why he had such a feeling of foreboding. "It's not alone."

"Derry?"

"There are two Shadows now," he said with a grimace of distaste and worry. "Linked still -- I think it's something that's breaking off from the original --"

"Oh no, we don't want that," Silas agreed with a glare at the door and the hidden world outside. "We had best come up with an answer here fast, my young gentlemen. We need this stopped before it spawns another."

"Yes," Derry said. He put his hands on the book as though he could absorb what he needed -- *I need your answers!*

He felt as though something had hit him in the head. He snapped back, crashing against the wall as Shannon yelped and grabbed him.

"What the hell --"

"I --" Derry began, and then he looked at the book with a touch of wonder and a lot of worries. "I think I found the answer, Shannon. I think, when I wished to find it and touched the book --"

"This is crazy."

"Magic," he said. "And crazy. But I think --"

"Derry?"

"Do you trust me?" he asked, his head tilted to the side. "Truly trust me, even with all the changes that have happened since I left?"

"Yes," Shannon replied. Not even a pause. "Even when you say crazy things. So, what do you want us to do, Derry?"

"We need wagons. People will have to push them because we don't want the horses near the creatures. They'd go crazy and take the wagons with them. The wagons can't be out in the open when the shadows arrive in town."

"What if they don't come to town?" Silas asked.

"They will," he said and smiled. "They'll come for me."

Chapter Twelve

The Shadows had moved closer to the village, lurking along the line of trees as they came cautiously closer. Derry could feel them trudging along the edge of the farm fields, anxious of the lights ahead -- but lured by a spark of life standing in the road. Derry waited patiently, glancing at the flickering of lights around buildings that kept the people safe.

Derry stood in the near dark of the road, though, and Shannon remained beside him. No amount of argument could dissuade his friend from that position. Derry did not want him here; he didn't want to see Shannon taken down with him. What he'd decided -- and the others had agreed to -- might well be insane. Could he really believe he had pulled the answer they needed from a book and without ever reading the passage?

Maybe his mind put together everything else he'd learned and found what did seem to be a viable answer. If Derry looked at what he proposed, and not at how he might have gotten the answer, he felt calmer again. He could also focus on what mattered right now, which was that everyone was safe for the moment.

Everyone but Shannon.

Derry turned to his friend, trying to think of something to get him to go anywhere but standing by him. It wasn't going to work, so he didn't waste time.

"That's better," Shannon said.

"You are insane, you know."

"Yes."

Another point they wouldn't argue over. "Get ready. We should see the Shadows at the end of the street soon."

Shannon had his hand on his sword. Derry wasn't sure what he intended to do with it. Maybe he hoped for the assassin to make a move so they could be done with that trouble as well --

Movement.

Derry tapped Shannon on the arm and nodded toward the end of town where something dark and vaguely mound-shaped moved like darkness within shadows. They had the road well lit, or so it seemed. Derry had created strategically placed spots of shade to draw the shadow closer. He watched the thing glide along the ground; they were aware of each other. The Shadow appeared to be larger than it had been, and sometimes when it moved, it seemed as though it had formed a shadow of itself. The second one had a hunger that felt far worse than the original's longing to take life. They did not dare let this thing loose!

The Shadows shifted slowly along the road and were difficult to see at times. The moon rose slowly behind the hills and not as full as it had been the night before. Wispy clouds left over from the rainstorm also obscured that light.

Derry could feel the creature's indecision -- an almost human emotion. His heart pounded with fear and pain as he stood his place. He had to wait them out. He knew that his fae blood drew them to him more than they wanted the others.

Then he feared they might retreat, thinking the morning too near. Should he let it go?

"Derry?" Shannon asked softly.

"I'll get it closer," Derry said. He lifted his hand and sensed the attention the creature gave him. "Come on then, Shadow. I'm tired of the game. Come for me now, or I'll join the fae, and you'll never have the chance again."

The darkness shifted slightly and then came toward them in a rush. Shannon hissed in surprise, but Derry had been ready. "Now!" he shouted.

Several dozen men moved; wagons rolled out from the sides of buildings, the dry hay already catching fire. Two blocked the way back out of town and two others blocked the side paths. Two more moved up behind Derry and Shannon -- and at the same time people stepped out of the buildings all around so that they made an impenetrable wall of flame.

The timing had been better than Derry had hoped, and the flames leapt up, filling the street with flickering light. A wiser person might have been standing behind the flames, but Derry worried that the Shadows would slip out, and he might not see where they went. Shannon had taken up a torch to protect them as well.

It felt as though the trapped Shadows became an overwhelming presence. Derry had to see the thing -- the two still joined -- to know where it moved so that he could keep it from any hope of escape. It hurt the part of him that was fae but the human -- and stubborn -- part refused to back away.

The Shadow moved, finding a bit of darkness between one flickering red flame and another. Odd how it acted intelligently and yet seemed to have no real substance. The Shadows were almost two now, distinct in shape and both giant-like, but still melded together for the bottom third. Derry studied them, trying to find a weakness

"What now?" Shannon asked.

"We wait while they move the fires in closer."

Shannon gave a grunt of agreement, clearly no happier with the plan then he had been when they had first discussed it over cider an hour before. This was not, Derry knew, a wise strategy, but no one could come up with another. That he still thought he'd pulled the plan, or at least the basics of it, from the book that he hadn't read didn't help him feel more assured.

"Trouble --" Derry said. He felt something in the air, like a touch of a wind that ruffled his hair, though it didn't seem to touch anyone else. Something tested him, and Derry pushed the ephemeral fingers away with a feeling of disgust. Whatever that had been, it didn't come from the Shadows. Hadn't Brian said there were other problems, though? Was he drawing them --

A sharp wind swept through the fire-lit village. The flames were fanned brighter and higher, and for a moment, he thought they'd found help. Then the breeze slammed down on the fires behind him like a giant hand smashing out the flames.

The Shadows charged straight at them.

Derry shoved his friend aside and leapt forward, his hands raised. He didn't know what he intended to do until it happened. Light bloomed in his fingers and flew straight at the heart of the Shadows. The creatures wailed in dismay and backed up again, arms flailing as the brightness weakened them. Derry tried to call it up again, but he shivered as though the first effort had taken every bit of heat from him and winter had returned.

Derry went to his knees, numb with the loss of power, reeling as he tried to regain his breath. The creatures were not dead. He could hear them howling, and he tried to lift his head and focus on the trouble. The others were in danger if he didn't move!

The fire behind him flared again while the men shouted with pleasure at their little win. The Shadows screamed as well, a sound of defiance without words as they swayed back and forth, clearly looking for another way to attack. The light closed in on them, the natural shadows lessening. The creatures changed shape, elongating, and twisting. Sometimes the light caught pieces of them, and those areas burnt away in a flash of gray smoke. Not enough, yet. Getting the fires closer was not easy and he didn't want anyone to get too near the things --

Shannon went past him, a torch in hand. Derry surged to his feet, though he swayed so much he feared falling on the Shadow if he got too close. He took a step towards the creatures and Shannon.

Brother Callen suddenly appeared and caught Derry by the arm, who bit back a cry of pain that swept from his wounded shoulder to hand. He'd forgotten that injury. The knife wound might have been bleeding again, as well. He couldn't tell as he swayed in the priest's hold and then tried to pull away again.

"Easy!" Brother Callen ordered and didn't let go. "Don't be a fool, Prince Derry! You can barely stay to your feet!"

"Back," he gasped. "Back! Let me try to hold them --"

"We're only going back if you are coming with us," Shannon answered. He waved the torch at the creature.

Two more men and a woman came with torches of their own and formed a semi-circle, though they were wise enough not to stand in front of him. The others moved the wagons in closer, narrowing any gaps. Derry could sense frantic fear in the Shadows this time as even the smallest shadowed areas began to disappear.

Shannon put a hand on his arm, drawing some of Derry's attention. "If you don't stand up to this, it won't matter if we're on this side of the fires or the other, you know."

Derry didn't like to hear that truth, but before he would say anything, a cold breeze blew past them, kicking up debris on the still wet street and rattling windows and doors. Derry looked up as ominous, dark clouds sprinted across the sky, instantly hiding the stars and the moon. He felt the rain on his face in the next moment. The fires would go out --

"No!"

Derry threw his will at the clouds, shoving them back. This proved harder than tossing the light at the Shadows, but if he didn't stop the storm, then the rain would drench all the flames, and he wasn't sure any of them would survive. The Shadows had clearly split into two now, and they were frantic. The priest shouted for more torches, but they were slow in coming, the panic of the people a palatable emotion in the air.

The sunrise, though, couldn't be far away.

Derry wasn't certain when Shannon had caught hold of him and held him to his feet. The priest had two torches now, and both Silas and Evan joined him. The others at least kept the wagon fires going and kept the buildings well-lit. Father Callan, Silas, and Evan kept the shadows away from Derry and Shannon. All Derry had to do was hold back the rain.

Where had he learned such a thing? The thought brought a moment of doubt, and the power behind the clouds pushed forward against that uncertainty. A spattering of rain won cries of surprise and dismay all around. Derry shoved the power back again.

Derry realized he was, honestly, fighting against another being. Fae? He didn't feel that in the magic, though he knew very little about the fae as a whole. There been wars between factions in the far, far past. Or perhaps it was not so distant for immortals. Leanora?

Was another group trying to take over Lynashin for some reason?

No matter what the cause, Derry didn't want them here, not when they killed -- killed indiscriminately. The anger gave him strength, and he pulled at it because he needed any help now. He shoved back against the clouds once more, sending them swirling back towards their maker --

Not so easy.

Something built in the clouds. Power grew, both natural and unnatural. The growing power tried to distract Derry, and he almost ignored it until he realized that energy was about to come straight for him.

The lightning bolt flashed out, and if Derry had been a heartbeat slower, he would have missed his chance. He let go of the clouds and focused on the light, curving it away from them, though they felt the heat. He drove a dozen of the lightning's tendrils straight into the hearts of the shadows.

The creatures howled and disappeared in a rain of gray ash, but in that same moment, Derry felt the shock and anger of two others who had sent the storm. Human, he thought this time. Derry tried to grab at the wisp of power that led to them, but they pulled away in haste.

The rains came in a deluge, drenching the fires. It didn't matter. The creatures were gone. The rain even cleansed the feel of evil from the air.

He went to his knees and pulled Shannon down with him.

"Gone," Derry whispered, too weak to even speak louder. Shannon took better hold of him, ready to stand again. "Give me a moment, Shan. I ache."

"There are better places to rest than in the mud and rain, Prince Derry," Silas said, leaning down to look him in the face. The older man's worry shown in his furrowed forehead and the set of his mouth. His shaggy white hair hung in wet stands across his face, but neither he nor anyone else seemed to notice the rain. "We're done now, are we? It won't come back?"

"Gone," Derry agreed, but he lifted a hand to make sure. His arm trembled, but he tested out the area where the shadow had been. "Like it never existed."

"Good then. Let's get Derry up, Shannon."

Derry tried to protest, but every movement brought sudden agony. He had the feeling he'd used powers that should never have been in his control. How? He'd just known what to do. It had worked. Nothing else mattered.

Derry closed his eyes and let the others take him away. The storm was fierce, but they'd survive it. They didn't need his help...

Chapter Thirteen

"A little more of the tea and honey now, Master Shannon," Brian said softly, a gentle hand brushing across Derry's face. "He's almost awake. Tired, aching, and weak -- but very much alive."

Considering how he felt, Derry doubted he should be happy about being alive. Moving even his eyes hurt. He felt the warm edge of a cup press to his lips, and he sipped out of habit, though it hurt to swallow. Sweet, though. Pleasant, but Derry still protested another sip with a soft moan, his eyes opening to slits. The room was too bright. He closed his eyes again.

After a few more sips, Derry felt well enough to open his eyes again. They had brought him back to the room above the inn. Shannon sat behind him on the bed, bracing his shoulders and carefully holding the tea so he could sip.

"Better," Derry managed to say though he doubted he sounded sincere. "What --" He couldn't find the words to ask. Even thinking hurt. "Trouble?"

"You utterly destroyed the shadows and nearly destroyed yourself as well," Brian said as he knelt by the bed and studied

Derry's face. "That was hours ago. It's almost sunset again, but it's a safe sunset this time."

"Nothing?"

"Nothing anywhere near that feels dangerous, though the fae are making certain."

"Fae back. Good." He didn't want to think beyond those words.

Brian and Shannon fell silent for a while. Derry took short breaths that came without pain after a while. His body trembled, but the pain subsided little by little. He saw the light of day fading from the window and regretted it. He would have enjoyed standing in the sunlight for a while and feel the warmth of the world again.

People laughed somewhere in the inn. Maybe that was good enough.

Derry slept, awoke several times in the dark of the night, worried -- but a candle burned in the room, and Shannon remained beside him and always urged him back to sleep. If Shannon wasn't worried, neither would he be. Derry slept, awoke, slept again, and again.

When next he awoke, Derry found a bright day, the shutters open, and a soft breeze brushing across the bed. A gallery of colorful birds sat on the sill, whispering their little chirps with a pleasant sound on a happier day. Derry carefully moved and found that the aches of the day before had settled into something tolerable.

Shannon was just coming into the room with a tray balanced in one hand, and for once, Derry wasn't going to argue with him about eating.

"There are back steps out to the privy," Shannon said. "Can you handle them? You're less likely to be seen going that way, and I don't think you're ready to deal with apologetic and still celebrating locals."

"Yes. Good idea." Derry stood and found himself steadier

than he'd expected as he started to the door. Shannon followed him. "You don't have to --"

"We still have an assassin to think about. I'll keep watch from the stairs."

Arguing would be stupid. Derry nodded, glanced at the food, and decided to hurry. The steps down were a little tricky, his body slow to respond, but standing out in the fresh air helped. Shannon kept watch from the top of the stairs, watching the room and him. Derry supposed he should feel better for it, except that Shannon's precautions pointed out that there were still problems.

Derry hurried back to the room. He cleaned up and sat down in a chair by the window while Shannon brought the little table and another chair over so he could sit down. Shannon also tore off bits of bread for the birds, and they sat politely waiting for more.

Derry felt exhausted already, but he was still hungry. He began to eat as soon as Shannon sat down, and he soon became aware of his friend watching him.

"Yes?" Derry asked.

"Nothing. Really. Everything is great."

"I'm hungry. You can stop staring at me like I'm a -- oh damn. I suppose I am a changeling, aren't I?"

Shannon hadn't laughed in a while. They had a nice, quiet meal. He could see people going on about their business in the street below. A wagon burnt down to the wheels sat across the road, the only real sign of the trouble they'd faced.

They had beat the enemy this time. The humans had worked with him, and they'd destroyed something evil. It had not been easy, but Derry felt as though they'd done something unexpected. Maybe he could feel a little tendril of annoyance out there, something testing the feel of the world much as he sought out trouble. Today the balance was in his favor, though.

A group of sparrows came to the window when the others left. They could have been the same ones from Tyleen for all Derry could tell. They sang bright little songs and gladly accepted crumbs from the lunch. Shannon watched them as though he only just now realized the extent of the change in the world. He also looked as though he mistrusted it, which Derry fully understood.

"This calm won't last," Derry said, and Shannon gave a grim nod of agreement. "We should take advantage of the peace while we can, Shannon. You look tired."

"If you are going to sit here, then I'm going to nap for a while," Shannon said. He all but threw himself on the bed.

"Good idea," Derry said with a smile.

Shannon quickly drifted to sleep, giving Derry some time alone to think. The battle with the Shadow came back to him in more detail. What he had done had not been natural -- or at least not so for a human. Was it for the fae? He remembered feeling the power in his hands as he fought and how he had instinctively known what to do. Was that the way fae felt when they did magic? Derry couldn't see the answer, but he suspected the fae would have had better control. They wouldn't have left themselves dangerously weak. He'd read stories of fae deeds, including some weather control. That had likely been what sparked mind on what to do, even though he'd never been taught.

Dangerous, he knew. Dangerous to the enemy, which was a bonus, but also risky to himself and to others around him. Derry looked at his hands and wished for control. For the rest of the daylight hours, Derry practiced controlling his emotions so that when he did act again, it would be with knowledge of at least some of his ability. He wanted mostly to talk to the fae, but that wasn't possible until they came to him.

In all, he passed a much-needed quiet day. Late in the day, the foxes finally took their leave, which Derry appreciated. He didn't want to take them on to new troubles. Shannon saw them out of the village, and Derry had watched from the window. The townspeople laughed as the animals danced along with Shannon, playfully trying to trip him. It was a good thing to watch.

As sunset neared, Derry felt a wave of anxiety and feared that reaction to nightfall was going to stay with him for some time. Silas and Brother Callen brought them dinner, though, and they had a companionable meal in the room. Derry was thrilled not to go downstairs and put himself on show. He'd been spotted a couple times in the window, and the people had seemed both awed and worried.

"If nothing untoward happens tonight, Shannon and I will be moving on tomorrow," Derry announced. They'd both decided it would be wise to get away soon, if only because more trouble was bound to find them. "I should like horses if they can be found."

"Where are you going?" Silas asked.

"I'm not certain yet." Derry glanced at the window, hoping one of the fae would come to him tonight. "I need more information."

They had a leisurely meal as the sun went down, discussing many things, except for the battle the night before. As the darkness fell, Derry heard bells and smiled as Brian came to the window. He looked better, as well. The rest had done them all good.

They moved the table out of the way. Only a bit of bread and cheese remained, which Brian accepted with a smile.

"Sit down and relax," Derry said with a wave of his hand toward the bed. "I have some questions, Brian, if you don't mind?"

"Not at all, Prince Derry, though I may not be able to answer them." He went to the bed and sat cross-legged on it, looking at ease and comfortable as he nibbled at the food.

Brother Callen still watched him with a mixture of happiness and curiosity. The priest's distrust seemed to have disappeared, at least for now.

"The fae blood gave me the power to hold back the storm and to take control of the lightning, but I have no idea how I did it, Brian. That worries me. I could have done something hazardous to those around me."

"Need," Brian said with a nod. "It has happened before with the fae who started as humans, though I've never heard of anything quite so spectacular. Queen Leanora herself shared blood with you, which is not usual. Normally the magic is passed a little at a time through spells and training, you see. You've had no training at all, and that may be a problem because you have unusual powers directly from her."

"Can I get training now?"

"I'll show you what I can, but the truth is that there's just too much trouble to stop for proper training." He looked to the window as though something might appear there and attack them at any moment. That reaction did not help Derry's state of mind. "Queen Leanora has gone to the south, Derry, and she's the one most needed to help you."

"Trouble?"

"Trouble everywhere, and truth be told, there just aren't enough of us," he admitted and gave Brother Callen a wistful glance. "We used to think there were thousands, didn't we, sir? Hiding in the woods, living in the wilds. But there's barely three hundred of us left, and we've spread across Lynashin as best we can to deal with the spread of evil."

"What should I do, then?" Derry asked.

"Rest. Mostly rest while you can. Travel westward. Something is going on there, too. A group of us are headed that way, and in all honesty, we'd like to have you close so that if there is trouble, we can help each other."

"Yes," Shannon said, and Derry nodded. "We can leave in

the morning. We thought it not wise to stay too long here, where enemies obviously know how to find us."

"There is that problem. The fae have been guarding the town and watching strangers, but we're few, my friends." He stopped and pushed a hand through his dark hair, looking bothered, and worn. "We weren't prepared for a war like this. Leanora hopes that other fae from the Elsewhere realms will answer her call for help, but the fae have odd ideas of time, you know. They may come at once, not at all, or in a hundred years."

"There is so much I need to know," Derry admitted and wanted to ask about the other realms. Not now. "I've learned most of what the humans knew about the fae. The more ancient the book, the less animosity I find towards the fae. I can't find what changed that set the two groups at war."

"We think it might ha' been a curse," Brian admitted with a frown. "I've heard such a thing from some of the older fae. A strong, quick curse that burnt itself out almost as quickly as it took hold, but once the harm was done, there was no chance to pull back the wrongs."

"I would like to know the truth," Brother Callen said.

"I'll see what I can learn for you, sir," Brian replied with a quick bow of his head -- a village boy again, facing the local priest. "It'll give us things to talk about again on cold winter nights, huddled by the hearth. I miss those days."

"Do you really?"

"Oh, yes, sir. There were many times I thought to come to you, but I feared how you might react."

"And what would your Queen think of you spending your winter nights at my hearth?" Brother Callen asked, his head tilted.

"What she's thought from the start when I told her about you. She said that such ties of friendship and obligation should not be broken, and that good deeds of my past life are as much of what made me as my father's evil. We don't really want to be apart from the humans, sir. It's just not safe, given the humans' attitudes."

"You never ask about your father."

Brian's face went a little harder, and Brother Callen lifted his hand as though to take back the words.

"I know he still lives at the edge of the village. I know he still drinks. He has no one living with him, praise the gods. I made certain of that -- yes, I'll tell you that truth. I didn't want him beating some other poor helpless child or wife, who might not have had the luck I did to survive anyway. My mother didn't, you know."

"I know. It's our shame that we never got you away from him."

"He would have killed anyone who tried, and I think you sensed that truth, didn't you? I can't say the law would have taken him for such a killing, either," Brian said. He sighed and shook his head. "That was another life. I spent what time I could with you and working for Silas so that my father could buy his drink and on good days, fall senseless into bed. That was the best any of us could do. He has a demon, sir. I sometimes think he has the soul of a true demon, and there is not that we can do except wait for the body to die. I'd be wary at his funeral, Brother Callen. I would really."

Brother Callen blinked several times and then nodded, accepting the warning.

"But enough of such things," Brian said. He waved the words away, and the faint sound of bells filled the air, as though they were purifying the area. He smiled again. "We won here, my friends. It was no small matter. The enemy nurtured the Shadow for over a year, but now that power is gone. That's no small win, you know."

"Are there other Shadows out there?" Shannon asked and looked towards the darkened window as well.

"None that we've felt, and they're presence is obvious to the fae," he replied. "That's not to say the other trouble you'll face won't be as bad, though. Just not the same."

"There is trouble to the west," Derry said.

"Yes. I don't know what it is, exactly -- but something that shouldn't be there. You'll go?"

"Yes," Derry said. "Where to the west, though? That's a wide stretch of land."

"A village called Riverton, southwest of here by about four days' walk. Maybe two by horse if you push them, but I don't think there is a need for such an obvious rush. It would be better if you were rested as much as possible before you face something new."

"Wise," Shannon said.

"We'll be near, Prince Derry," Brian said as he stood and crossed to the window. "I'll see what I can find out for you and for Brother Callen."

"Don't worry about me, Brian boy --" Brother Callen began.

"Knowledge is always helpful. You told me that yourself, you know. A curse that might have parted humans from fae -- yes, we might want to think about that right now and make certain it does not happen again. I'll see you as soon as I can. Now rest, Prince Derry. You've won a battle, but we have a long war ahead still."

Chapter Fourteen

Shannon rode out early the next morning to visit the local manor house and meet with the people who tended his father's land. Derry didn't mind that they would start their own journey a little later in the day. Shannon had to take care of some family business. If there was anything that needed his attention, they could delay heading westward.

Derry worried about letting him go off alone. Still, he also felt it was important that Shannon not be seen as his shadow, especially in his father's lands. He still fretted and sat alone by the window, feeding the birds and watching every movement on the street below. Shannon returned in the early afternoon and arrived with two beautiful chestnut horses, and from the looks of those packs, with supplies enough to see them through several days. Derry waved from the window, and Shannon quickly came up to the room to help gather their few things -- mostly gifts of clothing from Silas and Brother Callen, and more food from Evan.

"Not a problem, but you were right -- it was good I went there and alone. They were surprised you weren't along, and I had the feeling they thought I was somehow under your power."

"I feared it might have seemed so."

"You should have said something. I didn't need to waste time on their egos --"

"You did need to go, and you know it. I sat here and rested a while longer. We have horses and enough supplies between your people and Evan to last an army through a summer campaign."

"True -- even after I gave all the meat away to some villagers on my way in," Shannon said. He still looked bothered. "My father would have understood if we had just gone on, you know."

"I know, but you need to think about these people, Shannon. I believe there is going to be a time after these battles when we might come this way again. I don't want stupid problems blossoming behind us," Derry moved through the room looking for anything left behind. "This was an easy thing to fix."

"True," Shannon admitted and grabbed the last bag from the bed. "Let's go. We have another long ride ahead. I'm actually looking forward to it, though -- as long as there are no Shadows out there."

"None that I can sense. I'll let you know if that changes."

"Appreciate it," he said with a laugh.

They went downstairs, bade farewell to Evan who was alone cleaning up the common room, and then went out into the daylight. Derry had rarely left the room since the battle and stepping outside felt like being released from some constraint. He had done his best not to think about that damned cell in The Isles, but it had invaded his sleep the last few nights. Leaving this place behind would help get his own calm back.

People watched them prepare to leave. Silas came and shook their hands, Brother Callen came and bade them goodbye and gave a blessing, much to the shock of many people who watched. Derry thought the priest might have made a show on purpose to illustrate both his own change of heart and to prove that Daria didn't mark them as evil.

They rode away, Derry feeling better for the friendly farewell. However, as they neared the edge of town, Derry stared at a ragged cabin with weeds growing about the walls and the glowering shape of a wild-haired man standing in the darkened doorway.

"Derry?" Shannon said.

"Brian's father."

He looked and frowned. "You're sure?"

"Oh, yes. I can sense it, and there is evilness lingering around the man. He is on the edge of doing something in anger that would hurt others. Ride back and tell Silas and Brother Callen, will you? Don't worry. I won't ride on without you."

Shannon sighed and turned the horse to head back. Derry rode a little farther and stopped, still within view of the building. He dismounted from the fidgety horse that protested already stopping and took careful hold of the bridle, letting the animal know that the delay wouldn't be for long.

He hadn't expected the man to come shambling out towards him, and he wondered if he ought to retreat to Shannon's side. Derry couldn't clearly see the face through the shaggy black mane of snarled hair and equally snarled beard. The clothing appeared to be dirt-colored, whatever other colors they might once have been. His bare feet were covered in mud.

"Says you saw my son, the bastard. Says you and he be fae now." The man reeked of bad liquor and such a lack of hygiene that made Derry want to hold his breath. "Well, damn you? Yes?"

"I am Prince Derry SanOsen," Derry replied, meeting the man's bloodshot eyes, never looking away. "Do you know that? Do you know what kind of power I hold?"

"Not much as long as the Queen hates you, eh?" he countered, not a bit cowed --and very well informed, Derry thought, considering he was apparently disliked by everyone in town.

"You think so?" Derry said. He tilted his head a little. "And you think my Uncle, the King, means nothing?"

The man blinked at that one, mumbled something, and backed up a step. "You saw my son, yes?"

"If you had a son, you do not have one now," Derry answered and looked into the man's wild, gray eyes. "Be gone."

The scraggly-haired man glared as he backed away. He clearly didn't want to go, but the force of Derry's words left him no choice. Yes, there was fae power in what he'd said, and it left Derry a little breathless. He wondered if there was something more he could do as a fae that would make this man less dangerous. The best he could do was to wish it to be so, and not very hard since he had to be able to ride away.

Shannon rode back and Derry and mounted again. Brian's father had hastily retreated into his shambles of a cottage and scowled at them from the other side of the broken door, as though that insubstantial barrier would keep him safe.

Derry didn't much care. He and Shannon urged the horses away, and he gave a sigh of relief to be away from the man.

"They'll keep an eye on him," Shannon said. "That's the best we can do."

"Yes. Not a pleasant man, but one who was aware of my standing with the Queen."

"Was he?" Shannon said and looked back over his shoulder. Derry did as well. The man didn't like it much and scuttled into the shadows of his home once more. "That seems odd."

"He also knew I'd seen Brian and that we were both fae.

He could have easily heard that around town today. If he spends his nights drinking, then hearing about my relationship with the Queen is not a surprise, I suppose. However, it felt odd."

"Well, when we're done with everything else, I'll spend a bit more time finding out about him," Shannon promised. "I don't think he's going to follow us."

"Not a chance. He won't go that far from his liquor. Brian has moved on as well, so he's safe from the man." Derry felt another weight lift as the path turned, and he could no longer see the village through the line of trees. He fell silent for a little longer. "I think we need to talk to the King about when children should be taken away from cruel parents, and I don't mean taken by the fae."

"There's a big task," Shannon said. "Where do you draw the line?"

They talked about the possibilities for a few miles. They then drifted off to more pleasant conversations about the lovely spring weather. Deer trailed along with them sometimes, and squirrels chattered in the trees. They found a few people on the trail today; polite and calm people, though Shannon must have worried that each one was an assassin from the way he reacted. Derry often heard the distant sound of fae bells. The fae traveled in the same direction, which also made him feel better. He didn't want to feel as though they were heading into more trouble without anyone to back them up this time.

The flatlands gave way to hills and deeper woods that felt filled with magic and wilder than what they'd passed through before today. Derry could sense many odd things, including a place off to the northwest near the high mountains where neither mankind nor fae seemed to go. The location intrigued him, as though he might find a sanctuary from the world of strife there and a place where he might find rest.

Ah, but that would mean running away from the

problems in Lynashin, and he had matters here to handle. Besides, the more he touched on that area, the less welcoming it seemed.

"Derry?"

"Just thinking," he said with a laugh. "Press on to the village or camp out tonight?"

"Camp out," Shannon said, then gave him a narrow-eyed look. "Unless you can sense something out there --"

"Nothing," Derry admitted, glancing at the declining sun and glad they'd be stopping soon. "I have a sense of trouble far off to the west still, but nothing except calm anywhere near us."

"Good. I don't mind camping out. Fewer people to watch. You know the news about what happened in Glendalow will have spread this way, despite that there have been very few travelers."

"The news will spread everywhere," Derry said with a sigh.

They were already searching for a likely spot to stop. At least the woods here calmed him. Derry drank in the feel of the wild and knew his delight came from more than his fae blood. He'd always enjoyed the wilderness, though he'd also liked a good inn at the end of a day's ride. Derry glanced at Shannon, about to apologize for dragging him out into this -- and stopped before he said the words. Such a statement would be an insult to Shannon, who was here not because Derry needed him -- though that was true -- but rather because he wanted to help save the land as much as Derry wanted to help.

He could feel the problem in the west a little more clearly with each mile. This was not a situation like the Shadow. Whatever was out there seemed more natural, but --

"Derry?"

"Sorry," he apologized. He looked around, saw a small brook to the right, and a spot that had clearly been used by people on other nights. "You think that looks like a good spot?"

"Unless you tell me otherwise," Shannon said, looking at the area with some mistrust.

"Seems calm enough to me," Derry replied and turned the horse that way. He'd be glad to be off him for a while, though the ride had been pleasant.

Shannon still looked doubtful and mistrusting as they rode across the brook and to the little area that had been cleared of weeds by the people who had rested here before them. They found a much-used rock circle for fire and even a bit of wood set beside it, a kindness from fellow travelers to those who might arrive late and be too weary to gather firewood. Shannon left that wood and gathered some more, adding several pieces to the pile. Derry had divested the horses of their supplies but left Shannon to unsaddle the animals. He knew his limits.

Derry carefully helped Shannon with a little of the camp work. His side ached slightly, and he didn't want to argue with Shannon over something so trivial tonight. Derry stopped early and let his friend finish preparing the camp. They had a pleasant meal, the sounds of the forest quieting around them. The sun sank to the horizon, and no one had traversed the trail for a while. The fae must have settled somewhere as well, and he had only a sense of quiet contentment from everywhere around them.

Birds gave their last cries to the night, and somewhere far off, a wolf cried out for the company of others. Rabbits nestled down into their burrows nearby, and Derry could feel their warm contentment wash over him.

Derry hadn't realized how much he needed this wild peace until he sipped tea and let the worries of what they would face slip away for a while. He'd been tense in Keirkell, and it hadn't only been because of the dangerous creature. The people had bothered him, even when they seemed to be on the same side.

Out here, he sensed only the wild around him, except for Shannon. Shannon had never made him feel uncomfortable. Derry could rest tonight and recover a little out here away from everyone and all their troubles.

The nightmares still came that night, though they were not as intense, and he didn't even wake Shannon this time. They'd decided against trading off being guards since Derry would feel any intruder coming near. Shannon slept, trusting him.

They rode through two villages the next day. People stared at them with speculation, though he thought they might not be recognized. The locals were watching for a high prince and a fae -- not a weary man riding quietly by on a quite normal horse. They didn't stop, having plenty of supplies still, and on the second night found another pleasant camping spot. Sleep came easier, even though he knew that by the next night, they could be dealing with whatever trouble they headed toward. He could feel the problem, but he still couldn't understand the difficulty.

He started to dream about the prison cell that night and awoke with a start. The nightmare had felt different, and he didn't like it --

"Derry?"

"Sorry. Nightmare."

"Sleep. You'll regret it if you don't."

Derry gave a little laugh of agreement and settled back into the blanket. When he started to drift away, he felt the nightmare coming again, but this time he shoved the unwanted thoughts aside. Odd, how his subconscious reacted with what almost felt like a wave of annoyance at losing the nightmare again.

He slept and wasn't bothered any more that night.

Sometime later, Shannon cursed. Derry realized his friend was already up, and the scent of tea filled the area. Derry remembered pulling his head under the warm blanket at the first sign of light and now peeked out --

Rain.

An enormous, cold drop hit him on the forehead and ran down into his eye, startling him. Shannon threw more wood on the fire and glared up at the sky.

"It's not that bad," Derry said as he sat up, pulling the blanket up like a cloak over his head. "I've seen worse."

"Oh yes, far worse," Shannon agreed, but in no better mood. "Why is it that bad weather seems to follow you these days?"

"There is far worse than bad weather."

"Following you? Very likely." Shannon poured out tin cups of tea and handed one to Derry, his attitude improving. "We're not more than a few hours from Riverton. Any more idea of what's out there?"

"Trouble."

Shannon sighed.

"Sorry, but I really don't know anymore. I do have the feeling we'll find out soon."

Shannon looked up at the sky with more worry rather than anger now. "I kept hoping things would sort themselves out before we got there. I knew it wouldn't happen, but since the fae were heading that way as well --"

"And they have already gone on," Derry said, realizing they were nowhere around now. "I don't think that's good, Shannon."

"I'll saddle the horses. You get the supplies packed."

They quickly went to work. Derry did his part, but his mind worked on other things. They were closer to Riverton and the trouble, but he couldn't feel the substance of what they would face any better. He could sense the panic of people there, though, and that was going to affect him if he didn't start learning how to control that part of his new abilities.

The rain still fell when they crossed back to the trail, and even the little brook had doubled in size. Derry hoped to hear the fae bells again, but they were nowhere around now. Derry pushed damp hair from his face and watched the trail. "The fae are somewhere ahead of us still. Riverton would be my guess."

"Riverton, where we'll find trouble."

"Of course. We knew that."

Shannon drew his sword and laid it across his lap. Then he looked at Derry and gave a quick shrug. "I know. A sword hasn't been much help so far, but I'm willing to give it a try. It makes me hope there might still be a use for me in this mess."

"Other than shepherding me around?"

"Well, that's true. You do need a keeper. Maybe that is my true worth in this mess, but I'll hold on to the sword anyway, just in case."

"Shannon, I have to say this: you were crazy to get into so much trouble with Queen Alisia over me. What would you have done if King Nevin hadn't come back? He could have died in battle --"

"Yes, he could have, and we all feared it happening -- because then the good Queen Alisia would have taken over Lynashin, and I wouldn't want to be there under her rule. I would have had to go into exile anyway, Derry. She couldn't have trusted me, you know."

"True enough." Derry tried not to shiver at that thought. Everything had been out of his hands while he sat there in that cell --

The memory of the place came back to Derry with every unpleasant stink, and an unfriendly face turned his way. His breath caught as he shook his head and chased that darkness away again. Derry knew he needed to think clearly.

"Derry?"

He took a deeper breath and nodded. "I'm all right."

"Are you sure? You went pale, and your hands are trembling. Do you want to ride with me?"

"No, I'm fine." He sat up straighter now that he had control again. "Besides, I want you to keep hold of that sword."

"Excuse me? Would that be wisdom?"

"I'm sure I don't know any better than you do since neither of us has ever had any experience in it."

That won a snort of amused agreement. "Odd place to find ourselves in, isn't it?"

"I think so sometimes." He glanced around the woods. "Odder for me than you, but still ... maybe we prepared for this all our lives, Shannon. If we had played court games with all the others, we wouldn't be ready to face this kind of trouble. Can you imagine Egan riding through the country chasing after fae and dangers? We could have been like him if we'd wanted to stay in good with the Queen and her lot."

"So, fate set us on this path?"

"Fate and the gods," he said. "And probably the fact that we have always been wiser than people think. We chose our way rather than become Egan's sycophants."

"The thought makes me ill," Shannon admitted. "Egan got worse after you left, and the time in the temple with his mother did not improve his personality. I wish the fae had a way to fix him."

"They're still ahead of us, by the way. The fae haven't gone running off this time. They ran towards the trouble."

"Where we'll ride to join them."

"Of course. I admit I hope the fae and the locals have everything in hand before we get there."

"More wisdom. I don't know if I can handle any more of it today." Shannon stared ahead down the rainy trail for a moment. "I have gone odd, you know. I'm glad to know the fae are close by still."

"Another sign of the path we chose," Derry replied. He pulled his cloak up a little closer around his shoulders, glad to have the wind at their backs. "Though I would have been happier to have a path a bit less muddy."

A moment later, the storm struck harder, and the horses protested. Derry didn't blame the animals for disliking the weather. He thought he could hear distant thunder, though if there was lightning, it never pierced the wet gloom through which they rode.

The rain soon felt cold enough to be ice, and he didn't want to find himself in a late-season snowstorm. They were near enough to the mountain barrier that snow might slip down the peaks and catch them. The heights, though, stood off to the north, and the storm came from behind, so he thought they might stay lucky in that respect.

Derry realized he sensed magic in the rain. He thought that meant the fae had some hand in this weather, but he couldn't say that made him feel any better. Worse still, it obscured the feel of the fae ahead of him. He said nothing to Shannon, who rode hunched forward against the weather but remained silent and steady as he watched the way ahead of them. They were riding into trouble. They both knew it.

The day did not get any better. They traveled as quickly as they dared in the weather, but it neared noon before they came to the fields outside Riverton. The meadows were fast becoming ponds, and water rushed across the trail in places, making it treacherous to cross. They had to slow again while the horses carefully choose their footing.

Derry peered ahead, hoping to see the welcome outline of a building. Twice he thought he heard shouts, but he could sense nothing dangerous ahead. He did notice that the fae had moved off somewhere to the south and were not in the village itself, which couldn't be too far ahead. He could sense something --

Derry smelled smoke before he saw the first of the burnt cottages, the wood still smoldering, even in the rain. With a barely whispered curse, Derry urged the horse on faster. Shannon said nothing as he kept up with him. Rain and smoke obscured everything but the closest trees, and the two reached the edge of Riverton before they realized it.

They found more damage here with several fire-scarred buildings, although the village remained mostly still intact. Derry also found a line of people ready with weapons raised to beat them back; swords, shovels, rakes all lifted as the men gave shouts and several of them rushed forward --

"Hold! Hold!" Shannon shouted with a perfect combination of authority and panic.

"Human," one of the men said and lowered his shovel. The others lowered theirs as well, though they remained wary. "Not demons."

"Demons?" Derry asked as he held the horse in place. The animal sensed too many things wrong, and Derry had trouble calming him.

"Demons!"

"Creatures from hell itself!" a woman shouted, and she waved a rusted sword in her hand, looking toward the road behind Shannon and Derry.

Derry feared they meant fae, and that attitude would create a problem. Shannon had his sword firmly in hand now, though he still hadn't brought it up to fend off the worried people. No one had moved closer.

"Huge, hulking creatures with fur and horns," another said. "And stood on their back legs and spread fire with a wave of their great arms. We could barely hold them back, sir!"

"And then the fae came," the first man said. "We thought we was finished, then. We hadn't a chance to hold back them as well. But the fae attacked the monsters and chased them off. By the Gods, it's true, sir!"

"Oh, I believe you," Derry replied with a sigh of relief.

"Of course, you do, Prince Derry SanOsen!" A mud-spattered man trudged towards them, wiping dirt from his hands. "I've been hearing wild tales about you and Shannon, my lad. Almost makes we wish I still rode with the two of you."

Until the last line, Derry hadn't recognized the brawny man beneath the mud and unkempt hair.

"Farrin!" Shannon laughed and leapt from his horse, pounding the man on the back in greeting. Derry dismounted as well and took both horses in hand. "And what a fine, proper lord, you look!"

The others holding weapons moved aside now, relief and a bit of dismay in their faces. That probably came from realizing they'd stood against nobles who might not appreciate having swords and shovels waved at them. Not a few were watching Derry, and he wondered if that was because he was Prince Derry or because they knew of his connection to the fae. Since Farrin had heard tales, Derry had to believe the rest of the people knew the stories as well.

He did note that Shannon, for all he was acting quite happy to find their friend, had not yet sheathed his sword.

"I'm glad to see you, Farrin," Derry said and held out his hand.

Farrin paused for a heartbeat and then took it, winning a little hiss of surprise from the people nearby. Oh yes, they'd heard.

"You look pale, lad," Farrin said with a frown. He was only four years older than Derry and Shannon, but he'd always treated them like younger (and foolish) brothers. "This weather can't be doing you any good. We've saved the inn and her stores. Let's go warm up and maybe have a dram or two --

"

"Tea would be nice," Derry said, leading the horses forward. Shannon took hold of his mount, and the people scattered, though not without a few glances back at them.

"Tea, it is then," Farrin agreed. He glanced sideways at Derry. "They say you have fae blood now."

"I do."

"Well, then." Farrin walked a few steps, his head shaking from side-to-side.

"Is this going to be a problem for you?" Derry asked. As much as he wanted to go somewhere and rest, he would not put his friend in an awkward position with the people here.

"No problem," Farrin said, though he glanced at Derry again. "The fae did help us survive."

Derry saw others nod agreement, so let some of his worries go. The locals still gave him odd glances, but then so did Shannon now and then.

Farrin ordered his people to see to the horses while he led them through the mostly undamaged town and up into the rustic tavern. The place wasn't as crowded as Derry had expected, though quite a few others followed them in. Everyone appeared weary, and few were injured though none of those looked severe.

The place smelled of smoke from outdoors more than cooking meat, which suited him. The hand-carved furnishings were remarkably well made. A woman peered into the room from the kitchens and nodded at the intrusion. A dozen others followed them inside.

"Tea, Maisey," Farrin shouted.

The villagers whispered about princes and fae, giving their visitors wary looks, though they were unwilling to leave. They wanted to hear the news, and Derry felt a hint of hope that the strange visitors could help them. They'd already faced something dangerous and unnatural, and they had survived with the help of the fae. A fae prince was not nearly as disturbing to these people as he had been to others.

Derry followed Shannon over to a corner table by a window shuttered against the rain and settled into the chair closest to that opening. The storm had picked up again, and Derry was glad they'd made it to cover before it turned worse. He could feel a slight splatter of rain through the shutters, but that hardly mattered, as wet and muddy as he already was. Derry thought he could also hear the faint hint of ice as the wind plastered the water against the side of the building. There might be a little hint of magic in the wind. For all he could tell, though, it might be natural.

Shannon sat down with a sigh of relief. "I wasn't sure we were going to get here before the weather turned worse, or what we'd find when we did arrive," he admitted.

Farrin gave a grunt of understanding as he took a chair, dropping into it with the weariness of a man who had run a long race. He'd put on some weight, but mostly he'd aged since the days when he had run with Shannon and Derry. Farrin had inherited his father's lands the year before Derry's ill-fated trip to the Isles. Looking at Farrin now, Derry felt as though he and Shannon had somehow stayed in a bubble of time while the world moved on without them.

"Well, what happens now?" Farrin demanded. His grey eyes narrowed as he focused on Derry.

He feared that all the joy had gone from Farrin's life. There was impatience in those eyes and a little distrust that seemed to be his attitude towards the world.

"Derry?" Shannon said, giving him a nudge.

"Tea," Derry said, covering his lapse as best he could. "I'm sorry. I'm a little rattled still. I can't say what will happen next, Farrin. I need to speak with the fae and learn more about the trouble that has struck here."

"Then speak to them."

Shannon gave Farrin a hard look this time, but Derry patted his friend's arm and hoped he stayed calm. Farrin had been a long time away from court. He'd had hard work here since his father had abandoned the lands decades before he died, living a life of leisure in Tyleen. The man had not trusted his eldest son to go home and take care of things, either. Farrin had spent most of his life at Tyleen with little understanding of what would be needed when he took his father's place.

He'd learned quickly.

Life had changed, though. He was, Derry realized, unused to talking with equals any more. He was the only noble of any rank in a large swath of lands that were his holdings.

Farrin worried about his people and the danger they faced.

"The fae have chased these creatures away," Derry explained softly. Farrin sat back a little, perhaps reading Shannon's reaction and realizing he needed to play by old rules again. They'd never stood by formality, but they'd always been polite to each other, which marked them as different from Egan and the Queen. "I don't know where they've gone or what exactly they're doing. I don't think it either smart or safe for me to go blundering after them. They'll come back to me when they can."

"Yes, of course. That's wise," Farrin agreed. He pushed back his hair with muddy fingers. Surely that wasn't a sprinkling of grey that caught the light. "And you can sit back and relax, Shannon, lad. I'll curb my impatience and my temper. Now, are you sure you won't take a bit of ale or something stronger, Derry? You look as though you could use a bit to warm the body."

"Tea for me. I had better stay level-headed."

"Well damn," Farrin said with a shake of his head. "When did our wild Prince Derry get so sensible?"

"Apparently, when so much trouble began to fall his way," Shannon replied as he leaned his sword against the wall.

"Oh, aye. Yes, I can understand that."

So, they found some common ground. Farrin even surprised him by ordering the food and making sure there was no meat. He hadn't thought his friend would know even that much about the fae. Then he remembered how much Farrin used to read during the long winters at court, while the rest of them chaffed at being stuck inside. Derry hoped to have a chance to talk with him about it ... later. In private, because he didn't think the locals were really that sanguine about the fae, even if appreciated being rescued.

"Farrin, we just rode here from Keirkell, where we found trouble as well," Derry admitted. Best to get straight to the matter.

"We heard," Farrin replied, one eyebrow lifting as he nodded to continue.

Derry forced himself not to look around to gauge how the others reacted to the conversation. Remembering the trouble he had at the last inn didn't help, but Derry didn't feel the presence of magic pushing this group into a rage. He felt safe enough, especially since Shannon kept his sword in hand. It didn't even look unusual since some of the others had their weapons as well.

If an assassin had already arrived in town, Derry hoped Shannon spotted the man somehow. He would talk to Farrin about it, but later, in private. Right now, they had other problems to handle.

"What we faced in Keirkell was not the same as here, but I still suspect they are from the same source," Derry said and kept his voice steady. "We fear Lynashin has come under attack. The fae are doing what they can to help, but we don't have any answers about why -- not yet."

Farrin frowned, but then he nodded.

"It's not our way, magic," an old man said, leaning against the wall nearby, his dark eyes filled with distrust. "Not our war, is it?"

"It became our war today," Farrin said, his voice calm.

"Aye, yes, my lord. You are right." The old man still cast a look of anger at Derry, but he said no more.

Farrin had turned back to Derry with a different stare. Much was weighed at that moment when their eyes met. Shannon shifted, uncomfortable with this stare of evaluation, but Derry saw no distrust from his old friend. Farrin simply wasn't certain what to make of him, and in that Derry understood. He wasn't sure how to feel about the changes in himself as well, both the fae blood and the far worse that had happened in the prison cell. He had not left The Isles the same person as when he went there as the Queen's unwilling envoy. What had happened there, more than anything since, had created the differences in him now.

That thought made him bow his head and look away from his friend.

Farrin sighed and put a hand on Derry's arm. "The world has truly changed, hasn't it, my friends?" He sat back, clearly weary again, and the battle went out of him. "Some days, I think I would give anything to ride wild and free as we once did."

"I don't know, Farrin," Shannon replied. "I've been riding wild and free with our fine prince here for a few days, and I honestly don't know what we used to see in it."

That won a roar of laughter from Farrin, which brought laughter and looks of pleasure from the others. Derry realized that they liked their young lord. They appreciated him after the trouble they'd had with Farrin's father. Even King Nevin had thought the father worse than useless, but he had rarely stepped in unless the man's lands were in dire need. Nevin had always walked a thin line between his control and the rights of his lords.

They had a bit of tea and cakes while Derry and Shannon explained about what had happened back in Keirkell. Derry hadn't wanted to relive that trouble, but the others needed to realize the depth of problems.

"I can't say that standing stones would be a help against these creatures as they were against the Shadows. However, if anyone is caught out in the wilds, it might be your only hope," Derry said, looking around the area and trying not to show his nervousness. People watched him, entranced and worried. He felt odd at first to have their attention. Then he remembered he was Lord -- Prince -- Derry SanOsen, and they would have been watching him just as intently if he hadn't any link to the fae. "There is little more I can tell you -- ah, but I think I can get more answers now."

The sound of fae bells came closer, bright, and friendly sounds, but ones he was not used to hearing in the light of day. Derry stood, feeling weary and wishing he'd had a chance to at least finish his tea, but glad enough to find the fae here. They did need answers.

Shannon stood to go with him, and Farrin followed, which didn't surprise him. Farrin had always been the most daring of them. Derry was glad to see his friend had not changed.

But Derry had changed. Time to make that count for something.

Chapter Fifteen

R ain still fell when they stepped outside the inn, though not so hard as when they'd reached Riverton. The half dozen fae who stood on the street didn't look bothered by the weather. Derry held back his sigh. He didn't want to stand here in the cold, wet weather to discuss the fate of the world.

The fae gave Farrin and the two men who followed their lord looks of worry. Derry found that amusing since he felt much the same way when dealing with humans these days. Or maybe he mistrusted humans since there had always been a reason to worry about strangers in the past. He thought about the assassin again but suspected he was safe with the fae here.

Misty rain and smoke blunted the shapes around them, and the fae looked almost ghostlike in the waning light of day. Derry and Shannon went down the steps, though Shannon signaled Farrin to stay back. The man didn't argue.

"I'm glad you made it here safely, Derry and Shannon."

Derry had not expected to find Brian with the group. The young fae stepped closer; he looked exhausted and had a nasty cut that bled across his right arm.

"Are you all right?" Shannon asked, which seemed to surprise the fae as much as it did the humans.

"We sensed the trouble -- ran ahead --" Brian swayed, and Shannon took a step closer to keep Brian to his feet. "Thank you, my lord. I'll be all right. We fought a hard battle, and with so much trouble afoot, we dared not waste magic on small wounds."

"Well, then, maybe you should consider some old-fashioned human bandages," Farrin dared to suggest. A glance showed him more intrigued than worried. "That's a nasty enough cut, lad."

Brian looked up at Farrin and blinked before he gave a quick bow of his head, as though he only now came back to reality. "Yes, that would be wise, my lord."

Farrin looked a little startled by the response, but he signaled his people to get the supplies, and they left without comment.

"Brian used to be human," Derry said, which he suspected might help.

Farrin gave the boy another long look, questions clearly in his face though he appeared uncertain what he could ask. Derry understood that feeling -- as though they were all suddenly back at court, testing the rules with someone new in the mix.

"My father beat me and left me to die in the woods," Brian explained with a weary sound of a long-fought battle -- but was that from this fight or the old war with his father? Brian rubbed at his hand as though he remembered older wounds. "It was not the first time, but I would not have survived if the fae hadn't taken me in. I never expected to find myself back among humans."

"My fault," Derry began.

"Yours?" Brian asked and looked startled. "I don't think it is your fault that evil has struck the land, Prince Derry.

Somehow, I don't think you would wish this on us, neither on the humans nor on the fae."

"But you wouldn't be here --"

"Oh, but we would," Brian replied, far more forceful than he'd been in the past. "We just wouldn't have so fine a welcome with the humans without you, would we? Oh, let us be done with this -- we haven't time, you know. Let us go sit by yon tree, Prince Derry. We have much to discuss still."

"Yes, of course," Derry agreed. It had been selfish to try to make this meeting all about him.

Shannon helped Brian over to the oak tree that grew by the well, providing shade on sunny days and a little protection from the rain now. Derry heard Farrin send another person for tea, cakes, bread, and cheese -- his friend had always been quick to learn by example, and he did not include any meat.

Brian settled on the ground with his back to the tree, nodding thanks to Shannon, who had helped him. Some of the other fae were injured as well, but it seemed Brian was the worse. Derry couldn't decide if he had met any of the others before and realized he needed to start paying better attention. Suddenly, Derry thought he understood King Nevin far better than he ever had before, seeing him in all those gatherings of officials. Derry settled on the ground -- a bit damp, but he didn't care, glad to be off his feet again already. Shannon sat as well, but still looked worried. Food and bandages arrived, and the humans were delighted enough to hand both off to the fae. The fae might even have worried about poisons for a moment, but if so, they showed no sign. Food passed around, cups of tea followed, and Derry had a real feeling of momentary contentment. A fae woman quickly bandaged Brian's arm, and he gave a nod of thanks afterward. The tea seemed to be helping because Brian and the others all looked better. The few moments of rest must have helped. The rain had eased to nothing more than a mist, too. The day was no warmer for it, but they all seemed more comfortable.

"We came as quickly as we could," Brian said, mostly to the humans who had gathered around. "We had to skirt the Holy Woods, though -- that area just to the north where I think even humans avoid because of the power there."

Farrin have a quick nod of agreement, though he seemed surprised. "We always thought it was your land," he admitted. "A fae place."

"Something old and powerful lives there and protects the woods. It's a good power to have close, so long as we don't draw too much of it's attention." Brian stopped and shook his head. "The trouble here, though, is our concern. Queen Leanora and some of the fae have gone south to check that problem. The rest of us will help here."

"What do we do now, Brian?" Derry asked and cast a worried look back out into the rain. "This isn't over, is it?"

"No, it isn't, Prince Derry," Brian replied as he held the cup tightly in one hand. He glanced at the other fae, but, apparently, they left him to talk with the humans. "We will keep watch as best we can, though it is hard to say what we are dealing with here."

"Fire demons for one," Farrin offered as he dropped down on his heels beside Shannon.

"Oh yes, that, of course," Brian agreed with a bow of his head. "And they were dangerous, sirs. We chased them some distance and cornered them by a cliff overlooking the river --"

"More than twenty miles from here," Farrin said, surprised.

"Yes, sir. But we're fae -- the distance was not so troublesome. We fought them, both against their fire and their claws." He touched his bandaged arm where a little blood showed already. "We would have won, but at the moment before our triumph, they disappeared, and we couldn't trace what took them. That's powerful magic, sirs. It means they might reappear at any time. Whatever controlled the magic -- it was not the demons themselves - hovers nearby. We can sense something, but not find it. It wears at us, which is probably why Prince Derry is so distracted."

"No, he's this way all the time," Shannon replied.

"Always has been," Farrin agreed. "That's why he's always needed Shannon to lead him around lest he falls off a bridge or something."

"I only fell the once!" Derry protested.

The words won laughter from the fae and his friends. The day seemed far less oppressive for the sound. Derry wasn't sure the fae needed to know that much about him -- but by all the gods, they all felt better for the laughter.

And it wasn't as though Farrin lied.

"Do you think we might get back to the trouble at hand?" Derry asked -- and oh, how he sounded like his uncle the King just then. The other two hadn't missed it, either.

"Of course, Prince Derry SanOsen," Farrin replied with a proper bow of his head. "Whatever you command."

"There's no hope," he replied with a sigh, but hardly hid his own smile this time.

They were all more at ease. They spoke for a while longer, Brian explaining the battle and agreeing that any standing stones might be an excellent place to go if a person had to escape this danger.

"There are fae powers in such places," Brian explained. "Ancient powers and they don't much like what's going on here in the lands they've tried to protect for so long. Unfortunately, they are tied to where they are -- or maybe that's good. The Old Ones were far less fond of humans in general, though they'll help anyone in need. Unfortunately, there isn't much more that I can tell you. We are immersed in magic here, and the evil will strike again. Queen Leanora is searching out both information and trying to trace the source of this power."

"Why the attack on Riverton?" Farrin asked.

"Part of it is the cardinal points," Brian replied. "There have been attacks in the north, south, and east as well. We are trying to find out why. This has never happened before. We are keeping watch to the west, but Tyleen has ancient powers. The enemy may hold off anything happening in that direction until other points are secured."

Brian looked bothered and upset that he didn't have answers, but Farrin only nodded and accepted what was clearly the truth.

"If there is trouble elsewhere, will you be moving on?" Farrin asked, looking at Derry this time.

"Not yet," Derry said but didn't promise that he wouldn't leave if he had to chase after another problem.

Farrin nodded and understood.

Trouble struck again late in the afternoon. The fae had moved into the nearby woods, and almost everyone, including Shannon, rested. After a few hours, Derry walked through the village with Farrin. This was, more than anything, a show of trust. The others knew that Shannon was his guard, but Derry didn't want Farrin to feel as though they mistrusted their old friend.

Besides, he had rested for a few hours and then started to feel anxious again. Whatever danger was out there, it wasn't going away.

"I used to think things would never change, you know," Farrin said suddenly. They'd stopped at the southern edge of the village and stared out at fields, newly planted. The rain had stopped though everything still felt damp. "I thought my father would never die and leave the lands to me. I never, really, thought much of what I'd do if it did happen. My father didn't trust me enough to teach me anything about taking care of this place. Thank the Gods that King Nevin made certain we all knew what we were doing. He's also been less strict about me having to spend so much time at Tyleen since there is work to do here. I miss living at the castles, though."

"It's the downside of Tyleen," Derry said. "The King holds power and riches for the Lords there, and some of them are bound to get lazy. Paranoia might as well by a court game, the way they pass it around with whispers and glances. Just the same, I never thought it would change, either -- and now look at us."

"Changed in ways we never would ha' thought," Farrin agreed with a glance around. "And I don't mean the fae blood, either. Ah, but it is good to see you and Shannon back together. Just watching the two of you makes me feel young again."

"You are not that old!"

Farrin laughed and slapped him on the shoulder, but not very hard. "Next time I'm to Tyleen, we must ride to Glendalow if the inn is still there --"

"Oh, yes, it is. I stopped on my way home." Derry did not mention that it was where he had gotten tangled up with the fae.

"We best get back before Shannon wakes and comes looking for you."

"You'd think I didn't hold rank over both of you," Derry said. "Or that I don't have a mind of my own."

"I'll wait to see proof of -- what the hell is that!"

Derry spun and looked up to see something substantial flying low across the sky. Another followed. He thought they were large birds --

No. Too large.

"Shannon! Brian!" he shouted, knowing they had to hold this new enemy away from the others. "Farrin, get your people to cover!"

Farrin took off at a run but stopped a few yards farther

and looked back at him, realizing he hadn't followed. Derry waved him on, but Farrin only went back to shouting at his people when the fae arrived and headed straight for Derry.

They had weapons, too. Swords appeared in some hands and bows in others. Brian came to a skidding stop beside Derry and gave one wave of his hand to the nearest of the creatures, which was already only yards away. A bolt of blue light flashed from his hand, and the creature fell, but others followed too close behind. Fae used arrows and magic to take down two more. Derry saw three more appear above the line of woods: huge, dark-skinned things, with heads as long as his arm and wings as wide as a cottage.

"Find cover!" Brian shouted when Shannon and Farrin appeared on the road. He took hold of Derry's arm. "Back by the buildings and better cover! They can carry off a human!"

Derry felt helpless and useless until they reached Shannon, who handed him a sword he must have gotten from the locals. Shannon hadn't even grabbed his own cloak, and his shirt hung open. Derry thought they both ought to be cold, but his friend showed no sign of it.

"What the hell is it this time?" he demanded as the creatures flew closer, long wings flapping with dull thuds of sound.

"Gargoyles," Brian replied, his own bow in hand. He fired two arrows in quick succession. They both hit and another gargoyle went down, but more appeared from out of the tree line. "If they get close, cut their wings so they can't grab you and take off. Beware of their claws, though."

Farrin had gotten some of his own men out with bows, and they were not doing badly either.

"They are old enemies," Brian continued as he sighted another gargoyle and brought it down. "Long since locked out of this realm. Someone, though, must have opened the door and let them back in. If there are too many, the entire land might be in danger. I don't think this is so, though. I think these are the only ones. I can't feel more -- and it's like the demons. They just appeared out of nowhere."

"Someone opened a door," Derry said and lifted his sword as the creatures started getting closer. "And maybe closed the door again because the person didn't want to let too many of them through?"

"Maybe so. Maybe the enemy thought -- thought we'd be weak." Brian dropped the bow, which disappeared in a flash of light and lifted his hand instead. More blue light shot from his fingers, and this time scattered four of the creatures that had swarmed in together, making them all easier targets. Brian grinned as those four went down, but more were on them a moment later.

Derry had never liked to fight with swords, but he'd been trained to use the weapon skillfully along with the other young nobles at court. He'd never imagined he would fight side-by-side with Shannon, who'd had no better love for battles than him. However, having Shannon there made him work all the harder for fear that he would fail, and his friend would fall.

The scent of the gargoyle blood revolted him. Derry looked into the long-muzzled faces of the creatures; their red eyes glared with rage so intense that Derry suddenly felt it like a blow. The gargoyles hated both humans and fae, and they filled the air with the reek of their rage. He sensed some intelligence in these things -- they were not merely animals. However, there was no hope of any kind of truce. He could only fight and hope to win.

Some of his companions took wounds, though, and he felt when a fae died. He almost faltered then, but Brian must have expected it -- he came and stood beside Derry, sorrow in his eyes. He said nothing at first as they fought off two persistent creatures, but once they'd retreated somewhat, Brian dared to put a hand on Derry's arm.

"We mourn the loss, but not during the battle for which our friend gave her life. We must win this, or else her loss is wasted."

"Yes," Derry agreed. "I understand."

"They're backing off," Farrin said as he came to stand beside them. He looked bothered. "I don't think they'll hold back for long, though. Let's get the lot of you to the inn and rest while we can. They're going to come back."

"Yes," Brian agreed. He nodded to Shannon. "Let's get him inside."

"I can manage," Derry said and limped along with them, unsure when he'd strained his leg. He felt drained again.

Brian hurried off in another direction. The fae would have matters to see to now. The thought of having lost one of the fae bothered Derry more than he could say. He had trouble, though, just walking with his friends.

"Is he injured?" Farrin asked, looking at Shannon rather than asking Derry himself, which he found slightly annoying. He hadn't the strength for any stronger emotion or to argue the point. He also didn't argue when Farrin took the sword from his numb fingers and handed it off to someone with orders to have it cleaned. Derry didn't want the scent of that blood to follow him. "I don't think he took any new injury --"

"Only a couple scratches," Shannon said after looking Derry over. He had a hand at Derry's elbow now; he must have been slowing. "Nothing worse. He's weak, Farrin. The time he spent in The Isles nearly killed him."

He hadn't wanted to think about that old trouble -- but as soon as Shannon said the words, Derry felt as though he was being dragged back to the cell.

"Damn." Farrin opened the door to the inn and waved them inside before he followed. Guards stayed at the door. "With all else Derry's involved in, I forgot about his trip to the north. He's been home all winter, and he hasn't yet recovered?"

"No. How could he? There hasn't been much peace, you know. Derry?"

Derry tried to blink away the shadows of another place as they took him to the table by the window. "Alright," he mumbled.

"You look as pale as a ghost again," Shannon said and pushed him into a chair.

Derry looked up at him. For a heartbeat, the face of someone else had overlain Shannon's; a man from the cell had stood there, frowning at him.

Gods don't let it be true! Don't let my thoughts of home be a dream!

"Derry!"

He blinked and blinked again, calling this place back and making it real. A voice in his mind whispered that it wasn't true, though, and that he was still in the cell. The walls of the inn faded for a moment and became grey stone marked with graffiti carved by prisoners long gone. He'd left his name there as well, and he looked for it in the corner --

"Derry!"

Shannon pulled Derry to his feet and shook him this time. He came back with a gasp and blinding headache, but he reached up and stopped Shannon, uncertain if he should curse or thank him. The inn reformed in solid walls around him again, and he saw Farrin watching with eyes large and his face pale.

"I'm all right, I'm all right," Derry insisted and even pulled free from Shannon. "I'm sorry --"

"You need not apologize," Farrin said and pulled a chair over to sit down. "Sit back down before you fall down. Tell me what we can do to help you, lad. I don't want to see that happen to you again."

Derry hadn't considered what that reaction might look like from outside his head. He settled in the chair and gave a sigh of relief just to be still again. Shannon leaned against the edge of the table, looking too weary and worried to care much about his dignity.

"There is nothing that can be done, not just now," Derry admitted and stopping them when they both started to protest. "I suspect this is something I simply have to work out on my own. Or maybe -- maybe the fae can help when we aren't all fighting for survival."

Oddly, he must have said something that made sense. Shannon and Farrin both nodded, and Derry felt as though that darkness retreated a little again. Good. He needed to be more aware of the world so that he didn't make matters worse.

Did that mean he really believed in this reality and not the cell?

They didn't bother to go back to the room and try to rest. Brian arrived to say the gargoyles were still close, and there would be no long rest. They sipped cider and ate cheese and bread, Derry forcing himself to join them because he knew he couldn't keep going without food. Besides, seeing him eat pleased Shannon, and Farrin looked relieved.

When the fae battle cry went up again, none of them were slow to hurry back out. The swords stood by the door, and he took his back up again, trying not to feel weary or to wish this battle had moved on to somewhere else. He followed Shannon and Farrin down the steps and looked around, trying to gauge where they could do the most good --

Something odd. A flash of some magic behind him. Derry started to turn and --

A sharp pain shot through his left shoulder and he stumbled in shock.

He didn't go down.

Chapter Sixteen

Others shouted, a cacophony of noises and a surge of magic --

Shannon, Farrin, and Brian raced towards him, heedless of the gargoyles sailing above the village. Derry realized that his feet no longer touched the ground. Shock kept the realization of the pain away, but he knew something had grabbed him, claws sinking deep into his left shoulder.

The gargoyle must have been hidden by magic, huddled on the roof of the inn. He understood that much of what had happened and even knew there was more magic now, pushing the creature upward. Derry couldn't tell if the magic came from the beast or not. He didn't care. Derry tried to bring his sword around, but the agony through his shoulder nearly sent him unconscious. He still jabbed upwards into the creature's belly, and it howled in protest but didn't let him go. He jabbed a second time, but he couldn't hold on to the sword, and it tumbled away as they passed the edge of the village.

He could see the town laid out below him like an extremely well-painted map. The gargoyle circled upwards, gaining height as its broad, leathery wings flapped. The landscape looked like a drawing laid out in squares of fields and lines of trees. Just to the north, the direction they turned, he could see the vast stretch of forest.

Pure, bright blue magic hit the gargoyle in the right wing. The gargoyle -- and Derry -- dropped several yards and stopped so suddenly, Derry feared the talons would tear through his shoulder, and he'd fall. The creature found his faltering wingbeat again and kept going, though he didn't fly higher this time. That the beast was not doing well was obvious, but Derry didn't want to be dropped. He wished for the creature to land and let him go. Wished it very hard, hoping there was some fae power in the thought.

They began to descend, but they were over the forest now, and low enough that the tops of trees battered his legs. He tried to spot a glade, wanting down --

The gargoyle gave a hiss of anger.

And let him go.

Derry didn't have time for more than a heartbeat of panic before he crashed into the rough bough of an old pine. Fragrant needles sprayed everywhere, twigs snapping as he seemed to bounce. Derry hadn't fallen far; he grabbed at the tree slowed the drop, though he tumbled past the first, weak branch and kept falling, grabbing at the pine's outstretched arms.

Slowed. Derry's hands were torn from the rough wood and needles, but he still felt a surge of hope. He would survive the fall -- what happened afterward, he couldn't say. Just get down to the ground.

His shoulder sent a wave of agony through his body every time he tried to catch a tight hold of anything. He managed to stop for a few heartbeats on one branch, but it cracked, and he plunged downward again --

Down to the ground. Derry landed in a pile of old needles and stared upward through the broken trail he'd left behind in the tree. Gargoyles circled high overhead, and their angry shouts came too loudly in the silence of the forest.

They could not reach him here though the trees. He was safe, at least from them.

Derry stayed there, fighting to remain conscious and knowing that any movement was going to send agony through his shoulder and probably the rest of his body. He knew there were other dangers in the forest, even if the gargoyles couldn't reach him.

The gargoyle had specifically come for him and had been taking him somewhere else. The remembrance of flying almost made him ill, but he fought that back as well. Derry hoped the fae would come and get him. Would they have trouble finding him here in the woods? That they were not already here made Derry worry about what they might be facing elsewhere. Derry dared not wait for their help, so he slowly -- very slowly -- sat up. Every part of his body ached, but he could breathe, and he could move. Getting to his feet was not easy, but Derry found the personal resolve to do something to save himself.

Once on his feet, Derry stood with his back against the rough bark of the pine tree. Everything still appeared to move around him, and much of the world went precariously out of focus. He could do nothing for his wounds, though he did lift his left arm and secured it as best he could at his waist so that it didn't bounce quite so much. A few deep breaths later and he was ready to move.

But which way? He tried to feel out the magic he should recognize as Riverton and the fae -- but magic appeared to be strong in this forest, like a blanket of power everywhere around him.

Derry knew he would have to trust his instincts on this one. He looked right and left and then up at the gargoyles who still swept overhead. The right called to him more than left, so he took a couple steps that way, paused while his head pounded at the little effort, and then willed himself to move onward.

Derry quickly learned to watch his feet to avoid falling and trust his sense of direction. He had to keep moving. Eventually, he would reach the edge of the forest or find a stream he could follow. The trick was not to wait for something to spot him, either friend or foe. Derry would hope for a friend, but his luck didn't run that way these days.

The gargoyles were not directly overhead now, he realized. He thought maybe they couldn't find him in this vast mix of magic either, which gave him some hope. Something in these woods protected him, he thought. He dared to catch hold of that hope.

And he kept walking.

Sunset neared. Even as slowly as he moved, he must have gone at least a couple miles. Should he camp?

No. Derry knew that if he fell asleep now, he might not awaken, even if he sensed danger coming closer. There was also the danger of ... nightmares about other things. No. Keep moving for as long as he could.

Derry realized that his arm didn't hurt as badly as it had at first, nor did it still bleed. He took that as a sign of his link to the fae. That gave him more trust in the direction he had chosen to go, as well. Good. The others would be searching for him. Derry forced himself to keep moving, resting only with his back to a tree and never daring to sit down. The light shifted through the leaves with spots of bright colors here and there in a world gone mostly grayish green as night neared. He followed a deer trail for a while but somehow lost it and had to stumble through more brush that made walking difficult.

The woods seemed uncommonly silent. He'd seen no animals and hadn't even heard birds flying off. With the gargoyles sweeping overhead, he suspected anything wise had gone to ground and would do his best to keep out of notice.

Derry kept on.

He heard something move behind him, the slightest brush against a bush, and he spun, his heart pounding harder. The world went nearly dark, and he grabbed at the nearest tree, stifling a moan at the movement of his arm. If he went to his knees, he didn't have a chance --

After several shaky breaths, Derry found nothing behind him. He stared for another dozen heartbeats, but whatever had been there had gone still and silent. Something slight, he thought.

No gargoyle, at least. Derry finally pushed away, but he couldn't decide which way he'd been going. The frustration nearly brought a shout of anger from him, but he calmed and chose the direction that seemed most promising. It probably didn't matter if he kept moving.

Something moved in front of him, like a breeze through the bush. He felt magic, though like none he'd ever known before --

A young man stepped away from the towering trees where no one had stood a moment before. Dressed in green that might have been woven leaves, his long hair wood brown and his skin tan -- and magical. Oh yes, very magical -- but this one was not fae. The magic felt oddly pure and so potent that Derry wanted to back away from that warmth. He didn't have the strength to move.

"The woods are empty," the stranger said, his voice soft, though it carried well. He waved a hand towards the trees. "I want them back! Where have you sent them?"

"I didn't send them away," Derry replied softly. He bowed his head in belated politeness and locked his knees in hopes that he didn't fall. The stranger meant the animals, Derry realized. He'd wondered where they'd gone as well.

"You didn't?" The stranger frowned, and his hand moved. For a moment, Derry feared for his life, but he only felt a slight tendril of magic brush against him. Odd magic, but nothing dangerous. The stranger nodded finally, though a frown came to his face. "No, it is not you. There is something dark in the woods. It follows you."

Derry felt a shiver take him, and his mind swirled as he tried to sort out what to do. Brian had said something powerful lived in the woods, but he had thought it would be much farther away. "I am sorry the animals are gone. I -- I just want to get back to my friends. The darkness will follow me away, right? I can take it out of the woods, and the other creatures will return?"

"Yes." The man stared with eyes unnaturally green and bright in the falling shadows. "You wish to go to the humans? The fae?"

"Yes. Both. Either."

The stranger tilted his head and then looked up as a gargoyle swept overhead. "Found you."

"No friend of mine," Derry said. He looked frantically around, trying to guess the best direction to go. Derry didn't want to find himself trapped in here, with gargoyles in every direction and this magical being not happy with his presence. "I must go --"

"They helped scare my friends away." The words came like a whisper of a breeze, and leaves trembled around them. The gargoyle gave another shout and swept closer.

The young man pointed a hand at it the creature, and it tumbled, dead, to the ground.

Oh yes, very dangerous, this one. When the grass-green eyes turned back to him again, Derry fought aside his own panic. He couldn't run, and if this being, whatever he was, found Prince Derry SanOsen wanting, he would simply be dead like the gargoyle. The stranger didn't look angry -- but then he hadn't looked angry when he killed the gargoyle, either.

"Those creatures do not belong in my woods," he said.

And neither do I.

Derry gave a bow of his head. "I'll go, and they'll follow me. I'll do what I can to make sure the ones who belong here return. I am sorry for what's happened."

Derry took a step backward and another one before he gave one more bow and turned to walk away. He had gone several yards before he trusted that he might have survived the strange encounter. His shoulder ached again, and his body trembled. The night neared, but his sight didn't seem to fail him in the dark as he had feared it would. Another gift of the fae blood, he suspected. That meant he could keep moving. Gargoyles swept close again, no doubt called by the shout of the original, but he thought if he could stay within the thicker stands of trees they would not --

"How will you destroy this evil in my forest?"

The stranger stood a few steps in front of him.

Derry was in no condition for such a surprise. He gave one startled cry and stumbled backward, falling -- and darkness took him.

Chapter Seventeen

Derry drifted in a dark place for a while, his thoughts distant, and a sense of calm *almost* overlaid everything else. He did not want to return to the dangerous world filled with pain and enemies, but to remain in the darkness was a coward's retreat. Derry slowly pushed his mind through the depths, aware, in the end, of only one thing over all else.

"Damn, that hurts," he whispered.

"If you were more of the wild, I could help you."

Derry's eyes flew open, blinking at the dull light, and focusing on the stranger who knelt on the ground beside him. The man watched intently on Derry's face, as though he had never seen such a creature before.

That was an unsettling thought, and one Derry simply did not need to deal with right now.

"I'm sorry," Derry whispered. He somehow got his good arm under him and pushed upward so that, after a couple tries, he could sit. "I did not mean to --"

"Mean to be injured? I imagine not. Peace, Changeling. I know you are not the evil infesting my forest. I have studied both you and the trouble more carefully now."

The stranger seemed a little more coherent, though no less scary. Derry heard gargoyles not far away, too. This was not where he wanted to be.

"I'll -- I'll go now," Derry said. He got to his feet without any help. His odd companion stood as well, eyeing him with some curiosity. "I don't know yet what I'll do to help get the animals back, but I'll do whatever I can. I promise."

A true promise made with a touch of his fae power. Derry said those words with a full understanding of what he'd done. It was a little thing, really, since he would have tried to help anyway. The wild one looked him in the face. Even though this stranger looked human -- or fae -- Derry sensed an otherness that unsettled him again.

"I will go with you to see you safe," the man said.

"Oh no, that's alright," Derry replied and tried to slow the pounding of his heart. He did not want to walk the woods with this dire creature who could kill with a wave of his hand. "I'll be fine --"

"I will go with you. And you may call me Wild One. This is who and what I am."

There was clearly no arguing the point. Derry bowed his head in acceptance and glanced around, trying to decide the quickest way out of these woods -- at least the quickest way that did not include the talons of a gargoyle. He felt a little stronger again. Apparently, the rest -- and the panic -- helped.

"This way." Wild One tentatively put a hand on Derry's arm. "There. You are the first human I have ever touched. This was not such a fearful thing. This way."

Derry didn't argue. They walked in silence for some distance, and gradually Derry's calm returned. So did his curiosity.

"What are you?" Derry finally asked.

"I am the woods: the spirit of this place, the heart, and the guardian. Sometimes the fae call me a god."

Derry hadn't really needed to hear that last word, but he wasn't surprised. He fell silent again, sure that anything he said now would only add to the feeling that he was far, far out of his realm of understanding. He didn't slow, even though he had started getting dizzy. That might have been more from standing with Wild One, though, who radiated magic like a hearth gave off warmth. If Derry had been more fae, it probably would have helped.

Gargoyles yelled in fury somewhere behind them. Derry couldn't see their shadows in the dark night, but he suspected the two of them hadn't been spotted. Derry hoped they didn't even realize the direction he took, which seemed possible since they passed almost silently through the world.

"How far?" Derry finally asked, trying not to gasp at each step.

"To your friends? To the enemy who follows you? Nearly equal. Your friends are frantic. The enemy, which is not the gargoyles, but rather what controls them, is like water: impossible to grasp or hold still except in extremes. I would freeze this thing if it would hold still, but, unlike you, it wisely fears to come near me."

"Should I fear you?"

"Yes. Even so, I will do you no harm, neither will I hurt your frantic friends. You have done no evil here. The dark thing that sends my companions running -- and who does not care what damage it does to the woods -- that one I will not spare if I chance to catch it."

That was a promise of his own, and Derry bowed his head in thanks. He could hope that the trouble would end that way, and everything no longer in his hands. Derry wanted an end to the war and tried not to think about future battles and whatever might be preying on the lands.

As he walked with Wild One, the path grew easier. Bushes

moved out of the way, and limbs lifted above their heads. It did so without a sign from Wild One. The world simply moved around him.

"Humans don't come into these woods, nor do the fae. This is a sacred place, a sanctuary for the creatures who are hunted beyond my narrow lands. I give you leave to be here, so do not fear. If you had been a hunter, though, you would not have left.

"I never liked hunting much, even before I had fae blood. Humans rarely do so wantonly," he said. They might as well have the conversation. "And sometimes it even helps to keep the population in check. Too many deer can mean some will starve."

"This is true," Wild One agreed. "But even so, it does not happen in my woods."

"No, sir, not here."

"You are an odd man, I think."

"It must be the fae blood," he said.

"And you were never odd before your encounter with the fae? I can see what she has done to you, the Queen of the Fae. I even see why, and I think her wise. However, she must have seen an oddness in you from the start, Prince Derry SanOsen."

Derry felt his mouth went dry. He had not given Wild One his name, but then he supposed a God who knew what the fae had done months ago wouldn't be much bothered by such a trivial thing.

"Yes, I have always been odd, I suppose," Derry agreed. They could just talk because that made the encounter seem less strange, just the words between two passing strangers. Maybe that was good; he could say things to Wild One that he might not say to Shannon, who would take everything too much to heart. "My parents died when I was young, which was very difficult for me. I felt lost and desolate, but the King, who is also my uncle, took me in. I have been a ward of the King for most of my life. You know about kings?"

"Yes."

Derry looked around, uncertain what more he should say about his strange life. He thought there were far more critical discussions they might have.

"If I did not have any fae blood, being alone in the woods at night would have been scary, even without the gargoyles chasing me," Derry admitted. "Humans fear the wilds because unlike you and me, they cannot feel the world around them."

"And this is why killing innocent creatures and cutting down the woods does not bother them."

"Yes. Humans can only see what is around them. Sometimes it frightens them even when it shouldn't, and they kill out of a reflex to survive."

"Ah. If humans cannot feel the life, then killing is only an action with no consequence."

Derry agreed, as much as he thought Wild One understood. "May I tell you something more about humans?"

"Yes."

"Even if you come to understand mankind, you can never truly trust them."

Derry had startled his companion, and for a moment, the wind blew harder, and the ground trembled. Derry nearly went down, but Wild One took him by the arm -- a gentle touch, but the power that coursed through him still felt like fire. Wild One did not hold on for long, but it took a few deep breaths to get the feel of such pure power out of his battered body.

"How can you live, not trusting each other?" Wild One finally asked. Derry thought he caught a hint of sorrow for the humans.

"I have friends among the humans whom I trust with everything, even my life. Others I know I cannot trust because they are envious of my place in court -- of the power I hold. I am the nephew of the King --"

"The King gave a proclamation to protect the forest. He is not our enemy. Once, I even spoke to the King when he came to walk the woods."

Derry took several more steps in silence while he thought about an ancient legend. King Alain, almost three hundred years ago, had spoken with the spirit of the forest as he made a tour of his lands. The King later proclaimed the entire forest in this area to be held in perpetuity for the wild creatures living there. Derry remembered how he had thought it odd no one had challenged that proclamation, even centuries later. Now he knew why. The woods would never feel safe to humans, and if some thought to settle here anyway, he suspected Wild One would have handled that problem.

Derry looked at his companion and gave a slight nod. "There is a different king now," Derry offered.

"Yes, of course. Humans are like the other creatures who pass so quickly through the world. Is he a good king, too?"

"Very good. So are the King's heir and his younger son."

"But there are others who are not," Wild One surmised. His eyes narrowed, making him look more mature. Wild One looked at him again and Derry thought he could see connections forming in his face. Understanding seemed to surprise Wild One. "Some humans do not trust what they can't control, and therefore we clash still over the forest. They will never understand the wild that they cannot touch the way I can -- or even the way the fae can."

"Yes," Derry agreed. The conversation seemed too dire. He almost welcomed the sound of a gargoyle not far away.

"Something powerful compels them to follow you," Wild One said, glancing at the dark sky behind them. "The gargoyles no longer have no reason of their own. In their minds, there is but one quest, and that is to find you. Whatever controls them, it is not of nature. It is not something that I can track, but it drives them on."

"To get me." Derry put a hand to his shoulder, trying to measure strength. Even the slight touch sent a needle of pain through his arm and chest. The world spun around him again and he started to feel ill once more, but he kept moving with Wild One. Odd how his life kept taking such strange turns. He stopped trying to decide why. As Derry had grown older, he'd discovered that far more cruelty existed than he had ever imagined. He had attempted, in his little ways, to make things better for people, no matter what their rank. Perhaps that had brought him here.

Derry couldn't hold the thought for long, though, and turned his attention back to merely putting one foot in front of the other. Thoughts about his life came to him, disjointed and confusing. Then the memory of the cell tried to take him, like a raven sweeping down on him --

"No," Wild One said. "You do not wish to go there."

The memory retreated, though it held back like a cloud of smoke hiding a blaze that might soon take him.

One step after another. Walk. Nothing else mattered.

"We are not far," Wild One said.

Derry didn't know how long he had drifted in his own thoughts. He suspected the two had traveled a considerable distance, though looking around, he thought that this could have been mere yards from where they'd started. The feeling that he could have been lost in these woods forever nearly took him -- but then he wondered if that would have been so bad, as long as the gargoyles didn't reach him.

Derry ached and felt weak, and he didn't think that came entirely from his injuries. Had they traveled through the night? Was this another day?

He heard voices and quelled a sigh of relief, for fear of how Wild One would take the reaction. Wild One seemed unbothered by the sound. The others had to know they walked in a place they should not be. Derry could feel it himself, though perhaps that was his link to the fae again. He didn't think so, though.

"The others draw near. They see the gargoyles and follow, expecting to find you." Wild One looked up at the trees and somewhere distant came the cry of the creatures again. He had hoped they'd given up by now.

"I am grateful for your help. I would not have made it without you."

"This is true," Wild One agreed and finally helped Derry to lean against a tree. "Wait here. They are not far, and they worry about what is in the woods. Wise, for humans."

Derry looked at Wild One, measuring the look on his face. There was nothing there of emotion that he could have understood, he realized.

"I will do my best to help get your friends back," Derry finally said.

"I relieve you of that promise. You have trouble enough," Wild One said, which was not exactly reassuring.

"Nevertheless, I will do it because it is right. Besides, whatever chased your friends from the woods is my enemy, too. I will fight anyway -- but even so, I'll try my best to make certain this trouble follows me so that your friends can return safely."

The Wild One tilted his head, looking at Derry as though he had become some bizarre creature again.

"I have no magic to heal humans, and you are not fae enough for me to help more than I already have."

"My friends are close by. They'll help me. If you want to leave now, I understand. You need not deal with the humans."

"You are not what I expected."

Derry started to answer, but the bushes moved to his right, and figures came into the little open area. Shannon, Brian, and Farrin stopped, stone-still, starring at Derry and his companion. Brian's eyes went wide as he dared another step forward.

"Lord of the Woods," Brian whispered and won a regal nod from Wild One. "We are honored by your presence."

"He brought me back to find you," Derry said.

Brian looked shocked and bowed, as though he couldn't find the right words to say. Shannon and Farrin took their cues from their fae companion, realizing something very strange was happening here. Farrin looked worried, but Shannon didn't look too surprised at all. They both bowed.

"My friends who live in the woods have fled before the evil that hunted Prince Derry SanOsen," Wild One said and glanced from one to the other, clearly weighing each. "Derry says that he will try to get the creatures back. Will you help him, both human and fae?"

"Absolutely." Brian nodded vigorously. Shannon copied the move, and Farrin did as well, though he looked less sure.

"Those who help Prince Derry have my blessing."

Wild One turned, walked away into the woods, and disappeared into the shadows so quickly it seemed either unnatural or far too much a part of nature. Derry thought there should have been things to ask Wild One. How would they get the animals to return? The fae might know. First, though, they would need to lead the gargoyles and any other enemy away.

Derry stared where Wild One had gone for a moment, and then looked back at his friends. The tree at his back didn't feel all that substantial suddenly, and his knees refused to lock --

"Shan--non --"

He started to fall, and Shannon leapt forward and caught him. It might have been less painful to hit the ground. Nevertheless, he felt grateful to have his friends here, and to feel safe with them, even with the enemy still hunting. He had not been safe with Wild One, though he was very grateful for the help.

Somewhere a gargoyle gave a cry of attack, cut off in mid-sound. Derry suspected another tumbled lifeless to the ground. One less enemy to deal with now.

"Derry! God and Goddess, I thought we had lost you this time! You are going to drive me crazy!" Shannon said and pulled him closer.

"Not my fault," Derry protested with barely enough strength to say those words.

"No, of course not," Shannon relented and gently helped Derry sit on the ground and lean against him. "I'm sorry. Can you help him, Brian? His shoulder is torn up this time."

"And I fell through the tr-trees," Derry said, looking up at the sky. Oh, how that memory came back suddenly. Flying. Falling. "Fell a l-long way. The gargoyles -- never gave up. I was lost --"

"Easy," Brian ordered and knelt beside him. "Easy. Let's see what I can do. We must get back to the village soon. They still face danger."

Derry winced as Brian laid fingers gently over the worst of his wounds. He didn't look to see the injury, but Derry knew if he had still been fully human, he would never have lived to reach this far. Brian's healing magic felt warm and soft, and he let it take him away....

Chapter Eighteen

"**...** f ar, far older than fae or man. Keeper of the Woods is the title we gave him in myth long ago. No one seeks him out, but we know he takes different shapes to suit the need of the time. He does not come to the aid of humans -- or fae, for that matter. God and Goddess! When I saw him standing with Derry, I didn't know what to think!"

Derry listened to Brian, his eyes closed, and drifted in and out during points of the conversation as he tried to ignore the constant bouncing. He wanted to know more about Wild One and anything else the young fae could teach him. Derry needed to learn -- but what he caught was only disjointed bits of information from Brian and parts of conversations between Shannon and Farrin. They rested for a little while, blessed stillness, but then they moved on again.

The others fell silent after a while, but that didn't help. Derry wanted to hear them speak, to know he wasn't alone. Unable to still rest, Derry opened his eyes to see the trees moving oddly above him. He tried to sit up, only to find they had him on a stretcher of some sort, and movement nearly sent him toppling into the dirt.

"Easy, Derry!" Shannon warned from the area above his head. "Be still, or you'll tear open the wounds again."

"Shouldn't. . . shouldn't be carrying me," Derry protested and tried to get up again.

"Stay still!" Farrin ordered from the other end of the stretcher, and with far more force than Shannon used. It worked. Derry went still, mostly at the shock of being ordered. Few had ever done that in his adult life.

"We have to carry you, Derry," Shannon explained softly, though he grunted a bit as they went up a slight embankment. "We must get back to the village as quickly as possible."

"Trouble? Stupid question. There's always trouble," Derry said, breathless and trying to fight back the pain that came with each bouncing step.

"Trouble enough," Farrin answered with a growl. The anger in his old friend's voice unsettled Derry again, who wanted calm and to feel safe for a little while. "Whatever is making this trouble had no reason to turn it on my people!"

"My -- my fault," Derry whispered.

"Yours?" Farrin demanded, looking toward Derry with a snarl on his face.

"Not yours, Derry," Shannon offered and paused, catching his breath. Farrin must have been fueled by anger because he had no trouble with the terrain. "Farrin, he thinks every evil happening is suddenly his fault, but he didn't start this war. We're lucky he came back in time to help us fight it."

"I'll be honest, Shannon SanSota," Farrin said, looking over his shoulder to where his friend stood. "I don't trust this magic. It's not the human way."

"You can trust the fae," Shannon countered, his voice starting to take on a sting of anger his own, which was rare to hear. "They came to the aid of your people. Do you think you could have won your battle against those demons without them?"

"Magic attracts magic. I think there wouldn't have been a battle without the fae."

"You're right. It wouldn't have been a battle -- it would have been a massacre," Shannon replied with a snarl that bordered on rage.

Farrin's eyes narrowed, and he returned the glare.

"Please," Derry whispered.

Farrin looked down at Derry, and his face lost the cast of anger in one breath. He blinked and frowned. "We don't need any more enemies," Farrin admitted with a rueful shake of his head. "I don't know why I'm looking for more trouble."

"You are looking ... for an enemy you can face as a human," Derry replied, glad to have the trouble settled, as well as for the few moments while they remained still.

Farrin blinked and looked back at him, surprised. "When the hell did you get so wise, Derry SanOsen? You were the wildest of the boys."

Derry's throat constricted with fear as the dank, fetid darkness of the cell inched closer again. "They tamed me in the north."

Derry had started to tremble, although not from pain or weakness this time. He felt the darkness as though it stood behind a cloud, waiting, and patient for his weak moments. Now the memory tried to spring into him like something alive, to take hold with all the despair Derry had felt before he came home. Derry hadn't expected the memory to hit this hard; he could see the cell too clearly in the corner of his mind. It grew, trying to take over his sight, and he cried out, shoving it back again.

"What the hell?" Farrin demanded, his voice starting to take on a note of anger again. Farrin had never liked anything he didn't understand -- Derry grabbed hold of the thought, pulling himself closer to reality again.

If this was place in the magical woodlands could be real.

"Not now!" Shannon ordered though Derry couldn't decide if the order was meant for him or for Farrin. He tried to stop the darkness from coming closer, his hands moving against something that was not solid. He didn't want to upset Shannon. "Put the stretcher down!"

"Shannon, I apologize for my comments about the fae," Farrin replied. He didn't begin to lower the stretcher, and Derry felt as though he was caught between two walls of anger. "I wasn't even considering Derry's connection to them. I'll help you carry him, and I won't --"

"It's nothing to do with the fae. Put him down. He needs to be still and calm for a bit. It's because of that damned cell in Fairfall."

Derry saw Farrin's face -- the anger displaced by fear and sadness. Derry suspected that Farrin had looked to have his friend back, but Derry wasn't the same man. Derry closed his eyes and tried to remember the Derry from before his journey north. He didn't want to have died and been reborn in that cell, a different person. He didn't want to be the person who would have been created in such a place.

They did finally lower him to the hard ground. Derry put his hands on the earth, trying to make this place more real than the one in his mind. He thought Shannon and Farrin still spoke, but he had lost his connection to them, and the darkness of the cell tried to push in like something alive biting at his mind.

"Shannon," Derry whispered, reaching for him this time -- not to stop him from saying more, but to hold on to something real that he knew wasn't part of the cell. It was stupid and childish, but he desperately needed the contact.

Shannon put a hand under Derry's shoulder and helped him sit up. Derry took several deep breaths. He had trouble enough in these woods where no human should have been walking. He supposed that was part of Farrin's problem, in fact. They had to move on. Derry had to get control, but it wasn't easy. Nothing seemed real, not even the dirt beneath his hands as he clutched at it. Reality only came in little waves, like an ocean rolling across the land, and he was drowning in it.

"Madness," he finally whispered, lifting his head.

"Derry?" Shannon asked softly, still beside him.

"Madness. This is driving me to madness."

"You're exhausted and injured," Farrin replied from somewhere to the left. Standing guard, Derry hoped. "And you're under considerable pressure and stress."

"And I'm going mad," Derry added, daring a glance at Shannon.

"Along with the rest of us," Shannon replied, and sounded sincere. Derry wasn't sure if those words should comfort him, though he suspected, at least for Shannon, they were accurate enough. He'd pulled his friend into this mess, and now he didn't know how to get any of them out of it. "Peace, Derry. Just remember who -- and what you -- are. We need you. The cell is far away. You won't go back."

"I don't have to go back." He swayed a little and the darkness seeped in around him. "I never left it."

"Damn," Farrin whispered and sounded shaken this time. "Shannon, he needs help. He needs rest --"

"He needs green fields, bright sun, and peace," Shannon replied. He drew Derry back to his feet. "But you and I can't give those to him, least of all peace. First, we must defeat this enemy that stalks the land. He needs allies, Farrin. And you need his help."

"I know, I know. It was madness all my own that made me say those things about the fae. I hope you both can forgive me."

"It's forgotten," Derry said. He glanced around seeing the forest now and hardly any of the cell. He frowned again.

"Where's Brian?"

"Gone ahead to tell the others we found you and are heading back." Farrin stared into the shadows. "It's going to be dark before we reach the village."

"That far?"

"The gargoyle took you a long way," Shannon said. "Even with the Lord of the Woods bringing you back a good distance, we've several miles yet to go."

"Flew," Derry recalled and shuddered for a whole new reason.

"Easy," Shannon implored. "I know this sounds stupid but try not to think about it."

"Not stupid. The voice of sanity."

Farrin looked uncertain at the words, but Shannon knew enough to smile at the small jest. He also noticed how Shannon glanced nervously around at the shadowed bushes and tall trees. They didn't dare stay in one place for too long. The gargoyles, if nothing else, might still find them.

"Time to go," Derry said and tried not to sound discouraged.

"Let's get you back on the stretcher," Shannon suggested and nodded to the two limbs and capes they had somehow tied together.

"No, let me walk for a while. I need to get my feet under me again."

"You've taken a serious wound, Derry --"

"The Lord of the Woods and Brian both helped. It's not as serious as it could have been."

"As it should have been," Farrin replied and looked him over again. "And it wasn't just their magic that saved you, was it?"

"If I hadn't had fae blood of my own, I wouldn't be alive now. What does that mean to you, Farrin?" He stared into his friend's face and saw Farrin blink several times.

"It means I had better get damned used to changes in the world," Farrin replied and gave a nervous little smile to Shannon. "You don't have to glare, SanSota. And take that hand off your dagger. You know you could never take me, blade-to-blade."

Derry looked back at Shannon and found that he did, indeed, have his hand on the weapon, ready to draw. "Shannon!"

"Sorry. I'm nervous." Shannon took his hand away from the hilt and nodded when Farrin gathered up the stretcher, though Shannon didn't take a hand from Derry's arm. "Too many enemies, too much strangeness. No, I don't like it either, Farrin. The changes in Derry don't bother me -- he's still the wild prince we knew. What you see as changes are only brought on by illness and injury. The fae blood hasn't changed his soul. What I don't like, though, is this strange war we're fighting."

"Yes," Farrin agreed and shouldered the stretcher. "And from all I've heard, and what you've told me, we're lucky Derry has this link to the fae."

"Very lucky," Derry answered for himself as they started to walk. He glanced around the woods -- still too quiet and empty. He could have wished for some animals to give him the word of what was going on, even if it would have upset Farrin.

As far as he could tell, they were the only ones walking the woods. He didn't even hear so much as an insect.

"What can the fae do for us, then?" Farrin asked. He didn't sound belligerent, or at least not any more than usual. Farrin had always been a bit short-tempered.

"This is a magic war, Farrin, and something has turned dark magic on magic-less humans. We need the fae to hold back the enemy since we can't fight on their terms."

"And who is the enemy?"

"I don't know. Even the fae haven't been able to locate the source of this war. It hides with powerful magic."

"This isn't the kind of answer I like to hear," Farrin replied.

"There's no pleasing some people," Shannon said, and Farrin laughed.

"Seriously, Derry," Farrin continued as they walked along the narrow deer trail. Shannon moved in front and Farrin fell behind Derry; they meant to keep him in sight. "I like to think if I'm allied with the fae, that I can count on it meaning something in this war."

"Like how they saved your village?" Shannon asked.

"True again. I've grown short-sighted in my old age. I want to know what they can do for me right now. I tend to lose the past and future in thoughts like those."

"Right now, I'm hoping they can come and guide us out of these woods by the quickest route," Derry replied. He peered up into the darkening sky. "Have we lost the gargoyles completely?"

"Afraid so," Shannon said with apparent misgivings.

"There's something wrong with not having those misbegotten creatures from hell hovering over us?" Farrin asked and sounded very confused this time.

"They haven't given up, and yet they're not here," Derry said, glancing up at the darkening sky and hoping for a sign. "That means they're waiting for us somewhere ahead. Or they're busy elsewhere."

"Back at the village." Farrin's pace quickened for a few steps, a mumble of curses barely beneath his breath.

"Slow down. The villagers have the fae -- which is why the fae aren't here," Shannon reminded him. "Forgive me, but that's better protection than the three of us could give them."

"We do need to hurry, Shannon," Derry said with a glance into the shadows. "I don't want to be here in the woods at night."

"There's nothing left to hurt us," Farrin said. "Even the Lord of the Woods said so."

"He said all his friends had gone," Derry corrected. "Something sent them running from the woods, and I had the impression it was not entirely the gargoyles."

"There you go, making me feel better again." Farrin drew his sword and then looked down at the blade with a shake of his head. "Well, for all the good this is going to do us."

"Makes me feel better," Derry admitted. He finally put a hand to his wounded shoulder and slowed, the other two setting their pace to his. "I'll be lucky if I can handle a dagger if it comes to a battle. Damn, I wish Brian would show up again. I don't like the feel of this place."

"Don't like it as a human or don't like it as a fae?" Shannon asked.

"I think he doesn't like it because he's just the side of sane," Farrin said with a snort. "Human or fae doesn't matter. Or do you feel perfectly safe here?"

"Ah. Good point," Shannon conceded with a quick bow of his head. "I expected Brian to return, but that he hasn't makes me wonder what else is going on out there. I don't want to face anything like we did in Keirkell."

"There the fae were driven away by something that consumed life," Derry reminded him. "But it's not like that here -- something more subtle, which makes me uneasy. I think if I were wilder, I'd be fleeing from these woods with the rest of the creatures."

"Why would anything waste the power on something so trivial?" Farrin asked, glancing at the trees. "Why send rabbits and jays fleeing?"

"It's not trivial to the fae," Derry corrected. "The animals of the wild converse with the fae -- so the fae are robbed of any knowledge their little spies might gather."

"Which means the true enemy is somewhere in these woods," Shannon added with a quick glance around them again.

"You spend too much time with Derry," Farrin said with a sigh. "You're starting to depress me, too, Shannon."

Derry laughed. The three began to move faster while the darkness of night came too quickly.

Chapter Nineteen

Derry felt as though something dark and evil held its breath, watching them as they pressed on through the sunset and into the dark night. They dared not stop. They must have nearly reached the edge of the woods by now! He couldn't have flown that far with the damned gargoyle!

Shannon fell --

"Don't panic. I didn't see the limb," Shannon said and got back to his feet.

"Let's rest," Farrin said. He looked around with a nod. "We have a little open area here, so we're less likely to be surprised. It can't be more than a couple hours until dawn, either. I want to see where we are. I can't even clearly see the moon tonight to reckon our direction."

The cloud cover had created a diffuse gray light with no sight of the moon or stars.

"Best to stop," Derry agreed and wondered why they hadn't before this, except for their usual stubbornness.

Shannon started to argue. He changed his mind and settled on a log by the trail. The trees formed an uneven circle, and they were almost in the middle. It seemed as safe a place as any on this strange night.

Derry doubted either of his friends slept any more than he did. They dared no fire, which might draw unwanted attention. Besides, he didn't want to offend the Wild One. So, they huddled close together, and Derry felt more human for the contact. Farrin finally got the cloaks free from the stretcher, too. The extra warmth helped.

The rest helped ease aches and fears about too many things Derry could not control, let alone fix. He felt better just to know he was not alone --

The whisper of a falling leaf --

Derry couldn't be sure if his friends heard, or if his sudden surge to his feet brought them up as well. No matter. Both had swords in hand, and Shannon carefully handed Derry his dagger. Derry couldn't have handled anything heavier, so he was happy not to be entirely helpless.

Derry listened to the silence, and after a moment, he thought he heard breathing and took some comfort from that sound. If the enemy breathed, it could be defeated and die.

"If you are a friend, show yourself now," Derry said, lowering his dagger, though he kept it in hand.

Something moved, and leaves rustled to the right. They turned, weapons shifting and ready, but the sound stopped again.

"What the hell is out there?" Farrin demanded, his eyes narrowed, and his sword moving slightly as he tried to track the enemy.

Derry felt something cold at the back of his neck and spun in time to see something leap straight at them from across the little glade. He pushed his friends down and tumbled over them, mindful of the swords --

A shape swept over them, human-like but white and filmy and trailing bitter cold in its wake.

"What the hell is that!" Farrin demanded.

"It's dangerous. That's all we need to know," Shannon replied and won a grunt of agreement from Farrin as the two scrambled back to their feet. Derry moved a little more slowly in their wake.

It came back: faceless, elongating and twisting --

Shannon swept his sword forward as the thing -- ghost or worse -- came close to them again. Though seeming to lack any substance, the creature still screamed as the sword cut into the body, and it disappeared into a fine mist that fell like frost on the ground.

Shannon gave a quiet moan and went to his knees.

"Shannon!" Derry forgot all else and leapt to his friend, dropping to his knees as well. Farrin remained standing, though, his weapon ready -- for whatever good it would do if the attacker took injury, too.

Shannon dropped his sword and grabbed his wrist with his left hand. His right hand had turned bright red and bled from a dozen long cuts, as though the skin had cracked and broken open.

"Cold," Derry realized, already cutting a bandage from his own battered shirt.

"Very ... cold," Shannon agreed, his face pale, and his mouth clamping shut against the pain as Derry dealt with the injuries. He looked around, alert again. "Quickly Derry. There's still something out there in the woods."

"I'm on guard, Shannon," Farrin offered. "Not that it isn't wise to be quick anyway. Something knows where to find us."

"Amazing. I don't feel tired at all anymore," Shannon said, hissing a little in pain, and Derry tied off the cloth. Derry suspected the wounds went higher up under the tunic sleeve, but he didn't ask. Now wasn't the time to deal with anything worse. "Let's go."

Derry got to his feet without Shannon's help. Shannon

stood on his own as well, grabbing up the sword with his left hand, though he gave the weapon a dubious look. His friend looked pale but steady, and Derry noted how Farrin appeared worried as he glanced at them and knowing he couldn't carry both out if they collapsed.

Derry would not fail. He simply would not do anything that risked Shannon's life -- at least more than being with him put his friend at risk. They moved quickly down another deer track and into the deeper woods, Farrin taking the lead. Did this path lead where they wanted to go? Derry couldn't be certain anymore.

The silence felt both welcome and oppressive now. Derry knew his enemy wouldn't give up so easily. That little battle had been nothing compared to the troubles sent after him in the past.

A whisper of cold at his back --

"Down!"

Almost too late! Cold brushed at his back as they threw themselves at the ground. He felt a painful burn across his already wounded shoulder, but he rolled and prepared to stand again.

The creatures saw him down and circled in on him -- white, cold ghosts, their tendrils reaching --

"Shannon! Step aside!" Farrin yelled.

Shannon had been reaching for Derry, and he hesitated only half a heartbeat before he threw himself away. Something silvery flew overhead, dissecting at least four of the creatures. They screamed and dissolved.

Thrown sword. Very wise move.

The other three white shapes backed away as Derry drew the dagger Shannon had given him. He looked up into the creatures -- faceless, and yet seeing him and moving when he moved. Something directed them. Derry could feel magic by the trees nearby, and a thin line of the power connection from there to these dangerous creatures, no doubt directing them. Derry scrambled to his feet, grateful for Shannon's hand under his unwounded shoulder -- and for Shannon's far more substantial sword which he held left-handed but ready.

Farrin inched his way closer to his own sword, but the ghosts had other ideas. One swept down on him as he reached for the weapon --

But before Derry could give a cry of warning, Farrin drew a dagger and threw. One more of the creatures dissolved, and the others flew back in haste.

"Nicely done," Shannon praised.

Farrin grunted agreement, grabbed his sword, and surged back to his feet, ready to throw again. The ghosts had drifted back into the protection of the trees. They hovered there, far too close for Derry and his friends to turn their backs on them.

"What do we do now?" Farrin asked. He'd grabbed his two weapons and looked steady with his sword in hand, watching the ghosts.

"These things aren't the real enemy," Derry warned. He narrowed his eyes, trying to pierce the darkness where only faint moonlight gave any illumination.

"They're damn well enemy enough for me," Farrin answered though with a bit of humor in his voice.

Derry grinned, remembering that tone from old days, and how Farrin had been the toughest of the three of them, and always less willing to back away from trouble than he and Shannon. Derry kept scanning the woods for something that didn't want to be found. There. He wasn't sure exactly how he spotted the real enemy since that area of night-darkened woods looked no different than any other direction. Maybe he felt the malice directed at him like fingers grabbing at his heart, trying to kill him. This one had hurt Shannon. That he would not forgive.

With a slight sound of anger, Derry lifted his dagger and threw it towards the darkness.

Derry's move surprised Shannon and Farrin, and even more when the dagger hit something substantial where there should only have been night-bred shadows. They heard a growled curse, and for the barest eye blink, the illusion of emptiness disappeared, and Derry saw --

A human was all he knew for sure, a figure draped in a dark cloak, tall and forbidding. The illusion of darkness returned as the enemy fled loudly into the woods. All signs of attack disappeared with him; only a scattering of frost remained on the ground where the creatures had been a moment before. Shannon and Farrin slowly lowered their swords and stayed by Derry as he crossed to retrieve his dagger. Derry found a little blood on it and grimaced as he wiped it off on the ground. Then he turned and walked away again, and the other two fell in beside him.

"Well?" Shannon finally asked. "What was it?"

"Human, I think. That's all I saw."

"Human and not fae?" Shannon asked and sounded as though he worried about asking such a question.

"I can't be certain," Derry admitted with a slight shake of his head. The movement drove pain from his neck all the way down his arm, but he kept the sudden urge to curse from his lips because his friends would react badly. "Whatever stood there didn't feel like the fae, although perhaps I'm ascribing evil to men and good to the fae. Nothing personal, Shannon, Farrin."

Farrin laughed with a bark of amusement. Good. Farrin was finally starting to accept the situation, which would make him far more comfortable to work with during this mess. They needed Farrin to be calm in the face of these unnatural troubles. Derry didn't want everything to be in his own hands because he simply was not up to --

"Thank the Gods! There you three are!" Brian all but shouted. He stood amid the trees to their right and froze as two swords, and a dagger turned on him. He blinked. "Well, yes. That was very stupid of me, wasn't it?"

"Pretty damned stupid, yes," Derry agreed now that he was past the shock. He lowered his weapon first, and the other two copied his move more slowly, neither of them looking assured. "Where the hell are your bells?"

"I didn't want to upset Lord Farrin," Brian admitted sheepishly, looking downward.

"I like bells, Brian-boy," Farrin answered, though still looking nervously around. "I assume you can tell this is honestly your friend, right Derry? Not more foul magic sent do lure us off-guard?"

"This is Brian. Almost a dead Brian, mind you --"

"I take the hint." Brian waved his hand, and suddenly Derry heard the faint whisper of bells in the air -- a perfect, magical sound without corporal source. Just music, because the fae liked music. Brian's tune sounded a little frantic now, a mirror of the young fae's mood. Brian looked around with more worry now that they'd settled his chance for survival. "You don't fear the bells will draw attention?" Brian asked softly.

"Whatever is in these woods is already aware of our presence, Brian. I might have wounded it, though," Derry said.

"If something ghost-like appears, you can try magic, but we've found that good, old-fashioned iron thrown threw it does the trick," Farrin added. He, too, started looking around with worry.

"I'm just glad you're here. How far are we from the village?" Derry asked. He was tired of this walk, and he hoped Brian would have some good news, though just having him show up had helped.

"You are much farther away than you should be. I felt a

touch of a spell, obviously set to keep you wandering off the true path. I'm sorry I left you. I thought it important the fae start actions to get the animals back into the woods. We don't want to fall short on our promise to the Lord of the Woods. The other fae agreed. They're working on the matter already, and they hope to find whatever chased the creatures out of the area."

"I am grateful for whatever help they can give," Derry said. At least that was a problem that wouldn't fall entirely on his shoulders.

"You have done well to get this far," Brian said.

"We managed to survive. Barely." Derry replied. "Can you look at Shannon's arm?"

"No," Shannon said, holding the arm close to his side. "Let's just go. I'm on my feet, and I'm willing to run, if necessary. Let's get out of the woods and keep Brian magically strong in case we need him."

Brian nodded agreement, and Derry realized they were right. Besides, he knew Brian would help Shannon if it was needed. Now was time to get moving, especially with a guide who could sense magic. Derry was upset that he hadn't noticed the spell that kept them wandering through the night. He knew it was likely only because he wasn't trained in magic, but still -- he was the one they had come to find.

"How's the village faring?" Farrin asked after they'd gone a few steps.

"Quite well, my lord," Brain answered and sounded very much like the peasant boy he once had been, which sounded odd with the whisper of bells around him. "The gargoyles thought to make another attack, but your people and mine fought them back without taking any serious injuries."

"I'm grateful for the help you and the rest of the fae have given us, Brian." Brian gave him one startled glance. Farrin answered the look with a shrug. "A few hours wandering about the woods with these two, and I was either going to change my mind about the fae or else face Shannon's sword."

"You didn't think you could take Shannon, sir?" Brian asked.

Farrin roared with laughter, and Derry heard true acceptance in the sound. One battle fought and won, at least.

Chapter Twenty

D erry didn't want to leave the quiet, peaceful darkness where he'd walked, almost asleep, for some distance. However, he lifted his head at the unexpected sound of distant voices. Misty morning light illuminated a field and outlined the village beyond where others had spotted them. Derry hadn't realized they had left the towering trees. Now, with Brian in the lead, the group walked carefully across the ford of a small brook and into an open field beyond, ignoring water, mud, and muck.

"Ah, finally," Brian whispered. With a flutter of frantic bells, he went to his knees and then fell forward, unconscious.

The world spun, and Derry fell. He didn't care if it hurt.

"I wondered what kept our Prince Derry to his feet," Shannon whispered. Exhaustion and pain came too clearly in the sound of those words, but Derry hadn't the strength to even turn his head from the grass. At least this resting place was somewhat soft, and it smelled sweet.

"Kept us all to our feet," Farrin mumbled. "Brian's magic was it? Praise the gods for it because I think it means nothing else could keep up with us, either."

"True," Shannon answered. "Farrin --"

"Sit down before you fall as well! Damn, your arm is bleeding all over hell! Thank the Gods the fae are here!"

Those were not words Derry would have heard the day before, and the genuine acceptance he sensed brought a little smile as Farrin helped turn him over. He stared up into the sky where the sun lit the clouds with a hint of pink. Birds swept here and there in search of insects. Life everywhere again.

"Fari!"

Derry knew that voice.

"Maureen!"

Derry had completely forgotten Farrin had married. The two had been engaged when Derry left the court, and so the marriage had obviously gone ahead. Now, as Farrin stood, Derry forced himself to sit up, the call of old training trying to take over. It wasn't polite to roll around in the mud with a lady present.

Maureen SanKella still looked like the same fair, beautiful young woman from the Tyleen Court. She raced to the three and threw herself into her husband's arms, obviously caring little about the mud he wore over most of his clothing. She looked a bit scuffed as well, though.

"I came to Riverton yesterday, and the locals told me you had disappeared. I've been so worried!"

"I'm fine, my love," he answered and held her closer.

She looked over Farrin's shoulder and down to where Derry and Shannon still sat in the mud.

"Gods! Prince Derry!"

Maureen pulled away from Farrin and curtsied. The reaction took Derry so much by surprise that he stared at her, uncertain of what to do now. Derry couldn't stand and bow. He looked at Farrin with something that probably came close to panic.

"Let's get him up and to the Inn," Farrin suggested. He

nodded as several fae joined them. Derry didn't argue as two carefully gathered him into their capable hands, but only because others had already taken hold of Shannon and Brian.

"What's happened?" Maureen asked. "What is happening. There have been monsters -- and now this --"

"It's all right, love," Farrin assured his wife. "The fae will take excellent care of him."

"But their fae," she began to protest with a worried whisper. "He's a Prince of the Line."

"That means less to him now than it ever did."

True, Derry realized. He hadn't considered that part of his life now, and he never imagined it for his future.

The inn seemed very far away, another long journey while he shivered, watching for dangerous shadows to pass over them. Now that they'd come out of the woods, he expected the gargoyles to return, or the ghosts to sweep in and attack them all.

Derry didn't want to fly again. The fearful memory of what had happened set him trembling until he felt ill. The world went unsteady, and the sounds distant, while the fae took better hold of him...

Derry awoke in a bed, Brian sitting in a chair beside him. A half dozen candles lit the dark and pushed away the shadows. If he had awoken in nothing but darkness, he would have panicked, but the flickering light helped. Derry moved and stopped, his breath catching at a sudden pain.

"Better?" Brian asked softly.

"I think so. I ache. I feel bruised from head to toe."

"You are. Shannon's doing fine, too. He shouldn't use his arm for a few days -- but shouldn't and won't aren't the same things, are they? He likely won't have a choice. He and Farrin are still talking, but I came to sit with you."

"Thank you. Trouble?"

Brian paused for a moment, as though weighing what to

tell him, but he must have decided that the truth would be the best answer. Besides, Derry was fae enough to know the difference. "Something is hovering out there in the dark, waiting somewhere beyond the village. I don't know why it waits, and the fae are too few to risk going out and searching. I don't understand what's going on here, and unfortunately, neither do any of the other fae."

"That's not very reassuring," Derry said and understood Farrin better.

"Sorry." Brian bowed his head, but he grinned. "It's just that the fae always try to speak the truth in as much as we understand it."

"Is there anything you can tell me? Anything I should do?"

"You should rest. Some of our people are watching the woods -- carefully feeling around -- what's that!!"

Brian surged to his feet and took two steps towards the door before it flew open. The man in palace uniform slugged Brian, sending him sprawling. Derry had a moment to wonder if the fool realized he had just hit one of the fae.

"Lord Derry." The first guard gave a mocking bow, while the other three stayed in shadow. "Gather him up. We have an appointment to keep."

"What --" Derry began, finally comprehending the danger he faced. Not right. Something wrong with these men. Derry threw himself off the bed and scurried under reaching hands. Someone cursed and kicked, but he hardly felt the blow.

"Shannon!"

Shannon had already arrived. So had Farrin and a couple others, all with swords drawn.

"Hold right there!" the guard ordered. "I have a legal warrant to arrest Lord Derry. Unless you want to be named rebels here and now, you'll step aside."

"Fine. I'm a rebel," Shannon replied. He didn't even blink.

"Derry, can you see to Brian? Farrin, just back up there with the soldiers, boy. You know you never were a match for me."

Farrin gave Shannon an uncertain look. Derry hoped the guards took that for indecision about Shannon's ability and not on which side he stood. Shannon had been fool enough for both of them, and Farrin didn't need to leap into the morass with them. This had to be the queen's work, and they might yet need Farrin's help to get free of this new mess.

"We can take him," a guard said, a snarl of sound that made Derry very uncomfortable. "Shannon SanSota can't fight us all off."

"Not alone, but he isn't, is he?" Derry said as he knelt by Brian, who made a sound of coming around again. "And you don't want to face what I send against you."

They took him seriously and even backed up a step. Gods all, what was being said about him?

Brian opened his eyes, and Derry barely kept from sighing with relief. Their true fae companion was the only one here capable of exerting the kind of power Derry had used as a threat.

"Let's get the hell out of here," Shannon said with a wave of his arm. And yes, he did have a sword in the one he wasn't supposed to use. "Brian --"

"What the hell?" Brian sounded half panicked as he tried to sit up. He certainly didn't sound fae this time. "Where the hell did they come from?"

Derry thought his friend addled by the blow. Then he realized the guards should never have gotten into the village, let alone to his door, without being seen by the fae guards or the human ones. He felt a shiver crawl right up his back as he took Brian's hand and helped the unsteady fae back to his feet.

"I think we need some real answers here," Shannon stated and sounded far too calm. "Brian, can you call some of your people --"

The guard growled, seriously growled, and not a human sound at all. Brian grabbed Derry and shoved him behind as light erupted. Derry lifted his arm, blinded --

And something bore him down.

"Mine, changeling," a hot breath whispered at his ear

Pain.

The world disappeared, and he went away.

Chapter Twenty-One

Derry felt his breath catch and his heart pound painfully as he opened his eyes.

He sat in a shadowed corner of a dark place filled with stinking men and other filth. Something slithered nearby, and a faint shadow of light drifted through the high, barred window.

He knew this place.

"No!"

The cry of despair came from the depths of Derry's soul and escaped his lips, beyond his control. Derry could not be here again, back in that hellish cell. He tried to push the existence of this place away, just as he had when it came to him in the nightmares.

Nothing changed.

No, God and Goddess -- not here! Had everything been a fevered dream? Derry wanted to be back home with Shannon -- even back home fighting evil with Shannon at his side was better than this place. He tried not to retch at the stink around him and to call back the memory of the woods and the scent of trees, grass, and rain. For a moment, Derry caught the scent of that other world and closed his eyes, trying desperately to make it real again. He couldn't be here. This was a lie. He couldn't --

"Scared, are you, boy?" A rough voice asked and then coughed out a laugh. Calloused hands reached from the dark and brushed against the side of his face. Derry pulled away in disgust and revulsion. "Poor boy. Ours now. They give you to us."

"No!"

Derry tried to crawl away, but he found a heavy chain attached to his ankle, and it trapped him close to the wall. When had they chained him? There had never been chains before, and he jerked at this one, trying to work it free while hands reached for him again.

"No!" Derry shouted, but not in despair this time. He felt a surge of anger. Denial. They could not put him back in this place and leave him to suffer.

Derry had not expected power to come, fueled by his rage. Fae blood? He felt the magic come to his fingers, and for a moment, his light dispelled the darkness. The power sent anyone who had been near him fleeing into the darkness, like shadows afraid of the light.

Derry looked at his hands and the glow at his fingertips. If he had such power, that meant this scene was a lie. Derry was not back in Fairfall, and he wasn't helpless, either. When he heard a sound, he cast the light out once more and found no one in the cell, though shadows moved. Even the walls around him seemed less substantial. Nothing real. Derry had fought against nightmares before and won. This one would not stand before him --

Derry shivered, and the light in his hand dimmed and died.

"You haven't the power to hold us off forever, boy." The voice almost chuckled with pleasure, playing with him.

However, the voice was real, and that gave Derry new strength. He could fight against a real enemy. Someone stood close enough to speak to him and watch his moves.

Derry held up his hand again, and the light brightened. That person hissed in anger and retreated, but when Derry looked in that direction, he found only shadows.

However, he knew the enemy stood somewhere to the right. Human enough, he supposed, but with the taint of evil so strong that it nearly overwhelmed the feel of anything natural. Even when Derry had faced the mad king of the Isles, he hadn't sensed anything so dark and bereft of humanity. This thing in human skin was something he thought all humans would back away from in disgust.

Derry didn't possess the strength to hold onto his own power for long, though. Even knowing the cell wasn't real wouldn't make it any easier to face in the dark.

Coming, Derry! Hold -- light. Magic!

He'd felt Brian's touch in that whispered message, the fae's magic drawn to wherever Derry had been taken Derry looked around the little cell, trying not to shiver. The light dimmed. He felt ill and cold --

"Soon, boy."

Light flared again. The magical fire seemed to sap the warmth from his body, and Derry shivered, but he held on.

Derry!

Brian's voice had grown louder in his mind. Nearer. Stronger. He had to hold on to that link. They couldn't be far.

"No, you shall not draw them here."

The voice sounded closer. Derry turned and found a tall figure dressed in a cape and cowl, standing at the edge of the shadows at the far side of the room. He knew this one had to be the real enemy. Derry would have known it even if they had met in a busy market buying cloth. He could feel the evil like an ill wind.

With a sudden frantic jerk, Derry tried to break the chain that held his ankle to the wall. His light dimmed and then brightened in pure panic. The enemy obviously didn't like the illumination, so Derry fed it more power, desperately wanting to keep the man at bay a little longer.

"No more. I can't allow the fae to track you so easily. We have other plans for you, changeling."

Derry desperately wanted to know who that we included.

"Your friends follow your warmth, your power. Not to here."

A pale, thin hand snaked out of the cape and pointed at him. Whispered words --

Cold. The light flickered and died.

Der-ry!

Something touched his leg, and another hand brushed at his hair. Derry shivered and tried to pull away, swallowing back a whimper and a curse. He wanted to call the light again, but the cold had taken him now, and he couldn't touch the power that had burnt through him only moments before.

However, Derry wanted his friends with a desperation that could ignore the cold and brought the light back to his hands once more. He saw a face, leaning down close and gloating -- and then shocked as the man fled back into the shadows.

"Not that easy," Derry whispered as he finally fought his way to his knees, balanced as best he could despite feeling so weak. "I will not fall that easily."

"You know my face. I cannot allow you to leave."

Derry laughed. His light brightened, nearly filling the cell. He could see the figure and an odd red line of threads around him.

"I never believed you would let me go anyway," Derry replied with a shake of his head. Seeing the man's face was a power, though, even if he didn't understand how it would help him. Knowing he had won something of importance also gave him more strength. The light flickered, but it held.

Derry! Stay strong! Close!

"You've far more power than I was given to believe," the man said, his voice cultured behind the angry growl. The tone held the power of words like a knife's edge, ready to cut. "This makes things more interesting."

Derry heard a strange, whispery undercurrent to the words, like two voices speaking as one. Another here, too? Or not here, perhaps, but rather linked through those threads.

"You are no mage. You have magic, but only from the fae blood. She has strong blood, their queen. And now you have it -- and I will have it as well. You will give me that power, boy."

Derry focused on the one word -- give. They couldn't take the power from him, could they? He knew instinctively, like her gift to him, he had to willingly pass the gift of fae blood to them.

"I've no intention of betraying either the fae or the humans to you," Derry replied, so much control in his voice that he startled the dark-robed man into stepping back again. "I am Prince Derry SanOsen, and I understand honor."

"Honor!" Two voices laughed this time, clearly two voices, one a slight whisper before the man spoke. "What honor is there in a dark, dank cell, locked away forever --"

"You can't frighten me." The drain of power for the light made him feel icy now, as though his limbs froze in the worst of a winter storm. He still held on. "You can't frighten me more with this cell. I already believed I would die here. To accept again isn't so hard -- but I will not give you the fae gift that was entrusted to me."

"I can do far worse than this dismal little place, boy," the stranger answered and might even have sounded pleased at the idea, which meant nothing good from this man. "We've much to explore still, you and me. Pain, Lord Derry. Let us touch on pain, shall we?"

The man's arm moved, and the pain started at his feet and swept up through him like something alive. A heartbeat later, he fell forward, crying out. The light wavered, but he called it back, terrified of what would happen if the room grew dark.

"Ah, so very strong and brave," the voices mocked.

Derry!

"Quickly! Come quickly!"

The pain died slowly while the man laughed, and another, more distant voice joined in. Enemies here. Enemies elsewhere -- but he had friends coming, and he only had to hold on a little longer.

"No one will come for you here, boy," the man said, and pain started to sweep through him again.

The man -- mage -- was, quite obviously, wrong. The wall behind the stranger flew apart, a rock hitting Derry on the side of the face. He heard the voice's shriek in surprise and shock.

Shouts. Fire. A brief, blinding pain.

Safe?

"Derry?"

He wearily lifted his head and watched Shannon's concerned face. The walls of the cell still stood, except where his friends had come through. He could still feel it, smell it, though he thought that might only be in his mind. This place had the feel of somewhere long abandoned, nothing more than a convenient stage for those who wanted to torment him.

"I don't want to stay here, Shannon." Derry heard the unnatural calm that came from exhaustion more than any sudden bout of sanity. "Get me out of here."

"Careful," Shannon said. He helped Derry sit up. "We can't move you until Brian, and his friends get the iron off your leg."

Derry looked to where Brian and his fae friend used magic to tear the metal from his ankle. He wanted out, and that need overcame nearly everything else. Derry scrambled to his knees, viciously jerking at the chain.

"No! You'll hurt yourself! Be still!" Shannon tried to grab at him, but he pulled free, and the look he gave his friend stilled Shannon this time.

"I want out of here," Derry repeated, his voice still far calmer than the raging emotions in his mind or the actions he'd taken. Shannon stared at him, fear in his face this time.

Brian gave another try at breaking the metal apart, but Derry could tell that the chain had been magically reinforced. Some faint, distant whisper of logic kicked in. Derry wanted out, and if the fae couldn't break the chain, then he had to help. He reached out and sent a bright flash of power through the chain --

He heard Brian yelp with surprise just before the world went black again.

Chapter Twenty-Two

Derry awoke to find Shannon and Brian sitting by his bed in a room he didn't recognize. The door had been damaged in the old place, but he thought they must still be in the inn. Both of his friends bore bruises and bandages and plainly didn't feel any better than him. Candlelight danced through the shadows, but Derry had no idea the hour.

His friends looked worried, both watching the door and the window in turns. Farrin, he saw, sat close by the door with a sword in hand. Derry feared something more had gone wrong, but he hadn't the strength even to move a hand to push the hair from his eyes.

"Now what?" Derry whispered. His voice sounded scratchy.

"You rest," Shannon ordered and tugged at the blanket, pulling it up around Derry. Worry played across his face, but he still looked relieved to have Derry awake.

"Any sign of the enemy?" Derry asked. He wasn't going to sleep well with the thought of danger lurking nearby

"None," Brain replied, leaning closer. His hand lifted, the

fingers shaking as he spread a little helpful magic over Derry before he could protest. Breathing became easier afterward. "The man disappeared into the woods, along with the gargoyles."

That answer did start a surge of panic. "We can't leave the enemy in there! The Lord of the Woods --"

"We don't dare risk a battle," Brian explained, worry showing in his face. "The fae are exhausted. We haven't the power left to heal even minor wounds."

The news startled Derry. Shannon gave Brian a look of reproach.

"He needs to know, Shannon. Derry needs to realize that if danger comes again, we cannot rely on others to help us. Some of the fae are going to remain here and rid the woods of gargoyles as best they can. They are already doing their best to move creatures back into the woods and keep them safe -- but Derry, there are other problems that we must deal with, and we will need your help."

Derry looked at Brian with panic spreading from his head to his heart. He wanted to deny he had any importance, but Derry knew he stood in the center of the trouble. His only hope for peace was to defeat the enemy.

Well, at least that thought finally gave him a goal.

Derry blinked and found himself staring at Shannon, who looked as bruised and battered as Derry felt.

"You look like hell, Shannon."

Shannon blinked and then offered a tentative, but still worried, smile. "We've both gone through hell, my friend. Or at least we've entered into hell; I'm fairly certain we're not through it yet."

"Not yet," Brian agreed and rubbed at his own arm.

"Brian," Derry said, starting to straighten, as though to get up. Both Shannon and Brian dissuaded him of the idea. "I think I have a key to use against our enemy. It worried him at the time. I saw his face."

"Yes!" Brain laughed and clapped his hands with such delight that it startled everyone else in the room, including Farrin.

"What good will seeing his face do?" Farrin asked with a touch of annoyance, barely under control again. "We've not had any luck in our encounters so far."

"Yes, we have," Derry replied, surprising him. "We may have taken injuries and been worn down, but we've won every battle because the enemy hasn't stopped us. Those were battles on his terms. He doesn't want us to hunt him down."

"Derry's right," Brian said but gave him a worried look. "I don't know where you found such sudden wisdom --"

"I want to rest. I won't get it until we're done with this mess, which means that I want these fools destroyed so I can get some sleep."

Shannon laughed and slapped Derry -- gently -- on the shoulder. "Ah damn. I thought I'd never really get you back, Derry. Welcome home."

Farrin gave a little chuckle of his own. Brian still appeared to be uncertain, but then he probably didn't know what to expect from humans these days. Derry felt as though, in some strange way, the war suddenly lost the edge of importance. He would still fight with all his power, but he wouldn't allow the enemy to run him ragged anymore. He had his wits back, and he had no intention of losing them again.

"I haven't the strength to throw myself against this force." Derry settled more comfortably on the bed again, although he already felt stronger. "And we can't keep letting him wear us down."

"We can't reach any fae," Brian offered with another glance at the window. He probably hoped for the sound of bells and a friendly face. None came. "We can't tell if other fae are facing troubles of their own."

"Then we can count only upon ourselves. I wonder where the enemy is right now --"

And Derry saw the man, far too clearly for this to be a dream -- the well-made walls, tapestries, an elegant desk. The vision startled him. Derry yelped, and the man looked up in fear.

Derry found himself back on the bed, gasping for breath, and with Brian holding on to his shoulder, and luckily not the wounded one.

"What the hell happened?" Farrin demanded, standing with his sword in hand.

"Strong magic, my lord," Brian answered. "Uncommonly strong magic."

"Attacking Derry --" Farrin said, the sword raised as though to fight whatever came.

"Ah, no, my lord. This time it came from Derry's own magic. Prince Derry, did you see him?"

"Very clearly." His heart didn't pound quite as hard now. "And he knew I was there, somehow. I think I scared the hell out of him, which is only fair since it scared the hell out of me."

"Our enemy knows he can no longer hide. Rest, Prince Derry. We must consider how best to use this advantage. You will need to be strong when we take the next step. I'll ward you as you sleep so that you cannot go unawares to him, and neither will he touch you. You are safe. Rest."

Chapter Twenty-Three

S ilence reigned in the world outside while Derry rested, and he took that as a good sign. They needed one. He felt a little tingling of fae magic moving about the village, but there didn't seem to be any trouble. Good. The idea that the war might press in on them at any time troubled Derry because he still felt lost. He also worried that he could suddenly, and without warning, use magic to connect to the enemy. That couldn't be safe for Derry or for those around him.

Derry drifted in and out of sleep for a while, worried that he simply could not make the connection to whatever trouble lingered nearby. Had he missed something? By late afternoon, Derry laid in the bed and stared at the thatched ceiling as he tried to think the events since he arrived in Riverton. He needed a key that would help him find answers. They couldn't keep running around like this.

Sleep. Derry forced his eyes closed and tried to chase all the other thoughts away. He even slept for most of the day, aware that his body needed the rest. Derry thought the sleep would help, but his mind betrayed him as it had so often done in the past. Total exhaustion proved no deterrent to nightmares, especially those so recently reawakened by the return to the cell. Darkness swept in, and he sensed shadows within shadows reaching for him.

Not entirely a nightmare, though. Derry realized something did lurk there, on the edges of his thought, and it felt like the red threads he had seen attached to the enemy in the cell. Why hadn't Brian's magic kept this at bay? Had those strings already been part of him? Had he been carrying around a link to the magic that made the nightmare continue to grab at him whenever he weakened?

The thought angered Derry. The magic pushed a little nightmare his way, bringing a shadow of the cell back to his mind. He wished the fae could guard him in his sleep -- and the dream receded at the thought, hovering at the edges of his troubled sleep, like some unsure and angry man, denied entrance --

Man? No, not the man he had already seen. Someone else this time.

Woman?

For the first time, Derry stared into the shadows instead of away from them.

He saw her -- haughty as she bent over a desk, her hand moving across what appeared to be the surface of a mirror. A fire blazed in the hearth, casting light and shadows everywhere. She turned, startled to find him at her back. Her face paled, and with a start, she spun away -- but then she stopped and looked again. Fire brightened her eyes so that he could almost see a glow of red there.

"Too late, sweet Derry. Matters have changed. No, you cannot touch me through your dreams."

He tried anyway because he did have powers that were not human. She clearly hadn't counted on that, and his fingers brushed against her arm. She snarled and fled from the room and from his dreams.

Derry saw the strings she'd used to hold on to him, a red haze around the mirror. He brushed his hands across them as well, hoping to break that spell.

He awoke with a cry of surprise and annoyance.

"I can't do anything about the nightmares, Lord Farrin," Brian said from beside the bed. The young fae sounded apologetic. "I can't touch them because they are too much a part of who he is -- Derry?"

"Gods." Derry gasped and focused on the room, glad to find himself here. Farrin stood by the door, his hand on a weapon and his eyes narrowed in anger, but as Derry sat up -- all the way up this time -- Farrin gave a nod that showed relief. Derry pushed both hands through his hair, trying to regain control while he sorted through the vision of what he'd seen.

Shannon had been asleep on the floor at the foot of the bed. He sat up and looked worried. Derry, though, couldn't say why he wasn't panicked as well, except that he did finally understand the trouble at hand. Brian sat by the chair, looking worn and battered, but a touch of curiosity had come to his face. They had fought a damn long, hard war, and Derry was about to make things even more unpleasant for them.

"Derry? Awake?" Shannon asked softly, as though anything too loud might frighten him. Derry was not that fragile. Not any longer.

"Shannon, we need to ride. Brian, you must get back to your people and give them a message. I not only saw the face of the man that has attacked us, but now I have also seen the one who sent him. I thought I had sensed another when we were in the cell, and now I know the truth. We aren't safe here, but at least we have an enemy I can name."

He didn't name her yet, though. Shannon blinked several times, pushing away the blanket that had covered him, looking as though he still wasn't fully awake. However, he must have seen the change in Derry's face. Shannon stood and leaned over him, staring into his eyes for a moment longer. "You are finally awake, aren't you?"

"Completely awake for the first time in years. Damn, Shannon! I should have known who was behind this trouble from the start, especially when the attacks were so personal. A moment ago, in my sleep, I realized someone directed my nightmares, and I could take some control back. I looked into the darkness, and I saw her."

"Her?" Farrin asked, frowning already though he didn't realize the answer.

Shannon paled, though, and knew without being told. When Shannon shook his head, it was not in denial. He glanced around the room in frantic haste, knowing they would have to leave. Derry turned back to Farrin, who still stood guard by the door. Brian remained quiet and uncertain, but Derry had no doubt he would do whatever was needed.

"I don't know the man I first saw, but I do know he works for another. I've only ever had one real enemy in the world." He looked up into Farrin's face. Shannon cursed softly as he worked. "Queen Alisia."

Farrin crossed to stand over the bed, his brow furrowed, and his hand on his sword again. "You are certain?" he asked softly as though he feared she might hear. And maybe she might, but it was too late for Derry to worry about such things.

"Ah, that's the question." Derry swung his legs over the edge of the bed and prepared to stand. He couldn't say he was any stronger in body but having control of his mind did make a difference. How much had she played with him, keeping him confused and lost? The thought angered Derry more. They needed to move quickly because Alisia knew Derry had seen her, and he didn't want to give her time to act. She would no longer need to be as careful. "I'm certain I saw the Queen,

Farrin. I can tell the difference between a true nightmare and magic, and this was a link to her, not my imagination. She didn't expect me to understand that the hook she had in me could be used to see the other way as well. I think I'd gotten the feel of how to do so in the magic from her companion."

"Yes." Brian sounded assured. "There is no absolute certainty in magic -- however, I believe Derry's own growing abilities are blossoming quickly. He has startled the enemy before with what he can do; we saw that in the cell. This makes the enemy dangerous, my friends. The Queen will move against Prince Derry in haste before he can point trouble in her direction. He's right to want to ride as soon as we can move."

"She is planning to do something," Derry added and shook his head, still stunned by what had happened and fearing he would make the connection again. He didn't want to pull her to him. "She was upset that I had seen her, but she wasn't distraught. And that worries me."

Brian nodded and then turned to look at their other companion. "Lord Farrin, I suggest you say nothing of this news to anyone. Your silence is your shield. So long as she doesn't perceive you as a direct threat, you and your people should remain safe now."

"Because she's going to turn her full attention on Derry," Shannon said. He stood, already tossing their belongings in a knapsack.

"And you as well, Shannon," Brian reminded him. "You are linked to Derry. She knows he wouldn't keep this secret from you, especially when you go rushing off in the dead of night with him."

"Don't say anything, Derry," Shannon warned when Derry started to speak. "It's not like I was ever in the good Queen's favor anyway. If she's behind the dark magic, then I would surely have to face her sooner or later. Better to face her side-by-side rather than either of us alone."

"He's right," Brian replied, already moving to the window and looking out into the dark. Was she sending something against him tonight? Those guards who grabbed him -- the ones who hadn't truly been human -- had arrived without any show. He didn't want to face a group like that again. Derry pulled on his boots while Shannon did more packing, looking very much awake now. He mumbled now and then and shook his head, no doubt about having been so blind.

"She tried to kill me with the meat when I went back in Tyleen after staying with the SanSotas," Derry said and startled Shannon again, who gave another snarl of agreement. "It would have been the quickest, and least obvious way, to be rid of me. The Queen could have weathered the trouble if she'd been contrite enough -- and besides, some magic might have helped her smooth over anger from others."

"What of Egan the Pig?" Farrin asked, amusing Derry with that old term they'd used when the prince was a fat little boy. "Does he know what his mother is up to?"

"I don't know." Derry started to feel both more frantic and a little annoyed that he'd been so blind until now. Magic had probably played a part in keeping him from looking at the Queen. "He's never struck me as very bright, and I wouldn't think his mother would trust him with any knowledge that needed to be kept quiet. The Queen must be able to hide her magic most of the time or I think even I would have sensed something. I feel like a fool that I never realized."

"None of us noticed anything," Brian reminded Derry and the others. "And we started looking for the link to this trouble long before you even returned, Prince Derry. We knew there was power at Tyleen made of both fae and human magic, and no one ever considered that there might be something on the inside, having slipped through the wards. We also didn't notice anything during her exile from the court, and that means we need to take a good look at the place where she remained during that time."

"You really are convinced about the Queen?" Farrin asked. He didn't look like he really disbelieved, but rather that there was the hope of some other enemy. Derry could hardly blame him. Queen Alisia had been formidable enough as a human, but the idea that she had magical powers frightened him.

"I'm convinced," Derry replied and saw other incidents more clearly now. "It also explains the assassin in Keirkell and the magic that worked up the crowd against me."

"Assassin," Farrin said, his left eyebrow arched.

"Did we forget to mention that one?" Shannon asked as he shoved some bread into a leather pouch. "It simply got lost in the rest of this mess. I think you're right about it, Derry."

"I must go to my own Queen," Brian said by the window. He stopped there and looked back at them, worried. "Tyleen has always had a magic shield around it. Queen Leanora says it's as ancient as the castle itself or maybe even older. The fae couldn't easily pierce it to see inside, so she wasn't happy when you two went back to stay there last winter. She did think you were safe enough, though."

"No one has seen the magic in the Queen?" Shannon asked. "Can we be certain that we have seen it?"

"No fae has said anything," Brian replied and still paused by the window as though he considered all the possibilities. "She is clearly using magic to keep herself hidden, and because it is not fae magic, we have had a harder time tracking it. Yes, I think we know who the enemy truly is. I'll see the two of you as soon as I can catch up unless Leanora decides otherwise. The two of you should stay off the main trails. You might even forgo horses after the first few miles -- you'll want them first to get as far away as possible before she can move against you. Derry is now so much of the wild that she'll have trouble finding him."

"But she can find me." Shannon stopped in mid-stride and looked dismayed before he dropped the packed bag on a chair. His face changed; he calmed in a way that stilled anything Derry started to say. "I won't abandon him -- no, Derry, be quiet. Brian, our only hope is that I'm wild, too."

"Yes," Brain replied without hesitation. Derry and Farrin made sounds of disbelief, though neither argued. Derry thought Farrin was simply too shocked to say anything in protest.

Derry wasn't confident he could find the words to speak, to prevent Shannon from taking this step. He didn't want to stop Shannon, but that was for entirely selfish reasons. "Shannon," he began, his voice soft as he reached out, his hand touching Shannon's arm, uncertain --

Shannon put a hand over his fingers and gave a steady nod to his friend. "I've made the decision, Derry. I'd made it long before now, you know. This is just a good time to take the step since it will help. Be still."

Brian had remained silent, but he drew a blade from his belt and sent a little wave of magic over the metal so that it gleamed. He paused, though Derry didn't sense any doubt in their fae companion. "Children are brought into the fae differently -- at least most of the time. They adapt and accept more easily and absorb the magic just by being with the fae. It's a slower process, but not so overwhelming. When they found me, I was already dying, so I came to be fae much the same as Derry had, and as you will, Shannon. It's a faster introduction to magic, but it will be disconcerting at first."

"I watched Derry changing," Shannon said and put a hand on Derry's shoulder before he could speak again. "I understand."

"Good. My gift of magic isn't as strong as my Queen's, but it will make you fae enough to go unnoticed out in the wild. Eventually you will begin to touch the powers, though probably not as fast as Derry has started to gain control of his. If you do this, there's no going back, Shannon SanSota."

"I never intended to go back anyway."

"True," Brian replied as though he had known this truth all along. Derry realized he had known as well, and when Shannon finally dared a glance his way, he didn't protest, though his heart beat a little faster. Did that come from worry for Shannon? Or did he feel joy that his friend would still be with him, and that they might yet be truly wild boys again? "If you were one of the lost, we would do this by rituals, rites, and adoptions. However, by blood is quicker. And we need speed."

Brian cut his own left wrist as Farrin made a startled sound, though he fell silent at Shannon's shake of his head. Brian took Shannon's right hand and made a quick cut in the wrist. Brian pushed his arm against the wound.

Shannon took a breath -- and then looked startled. Derry remembered the same moment when the world came awake around him. By the time Brain drew back his hand, Shannon's little cut had already half-healed.

"You'll do very well among the fae, Shannon," Brian said with a bright smile. "We love music. Go quickly and be careful."

Brian crossed back to the window and slipped out into the night. Wise, not to go through the inn and draw attention. He and Shannon would make enough of a scene on their own. Derry heard bells ... close below and then drifting away. Brian obviously did travel alone either, praise the Gods and Goddess.

"Damn! You two are enough to drive me crazy!" Farrin finally exclaimed.

Shannon grinned. He still looked dazed.

"Just remember what Brain said," Derry reminded him as he took a pack from Shannon. "Keep silent about what's been said here in this room. Shannon and I are certain to keep her interest, but we don't want the Queen to wonder about you. If we fail, you at least know the face of the true enemy, and you know you can trust the fae. This is the best gift I can leave with you."

Farrin nodded and looked as though he considered the future in which he might be at war with Queen Alisia. That would not have been a happy thought even if she didn't have magic. "You two take care. Take damned good care, and even if you go fae and wild, don't forget me. I want to see you again."

"We'll be back," Derry promised. Shannon gave a distracted nod, which Derry found almost amusing.

Farrin rushed downstairs ahead of them, doubtlessly startling everyone, but he could get both horses and trail food ready.

By the time Shannon and Derry reached the stables, the sun had started to rise into a bright and cloudless sky. Derry looked towards the woods and did a quick search but found no evil lurking there. In fact, he could feel the little lives of small animals nearby, and some headed back into the woods. Derry wished them to go home quickly and please the Lord of the Woods.

"So, where are you going?" Farrin asked with sudden worry as the two mounted their horses.

"There's only one place to go." Derry looked around -- felt out the area -- and knew they were alone. "We're going back to Tyleen."

"Are you crazy? To her own place?" Farrin demanded and reached to grab the bridle.

Derry eased the horse out of his reach. "Tyleen is my place as well," Derry reminded him softly. "We don't have a lot of choices left, Farrin. We must get to the King and tell him the truth. If Alisia is behind this trouble, then I suspect her favorite son is involved as well, which puts the King and the crown prince in considerable danger, doesn't it? And Roe as well, since she wouldn't want to leave him as a better choice for the people to follow. This may well be why she sent me north -- an easy way to be rid of one possible heir and thinning down the possibilities without drawing too much attention."

"God and Goddess, of course. She wants to rule!" Shannon said with sudden understanding. "She can't rule on her own -- she's foreign -- but she can through the toad. We must go, Farrin. Gods grant that we meet again in better times."

Farrin nodded and offered his hand. Derry leaned down and took it. "Don't forget that the fae are your friends. If things don't go well for Shannon and me, turn to Brian and the others. It's a trust I give you, my friend. It is the second line of hope if I fail."

Farrin nodded with a new look of worry and said nothing more as the two rode away.

Heading for home and heading for war.

Chapter Twenty-Four

The three of them sat around a meager fire, a little flare of flame brightening the area now and then. Brian had rejoined them before sunset and now hunched over with his fingers tight around a battered cup filled with tea. Derry felt cold just looking at him, which didn't help his state of mind.

"I had hoped some fae blood would help me feel less involved in the weather," Shannon said with a shake of his head. "I feel colder than I ever remember in the spring!"

"This is colder than usual," Brian replied. He looked up and shook back his long, dark hair, a moment of unease showing in his thin face as he glanced around again. "This isn't the physical cold we're feeling. It's getting darker out there."

"And not the darkness of night," Derry added, looking at the shadowy trees and bushes. He shivered again.

"No, not anything as pleasant as the coming of night," Brian agreed and sipped the tea.

Shannon sighed. Only six days had passed since he'd become blood kin to the fae, and Shannon didn't quite have the feel yet. For that matter, Derry had months of experience on him, and he didn't fully understand what he felt.

Brian had been a fully human boy. No one would mistake him for human now, even without the bells: wildness clung to Brian, making him more akin to the forest than the village.

Derry wondered if he and Shannon would ever reach that stage. He wanted away from the humans and their cruelty, and their dark places --

Small, dull, rat-infested cells with the stink of humans and their touching hands --

"Derry! Derry!"

Shannon viciously shook him and had been shaking him for some time from the feel of his pounding head. Brian stood behind Derry, hands on his shoulders, and chanting magic that swept through him with unexpected warmth.

The magic surprised and shocked him, but Shannon finally stopped shaking him, at least.

"Brian! Stop! We'll draw attention!" Derry gasped and pulled away from the fae.

"We already have!" Shannon warned. He kept tight hold to Derry's arm and started to pull him to his feet. "What the hell do you think happened to you?"

"I think ... I had a nightmare? No -- too real. Too quick, and it sucked me in too far."

"Something pulled you straight down into an abyss, friend," Brian said as he finally stepped back to the fire, though he quenched that friendly flame with a wave of his hand. "I severed the spell, but they know where we are. The spell almost got us all that time -- it wasn't just aimed at you, Derry. I think it was meant to call up all our worst nightmares, but you were more susceptible since you'd been under such a spell recently. For a heartbeat, I was with my father again, but I realized the trouble before it sucked us in. We're lucky Time to move on."

"Quickly," Derry agreed while the other two scrambled to

do the work of gathering up their supplies. Derry still suffered from old injuries, especially the one to his shoulder. Brian and Shannon gave him nervous glances as though afraid he would take off without them. "We don't dare head straight for Tyleen now if she's found us here. Let's double back for a few miles and circle at the edge of the valley."

Neither argued nor complained about how hard they'd traveled to get this close. They had always expected to be discovered and planned on retreating in hopes the Queen would believe they feared her too much to test her powers.

They did fear her. Contrary to what any of their acquaintances likely thought, the three had found unexpected wisdom of late. They headed into the darker woods, moving at a pace only slightly less than a jog. Derry wouldn't be able to continue for long, but he wanted some distance before Alisia came sniffing around. They were not ready for battle.

Damn. When would they ever be ready? This wasn't the first time such a thought occurred to Derry, and he still didn't have an answer. He wasn't fae enough to feel confident in a magical battle --

Well, but they had Brian, moving right along with them as they rushed away from the face of danger. Maybe Derry's lack of fae abilities was not the real problem since no other fae had leapt to the attack, either.

The three rushed through the woods for as far as they dared before Derry began to stumble. His companions stopped, and Derry didn't complain, though he wanted to keep going. Want and ability were two different things, though, and he gratefully stumbled to a stop and leaned against the nearest oak, his eyes closed as he gasped.

Everything remained still around them. Derry could feel no intrusive magic following their path, though he felt an odd throb of magic, neither good nor evil, at Tyleen itself.

"Derry?" Shannon asked.

"Couple breaths. I'll be fine."

"Nothing is coming after us," Brian said and lowered his arm. "I think your plan worked, Derry."

"Good, but we dare not stay this near. I can still feel something out there, though it doesn't seem to be moving."

"You probably feel Tyleen itself. There's old, old magic there," Brian reminded them. He still leaned back against a tree and looked no more at ease than the other two. "That wasn't much of an attack, considering how close we are to her lair."

"Makes me nervous, wondering what she's doing in there," Shannon admitted and looked toward Tyleen as though he could see the city through the forest and rolling hills. "I feel like a rabbit about to test the skills of an alert and eager hawk."

"At least there are no gargoyles," Derry replied. He took an instinctive look upward, fearing he might be wrong in that pronouncement.

"Sorry, Derry. I didn't mean to make you think about --" His hand waved vaguely towards the sky.

"About being a rabbit in a gargoyle's hold?" He grinned, surprising, and calming Shannon, who didn't need to worry about such useless troubles. "That's something not often out of my thoughts. However, I was thinking more that we were flies before a spider's web. I know there are traps, but I keep hoping for an opening wide enough to slip through."

"So, what's your analogy, Brian?" Shannon asked with a laugh.

"Me? How about feeling like a fae trying to slip past human guards?"

Shannon smirked, and Derry laughed, making the night feel far less fierce. Brian was right, though; Queen Alisia wasn't showing much fire in her pursuit of them, considering the circumstances. Derry didn't trust this at all, and every time a breeze blew close by, he prepared to bolt. She had seen him looking at her, and she had to know --

"Maybe she doesn't realize it's us," Derry suggested with a bit of hope. "Maybe she thinks that was just a few fae coming closer to Tyleen."

"Oh, there's a good thought," Brian said and sounded relieved at the idea. "She'll be looking for Shannon, you know. Testing for a human to be with you."

Shannon smiled brightly and showed no sign of regret. Once this problem was over though -- well, they'd deal with that time when they reached that point. Derry could see no end to their troubles, so he didn't worry over it yet.

"Let's back away from Tyleen," Derry suggested. "We can stay close enough to observe. I want to know what's happening in the castle before we walk up to the walls. I'd like to have a word with King Nevin, Tevin, or Roe in private, if possible. So, let's watch for a couple days and see if we can stumble on any weakness. Maybe the fae can somehow make her think we're somewhere else, too."

"Good idea," Shannon agreed.

"We need to speak to a few fae around here," Brain added. He lifted his hand and frowned. "There aren't many, and none appear anxious to come and see us, which makes me wonder all the more about what's going on."

"I know the best place to get gossip if the two of you are game," Shannon said.

"A village tavern," Derry agreed with a nod, though he didn't sound very enthusiastic.

"It wasn't that bad! You're giving Brian the wrong idea!"

"Ah no, I remember human taverns too well on my own," Brian answered, and he slipped again into being that human boy. "Me father liked them much too well."

"We went more for the company than the drink," Derry said with a shake of his head. "Though there were nights when I drank more than my fill."

"And regretted it every morning after," Shannon

reminded him with a laugh. They had already started to walk away, which Derry appreciated. He didn't think staying in one place was a good idea in case Alisia looked closer at what had tripped her spell.

"But apparently I never regretted it enough," Derry replied as he moved up beside Shannon. Brian trailed behind like a guard at their back. He felt safer since their fae friend would be more likely to notice magic coming than either of them. "I went back and did it again far too often, you know."

"Just wasting time back then," Shannon said with a little frown. "And it was a damned waste, too. If we had spent more time around Tyleen, we might have noticed something odd about Alisia."

"Probably not," Derry countered. He stepped over a rabbit that had appeared in front of them, oblivious to where they walked. "It's obvious the King hasn't noticed."

"You're certain he doesn't know?" Brian asked from behind, his voice touched with worry.

"Yes," Derry and Shannon chorused.

"Good. I trust your judgment. Even when I was human, I had no contact with your King, you know. We thought him a good man, but still, it is hard to judge a man by rumors alone. The fae never spoke ill of him, though, and they had never been that kind about Alisia."

"I suspect they must have sensed more than they realized," Shannon surmised as they crossed a small brook. A deer looked up, head tilted, and then went back to drinking. "Obviously she's worked at this magic for some time. Magic can't come easily to us. To humans, I mean."

"It is a bit disorientating, isn't it?" Brian asked with a little laugh, and his bells rang brightly for a moment. "You still feel mostly human. Eventually, though, you will accept the fae powers that link you to nature. Once you accept fully, you will be fae."

"No regrets?" Derry asked, glancing back at him.

"Me? Brian laughed again and more brightly this time. "Absolutely not. But I was neither a Prince of the Line nor a Lord."

Derry felt an unexpected shiver at the words, though he couldn't decide why. "I can't remember that being a prince ever mattered much to me."

"Not so much that any of the rest of us could tell," Shannon agreed with a shrug. "Are you going to tell me that it matters to you now?"

"Not for the power," Derry said and shook his head. "However, I did have opportunities back then, and I never realized. I could have helped people."

"Oh, and like you never did such a thing." Shannon dropped a hand on Derry's shoulder when he started to slow. "Like giving a horse to that young man pulling a cart to the market. Or paying to rebuild half a village destroyed by fire -- a village not even on your lands."

"Little things." Derry waved them away.

"Little things counted ta' us, Prince Derry," Brian answered, surprising him. "They counted a lot when I was human, and even the fae noticed from all I heard later. No offense meant to the good King -- he keeps the lands safe and quelled the civil wars of the south -- but he rarely notes the lesser people, and that's why so many children go to the fae. Ah, but there's cruelty in the best of human lands, so it's not that Lynashin is any worse than the others."

"And there is a chance we might yet make it better," Shannon added. He sounded intrigued at the thought.

Derry hadn't considered that possibility. He had powers now that went beyond that of being the nephew of the King. The fae had been saving children already. Maybe he could help people who were not lost, but who were still in dire situations.

"There's no cruelty among the fae?" Shannon asked,

daring a glance at Brian as though he either feared to ask the question or feared the answer he might get in return.

"Not like humans. At worse, some of the fae are indifferent. They would never do anything purposely cruel, though."

"Good." Shannon sounded strangely sincere. "I like to think there might be better in the world than what humans have done." He looked around at the trail Derry had chosen. "Are we going to Glendalow, then?"

"Near to it, at least. I don't think we dare the tavern tonight," Derry said. "We're known there, and even if they didn't feel us as fae, they would have heard about me. I think we can get close enough to hear things. Maybe a little magic might help, Brian. We know the people at Glendalow, and we should be able to judge their moods and words better than we could elsewhere."

"Good," Brian agreed. He probably knew the people better than any of them, in fact.

Having a destination other than Tyleen and Alisia's lair made the walk more pleasant. Brian had taken the lead, proving he knew this area very well. When Shannon began humming a bright little tune, Brian looked around at him in shocked surprise.

"Oh, sorry," Shannon said, bowing his head in embarrassment.

"It was nice! I love music -- all fae do. And you hold the tune so well!"

"He used to play harp for the court," Derry said. "They even liked him, and that's a hard audience to impress."

"No doubt." Brian nodded enthusiastically, which seemed an odd reaction to the little tune. "Music can make unique magic. Creative magic and healing magic. Not all the fae have that ability."

"Ah, so you're excited because you finally found a use for

me," Shannon said with an entirely serious nod.

"No, my Lord! I did nay mean --" Brian looked at him with shocked dismay, nearly tripping as he struggled to find something proper to say.

"That was a joke, Brian!" Shannon slapped him on the shoulder. That surprised the fae even more, but he did smile. "You need to relax a bit around us."

"Besides, it's not like he's ever had a use before," Derry added.

Shannon laughed, and Brian finally joined him this time. Birds sang at the sound, and Derry thought the world seemed brighter around them. Derry wanted to be fully fae like Brian. He wanted to be done with the rest of this madness and move on to an adventure that did not include worrying about how he would fail everyone else.

Derry kept those thoughts to himself. Doubt had lingered in his mind ever since he returned to Lynashin, and now was not the time to pull those fears up into the light again. Derry tried to remember, though, if he'd ever felt doubt before leaving his safe little world. He thought his doubts must have been simple things back then. Would he ever have that peace again?

He looked at Brian, trying to imagine what life had been like for him before he went to the fae. Brian gave him the hope that everything would work out well.

When Derry finally heard the village ahead, he suddenly didn't want to go there. He wanted the peace of the forest and the calm that had traveled with them for this little time. The war seemed too big; the trouble too diverse for him to handle.

"Derry?" Shannon whispered.

Derry kept spending a lot of time ... not here, and it probably drove poor Shannon mad, trying to keep him from wandering off or stumbling into trouble. Derry vowed to pay better attention, and not wish for those other changes to come too quickly. He still had work to do here. He wanted to do this right.

Derry admitted that having Shannon with him (the fool), meant he didn't have so much to hold in the human world. He loved King Nevin, of course -- but the man had always been King first, no matter what their relationship. If King Nevin had been his father, Derry would have wanted to follow in the man's footsteps. However, there was Tevin for that job, and he'd do very well at it. Or Roe.

Derry felt a surge of unease at the thought of Egan, there between Tevin and Roe. His mother's child, and did he know magic as well? Not that knowing magic was evil, Derry reminded himself with a bit of a smile -- but what a person did with the power could change whole worlds. He would never trust Egan to do right.

The Queen had three sons, but she'd lost her connection to Tevin very early. Maybe, in fact, she'd let him go on purpose, to keep the King from looking at the other two. King Nevin had his heir, and he didn't bother much with Egan and Roe. King Nevin had limited time to train the boy, and Tevin had been a handful the first few years

Queen Alisia had concentrated on Egan. Roe had turned out to be too much like his father, Derry supposed. A smart boy. What did he suspect of his mother? Probably no more than the rest of them. Everyone in the castle had walked carefully and avoided the spider weaving her webs around them.

He had heard castle rumors, and thought little of it -- but hadn't there been a whisper of fear from some of the servants?

Not his job to pay attention to the servants who served the King and Queen -- he couldn't have done so, even if he'd tried. There had always been a plethora of servants from the kitchens to those who served Nevin and Alisia personally. He did know that few stayed very long in her service, and the

King was happy enough to let them go, even over the Queen's protests sometimes. Did she want to keep them close? Did she fear what they might say?

Hadn't three died in the last two years before he went to the Isles?

She'd been exiled from court.

What had the Queen really done during that time?

Derry shook his head and called himself back to here again. They were closer to the village, and he shook himself out of those thoughts to pay attention. Derry could see buildings just beyond the row of trees. He could hear voices -- a constant whisper of sound that was only slightly louder than the breeze. People moved quickly around the buildings though without the frantic worry he'd last seen. It still made Derry uneasy to see it, though. In fact, the entire place made him uncomfortable suddenly.

"Something wrong." Brian stopped and held up his hand as he frowned. "Agitation in the village. I don't want to walk into trouble there. We had better move more carefully."

"Something is going on." Derry stopped and looked down the long road that led through the village. People moved there, but they all seemed in a hurry again -- and it wasn't nightfall yet. "I think I feel fae close by, too."

"Yes," Brian agreed. "And they're upset as well."

"Not good," Shannon stopped to lean against a tree. A bird came down and chattered at him, and he looked startled, probably because he understood the little creature's unease, if not precisely what it said.

They crept to the edge of town, where the trees grew almost to the first cottage. Glendalow looked like a hive of activity, and the frantic energy didn't make the place look very safe at all.

"Every village I visit lately has a problem," Derry said with a sigh. "I feel like a harbinger of disaster. And it doesn't help that trouble travels with me."

"I thought he liked us," Brian said, looking at Shannon.

Nice that the two of them still had a sense of humor.

"Anyone here that you two can trust?" Brain asked, peering around the brush and looking worried.

"Trust. As in trust with our lives," Shannon said. "I'd say Finil, the innkeeper, but he'd be impossible to reach without being noticed."

"We might be in luck." Derry pointed towards a soldier standing at the edge of the village, obviously working as a guard along the road. "I know that man. He's Captain Killough, and he escorted me back to Tyleen when I first came home."

"The one who came running after you when you went to the fae," Shannon added with a glance at the man. "And the fae made him very nervous, as I recall."

"I'll stay out of the way then," Brian offered. "Won't hurt to have back up anyway. If you intend to talk to him, you better do so quickly."

Brian was right. Captain Killough looked as though he prepared to head elsewhere. Derry didn't waste time as he moved out of the trees and to the edge of the road, drawing the man's immediate attention. When Shannon joined him, Killough's shoulders straightened, and he took a few quick steps their way with a nervous glance down the road.

""Get back to the trees," he warned softly. "Don't let them see you, Prince Derry! Nor you, Lord Shannon!"

Worse than Derry expected. He darted back to the trees, Shannon at his side. Captain Killough had come closer, but someone else arrived at a run.

"No, not fae or humans," Killough said with a laugh. "A couple of deer, but they startled me."

"Could have been fae spies," the second man said, glancing into the woods but obviously seeing nothing.

"Damn poor ones since they ran so fast." Killough laughed, and the other man did as well. "I'm going to walk into the edge of the trees, though, just to be certain. You stay here and keep watch on me."

"Yes sir," the man said, obviously pleased not to be the one sent to have a look.

Killough strode out along the road, and then within a yard of where they were, stepped aside as though checking things out. The other soldier watched carefully but didn't come any closer.

"Stay hidden!" Killough warned, his voice soft and harsh. "Come to the room after dark. Quietly. Discreetly."

He started to step back. Derry panicked and nearly gave himself away by reaching for the man.

"The room?" he whispered, frantic because he didn't understand.

"The room you had at the inn," Killough said. "Stay hidden!"

Killough turned and strode back up the road where he patted the man on the shoulder and then headed away without ever looking back. The man stayed his hand on his sword.

"My, that was inspiring," Shannon said with a sigh. "It makes me feel incredibly safe."

The three quickly moved well away from the road, settling at last in a dense stand of tall old oaks. It wasn't until then that Derry felt safe enough to speak. No one could come upon them without warning.

"Here's the question," he said as he leaned against a solid trunk. "Is this problem directed at the fae, or is it just at me? I had the feeling it might be both from the way Captain Killough and the other acted."

"I might go speak with some fae," Brian offered, though he frowned. "I don't want to leave you two alone --"

"We're safe enough," Derry said. "And I won't go to town

until well after dark."

"Good." Brian stood and looked both weary and worried. "I don't like what's we've seen here. I don't know why the fae haven't come to us, but they aren't hiding either. I think they are just busy with something else. I don't like feeling as though we haven't an ally in the world tonight."

"We have Captain Killough. We have friends, even if they aren't here with us. Don't despair, Brian."

Brian smiled, and bells rang around him, loud enough to make the birds sing again. "Despair is hardly a fae emoting, is it? Must still be some human blood in me after all!"

"More likely, it's the company you're keeping," Shannon offered.

Brian laughed, gave them a little bow, and moved off into the woods, the bells and the birds traveling with him. Derry leaned back, glanced at the sky -- already growing darker -- and closed his eyes, savoring the moment of peace.

"Can I get you anything, Derry?"

"You are not my servant, Shannon."

"No, I'm your friend."

Derry opened his eyes, considering the actual weight of those words. Shannon made himself enemies by associating with Derry. Now he had also taken the step to become fae as well, just so that he could stay with Derry at a time of danger. Oh, chances were that he would have made that change anyway -- Derry should have realized it before now. Shannon had been no happier at court than he had been, after all.

But still, he had cut himself off from his family, and he couldn't go back. The reality struck Derry like a blow.

"Oh damn, Shannon. What are we going to tell your family?"

"Tell them?" Shannon asked, sitting down by the tree so that Derry did as well. Shannon held out a piece of apple. "Derry?"

"Shannon, you know ... you can't go back to being what you were --"

"Cannot go back to being human," Shannon said with a nod and then a look of exasperation. "Of course, I know, Derry. It's not as though I didn't have plenty of warning with you as an example. I don't want to go back. Oh, I love my family, but I drifted away from them over the last few years. I didn't belong there."

"Changed when I took the Queen's errand to the north," Derry ventured, forcing himself to stay calm while he thought about that ill-fated trip. All of this was his fault --

"The big change happened then, but that wasn't the only cause," Shannon replied and finally forced the piece of apple into Derry's hand. "I was changing before you left -- and so were you. We had talked of it now and then, wondering what we were doing, what we should be doing."

"Yes. I remember." One memory came back, sharp and clear, of Shannon sitting beside him on the banks by the river, watching craft go past. They had both wondered if they were simply letting the current take them or if they ought to be choosing their own destinations. Was this better?

"I stopped playing the harp years ago, long before you left. That was the sign, Derry, but no one really noticed, not even me. I can hear music again. I haven't heard it for a long time, and this feels as though I am coming awake."

Derry took one deep breath, calming himself once more and accepting that Shannon did have his own mind and his personal reasons for becoming fae. He even understood. After all, they'd always been very much alike. Looking at Shannon, he wondered if his companion didn't have a better reason for becoming fae than he did.

"Eat the apple, Derry."

Derry grinned and obeyed, glad to have a friend along on this long and extraordinary journey. He tried not to fret about

Brian and what his fae friend might face, especially since that was far out of his hands. Derry slowly relaxed, letting the peace of the forest ease the tension from his body. He could almost believe nothing mattered beyond these trees. He could find eternal peace here if he stayed.

Not yet, not yet.

The dark night came, and Brian hadn't returned. They heard fae bells twice, and not far away, but none sought out the two. No moon rose, and the stars remained obscured by leaves so that the night stayed very dark. He and Shannon could see well enough, though, which was undoubtedly a gift of the fae blood. Derry couldn't guess at the time, but he couldn't ignore it, either.

"Let's start heading toward the inn," Shannon finally suggested as he stood. "Brian can find us there. I don't want your Captain thinking we don't intend to show up. He has the answers, and we need them."

"Good point." He let Shannon help him up, though he felt considerably stronger after the long rest. He didn't worry about what the Captain was going to tell them. He already knew it wouldn't be good, but he would deal with it.

The woods remained quiet, and there was no feeling of trouble there. Distant fae moved off somewhere to the north, and there might have been some agitation within that group. Derry could sense them better tonight, but he couldn't tell more than the hint of unease there. He wished Brian had come back because their fae friend might have an idea of what they should do.

He and Shannon would have to trust themselves, Derry supposed. Derry had managed a lot of rest on this journey back to Tyleen, and he considered the changes that had taken him since that fateful last night in Glendalow. It was the time that Derry started thinking clearly and face the trouble, rather than assuming everything was fae-related and nothing Derry could really deal with yet. Now that he knew the Queen was involved -- never mind if she had magic or not -- the trouble came fully back into his own realm. He knew what they faced, magic or not.

They had finally found the real enemy.

Chapter Twenty-Five

Derry and Shannon entered the quiet village long after dark. The shadows worked for them as they went from the edge of the wild woods to the first of human buildings, avoiding the road and the guards. Glendalow looked calmer in the dark of the night, although Derry could sense worry and dread behind the closed and bolted doors.

Derry and Shannon arrived at the inn undetected. A large dog lay in the yard. If he was meant to be a guard, the people weren't thinking very clearly. The dog certainly didn't bark at the two almost-fae, and Derry rubbed the big creature's ears, winning a friendly swish of the tail. Shannon grinned.

Brian caught up with them at the side of the building, giving a silent but worried nod to the two. Derry couldn't tell if his friend had learned anything troubling, or if the attitude came from being in the village.

Derry spotted the window up high on the side of the building and wondered how they were going to get to the room without going through the inn's main door and the common room. The building was made of wood, though. No matter how long removed from the forest, it still held a touch of nature. Derry began to climb, and it proved effortless work. His fingers touched the wood and held on, though he had a harder time through the boots. That might be why the fae were often barefoot, Derry thought. He heard Shannon's little gasp of surprise before he followed Derry up, Brian right behind.

Derry caught a feel of the building, the layering of emotions down through the years: more good than bad had happened within the walls. Derry let himself borrow a little of that peace, reminding himself that what was happening today was transitory. They would get past this trouble and move on. Derry only hoped to help them move to a better place. He did not want to leave the Queen to complete whatever plans she intended.

Queen Alisia had said he was already too late, though. Finding trouble at Glendalow made Derry fear what he would learn but running away was no more of an answer now than it had been from the start. Derry reached the window, knew there were people inside, and still didn't pause. The shutter opened at his touch and the faint light of a single candle shown inside.

"Come in lads," Captain Killough whispered. "Quickly and quietly now."

Derry obeyed, noting someone else in the shadows -- an anxious, but not frightened person. He reached back to help Shannon, ignoring the fact that his shoulder still ached when he lifted anything. Shannon hadn't been quite as 'sure-footed' on the wall, and he came into the room and put his feet on the floor with a definite sigh of relief. Brian slid in last and pulled the shutter closed behind them.

They all paused there, Derry, Shannon, Brian, Killough, and someone else Derry couldn't quite see past the soldier. Sounds came from outside: a distant shout, a dog barking somewhere at the other end of the village. Laughter rose from the room below, nervous and uneasy. Silence fell slowly while no one in the room moved or even breathed very loudly.

"Your lordships," Brian said softly, sounding all too human, and like the peasant boy he'd been again as he bowed his head. The little candle was almost gutted in a bowl of melted wax "I can use a little magic to protect us from sight and hearing if you don't object."

"Ah, well." Captain Killough shrugged, a shadowy movement in the dark. "I've gone this far -- we both have. Best not to take any chances now. Do your magic, lad."

Brian whispered words, soft and melodic, and accompanied by the little whisper of bells. Derry felt the change in the air and sensed a seal slipping around them. A moment later, a glow of yellowish light brightened the area. Brian sat a glowing globe in the air above them, and it hung there like a giant summer firefly tethered by some invisible leash.

"We're safe now," Brian said and sounded relieved.

"I can't say I'll ever get used to this magic," Killough replied, shaking his head as he looked upward and then at the three of them. "But I can handle this tonight. I'm glad to see you both, Prince Derry, Lord Shannon."

"And this is our friend, Brian," Derry said, waving a hand toward the third member of their group. "He's fae."

"I had noticed that part almost right away."

Derry laughed and noted the other man in the room turned out to be Finil, the innkeeper. The man gave a bright smile when Derry looked his way. Shannon pushed Derry into the chair by the window, and Brian stayed nearby, listening for trouble outside -- and ready if magic came their way. Shannon sat on the floor. Derry could tell that both of his friends relieved to be inside the building and safe for the moment.

"I took Finil here into my confidence when I asked for this specific room. He showed kindness to you that night we rode through, Prince Derry, and I could tell he was a true friend."

"You made a fine choice in ally. So, what is all this madness? Brian, did you learn anything from the fae tonight?" Derry asked, glancing back at their quiet companion.

"Some," Brian said, still sounding uneasy. "What I learned isn't particularly good, either -- but nearly everything is human-related. Perhaps you should hear the tale from the Captain, who likely knows more than the fae in that regard."

"Fine," Derry said. He looked back at Captain Killough, feeling a touch of frustration since no one seemed willing to tell him anything at all -- which meant this had to be terrible news.

"You've been out of touch for the last few days?" Killough asked, settling on the bed, though he looked uncomfortably again.

"Completely. We couldn't even find fae to give us the news."

"Ah, well, then, here is the worst of the news. King Nevin, Prince Tevin, and Prince Roe have disappeared. Queen Alisia and Prince Egan have assumed the rule, and they've spread the word that Derry is responsible for their disappearance. Egan swears he saw you using magic to do the three harm and only barely saved his mother from the same fate."

Derry felt his heart thudding hard against his chest as he stared at the man. "Gods -- Uncle Nevin, Tev, Roe -- what did she do to them?"

"And not a worry about what harm she's trying to do you," Killough said with a soft smile. "You're a fine young man."

"Their attack on me was inevitable," Derry replied with a wave of his hand. "But I didn't expect the others --"

We don't know where they have gone, lad. We fear the

worst, but she's not produced a body, our fine and treacherous Queen. I mistrust her for that one. Let's hear what your fae friend says before we try to guess at what's happened."

"We do know where the King and Crown Prince are being held," Brian replied with a quick nod.

"Alive?" Derry asked softly.

"Yes, they are alive. The Queen wants you there, Derry -- and they are the bait to draw you into her trap. If they were dead, she'd hand over the bodies and hope to convince everyone of your guilt. We have Prince Roe, though he suffered such serious injury that even our magic barely kept him alive long enough to begin healing."

"How was the boy injured?" Finil dared ask.

"The Queen tried to kill him and blame the death on Derry."

"No big surprise there," Shannon said, the anger in his eyes showed more clearly than he allowed in his voice.

"Lucky for Roe that he and the fae had remained in close contact since you left Tyleen, Derry. The fae sensed something very wrong and barely reached Roe in time, foiling at least one aspect of her plan. Queen Alisia meant for Prince Roe's body to be found with clues pointing to you as the killer."

"I wasn't anywhere near Tyleen until today."

"Doesn't matter," Killough replied with a wave of his hand towards Brian. "Everyone knows you deal in magic, and you have fae blood. They think anything is possible with such powers."

"Oh, damn. You best tell us what happened to King Nevin and Prince Tevin," Shannon said, looking at Brian again.

Brian bowed his head once before he spoke. When he looked up, his eyes blazed with unexpected anger. "She has them held safely in the castle, your lordships, and they're still alive. However, the trap she's laid makes it impossible to free them. If any of the fae go near, it'll kill both the fae as well as the King and Prince, and then she'll have the proof she wants that we are all evil."

"What kind of trap?" Killough asked, though he obviously had guessed the implications already.

"Magic," Derry answered. "She adept in the art."

"Is she fae then?" Finil asked, looking confused.

"No," Brian said, with a shake of his head. "Dark magic. Evil. And very, very powerful."

"I don't understand." Finil looked from one to the other, staying for a moment on Derry. "Why would she do these things? Why would she even learn such magic?"

"She craves power," Derry said. "Human power and magic power. We've known about the first from the start. She made it clear that she intended to have her hand in how Lynashin was ruled."

"She can't take the throne, though. Egan rules now," Killough protested. "She's foreign!"

"Egan is her son," Shannon reminded them. "We've never thought much of his mother's little lamb -- but she's always made it plain that she was the one who ruled Egan. She can't rule if there is another prince of the line to take Egan's place. Beyond Derry, no one outside of the immediate family counts. She's not had any good luck killing Derry, so now she's making certain he can't inherit the throne when the people look for an alternative to her and the dog she raised."

"Damn. Too true. God and Goddess! It's bad enough the woman is evil, but a hypocrite besides --" Killough said with a shake of his head and a snarl on his face.

"You believe us?" Brian asked, sounding surprised.

"I wouldn't be here if I wasn't inclined to believe you from the beginning."

"True. My apologies. I'm not used to dealing with humans." Brian offered such a bright grin that Derry couldn't guess if he joked or not.

"What are our options, Brian?" Derry finally asked.

"You should set sail for a friendly land."

He hadn't expected that answer from Brian. "You know that's not going to happen," he said.

"You might be the last hope of a good ruler for Lynashin. We have Roe, but ... he's been badly wounded, and there is still a chance he won't pull through. You are an option, Derry. You are a hope --"

"But I am already too closely tied with the fae," Derry reminded him. "I can't go back, and if people learn about Queen Alisia and her magic, they are going to be even less likely to trust me. I'm here to help, my friends."

"None of us want to see you dead, Derry," Shannon said with a shake of his head, but then he turned away. "How many humans can we count on, Captain Killough?"

"It's difficult to say. People fear to say anything but what pleases Queen Alisia. Some villagers are grumbling, and there's even been sharp in the city of Tyleen itself, so she's put the guards out to supposedly protect everyone from the fae. It is obvious that most of the guards are her spies. The clan lords -- she's keeping them under even tighter watch, there in their nestling castles around Tyleen." Killough stopped and tilted his head, blinking several times. "Forgive me, Lord Shannon, but it suddenly occurs to me that ... you are different."

Shannon grinned very brightly.

"You did join the fae, then," Killough said and didn't sound at all surprised or shocked. "I thought as much. Is this a new phase the nobility is going through?"

"I wish we could get that lucky," Derry said with a laugh. "Queen Alisia would have a hell of a hard time dealing with more of us!"

"Not to mention that the fae couldn't well handle it," Brian added and looked alarmed by the idea. "What a frightening concept!"

They all laughed, even Killough and Finil, who had stayed quiet but attentive. Derry didn't see any distrust in either human face. If anything, he thought there might be a little hope lingering in their eyes. That bothered him, fearing these two might expect salvation from the evil Queen. Ah, but wasn't that what they meant to do anyway? Maybe it was good to have someone on the outside reminding him of his purpose.

"What about the king and Tevin?" Derry dared to ask, fear settling in his stomach. "How safe are they in her hands?"

"Safe enough, Queen Leanora thinks," Brian replied. He glanced toward the window. "Alisia has spread the word that you and the fae have them and mean to do them evil. She doesn't want either dead without you there, and she's using them as a lure to draw you in. She's committed too much magical power to back out now without good provocation. When she does, she will have to kill both and hope the murders don't point to her. For now, she'll wait for you, Derry."

"And if I don't' show up?"

"The King and Crown Prince languish in her hold while she runs the country to hell," Brian answered. Killough and Final nodded agreement. "She's already let her allies loose in places, as we have seen. Eventually, people will give the Queen anything she wants to make the evil stop. Alisia made a mistake with Roe, Derry. She tortured him and then put him out to be found dead near the forest so she could point at the fae. Alisia claimed that Roe had fought us and taken injury. We found him before he died -- a matter of heartbeats -- and she knows his body was never recovered. She still has the upper hand, Derry, but she hasn't won the war. Queen Alisia has time, but we have -- collectively -- far more power. Alisia made one serious mistake by making her trap so obvious. She didn't want you to miss it. However, this gives us an excellent chance to study what she's done. The fae have far more knowledge in the arts of magic than she ever will. We hope to quickly find a weakness in her trap."

"Time," Killough said. He looked from one to the other. "It doesn't mean much to the fae, does it?"

"Some of us were human once, Captain," Brian replied, and his hand traced a scar on his arm. "And not so long ago. I remember human time very well. I do mean quickly in a human sense."

The entire turn of conversation took Derry quite by surprise, and Shannon, too, from the look of shock on his face. Time? Fae? Of course, he knew the fae didn't age -- but he had never applied that part of the myth even to Brian, let alone to himself or Shannon. The world got stranger every day.

"We better call this a night, and each group learn what we can," Shannon said. "We'll meet back here in five nights."

"If it's safe," Derry added as he glanced at the window. "She can sense the use of magic, can't she?"

Brian looked out and nodded. "Yes. However, I arranged for many fae in the area to use a little magic tonight. I'm just another little spot in the crowd. We can do this again when need be. Take good care, Captain Killough, Master Finil. Don't let anyone suspect you of complicity with us. Obey the Queen and Prince Egan as best you can. However, if you do need help, you need only call out to the fae. We'll listen for you."

Finil looked uncertain, but Killough appeared strangely at ease with the offer. He seemed a different man from the night they had both faced the fae Queen.

The world had changed so quickly...

Brian dulled the light to darkness and dropped their protective shields. He pulled the shutters open on the night that still seemed moonless and unfriendly. Derry moved towards the window, wishing he felt more assured. Wishing he had a plan --

Killough put a hand on Derry's shoulder, holding him back. Then, unexpectedly, the older man silently embraced the fae prince and gave him a nod that mingled both appreciation and friendship. The warmth of that contact stayed with Derry as he climbed down the building and followed Shannon and Brian to the protective, though not safe, woods. They were far away from the village before Brian dared speak.

"Let us head north. We've not much of the night left, and I do want to get some rest before morning. I fear the days -- and nights -- will be long before this mess is finished."

Derry nodded and felt worn already. Shannon only sighed as they began to jog northward.

Queen Alisia had made her move. They had a chance, finally, to act against her, but only if they moved wisely.

Chapter Twenty-Six

Songbirds offered their sweet music as Derry awoke. Both the sound and the fact he had slept through the dawn without any nightmares, immediately brightened his mood. Derry turned and smiled, finding a half dozen fae sitting around their small camp. He had sensed they were there and had felt their protective shield around him while he slept. He felt far better than he had in a long time.

Then he saw a few more fae arrive. They brought Roe with them, carrying him on a stretcher and bundled in blankets. The boy looked worn and gaunt, and Derry could see bruises on his hands, arms, and face.

"Roe," Derry greeted him and brushed his hair back. He looked around the camp and grinned. "My. I bet two princes of Lynashin have never met like this before. Not a servant in sight. That's the worst of it."

Shannon and Roe laughed, and the fae looked amused.

"They thought we might come and discuss this mess," Roe said as he and the fae settled nearby.

Derry watched with growing worry. Roe looked exhausted, and his hand shook as he accepted a cup of tea, but

Derry said nothing. The others doubtless babied him too much. Derry knew Roe wouldn't like it any more than he did.

"We must stop her," Roe finally said, looking back at him. The hurt and anger grew in his eyes, though Roe tried to keep the emotions from his face. "We must stop her and Egan. I didn't know they were evil, Derry --"

"None of us did," Derry assured him.

"But surely, after everything she did to you --"

"I disliked her, but for personal reasons, Roe. I thought she treated me the way she did for the same reason. Even after I gained my link with the fae, I didn't realize she was anything more than an unpleasant woman. Queen Alisia couldn't hide her essentially cruel nature, but she did well at masking the magic. No one knew Roe, not even the fae."

Roe glanced around and appeared relieved as his body relaxed. Derry suspected the boy felt guilt, knowing he survived while the King and Crown Prince remained in her hands and might not come away alive. Derry suspected Roe also knew how unsuited he was to this unusual battle. He and Roe had a lot in common these days.

"I wish --" Roe whispered softly, his head bowed and his hands still. Then he looked at Derry with something wanting in his eyes. "I wish I could go to the fae, go completely, and escape the world of humans. I never knew there were such wondrous places just outside my door until I traveled with the fae. It's so free, Derry."

"Roe --"

"I can't go. I know." Roe gave him a wane, half-hearted smile as he leaned back against a tree, apparently worn out just from the little talk. "With my father and Tevin in her hands and Egan, her accomplice, the throne might yet come to me. Or to you."

"I'm already too much a part of the fae. The people would never allow me to rule with those ties. Don't despair. Your father and Tevin are still alive, and we'll get them free. Your mother has power, but she can't stand up to the fae once we find her weakness."

"How can you be so certain?" he asked, tilting his head to the side.

"Queen Alisia fears the fae. She hasn't tested her magic against them and has avoided any confrontation. That means she has something to fear from our fae friends."

"That's true." Roe looked better for the conversation. He suddenly grinned. "And she especially fears you, Derry. She wanted to blame you for my death." His eyes flickered a little at the statement despite the smile. He lifted a hand when Derry started to speak, a surprisingly regal movement. His young cousin had always stood far closer to the throne than his position. "I'm all right. It was a horrendous experience, but I survived, and I'll help defeat her as best I can. I have begun thinking she underestimates everyone, Derry. She wanted to turn people against you, but I don't think it would have worked even if I had died. Most everyone at Tyleen and beyond still spoke well of you, even after this business with the fae. I think she miscalculates the ability of people to reason for themselves."

Derry realized he had badly underestimated Prince Roe, though he didn't say as much aloud. Roe hadn't gone running back to his mother when she returned from her exile. Roe had done better at watching the court, too. Not a child.

Derry gratefully accepted a cup of tea from Shannon. Brian handed another cup to Roe. Derry sipped and savored the morning warmth, including the sweet and the bitter. They still had peace this morning, but it would not last.

"How long will you stay with the fae, Roe?" Derry asked.

"They suggest I stay until I'm strong enough to stand on my own," Roe replied. He grinned, making a joke of his weakness. "Then they'll deliver me to Kelkass Abby. They say the place is holy enough to keep me safe."

"Is it really?" Shannon asked and looked at Brian, obviously curious about the statement.

"The brothers of Kelkass live on a fae holy site -- like the standing stone sites, but more powerful by a thousand-fold. And yes, they know about the power. Of all the people in Lynashin, they alone maintained contact with the fae. That's a secret kept for hundreds of years, my friends."

"No one will hear it from us," Roe said, reassuring him.

"Kelkass is a wild place," Derry said, recalling the time he had visited once, just after his parents had died. The King had taken him there, the two of them alone -- well, except for all the guards. Derry remembered that being there had helped, though he hadn't expected it to. "It's far up in the hills without a settlement of any sort nearby, which would make it easy to keep the secret there."

They spoke for a while, and a little later, Roe's companions gathered him up and headed away, taking the prince to safety again. It probably wasn't wise to have him too near to Derry and Shannon for long, but Derry still wished he didn't have to go. He watched as the group disappeared into the shadows of the woods, and then looked up with surprise when Brian put a hand on his shoulder.

"You did very well," Brian praised, confusing him.

"I did? How?" Derry asked.

"Since his mother's attack, Roe has felt inadequate. You didn't treat him like the unneeded prince whom even his mother and brother obviously found worthless and easy to turn away. You gave Roe the dignity of treating him like the possible next holder of the human throne. Besides, he needed to know that what has happened isn't his fault. He is not alone in misjudging the true depth of evil in the Queen Alisia."

"Ah. Of course."

"A shame no one ever did the same for you," Shannon

said with a sigh.

Brian gave a quick nod and a fleeting smile. "Time to move on," he said. "Our people sense Alisia's magic questing again."

"Do we have any better idea of how to defeat her?"

"None. We're working on finding answers now that we know at least whom we face. When we have an answer, we'll tell you."

Derry gathered up his belongings as they broke camp and headed into the woods. There were worse ways to spend the day than wandering the wilderness with his two friends. He only wished they could, perhaps, wander more slowly. The three raced from one glade to another, with the feel of trouble quite literally too close behind them. Derry could sense Queen Alisia seeking and searching for her prey. As the day grew later, her aura became more frantic and irritated. Good and bad --

And Shannon walked right into a trap. A bolt of magic hit him in the chest with enough force to send Shannon tumbling backward, too stunned to even make a sound as he slammed against a tree.

Before Derry could react, her magic swept all round them. The world trembled as creatures surged out of the ground, crawling and slithering -- dark gray and bloodless white things as long as his arm, and with claws and teeth. Derry kicked one aside, drawing his dagger and moving to protect Shannon.

"Unfocused magic," Brian said. He gave a wave of his hand that sent one of the monsters squealing back into nothingness. "Alisia's magic, but just a trap hoping for fae prey. She's not here. Yet. Too many of them!"

"What do I do?" Derry stabbed one creature, but others moved closer to Shannon. He could sense that his friend was not severely injured, but Shannon did not respond to the danger. Derry had to protect Shannon, but nothing he did seemed to work against these creatures.

"You must use your will against them, Derry," Brian advised as he moved in on the left of Shannon and Derry to the right. Brian was breathless already, trying to hold back dozens of the creatures. "Tell them you don't want them here and be more forceful than Queen Alisia's wish that they remain." Brian waved a hand again, and another two disappeared, but he had to step back and gasp for breath this time.

Derry believed in Brian far more than he did in his own nascent fae abilities, but he would try, nonetheless. He waved his hand toward the closest stand of the creatures and very much wished them away. He felt an odd connection between them as a line of his will snapped out and engulphed the ugly things in a circle of shimmering light.

Over half of the entire group disappeared.

Derry found himself falling to his knees, extremely weak and very ill.

"Oh damn, oh damn! I didn't know you'd be that well the first time!" Brian leapt to protect both he and Shannon now. He sounded frantic and breathless.

"I did well?"

"You need lessons in control, Prince Derry. You put far too much of your personal power into that wish. Though this time -- appreciated it --"

Brian desperately tried to ward off another half dozen of the nasty creatures. Trying to protect Derry and Shannon made him careless of his own safety, and something long and gray wrapped itself around the fae's ankle. Brian yelped in pain.

Derry lifted his hand and weakly waved it away. He hadn't the strength for anything more strenuous. However, the creature did disappear, along with several more of its companions. Brian stepped back, limping slightly, but with a nod of thanks. The shadows continued to shift, though, and

Derry could see more of the creatures would soon be on them.

"Help -- on the way," Brian gasped. Derry could barely hear distant bells. "We must get moving, though. She'll have noticed the trap was sprung."

Derry didn't think he could run. And Shannon -- God and Goddess, Shannon still hadn't gotten up --

Brian waved away a few more of the creatures and looked frantically around. "She knows where we are, Derry --"

The realization frightened him. Derry didn't want to lose his friends to her wrath. Panic made him reach for Shannon, desperately wanting his friend to be well --

Blackness.

Chapter Twenty-Seven

"I only told him once what he should do," Brian whispered. His voice hinted at worry and awe. "He banished a good many of her creatures with a single thought. However, then he feared for Shannon, and he wished his friend better, calling up more power far too soon after the other magic. It worked."

"Worked very well," Shannon agreed.

Shannon's steady voice drew Derry closer to the world again. He couldn't be sure he really wanted to regain full consciousness, though. He could already tell he ached, and even the act of breathing made him feel ill. Derry twitched slightly and then stayed still again.

"You are a fool sometimes, Derry SanOsen," Shannon said softly. He laid a warm hand on Derry's arm, pulling him back to reality and probably another crisis.

"He didn't know what he was doing," someone else said. Derry didn't know the voice, but he could tell a fae spoke. New bells mingled with Brian's melody. Safe. "Prince Derry already has the fae ability to instinctively use his new powers. Now we must teach him to temper the amount of power he uses each time. If other fae hadn't been so close, and able to stop him, he might have released all is life-energy into that last wish to make you well, Shannon."

"Might have killed himself is what you're saying," Shannon said, his finger's tightening on Derry's arm.

"Yes. Prince Derry is dangerous to himself at this point. There is only one other way that we can hope to teach him what he needs so that he will survive."

"Teach him by magic?" Brian asked and sounded oddly worried by the idea.

"Yes, by magic," the other man replied, his voice quiet and calm. A fire crackled nearby, the warmth welcome, and the feel of peace helped. "It won't be easy, but we dare not let him go blundering on in this way. This boy is far too powerful, and I'm beginning to think this comes from more than our fair fae Queen's blood."

Those words intrigued Derry. He finally eased his eyes open, grateful for the pleasant fae light suspended overhead and surprised to find they had crowded into a small cavern. How odd. He hadn't realized they weren't out in the open. The air tasted fresh, and the walls of stone were smooth and dry. Magic lingered here.

"What do you mean, more than her blood?" Shannon asked. "Do you believe he has some magic of his own?"

"Latent," the unnamed fae answered. He sat opposite Derry, sitting cross-legged, and his long, silvery hair hanging to his waist. Derry had never met this one; the fae radiated magic and calm. "I suspect there might be fae blood somewhere in his background. What's known about his family?"

Brian, who had slumped against the wall by the stranger, sat up his eyes gone wide with shock. Shannon, though, laughed.

"This is Prince Derry SanOsen, Kyrian. He's the son of the High King's own brother and a Prince of Lynashin. The

SanOsens can trace their family back at least fifteen generations, and his mother was a noble with almost as long of a family history."

"Ah, well, of course." Kyrian grinned. "That's fine and good, but humans came to Lynashin more than thirty human generations past, and we were closer to some in those early days. You came as refugees running from the cruelty of other humans. It made you less inclined to cruelty toward us, and more open to our help."

"But we became cruel," Shannon said with a weary shake of his head.

"No, you never have been a cruel people. In many places, humans have enslaved and murdered the fae. We may not live in perfect companionship here, but our wars were brief, and both fae and humans have survived. We can work together against a common foe in times of need, as we've proven lately. The other humans don't realize about their Queen and her magic, but I don't think it would make much difference if they did learn. They mostly despise her, you know."

"This is true," Shannon agreed. He didn't look as comfortable as Kyrian or Brian. "I don't think she can have made friends. She can't hide her true nature, and no one really trusts her."

"In many places, the humans fear the fae and magic," Kyrian added. "There are more fae in Lynashin, both true and adopted, than almost anywhere else where humans live, though. Despite fears, we've done well together."

Strange news, Derry thought. His world had always included the fae. The thought of places where they had been destroyed would have appalled him even before he became a part of their world.

Derry moved slightly again and made a sound of discomfort, though he thought he ought to feel worse.

"Derry, are you with us?" Shannon asked as he leaned

closer. Shannon looked very good, and that relieved Derry of other worries. Whatever he had done had obviously helped his friend, but he still hoped this fae -- this Kyrian --could help him with some control. Blundering around didn't help, especially when he faced Alisia.

"Derry?" Shannon asked again.

"Sorry." Derry realized he had been staring, trying to sort through his worries and thoughts. "Not all here."

"You are better," Shannon said with a nod of relief. "At least you're talking this time."

"This time?"

"You awoke twice before, but we couldn't get any reaction from you." Shannon looked worried at those words, a remembrance of something Derry didn't recall.

Derry finally started to sit up, marveling at the soft pillows and blankets where he had been sleeping. They were entirely made of magic. He brushed his hand over the pale blue fabric, amazed at the feel, and finally had to pull himself away to face Shannon again. His friend had started to worry, the feeling clinging to Shannon like a shadow.

"I don't remember anything except the battle," he said and tried to remember what had happened afterward. "Where are we?"

"A cave," Brian said softly and looked worried as well.

"I can tell that much," he answered with a little laugh. He felt strangely light-headed and oddly clear-headed at the same time. Calm. Calm as though this place made them safe from all the evils in the world.

"Derry, you're not listening to me," Brian said with a hand on his arm.

He looked back at the fae with a start.

"You're feeling attuned to this place," Brian explained, and Derry forced himself to listen and keep focus on his friend. "This is a very magical place, where the powers of natural magic exist and are at peace. There is a standing circle on the hill above us."

"Peace," Derry agreed and still had trouble staying focused. Sleep might have been better. He could have settled down and slept for a long time. His eyes even began to blink at the thought.

"This place is dangerous," Brian added his fingers tightening on Derry's arm, the hold almost painful. "The peace can calm a fae beyond a point where they can recover enough sense to go back out again. We're safe. The four of us together will keep each other aware, and the others outside will come in for us if we stay too long. However, this was a good place to bring you. The powers helped you recover, and the peace kept you calm -- and Queen Alisia can't sense you here. You need to wake up now, though. It isn't safe for you to sleep any longer."

"Nothing is safe," Derry replied, and the others gave reluctant nods of agreement, even Kyrian.

"That's the way of life, my friend," Kyrian answered as Derry sat up straighter with a sigh, forcing himself to feel less comfortable now that he understood the nature of the place. "No extreme is ever completely safe. However, this is a better place to rest than others. Your Queen will not find you here. Her powers are directed towards the dark and at the taking of power from others. Nature itself rejects her. Those of us with fae blood can find sanctuary here, and as far as your Queen can tell, you have simply disappeared."

"She could have tracked me to here when you brought me, though," he said. "And it would be plain where I had gone once in the area."

"If she had that much of a link on you, yes," Kyrian replied and seemed pleased that Derry had thought that through. "When you realized what Alisia had been doing with the nightmares, you severed that link to her. Alisia had no other connection, so she couldn't find you out in the wilds. Your battle with her creatures might have alerted her since you used so much power. However, we made certain she was not tracking us to this place, and it is not the closest circle of standing stones to where you fought. More fae are keeping watch. She has not seemed to look this way."

"This gives us a little time," Shannon said and sounded relieved.

Derry borrowed that reaction from his friend since he still felt a little too muddled to think clearly. The small cavern felt close but steady and stable. Derry felt a bit ephemeral himself.

"If we stay too long in here, she will recover too much of her own power," Kyrian continued. He looked toward what must be the opening, though covered in magic. A bit of a breeze blew through, and the fire flared up for a moment. Derry thought there might be glyphs worked into the walls around them. "Queen Alisia still wastes power on her traps. After a while, those traps will no longer need attention and become self-sustaining. Dangerous. If they reach that point, we'll be hunting them out for years. To stop it from happening, we must stop her and soon. We need --"

"You need to teach me magic by using magic," Derry said. "I heard that much."

"And that won't be easy for you," Kyrian explained. He looked at Derry for a long moment. "But you are ready. You know you're needed, and you've accepted the changes in you and the growth of your power. What would have taken years in others, you've accepted so that you can help others. This, my friend, is an essential first step."

The fae's wild, dark eyes had softened as he spoke. Looking at Kyrian, Derry realized this was an ancient fae -- perhaps so old that he'd been here when those first humans stepped foot in Lynashin. That realization almost made Derry uneasy. He was uncertain where he stood before such a being.

"Shannon, hold him in your arms," Kyrian instructed. "Make certain he has contact with you. You have always been his anchor to the world."

Shannon moved to pull Derry back against his chest. Derry felt protected again. Safe. He could have rested here for a long time, but he chased that thought away. Instead, he looked at Kyrian and nodded.

Chapter Twenty-Eight

Derry had barely looked into Kyrian's eyes and immediately found it impossible to look away, compelled by the magic that drew him to somewhere else. He felt as though fell -- and he hated falling, remembering the drop into the trees, the pain -- but no. This was a fall through time, back into ages. This was Lynashin before humans arrived.

Kyrian had brought him here, stood by him. The fae looked no different, although he felt younger. The fae held out his hand to a world filled with brighter greens and truer blues than Derry had ever seen.

Knowledge. Earth Magic.

Kyrian gave him that knowledge with blinding swiftness and an odd combination of want and need. Derry lost all sense of how long it took to learn the feel of a world with magic everywhere, and this underlaid his own world. Derry soon found how to touch and hold power. He learned the different types of power he could call upon, but Derry wanted to know more. Needed more, and so he raced ahead in a reckless push to grab every bit of knowledge he could find. Derry thought

Kyrian might be trying to tell him something, but he couldn't quite hear. He paused a moment -- and lost the thread he had been following. Then he looked around, stunned to find a place of jewel-like beauty, colors swirling and moving around him so that he didn't know quite where to reach to find the knowledge he wanted again.

Kyrian took hold of Derry's shoulder and led him out.

Derry came back to the real world with a cry of dismay at all he still had to learn. He almost pushed back in, but Kyrian stood at the portal, and with a gentle nod, directed him out again.

Derry came fully back to the world this time, gasping for breath and with Shannon's hands holding him tightly. He could sense anxious people all around, and when he looked at his fae guide, Kyrian suddenly leaned back against the cave's wall, shocked.

"That was not planned," Kyrian whispered and sounded as unsettled as he looked. "Prince Derry took control because he wanted to learn. I was unable to pull him out until he lost his way. My friends, most born fae don't have that much control!"

"I am sorry," Derry whispered, still feeling the whirl of knowledge and magic within him. He tried to sort out the basics and decide what might help. So much he had never known --

"By the Gods of all the peoples!" Kyrian exclaimed, and the intensity of is words drew Derry's wandering attention again. "Don't apologize. Your magical abilities are phenomenal, and we need such a gift now."

"You just scared the hell out of us again, Derry," Shannon said, and helped him sit up straighter. Shannon shifted his own shoulders and stretched. "At least it was in a good cause. You should sleep for a while. That was a damned long ordeal, even for Brian and me."

"Long?"

"You linked with Kyrian for over half a day," Shannon said.

"Seemed like only moments," Derry confessed. "But I am tired --"

Shannon nodded and helped Derry get comfortable amid the magical blankets and pillows. Not safe, Derry reminded himself, but just the same, he felt so tired that he fell instantly from consciousness to dream.

He knew this was a dream because he didn't usually walk up and talk to badgers and squirrels in everyday life.

"Not good," the squirrel chattered. Excited, and his tail flickered back and forth as he danced from foot-to-foot. "Not good. She takes too much. She is killing life."

"Too few young this year," the badger moaned as she stood on her back legs, and intently stared into Derry's face. "She takes their lives, and she doesn't care what she destroys."

"Queen Alisia," Derry ventured, hoping he understood the problem.

"Evil woman!" The squirrel danced about and chattered, nervous and afraid. "Dark woman! She wants more than just the rule of humanity. She wants power over everything. And she'll destroy it all. You must help!"

"I'll do all I can," Derry promised. "I don't know what that will be yet --"

"You learned quickly," the badger said, still looking up into his face. "She knows power, but she doesn't know cooperation. She doesn't understand trust -- and she doesn't believe in the strength of the power that comes from life and earth."

"Ah."

This was making a damn lot of sense for a dream, which made Derry uneasy again.

"You shouldn't be afraid," a familiar voice said.

Derry looked up to find Wild One standing before him, the squirrel and badger at his feet. Despite being glad to see him, Derry knew that Wild One's appearance, even in his dream, meant more trouble. The man didn't seem annoyed that they had not yet fully returned his wild friends to the woods. Derry hoped the fae still saw to that work.

"You are more of the wild now," Wild One said with a nod. "You understand better, and the warmth of your power even calls to me. What are you, changeling?"

"Only that," Derry insisted, giving this strange being a belated bow. The fae thought of Wild One as a god, and he was something even older than Kyrian. "Only a changeling still moving from one world to another. The fae say I have unusual power. None of us understand why."

"Nature provides from need. You are strong because we need your strength. You are our hope. If you fail, then the fae will disappear from Lynashin. You stand as the only guardian between them and your Queen, who will, eventually, find the powers she needs to destroy her enemy. She could not let them survive."

This was not a position Derry truly wanted. He would have fought Alisia without this added knowledge. To lose the fae --

He began to shiver.

("Easy Derry. Rest. Calm. I'm here," Shannon whispered somewhere else.)

"She knows that as long as the fae survive, she will never be safe despite her power." Wild One tilted his head, looking sad and old. That unnerved Derry. "Queen Alisia will destroy the land, and all the wild places will be gone. We'll all disappear when the ancient wilderness is destroyed. She does not trust the wild. She can't control it."

"Ah." He understood now. "Tell me what to do, Wild One."

"I cannot touch her. Since we met in my woods, I sought out the evil that besieged you, and I found her. She wards against such wildness as me. You and your changeling companion remain human enough, though. Use ... use humanness against her."

Derry wished for a better answer -- even in a dream -- but he accepted this help. "Thank you. I will consider this and find a way to use your wisdom," he said, admitting that he didn't quite understand. He still hoped for a better answer.

"You have helped my friends," the Lord of the Woods said with a little smile. "You put yourself in danger for the sake of the fox and her kits."

Derry started to shrug, but the wood spirit's hand reached out and rested on his shoulder. The contact felt very real, warm, and comforting -- and utterly alien.

Extraordinary dream.

"There are powers more easily reached by the inner mind," Wild One explained. He titled his head, looking uncertain. "So much power and ability, but so little understanding. Maybe that is power of its own. Maybe to understand too well would make you fae, and in that change make you more vulnerable to her own magic. You need your humanness defeat this mortal human Queen."

"This is not a dream," Derry suddenly realized.

"You felt a need. The children of the land called out in despair." The Lord of the Woods knelt and gathered both the badger and the squirrel into his arms. "Only the fair fae Queen ever speaks so easily to the wild creatures in words rather than just emotions."

"It's her blood that makes me fae."

"But your own strengths give you power. Your inner mind is strong. Rest now, my young changeling friend. Rest safe. You cannot face her until you are strong enough to defeat this human witch. Take care. Take time. Let her waste her power in a fury of anxiousness as time passes, while you rest and grow stronger."

"My friends -- the King, Prince Tevin --"

"She holds them in her power, but they live. The trap is set for you and rushing to face it without knowing how to deal with the problem will only get you -- and her prisoners killed -- which is her intent. Move slowly. Move wisely."

"Thank you for your advice, Wild One. I shall take it to heart."

He smiled and bowed his head, turning and walking away. Creatures followed him, including the foxes. Good. They would be safe.

Derry slept peacefully. Strange thoughts passed through his mind, and through some troubled him, none lingered for long. When he finally awoke, he could feel the start of a new day beyond the cave where birds and rabbits came awake. Brian was also awake and grinned silently at him.

Although Derry knew he still faced trouble, everything felt less pressing today. He took Wild One's words to heart and didn't feel the need to rush out to do battle with Alisia. Besides, he had no idea how to defeat her. Wild One wanted them to take their time, but there was another problem Wild One didn't quite understand. Kyrian knew that they would have to move soon to stop her traps from becoming self-powered.

"We need to know what she's doing," Derry whispered. Brian nodded and Shannon shifted slightly. He wasn't certain Kyrian really slept at all. "We must understand more than just the magic she employs. I want to know who her allies are as well. Have any of the clans rallied to support her, or are they only opposed to me and what I represent?"

Kyrian nodded as he sat up, and Derry was sorry to have awakened them. Derry had, however, come fully awake with thoughts he had not considered before. Shannon didn't look bothered.

"Fae," Shannon offered sleepily. "I don't know. Alisia never was very well-liked for herself. If she hadn't given King Nevin three fine male heirs, I suspect she wouldn't still be Queen."

"Ah, well. A woman of her wants would have found a way to power anyway," Derry said.

"Which leads to other dark thoughts about Nevin's first wife and son -- the ones who died of fever before we were born," Shannon said with his eyes narrowed. "Where was our fair Alisia then?"

"Short of a confession from her, we can't know the answer," Derry replied. He thought about those two, but then gave a slight wave of his hand, dismissing those ill-formed ghosts from his thoughts. "And forgive me, but I never knew the first Queen and her child, so they seem unreal to me. Whatever else we may think of Alisia, our world would be poorer without Tevin and Roe."

"True, true. They even make up for that prig, Egan," Shannon said with a smile. He brushed his hair back and looked better for the rest. "You realize he's disliked even more than his mother, right? People will forgive a certain amount of pretentiousness in a Queen. In a second Prince, though, it looks far too much like..."

"Like aspirations to take something he could only have at the death of his father and his brother?" Derry answered. "I think we know she always intended Egan to rule, and he must have taken that to heart."

"Why is it the King remained blind to her?" Brian asked.

"We were all blind. Remember, humans don't normally look towards magic for answers to things they dislike or don't understand. It's not as though she weaved spells to entertain us at the feasts. We might have liked her better for it."

Shannon gave a snort of amusement but nodded

agreement.

"Sometimes, it's easy for me to forget even that much about what I once was," Brian admitted. "I never thought to deal with humans again, but I don't regret it. Magic is so much a part of my life now that I can't imagine existing without it. I don't always remember what it was like back then."

The magic Derry now felt brought him closer to the life around him, and he wouldn't willingly give that connection up, even if it were possible. Derry understood how Brian felt, and he wondered if there really would come a time when he wouldn't want to deal with humans anymore. Derry couldn't say since he still had King Nevin, Prince Tevin, and Roe. He couldn't imagine not having the connection to them.

"How do we find out what Queen Alisia is doing?" Brian asked. "Any use of magic to spy on her would certainly draw her attention."

Shannon suddenly stopped fiddling with his clothing and smiled. "We'll go in person," he answered. Kyrian and Brian stared with shocked disbelief, but Derry nodded, already understanding what Shannon had in mind. "We'll go to Tyleen and to my family castle. Derry and I know at least one secret way into the building. We can listen long enough to hear a few secrets, even if we decide it's not safe to show ourselves."

"Good plan," Derry agreed, glad to have some action they could take. "Safer than using magic, as long as the mere presence of fae blood doesn't alert her."

"I don't think it will," Kyrian replied, though he still didn't sound pleased by this idea. "She apparently has to make an effort to locate any fae, and she has set spells to her traps, so they spring when a fae comes close. If she could simply sense us, she wouldn't need the traps. The closer you get to her -- without tripping any of the traps -- the less likely she is to notice."

"I'll go with you," Brian said.

"This isn't a place for a true fae, especially if we run into trouble," Derry replied with a shake of his head.

"There is no safe place. We each must do whatever is necessary to save both the fae and the humans from this woman. I'll come with you. I'm closer to being human than any but the younger children. I know what we're heading into, and if there is a need for magic to get free, you will want someone who knows what to do."

Derry reluctantly agreed, which ended any protest from Shannon. They began to gather up their little supplies, ready to make this journey into the lair of the enemy. Kyrian would travel with them and help make certain they didn't find any more traps, but he would not go within the city.

Derry and Shannon, however, would go on straight to the enemy's door and hope she didn't see them scurrying past in the shadows.

Chapter Twenty-Nine

Kyrian would leave them in the hills with only a short walk from Tyleen. The older fae would then head to Queen Leanora to deliver his news in person. Brian had been worried that Queen Leanora might not be happy with this plan when she heard it, but Kyrian appeared far less worried about such things. He did insist again that they take care on this journey.

As soon as the sun began to set, Brian, Shannon, and Derry planned to cross the last line of trees, mindful of any traps, and head quietly down to the city.

"It seems odd that she hasn't set any traps closer to the city," Derry said as he stared down at the town.

"Not really," Kyrian said as he prepared to leave. "She wouldn't want her own people to sense them, and even magicless humans can sometimes feel the pooling of power. That's why they avoid the standing stones."

"Good point," Derry replied softly, half fearing she would hear them.

"She has power, but she hasn't much control." Kyrian looked at the three, shaking his head with obvious worry. "I'll leave you here. Be careful. Count on your wits and not your magic, none of you. Derry feels his powers better, and Shannon has started to awaken some of his -- and Brian has always had a good grasp of magic. However, only use magic if you must get away from the place. She'll feel the power, even if she doesn't sense you otherwise."

They parted company. Kyrian still looked worried, and Derry thought he might be regretting his agreement to this plan. Not long afterward, the three reached the edge of the trees just as dusk settled across the hillside, and the city and castles took on the last glow of sunset light.

"God and Goddess," Brain whispered. "I'd never seen it, you know. I didn't know humans possessed anything so beautiful!"

The words made Derry's heart beat harder as he, too, accepted the beauty of this place -- and admitted that he would always belong here. Even after he went all the way to the fae, he would remain Prince Derry SanOsen, and it meant something in this battle just as it would in the future when the people might need him again.

He was a Prince of Lynashin: human or fae made no difference to the duties that came with that position in life. He hadn't dishonored his family name by joining with the fae.

The three carefully made their way down the hillside, moving cautiously through the summer grass. Derry prayed they found cover before any of the guards' eyesight adjusted to the growing dark. They avoided the road, which appeared to be nearly empty anyway. Sunset should have been the time when people headed out of the city and to their farms and cottages. However, only a couple people moved along the road, and they looked anxious to be away.

The town appeared dark and uninviting, which it had never been before. The three reached the outskirts and moved along the shadows, darting from building to building and avoiding anywhere with loud noises. Shannon led the way, growing more cautious as they moved closer to incline that led to the taller walls of the SanSota Castle. Derry looked toward Tyleen Castle, worried still about Nevin and Tevin, and wishing they could just go there and finish this war. He did not wish too hard, though, for fear of what his magic might do. He'd made that mistake when he feared for Shannon.

They reached the south wall of the castle without incident. Shannon's hand pressed against his arm, and Derry sensed the worry. Though they could see movement and some torches lit to banish the coming dark, Derry couldn't hear much activity within the building.

Shannon led them around the edge of the wall, carefully looking for the old way in and avoiding disturbing the bit of brush along the way. It had been far too many years since the two young, wild boys had found the way out and slipped off into the woods to find adventure.

Older now.

And wilder.

Because of the nature of the Tyleen castles, all except the more massive castle possessed minimal defenses to discourage feuds among the lords or attacks on the rulers. The SanOsens maintained military superiority at the higher position to enforce their rule and to stop any trouble among the others. That gave Alisia an edge that didn't come from magic.

It also made minor wall repair on any of the lords' castles unnecessary until the problem verged on a dangerous collapse. A few loose stones didn't warrant much attention, except by curious boys.

Shannon located the spot, now hidden behind a spreading vine. He pulled that away and carefully slid the first stone back. The slight sound of stone against mossy stone sounded like thunder in the silent night, and even Brian glanced nervously around. Using magic to mask the work would only draw

Alisia's attention.

The hole came open, though it looked dubiously small. Derry and Shannon had come this way perhaps half a year before his ill-fated journey to the north. Nevin had already been on the campaign in the south, and with Alisia in charge, discretion about their occasional jaunts had seemed wise.

Shannon knelt, peeked into the hole, and nodded. Derry shrugged and silently began to crawl through. He fit easily enough. Probably, he'd lost so much weight since the last time he'd done this.

The narrow passage was blessedly short but filled with the scent of damp rock and musty dirt that Derry still associated with the cell. He shoved aside some small debris, and his head emerged into the darker room. Derry pulled himself through with haste. He couldn't decide, standing in the dark, if he should feel safer or not. They had slipped in through a back door while Alisia watched the front, and at any moment, she could turn around and see them.

Shannon followed him in and put a hand on Derry's shoulder before he struck a flint and lit a small candle he found on the shelf where they'd left them so long ago. It flared with dust and cobwebs, but then held steady. That helped since the room became larger and less cell-like.

Brian came last and looked around, obviously curious. More light came from a torch-lit somewhere high up the curving stairs at the far side of the room. This area was used for storage, though there wasn't much in supplies here now. Derry took the candle while Shannon covered the hole where they'd come in. The three remained silent as Shannon led the way up the stairway that looked as though it hadn't been cleaned since last they'd traveled these steps. That made Derry feel better because it meant they were not likely to meet anyone. Poor Brian looked ready to bolt.

Derry didn't feel any magic ahead, and he nodded to

Shannon when his friend stopped at the top of the stairs before heading into the busier part of the castle.

Only it wasn't busy. Derry wanted to find some sign of normality. They did, finally, see someone: a guard in the King's colors stood in an archway to the right, looking into the kitchen opposite them. He was one of the Queen's men now.

They slipped back and headed down another hall before Shannon stopped and looked at Derry, frowning. "Something is wrong. Where is everyone? I don't like this."

"Me, either," Derry agreed. This had been his home, a riotous and joyful place. The silence unsettled him as much as it did Shannon.

"My family should still be down at the hall, finishing dinner. Let's see how close we can get and if we can hear anything."

"Your place. You lead the way," Derry said.

Shannon didn't remind Derry that he knew this building just as well. Derry silently followed his friend, and Brian trailed behind the two. Their fae friend obviously felt uneasy and out of his element. Even as a human, Brian never would have walked the halls of one of the castles.

Looking at all of this from Brian's point of view made Derry realize how much he still took for granted. Derry enjoyed his new life with the freedom of the woods, though perhaps that was only because he knew he still had strong walls and warm beds within reach. That made him too human, he supposed.

What was it that suddenly had him thinking about human comforts? Or did he think like a fae while in the wilds, and like a human when in civilization? Maybe each part of him grew stronger, depending on where he stood. He'd have to ask Kyrian if he had a chance. Perhaps this was even good since it seemed that there was something about being human that would still help in this war. Both the Queen of the fae and

Wild One had said so, though he wished they could have been a little more informative   --

"She had no right!"

The shout bellowed from the dining hall ahead, followed by the explosive sound of something hitting a table. Dishes rattled. Derry recognized the voice of Arlis SanSota, Shannon's father. Derry knew from experience that it took a lot to anger the man. By his words, Derry guessed the Queen had annoyed him -- but they didn't rush forward to find out how or why. Shannon eased closer to the opening, and Brian hovered behind them, looking a little pale, and likely having second thoughts about this entire insanity.

Derry dared a glance and found the room mostly empty. A couple servants stood at the main table where it looked as though all the family had gathered for a meager meal. Only two of the lower tables held anyone at all, and those sullen-looking cousins. Odd. The SanSota Clan prided themselves on extravagance for the evening meal.

Shannon gently nudged Derry and pointed past the main table. More of the royal guards stood there, and at the table sat a Daria Priest who was clearly presiding over the meal. The priest didn't look any happier.

Derry made another quick look around the room. All of Shannon's immediate family were present: father, mother, two sisters, and three brothers. So were wives, husbands, and children. Even the youngest looked glum.

The priest leaned forward and glanced their way but obviously saw only shadows. The three quickly retreated anyway, far away from everyone. That was easy enough since most of the castle appeared to be empty. Down one hall, then another -- avoiding the kitchens where there was some activity and finally to the shadow of the stairs leading upwards.

"We should have realized Alisia wouldn't trust your family after how close I've always been to them. I'm sorry," Derry said with a slight gasp for breath. Were there more guards? He could hear nothing.

"Given the circumstances, I think we made the right choice," Shannon answered. He smiled now, though there was still fire lingering in his eyes. "And I seriously doubt Da is going to feel any differently."

"Your entire family is here. Who do you think is running the estates?"

Shannon glanced back into the room and then shrugged. "Maybe the estate manager or some of the Queen's people. That's not very important in the wider scheme of this mess. We have all Lynashin to worry about, Derry. Even my father would agree."

Derry nodded and leaned against the wall, letting himself accept the little bit of peace and knowing it wouldn't last. Damned mess. He started to worry about standing around in the hall or very long.

They needed a destination, but one that would keep them out of sight still.

"Let's go up to your father's rooms. He'll turn up there eventually. We should have a chance to talk then."

"Good idea." Shannon looked back towards the dining hall and shook his head. "That's not a happy man. I hope Alisia doesn't insist on a guard going into the room with him."

"We'd better be careful. We can go out of the window and down the side of the wall if we find that it isn't safe. Let's go."

Even the upper halls of the castle proved to be empty, though they found signs that the servants had come through and hastily lit the torches. Some barely flickered, and one with oil spilled on the floor. They still saw no one and reached the upper level of the main tower without a single incident. Finding no guards gave Derry hope, though he supposed the guards would return with the others from dinner.

The doors all had newly installed bolts that would lock the

people inside. At seeing them, Shannon finally showed a sign of anger. "The guard locks them in at night. This isn't right --"

He started to reach for the door and stopped, pulling his hand back and looking puzzled.

Brian had reached to stop him and now smiled instead. "You can feel it -- good. Magic, and attuned to anyone with fae blood. The moment you touched that door, she would know we're here."

"She must have hoped I would touch one of the doors," Derry said and stepped back, least he set it off just by nearness. "Like all her other traps set on the hopes of one being tripped. We can't stand out here in the hall. I can feel the trap on all the doors. What now?"

"We can crawl around to the side," Shannon said, waving toward the window at the far end of the tower. "She hasn't put her touch on the windows as well."

They hurried to the far end of the hall where the window stood open to the spring night. Walking between the barred doors felt like walking between a line of pointed javelins, any one of which might pierce him. Derry didn't like the tingle along his arms.

Alisia held power. Alisia had a far better understanding of how to use magic than he did, which meant he must not become careless.

Derry glanced back at the bolted doors. They were putting too many people at risk by being here, but just the same -- they needed answers, and there were not a lot of people they could trust right now.

Chapter Thirty

Brian gently ran his finger along the edge of the window and gave a tentative nod. "Safe, though that may only be a trap to lure us out where we're more vulnerable."

"Or it may have been opened as a lure to draw us in," Derry said and thought back to their walk through the castle. "I saw many of the hall windows open to the night. Alisia doesn't know we already had our own secret ways into the building."

"That might be," Brian agreed and sounded more assured now that they dealt with magic again. "She can't watch everywhere, and even all the little traps she set take energy. Let's go. We don't want to be caught standing here."

Climbing on the rough stone of the tower was a trick Derry and Shannon had managed before to escape notice, though they had headed for Shannon's rooms, not his father's quarters. Not that they ever really fooled anyone. They played a game; everyone made jokes about it the next day. It had been dangerous, of course. Not as terrible as now, but in a different way.

Those were bright days, Derry suddenly realized. Good

days.

Tyleen Castle rose before them as they started their way around the wall. Being fae helped, even without using power, and he had little trouble holding to the stone. Guards walked along the high walls, but they wouldn't see any movement in the dark unless they had magic as well. Derry doubted it. Alisia would be hoarding power to herself and mistrusting everyone. She would have no allies except for that one man who must have had some link to her power. Oh, and she had Egan, of course -- what little good the toad would do her.

They had only gone a little of the ways when Derry's shoulder began to ache, and that reminded him of flying. This wasn't a good time to recall the horror of being carried through the air by the gargoyle. Derry began to tremble as he considered the long drop to the courtyard. Had it ever frightened him before? Shannon's brothers had called them fools. He supposed they had been --

His hand missed the next hold on the dew-slick rock, and he started to slide. Brian, though, caught his arm --

The sudden stop wrenched his already aching shoulder. Agony flared from his neck to the tips of his fingers. Brian, held tight to his hand, must have felt an echo of that pain as well. He gasped --

"Derry -- Brian!" Shannon sounded afraid and perhaps too loud. That frightened Derry into movement again. He fought away the shock of pain, and his feet found holds, easing the pressure on his shoulder. Brain gave a little gasp of relief and helped guide his fingers to the proper spots.

And there they all remained, still and silent, for several dozen heartbeats.

"We might as well go on," Derry finally gasped. "I'm not going back."

"We're closer to his Lordship's window anyway," Brain said softly. "Let's go."

Derry forced himself to move again. He wanted a solid floor beneath him and solid walls at his back. He wanted in that room, no matter what other dangerous they might face.

They reached the window only moments later, Shannon reached for Derry and got him to the window to go in first --

They heard a muffled voice from the hall as the door opened, a growl of sound, and steps heading inside.

"Bastard Guard! Lock me up in my own castle --"

The door slammed shut, the bolts going loudly in place. The man stalked across the room. Derry just held on and looked up into Lord Arlis SanSota's face as the man took a deep breath and nodded.

"So, there you are. Best get inside."

Lord Arlis turned around and stalked back across to the door and stood listening.

Brian grinned, obviously liking Shannon's father already. All three scrambled into the room and away from the open window.

The room was cold and barely lit. Derry thought it might be sparse and wondered if Alisia had collected anything of worth. She could be petty that way, disliking the idea of someone having something she didn't.

Brian rushed past the other two, heading towards the door, silent for a moment before he pulled away and nodded.

"There is no guard in the hall," he announced.

"No, there wouldn't be," Lord Arlis said with another growl as he threw himself into a nearby chair. "The bastard is downstairs by now, drinking himself blind and terrorizing the few remaining servants. He doesn't have to worry once he locks us in for the night."

"Mother --" Shannon said, with a wave toward the connecting door.

"She's staying with Bethy in her room. One of the guards has been eyeing the child, and we don't want her alone."

"Damn," Shannon said, shaking his head and looking worried again.

"This is because of me, isn't it?" Derry said, leaning against the wall by the window.

"No. This is because we have a mean-spirited Queen who mistrusts any friendship. I'm not the only noble she's terrorizing." Arlis stopped and shook his head, worry and loss coming to his eyes this time. "And I suspect you know she's blamed you for the deaths of King Nevin, Prince Tevin, and Prince Roe."

"None of them are dead," Derry said.

"Ah, and since you know that, it means you've seen them?" he asked, looking hopeful.

"Not King Nevin or Tevin -- she has them prisoner -- but Roe is with the fae. She tried to kill him, but the fae got to him in time, and they're taking care of the boy."

"And there's more to this than what you've said," Arlis added and sighed. He leaned back and glanced at the meager fire as though he needed to regain some control. When he looked at Derry again, his face had calmed, but Derry could still feel the rage of emotions. "I can see things in your eyes, Derry boy. She's dealing in magic, isn't she?"

"Very dark magic, your lordship, sir," Brian said softly.

"Many of us had begun to suspect so," Arlis admitted. He looked at the three and finally focused on Shannon with a soft smile that tried to hide a hint of loss in his face. "And it's happened, hasn't it? I can see the change in you, Shannon. You needn't squirm. I hope ... I hope that you won't forget us."

"He won't, sir," Brian replied with a bow of his head. "For good or ill, we always remember our human lives."

"Strange times, strange times," Arlis whispered and shook his head. "To tell you the truth, your mother and I thought this would be your choice the very night Derry came home from the Isles. I said you would follow him this time for sure."

Shannon smiled, and Derry felt better as well, relieved that this part had gone so well. He wasn't surprised by Arlis SanSota's acceptance; after all, he hadn't made much of Derry's change and allowed him to stay in this castle all through the last winter. Still, Shannon had always been a favorite son, and Arlis had to feel the loss though he hid it well. Derry wondered if his own father would have felt the same or if King Nevin had.

"Father, we came to you to try and learn who will stand against the Queen when the time comes."

"It's not to be a battle of magic against magic? You think there will be work for the rest of us?"

"Some of us will face her with our magic," Brian replied. He sat on the floor by the fire, and he sounded more assured. "As soon as we puzzle out the source of her powers, we'll learn her weakness. However, we must reach the Queen first to fight her. If she has an army to hold us off, we'll need every bit of help we can get -- human and fae."

"Oh, aye," Arlis said, and he even looked relieved to know humans could still help. "I'll have to think hard on this and figure out who might stand with us against her. To be honest, I think some of her allies are less happy now. From what little I saw right after the matter with the king and his sons, I don't think anyone really believed her when she said you were involved."

Derry left the discussion about the possible allies to Arlis, Shannon, and Brian. He settled in a chair and leaned back, letting aches ease from his body again. Shannon even brought him a blanket and told him to sleep for a while if he could. Shannon and Brian had this part of the trouble handled. Amusing to realize they were probably safer now that they were so close to Tyleen Castle than they had been out in the woods.

Derry didn't sleep soundly, though. Parts of the

conversation intruded and triggered little nightmares. They spoke about what was happening in Tyleen, and Brian explained a great deal about the fae. Arlis listened quietly, asking astute questions about the nature of fae magic and how it differed from what the Queen did. As the night drew on, they talked about the other Lords and all that happened within those clans. Arlis got his news through the servants who traded bits of information in the marketplace when they could get free of the guards for a moment or two.

Familiar names, now friends or enemies ... or just too uncertain of the fae to be trusted. Even among Shannon's own family, Arlis admitted there were some he wouldn't trust who considered it unfair to be out of grace with the Queen because of Shannon's friend.

"Personally, I like to think we'd be out of grace anyway," Arlis said with a quick laugh.

Shannon laughed agreement, a wonderful musical sound that drew Derry entirely from his rest. When he looked up, he found Arlis staring at his youngest son with wonder and a little delight. Derry could only imagine how hard it must have been for Arlis to watch his son during those years while Derry languished in the north, and see the anger change him far more than going to the fae had done.

"I fear I've led your son very far from the path, my lord," Derry said, sitting up and trying not to wince at the movement of his arm.

"Oh, have you now? Well, truth be known, I'd rather he was fae than dead, Prince Derry."

"Pardon?"

"Queen Alisia obviously intended to take over. How long do you think my Shannon here would have lasted under her rule, even if you had not come home?"

Derry couldn't argue with his logic, and it at last put to rest the fears that Shannon would hear harsh words from his family. The others didn't count as long as Shannon's father still loved his son. A couple of his brothers had always been stubborn and jealous that Shannon rode with Prince Derry. He imagined those emotions had just carried over.

"The morning is drawing near, your lordships," Brian warned. He sat by the door and looked very relaxed. "We've barely enough time to get clear of the city."

"It's so peaceful here. It's a shame we can't stay," Derry said with a sigh.

"Why can't we?" Brian asked and drew startled looks from both Shannon and Derry. He smiled. "We're well inside her defenses, and obviously, if she hasn't found us yet, she's not looking."

"Food," Lord Arlis said, frowning. He'd stayed awake talking, and Derry thought it might have done him some good. Derry wasn't sure they'd learned anything of importance, though. "I hate to say I canna' offer hospitality even to me own son and his friends. The damn guard counts every crumb and bone to make sure we're none taking more than our share -- and that in my own house!"

"Food isn't a problem for us. Birds will bring us fruit if we ask, and no magic needed for it," Brian said.

"Ah, well, then you'll likely eat better than the rest of us," he said in a half-hearted jest. The captivity obviously weighed on the man.

"You do look better for having rested, Derry," Shannon said. "Maybe we can stay until nightfall."

"And you are welcome here," Arlis said with a bright smile. Obviously, he'd be glad to see his son for a while longer.

"My lord," Derry said with a little shake of his head. "I don't mean to be impolitic, but you might be wise to curb your joy once you leave this room. Whether we remain or not, you don't want to give yourself away."

"Ah, good point, lad. Good point. No doubt one look at

the guard who comes for me, or that damned Daria Priest -- may the gods forgive me -- and I'll be in a bad enough mood again."

"I thought of another reason to stay," Shannon said and looked toward the window. "We can see a good part of Tyleen Castle from here, including the front gate. We might learn something by watching who comes and goes and how they react."

Derry agreed, and Lord Arlis gave his son an appraising look as though he hadn't expected anything so logical from Shannon. It didn't surprise Derry, though. He and Shannon had often found themselves in odd situations, and Shannon was good at thinking out the problems.

Lord Arlis looked at the window and gave a thoughtful nod this time. "None of us can stay in the rooms during the day where we might watch. She is hiding something."

"Well then, we can't go," Brian decided. "We will want to know anything this woman tries to hide. I'll get word to Kyrian via the mice or something. We apparently have found our work."

Derry agreed. He wouldn't turn down a chance to rest, especially when it looked as though they would get some important work done as well. The others looked relieved, and Brian thoughtful.

The sun would be up soon. He wondered what the light of day would bring for them.

Chapter Thirty-One

"Another priest!" Brian whispered in surprise. "What does she want with all of them? Does this happen every day?"

"We might have to stay to find out," Shannon replied and didn't sound at all happy. "It's odd no one else goes in. And don't the priests seem to be acting oddly?"

Those words sent a shiver of foreboding up Derry's spine. He sat forward, glancing from the shadows towards the window. Brian had a better view. All Derry could see was the top of a high tower and the curtain wall surrounding it. No guards moved there, closest to the Queen's own tower.

They knew Alisia had ties with the Daria temple, but he had assumed it was only because those of the temple didn't realize the true nature of the woman. Now, with fifteen men from various priesthoods in her castle, Derry began to feel uneasy. Hadn't anyone been holy enough to detect the magic and the evil?

What did she want with them? Brian glanced his way as though hoping for an answer, but Derry could only offer a shrug. Shannon watched for a bit and then went to rest on his father's bed, sleeping soundly. Derry leaned back in his chair. He wondered if they could really hide here for a few days. Would they really find any answers, or was this just an excellent place to hide and rest?

Could they get into Tyleen itself? Derry and Shannon had never tried to breach the place, but they had new skills now, and climbing those walls wouldn't be any harder than this one, except for the presence of the Queen and what she might sense.

"The priests are coming up to the curtain wall," Brian whispered, his voice soft and trembling. "If they know we are here, it's going to be dangerous for us and for everyone in the castle. Shannon, what should --"

Derry crawled to the window and peered out like a child trying to see outside. He could see the priests, conspicuous in their various gray and black cowls. "They're not looking this way," Derry said. "Something else is going on. I don't like how they're moving."

Shannon joined them. The priests moved slowly, staring ahead, each step like a toddler just learning to walk. While they might yet turn in their direction, Derry didn't feel that would be a danger.

"There's Queen Alisia. Who is that with her?" Brian asked.

Whoever the man in the long, hooded robe was, he clearly controlled the scene. He brought the group to a halt with a wave of his hand.

"That's the man I saw in the cell," Derry said. He had to be very careful not to make an accidental connection to the two.

"Is it?" Shannon said. He shook his head. "I can't see his face, but my guess would be the head of the Daria Temple here in Tyleen. He took over while you were away, Derry -- but after Queen Alisia came back."

"Ah, now there's a bad sequence of events," Derry said. He kept watching as did the other two, but the priests simply faced the Queen and her companion. "I don't trust it since she went to a Daria temple in the north. Could she have arranged to go there?"

"The king's rage as real," Shannon said. He even winced at the memory. "She was going into exile -- but maybe she used magic to influence where she wanted to go."

"Something is about to happen," Brian said. "Magic is building out there."

Derry could feel it too, like the heat from a blaze growing brighter. The Queen stepped forward, placing herself halfway between her companion and the other priests. For a moment, she stood still, but then she lifted her hands above her head. A globe of light enveloped her.

The Daria Priest swept his hands out, and lines of power, bright even in the daylight, snaked out to touch each of the unmoving priests in the forehead. The colors of those magical strings began to change, and as each went from white bright to dark blue, the priest transferred the line from his hands to her globe.

"She's taking magic from them," Shannon said softly.

"More than that, I fear," Brian said. "They're draining away life itself. Not so much that it will kill them outright, but they're going to be weak and confused for a long time."

"Is that why she has so many?" Derry asked.

"Take a little from each? Dead priests would be hard to explain," Shannon said.

"Unlike Kings and Princes," Derry replied with a shake of her head. "Which she can blame on me."

"The King and Tevin aren't dead yet," Shannon reminded him. He glanced toward Queen Alisia and shook his head. "At least now we know why she doesn't allow anyone to watch the castle from here during the day. This is the only place with a view of that stretch of wall. I assume this ... rite ... must be performed outside?"

"It would probably be too dangerous within walls," Brian agreed. "I don't understand human magic, but I suspect the power transmitted this way is unstable, and they don't have a good feel for what they were doing. If that force got loose, the chaotic destruction would be difficult to explain, even if any of them survived."

"She's gaining power," Derry said. "And we don't dare stop her, do we?"

"Right now? No. With that much raw power available within a hand's reach, trying anything would not be wise." Brian stared for a long time again. "That's all right. We can use this knowledge against her."

"How? Tell my father? He's in no position to make any accusations against her or the priests."

"True," Brian agreed. He watched the spectacle, but he looked calmer for it. "I had a different idea. We're going to go to Kelkass Temple and speak with the priests there. They won't be in her control."

"Looks as though they're done, and in a hurry to get clear," Shannon remarked.

They watched as Alisia and her people headed back towards the stairs, the magic show over. At the last moment, Alisia waved everyone else on. She went back and stood at the wall, clearly waiting.

Egan arrived. He looked uncomfortable in his starch and lace, and even from here, Derry could tell his face had gone red. The two argued about something, and then they both left and disappeared back into the castle.

"So, she doesn't want little Egan to know what she's doing. I'd find that interesting if I thought there was any chance at all we could turn him to our side," Shannon said as he stepped away from the window again.

"We should leave tonight after all," Brian said. He looked at the two as though he expected some argument. "We have to get to the others and make a plan. If she is pulling magic and power from priests, that's going to make her too strong. We don't dare wait.," Brian stared at the castle, silent for a moment. "We don't dare let her grow any more powerful. Besides, if we save these priests, they might realize enough to come to our side. We finally have a key to her power."

For the first time during this long ordeal, Derry felt a genuine surge of hope. This chance at finding one weak link in the Queen's magic meant they would finally have a way to deal with her. Any question of what she did with the priests would draw attention, but they had to turn the right people to look at her. The priests at Kelkass seemed the wisest choice. Those priests lived at their temple, accepting into their pantheon any god or goddess of genuine kindness. Their leader was renowned for his piety. Even so, if the fae hadn't vouched for them, Derry would never have turned to a priesthood for help. There had always been a distrust of magic -- and fae -- within the temples.

The Temple of Daria had been best known as secretive about their practices. Thinking back on all he'd known about the Kelkass priests, Derry realized they were quiet about anything but the praise of the gods. They only had the one temple, unlike the other ones that scattered small temples all through the land.

Alisia presented a queenly enough façade at court, keeping everyone from guessing at the state of her soul, though no one thought of her as kind. If the others learned about this, Derry could turn humanity against her, even if they remained distrustful of the fae.

"Let's rest while we can," Derry suggested as he stood again. "The sun will be down in a couple hours. We'll wait until Shannon's father returns, and then we can make our escape."

"We don't have to wait just to be polite," Shannon replied. "Or do you intend to tell him what's going on?"

"I would like to ask him about the priest we saw at the table last night and about any contact he's had with others. We should gather all the information we can."

Brian and Shannon both agreed. Derry settled into the chair once more, knowing he needed to rest to be ready for anything more strenuous. Brian sat by the door, and Shannon watched Tyleen.

Queen Alisia held to the protocol in some ways. The woman whose husband and sons were missing did not give a nightly feast, though a few people arrived for the evening meal. The three made a note of the company she kept, suspecting those would be her closest supporters. Perhaps they only supported what they saw as the legitimate representatives of the SanOsen royalty. Derry didn't want to make any mistakes and drag innocents down with the Queen.

None of them stayed long, and they didn't look happy when they left.

Derry was glad they'd remained just for the joy of Lord SanSota's look when he found them still there. They had been hiding behind the bed, and he all but laughed when the three popped back out.

"Well, you do look better than you did last night," Arlis confessed as he crossed to the chair and threw himself down. He looked bothered, but that seemed to be more about the captivity again. "You gave me quite a start, Derry. You looked closer to dead than alive."

"I've had a long and difficult journey from ... Gods, I can't even remember where all this began," Derry admitted with a shake of his head as he sat on the bed by Shannon. Brian had gone back to the door, and they had the shutter closed on the window.

"No matter." Arlis gave a shrug and appeared to be less tense then he had been. "It's where you end a journey that truly matters."

"Wise words, my lord. I'll take them to heart."

"You don't need a poor old human who can't rule his own house to guide your steps, Prince Derry."

"Prince?" he said with a shake of his head.

"Prince. I'll say it now and later, too. We lived by convention here, and I'll be damned if I'll call that pig Egan by the title of Prince and not give you the same courtesy. I can't think good King Nevin would disagree, even if he did give way to keep peace with his wife. It is plain we only kept to the old title to keep the Bitch Queen from getting upset that someone might steal some glory from her sons. Or, at least, from Egan. Sniveling little bastard. But tell me how I might yet help you three."

"Last night we saw a priest in your hall," Derry said, glancing towards the closed window and remembering the scene they had seen enacted out there. "Is he the Queen's man? Are the temples fully behind her and Egan?"

"The gods alone know what the heads of the temples think," Arlis replied with a shake of his shaggy hair. "The priest is here to watch us, aye, because of the taint of the fae. Truth be known, that's a perplexed and uncertain young man, and every day he spends at Tyleen Castle before coming back seems to make him less coherent. I think she'd driven the man daft."

Arlis SanSota was obviously an astute man. Derry even suspected he caught more in the simple question than Derry had intended. Fine. Let him be wary of the priests.

"The Queen has several priests in her power. Literally in her power," Derry said, and the man looked shocked, but not surprised. "She is getting some of her power from draining them, though I seriously doubt they realize what is happening.

We saw at least part of the rite this afternoon. Do not trust the head of the local Daria temple, either."

"Oh, now, that's how it is, is it? The exile gave her more of a chance to gain power?"

"We think so," Shannon said.

"And you dare not say this to anyone, Lord Arlis," Derry reminded the man. "Not unless you think we have already failed, and you have nothing to lose. There is no telling who else might be caught in her web."

"Yes, true," he agreed. Shannon's father was a good, thoughtful man. He wouldn't do anything rash that might endanger his family or his friends.

"We have a long way to go tonight," Brian warned softly and moved away from the door. "Now is the time to head out."

Shannon nodded reluctant agreement, and Derry worked to curb his anxiousness at the idea of leaving. He did like it here, and he'd always enjoyed the company of Arlis SanSota. As they stood beside the balcony door, Brian gently laid a hand on Derry's shoulder and drew his wandering attention.

"We'll head straight down this time and head for the wall. It's less of a climb since we can bypass the main hall."

"I'll be fine," Derry promised. He felt embarrassment surge leaving him red-faced.

"Shan explained about your injured shoulder," Arlis said, leaning forward as they gathered by the window. "Magic is all fine for healing lad, but you take care anyway."

Derry nodded and wisely refrained from saying the wound didn't bother him nearly as much as the memory of how he got it. This was not the time to think about falling!

They slipped out over the edge of the window, Brian first, then Derry and finally Shannon, who whispered a private farewell to his father. The night proved warm and fresh, the scent of the forest not too far away. Derry found it hard to believe in danger, or that evil lurked so near to them.

Then he felt the little tendril of magic from Tyleen. That evil did not belong there, the dark whisper that came on the breeze and tried to draw his attention. She still held the King and Prince Heir somewhere inside that castle, and if he'd been any more daring -- or stupid -- Derry might have reached the ground and gone to see if he could free them.

While it was wise not to forget that Alisa was nearby, it was still necessary to remember she wasn't everywhere. The woman had limits to her powers.

They left both the castle and the city without an incident.

Chapter Thirty-Two

Kyrian waited at the edge of the woods overlooking Tyleen and the castles. He was not alone. Derry suspected the other fae had come to help if things had gone badly. This position had been far more dangerous than staying in the SanSota castle since Alisa still looked for an attack from the woods. However, nothing had gone wrong, so Derry didn't worry about what might have happened. They had enough trouble with real problems.

The group abandoned their post and immediately headed toward Glendalow. There Derry managed a few words of encouragement for Captain Killough, who still had the room at the inn. The man looked glad to see them -- and just as pleased to see the group leave again. Derry didn't tell him more than that they were going for help. The soldier lived in a dangerous world where he served the Queen but helped her enemy. Derry remembered the stories about the man's family and wondered why he dared.

Or maybe Killough dared what he did because of his family. Alisia was not a safe choice under any circumstances.

Derry felt at peace when they finally reached the deep

woods. The group slept in turns for the last few hours of the night and stayed in camp past the dawn. Derry knew they all needed rest, but he felt as though every moment he slept put someone else at risk.

How long would she hold Nevin and Tevin? She would need to show the bodies before Egan could legally rule. Otherwise, ten years must pass in a regency controlled by the lords before a new king could be chosen, whether Egan or not. That would limit her powers, and Alisa wasn't the kind of person who would be content with less than full control.

Would she decide she could defeat Derry without bothering to turn the nobility against him first? He knew it wasn't just him that she wanted to discredit. Alisia meant to start a war with the fae and destroy the only others who would be a threat to her magical position. So much of what she had done made more sense now. The sooner Egan took the throne, the better for her. Too long without a real king, and the land would start falling into anarchy. Alisia wouldn't want Tyleen on the verge of ruin.

Derry didn't know the fae ever rode horses until Kyrian one arrived with the beautiful animals. Because of the fae's affinity with animals, they willingly took the riders. A dapple grey made Derry his rider, and despite the animal's wildness and the lack of the saddle, the journey proved very smooth. Derry held lightly to the mane with his left hand, resting the strained right shoulder by cradling the arm within his ragged vest.

Looking at his clothing, Derry realized he didn't appear much like a Prince of the Line these days. Unfortunately, he hadn't acquired the grace of the fae either. He looked very much like a beggar.

Shannon, somehow, still looked very fine despite the dirt and rips in his clothing. Kyrian and Brian looked wild and fae. Derry studied Brian for a long time. The young fae wasn't far removed from this humanity, and scars showed on Brian's back, visible sometimes at the edge of his shirt. Derry thought about his own scars -- more mental than physical -- and what had driven him to run after the fae on that fateful night in Glendalow.

"You are too quiet, Derry," Shannon said with a sigh. "I always know when you're having dark thoughts."

"Dark enough, I suppose," he confessed. "I just ... wish I looked a little better."

Brian and Kyrian both gave him curious looks. Plainly this wasn't something fae worried about, least of all amid such madness as this war. Shannon at least nodded, making Derry feel a bit less stupid. He should, he supposed, worry about the battle --

Derry couldn't. He had to turn his mind to simpler things for a while since he had no answers for this war. Thinking about what he couldn't do wasn't helping his state of mind.

Maybe that decision might even pass for wisdom.

Derry turned his interest to the woods instead. They didn't travel the main trail, which suited Derry very well. He didn't want to meet people who might suspect him in complicity at the disappearance of the King. Besides, while in the woods, small creatures danced around the hooves of the horses, chattering to the fae. Derry understood little of it, but he did realize that the farther they moved from Tyleen and the Queen, the less worry the little creatures showed.

The third day proved amusing. Shannon suddenly realized he had begun to understand the squirrels. His friend's sudden delight made the journey go too quickly. Even though they rode all day and into the night, Derry wasn't ready to stop until the large solid walls of the temple came into view. Then he felt weary.

"Rest at last," Kyrian said. "Though I fear this place is even more persuasive than our little cave --"

"It's not safe to rest?" Shannon asked and plainly tried not to sound tired or disappointed.

"We'll rest. The good priests will rouse us again. Come my friends. We'll turn our horses loose at the gate. They won't wander far. We'll need them for the journey back to Tyleen."

"Back and forth, back and forth," Derry said with a shake of his head. "I once loved travel, you know. Now, I'd like to remain somewhere long enough to bathe, eat, and sleep, all in one visit."

"Prince of the Line," Shannon said with a grin. "They're so fussy."

Derry laughed but didn't disagree. When they slipped from the horses, he tried not to stagger or show the sudden pain through his shoulder. However, even the fae looked worn this time.

The gate to Kelkass Temple stood open to any visitor, which made Derry uneasy about their safety within those walls. However, as they passed through the portal, he sensed an extraordinary surge of magic --

"What was that?" Shannon asked, looking confused.

"Warning to the priest and any fae within," Kyrian explained. "It lets them sense the potential for magic from fae or human, so they know what kind of trouble just walked in the door."

"Isn't that dangerous?" Derry asked. "Because anyone with magic knows they went through a spell. That would alert them as well, wouldn't it?"

"Oh yes, but it's an ancient spell, and the priests certainly wouldn't claim to know anything about it. Also, the person coming through would have to admit to knowing magic to speak about it, so if that ever happened, they all act ignorant. And here is Brother Milin now."

"Ah, Kyrian!" A grey-haired priest hurried to meet them. The man held up a shielded candle, squinting into the faintly lit night. Derry remembered Milin who seemed little changed from the time when he came here after his parents had died. "You gave us quite a start, a party with so much power arriving unannounced. No need to worry, though. There's no one here that would be a problem."

"Good. We dare not advertise our travels, friend," Kyrian explained. He let go of the horses, and they walked away. Derry watched them, worried about what would happen if they had to ride quickly again. A great deal of his recent life had involved rushing somewhere else as fast as possible.

"I dare say not since I see Prince Derry with you," the priest said, looking him over. Derry brushed at his clothing again. "Ah, and his companion, Shannon SanSota. My -- and he touched by the wild as well. Welcome, welcome. Prince Roe will be thrilled to see you."

"Is he better?" Derry asked. He managed to keep pace with the priest, thought the man appeared to be in a considerable hurry.

"Better in body and soul. This is an excellent place to heal and find peace, Prince Derry. I hoped you would come to us since you obviously are in need."

"We come because we have grave news concerning priests and the Queen," Kyrian said, moving up to the other side of the priest.

By the time they reached the heart of the temple, Brother Milin had heard the tale and looked grim-faced at the news. They entered his well-lit warm suite in silence. Milin sent the three priests off to bed with word that they would have an important meeting at dawn.

He must have heard Derry's sigh at those words.

"Don't worry, Prince. You need not attend --"

"No, no. I didn't mean --"

"You meant only that you are very weary," Brother Milin interrupted. "Truly, you look as though you need rest, Prince

Derry. My meeting in the morning concerns only temple affairs as it pertains to this matter. Not even Kyrian is expected to attend."

"Ah, then I shall be very grateful for some corner where I can curl up for a few hours, sir."

"I think we can offer a prince of the line a bit more hospitality than a mere corner!"

"Titles mean nothing to me these days. My wants are few. I only want somewhere to sleep."

Brother Milin looked at Derry for so long a moment that he felt distinctly uncomfortable beneath the stare. Even Shannon seemed to find it odd since he came closer and put a protective hand on Derry's shoulder.

"Milin?" Kyrian ventured.

"Just realizing the weight this young man carries and how simple are his wants."

"I'm just tired," Derry said and looked around. "Any corner would do. A blanket would be nice."

Shannon laughed, but the priest shook his head as though uncertain how to handle a prince with so few wants. Derry didn't care. He wanted to sleep. He needed to lie down -- right here --

"Derry!" Shannon grabbed his friend as Derry's legs gave way. "No, it's all right, sir. He is exhausted."

"Worn to the bone," Milin agreed with a perceptive nod. "As pale as a ghost and just as thin. This boy needs rest if he really is to help you. He couldn't stand up to a determined rabbit the state he's in."

Derry chuckled and let the priest take him ... somewhere. The trip proved mercifully quick. When Shannon and Brian deposited him on a bed, Derry forced himself to open his eyes, worried that they would need him for something more.

"Go to sleep Derry," Brian insisted. "Like the cave, this is a place that heals and gives peace. We'll be here to awaken you again."

"I'm not afraid to sleep," he said with a sigh. "Just damned few opportunities. Your pardon, Brother Milin --"

"Sleep," the priest insisted.

And he did.

Chapter Thirty-Three

Derry awoke feeling as though every inch of his body tingled with anticipation.

"You know I'm here, don't you?"

Derry recognized the soft voice, though he had only heard her speak that one night. He sat up with a start and found the Queen of the fae settled in a chair by the bed. Tongue-tied in her presence, Derry only managed to bow his head in greeting. "My Queen," he mumbled.

"And why so formal?" Leonora asked and laughed. "We didn't bow to one another when we first met."

"I didn't know you were the Queen then," he answered and felt bolder as his wits overcame the last vestiges of sleep. "Have you come to tell me what I've done wrong?"

"What makes you think you've done anything wrong?" she asked with a frown and a look that said she didn't understand.

"I haven't defeated Alisia yet."

"Neither have I," Leonora reminded him with a wave of her long-fingered hand. "And without your help, we wouldn't have known she was our true enemy. Don't despair, Derry.

Peace. I am only here because I wanted to see you again. We are allies-- and I hope, someday, we will be something more. Ah, but now is not the time to think on such a future. You do blush well, though. Never mind, we have enough to occupy us at present."

Derry nodded, relieved to have her turn attention to less personal matters. He didn't fear the future with her, but he needed all his wits for the trouble at hand. If Derry didn't settle the problem with Alisia, there wouldn't be a future anyway. The fae would disappear from Lynashin, and he would likely be dead at Alisia's hands by then.

"What should I call you?" Derry asked as he sat up. Praise the gods he had been too tired to undress last night, though he could have wished for a bath and clean clothing sometime in the previous few days.

"I am Leanora, and you may certainly call me that, forgoing all formality. Sometimes others insist upon my title. I do not."

"That makes us more alike again," Derry admitted and slowly stood. He felt better for the sleep and for seeing her, but that didn't mean he also didn't still ache. She gave him hope and help, both of which he badly needed. "And it makes some of our acquaintances, both human and fae, more alike than they care to admit."

She laughed. The sound reminded him of birds, flowers, and bright spring days. Derry felt cheered by the response. They had battles to fight, but the war would not last forever. He had to believe they would win.

He brushed ineffectively at his clothing and hair, but Leanora gave a wave of her hand that mended, cleaned, and brushed all in one sweep.

"Now there is something I need to learn," he admitted. "Thank you."

"Your friends are breakfasting with Prince Roe," Leanora

said. She crossed to the door. "Shall we join them? I should hate to ruin your reputation by spending too much time alone in your bedroom with you."

They both laughed this time. Derry took a couple slow steps toward her, still weak and sore, although not so much as before. Leanora offered her arm, and Derry wrapped his own around it. He felt life and hope in the warmth of being near her.

Everyone looked up when they entered the room. Brother Milin looked surprised, Shannon amused, and the others pleased. Roe grinned brightly, making the boy seem young again. Derry hadn't asked what Alisia had done to her youngest son, but he could still see something haunted and lost in the boy's eyes even when he smiled.

"Make room for them!" Milin urged and waved a space on the bench by him. "Come and eat! Prince Derry plainly needs some strength!"

"You needn't all baby him," Leanora said, leading Derry to a chair. "I'll do that myself."

Shannon laughed, and Roe, still too close to court life, grabbed a glass of water to hide his grin.

Despite the show, they had a pleasant breakfast. Derry felt the safety of this place like an impenetrable shield, and he knew Alisia would not find them here. The war wouldn't wait for long, but that worry could stay in the background for the length of one pleasant morning meal.

With the plates finally cleared away, they turned to the trouble at hand. After the calming effect of the night and the meal, the problem didn't seem as menacing and immediate. They could look at everything logically and discuss it without fearing that Alisia would destroy them all before they could act.

Roe proved an invaluable resource, filling in reports on his mother's usual daily activities, like the time of day she always insisted upon her solitude, and where she spent those hours. That would most likely be the time she cast her spells and renewed her powers.

"How could she do this and not draw anyone's attention, let alone not alerting the fae?" Derry finally asked.

"Tyleen possesses special magic," Kyrian reminded him. The older fae shrugged. "The castle is ancient and has held magic for centuries. That power hides what she does."

"Could she tap that power?" Milin asked.

"No human has before, but that doesn't rule out the possibility. She's learned to utilize other, unusual sources of power."

"Priests," Brother Milin said with a sudden show of anger in his face. "Do they choose to serve her, or are they under magical control? Has she bought their souls or only captured them?"

"Captured at least some," Shannon replied. "We watched, and they were not moving on their own on the curtain wall. Sleepwalking, really. My father said the priest assigned to watch over him appears confused quite often. I suspect he doesn't know what happens during those times he spends with the Queen."

"So, we can probably turn her captive priests against her, given the right tools to break her hold." Kyrian leaned forward, one arm on the table. Derry again noted how Kyrian differed from the other fae and wondered if Leanora was his Queen, too. He didn't ask. "If we get the priests free of her, it will deprive Alisia of some power. Anything we can do to weaken her is essential, even if it doesn't lead to her immediate defeat. We must also look at freeing the King from her hold and disarming her other magics before they become perpetuals, without the need of her notice to continue."

"Then we must strike at the only weakness we know, and soon. We must deprive Alisia of the priests," Milin stated with more force than usual. "I'm only uncertain how we can do it. I suspect ordering them away wouldn't work."

"No, it wouldn't," Derry replied with a shake of his head. "We would only alert her that we know what she's doing. We don't want to give her an edge before we're ready to take her on."

"Catching Alisia in the act of draining them would be the best hope," Kyrian said and grimaced at the words. "But probably the most dangerous as well. We would need to be very close to make certain she hasn't time to turn the magic against us."

"The only way to do that would be to enter Tyleen in disguise," Leanora added.

"As priests," Milin said, surprising them all. "It is important enough that I think I must take my side openly with you. Given the situation, with the King missing, there is good cause for me to go to Tyleen to talk to her and offer what help my temple can give. We will all go as priests, and I will go with you -- because if I am there, she will not look too closely at a group of lesser priests with me, right?"

"True," Roe agreed, though he didn't look any happier about the situation. "She is always drawn to the most powerful person present. You'll look like a tasty tidbit of more power."

Brother Milin nodded in agreement.

"How do we hide the fact that we're fae?" Derry asked, surprised that anyone would consider such a rash plan.

"It can be done, though the work is dangerous in its own right, especially for those of us who have never been human," Leanora explained. She gave a little shudder and Derry almost suggested the real fae remain outside -- but no. They would need the power to face her. "It will make us vulnerable. However, I don't see any other way that we could get close enough -- at least not without destroying all of Tyleen castle and most of the city as well. We have the power to do so, but we wouldn't. It would destroy us to kill so many innocents in order to destroy one enemy. She would not need to kill us since we would have done the work ourselves."

Kyrian bowed his head in agreement. "We must also find a way to reach the prisoners. Destroying the Queen and Egan will not help if we can't bring the King back to the throne to replace her. That's no reflection on you, Prince Roe --"

"I don't want to be King!" Outright panic came with the words, and he put both hands on the table, steadying himself before he dared speak again. "I won't let Egan have the throne without a fight, but I don't want it to come to me."

The others nodded at the honesty of the answer. Derry understood. If he had not already gone to the fae, Derry would be standing by Prince Roe as a possible alternative for the throne. The idea left him queasy, even now.

"Then the plan is simple." Leanora leaned back in her chair. "Now that we know she is the enemy and some of how she gains her power, we can move on her. We disguise ourselves and mute our powers before slipping inside her fortress. What we do afterward depends on what we find."

"That sounds a bit nebulous," Shannon said, looking worried.

"As it must be. We don't know what traps the Queen has set within the castle, except for the one we felt that is specifically for Derry."

Shannon nodded, though he didn't look mollified by the answer. Derry had misgivings of his own, but then he suspected they all did. No one wanted to confront Alisa, and especially not in the place where she felt secure.

However, the Queen wouldn't come to them unless she knew she would win the battle, and they dared not wait for that moment.

At least no one suggested they rush off to the castle. Leanora wanted to spend time with Roe discussing his mother.

Shannon, Brian, and Kyrian worked on maps and the layout of the castle. Brother Milin addressed the situation with his priests, preparing them for what needed to be done if he didn't return.

That left Derry with little to do but rest. They had doubtlessly planned everything that way, and he didn't complain. Derry would have time enough for his pride after they settled this damned business.

Derry wanted to believe it would be done.

He wanted to --

Sitting alone on a bench in the temple garden, he finally considered what he really wanted. Rabbits played at his feet, and birds settled on his hand; he had accepted their presence with only a smile.

They presented him with a clear picture of how much he had changed.

Derry had come home from prison a broken man wanting only his old life ... but he never found the mythical place he'd kept in his heart for so long. Alisia's evil had already changed much, although so subtly Derry hadn't noticed at first. No one had noticed, though he suspected the threads of darkness had already been clinging to the castle -- a small web, growing each day -- even before she sent him to the north.

Derry had changed and more so by the prison than by the fae. Now he couldn't go home, and that was all right. He wanted to go to the fae and be at peace, but he couldn't do that until he made his old home safe.

They would leave tonight at sundown, taking another wild ride back to Tyleen. Then his part in this madness would come to an end. Derry had no doubt that if they didn't defeat Alisia, he wouldn't walk away from the castle again. Derry did want to survive -- he could admit to that much these days, and the thought helped him prepare for the coming battle. Strangely, he wasn't afraid.

Not yet.

Chapter Thirty-Four

The group approached Tyleen late in the afternoon a full three days after leaving Kelkass Temple. They came in the disguise of priests, with the famous Brother Milin as their leader. He brought only two of his priests, and the rest of the party was made up of Roe, Derry, Shannon, Brian, Leanora, Kyrian, and three more fae who joined them as they neared the city.

Milin told the guards he had come to speak with the Queen about the menace of the fae. They might well be a menace to her right now with Leanora, Kyrian, Brian, Shannon, Derry, and the other fae standing in long robes, heads bowed beneath cowls. The fae were only temporarily bereft of their magic, but even for Derry, it felt odd.

Those powers rested in small mirrors, wrapped in black cloth so that no light could hit the surface. Each fae kept their own little mirror placed over their hearts and hidden from sight. Derry felt naked and dull without the fae senses he'd already learned to appreciate. He also had begun to suspect walking right up to Alisia in the throne room seemed the height of insanity and maybe hinted at suicidal tendencies among the fae.

Nonetheless, there he stood, Shannon a few steps away, while Brother Milin made his greetings to the Queen. The priest sounded kind and concerned about her safety and the welfare of the country. Derry dared to look at her from beneath the fall of his darker hair -- wonderful what a little nut dye could do. Derry watched her while Milin explained how the disappearance of the King and two princes, and the involvement of the fae, greatly bothered some members of the temple. Alisia nodded, and Derry could almost see the hunger in her eyes. Milin had been right to come along because he kept her attention from everyone else. She looked like a hungry wolf watching a meal about to be staked out for her pleasure.

When he admitted to exhaustion, she assigned the group to meager guest quarters a reasonable distance from the main areas of the palace. Even better. She might not want them around to guess at her activities, but they didn't want her to see them, either. They didn't trust their quarters to be safe from her magical prying, though, and carefully kept to forms, praying, and discussing what they had seen on the long journey.

They also fasted. That was the only way to safely avoid meat without alerting the Queen to what she harbored inside of her own lair. Milin had told her they were going follow temple observances because he believed the Gods were punishing them for not following the strict rules. Tonight, was a fasting night, though he would be happy to have breakfast with her after dawn the next day.

They dared not stay too long. The fae, including Derry, all looked exhausted. Shannon, who was still the least fae among them, looked uncomfortable and unsettled.

They had to wait through the long night.

At the hour before dawn, Derry and his companions

finally took their first steps against her. Roe had said the Queen always spent the hour after sunrise privately conferring with a priest -- never the same one in any ten days. With her occupied, they dared a little exploration, careful to avoid her few guards. They had to get closer to where she kept the King and Prince -- because she might kill them out of spite if she was about to fail, especially if she could implicate the fae.

They located the King and Prince in the little-used dungeons King Nevin left empty for years at a time, preferring either exile or execution for someone of real trouble. The King had never kept people locked away for long.

Milin led them in mass to the lower floor, chanting as they moved along. The guard at the top of the stairwell looked surprised and worried -- and then shocked when Kyrian slugged him.

"That was our last chance for finesse," Leanora mused.

She threw aside her cumbersome robe, and the others followed suit -- except, of course, for Milin and his three people. Derry's hand touched the outline of the mirror beneath his tunic and saw the others do the same. However, they dared not reveal themselves yet.

"Milin, please get your people to safety," Leanora said and lifted a hand when Milin started to speak. "No, don't argue. You know what's going on here, and this might yet become a human battle. Roe, you must lead me now. Derry and Shannon have other work."

Roe nodded and, at last, shed his own robe. Kyrian and Brian moved to go with Derry and Shannon while Roe prepared to take Leanora and the other fae down to the cells. If Derry and his people could take enough of the Queen's notice, Leanora's group should have a chance to free King Nevin and Prince Tevin.

Roe looked back at Derry and Shannon with the first appearance of genuine fear Derry had seen in the prince. "Be careful," he whispered. He looked from one to the other and took a deeper breath. "Be very careful when you face her."

"We're going to win," Derry said and even meant those words, which seemed to shock everyone. "Look how far we've come already, and she has no idea we're within her walls. Before this she had surprise and secrecy on her side. She can't use either of them against us again."

Roe gave a nod of agreement before Derry turned away. He and Shannon hurried through the labyrinth passages of the castles and took halls that were less likely to be traveled. Kyrian and Brian had trouble keeping up, and Derry could tell they suffered for the lack of powers. So did Derry, but an inner fire drove him as they drew closer to his real enemy -- to the enemy of everyone. As they reached the top of the stairs, Derry paused only long enough to move so that the others could see the door.

"No guards on the upper levels," Shannon noted. "She wouldn't trust them here."

"I never would want to be a human for long," Kyrian whispered. "They're so blind! They can't touch the world the way we can."

"Only a few more steps, and we can all be fae again," Shannon answered in a soft whisper. He pulled out his cloth-covered mirror. "That's her room. God and Goddess help us beyond this point."

Derry didn't want to take his companions beyond that door. He would rather have faced Alisa alone, but he would risk too much if he lost. The fae could be destroyed, and likely all Lynashin before she was done. Maybe the world would fall for all he knew. He didn't stop Shannon when he started forward. The others followed. They stopped beside the ancient oak door, embossed with the SanOsen coat of arms. Derry's fingers tightened on the mirror.

Not quite yet.

Derry pushed the door open.

They did surprise her. She started at the sound of the opening door, and the magic binding the priest to her fell away in a flash of a dozen small lights. The priest cried out in dismay and disgust as he scrambled away from the Queen. He had been kneeling with her bent over like some creature sucking the life out of him.

She screamed in rage.

Derry grabbed up his mirror and looked into his own eyes --

The surge of power came as a shock to his system, disorientating for a moment -- bad timing, he knew, while Alisa got her wits back. When he looked up, she had shoved aside the priest and threw herself from the chair, her hands lifting.

Derry leapt at her.

He had thought to distract Alisia, but he never considered that he'd actually hit her. They collided, her soft flesh yielding with a grunt of surprise, but her unfinished magic hitting him with a fiery surge that did more than just unsettle him this time. He fell like a rock, landing at her feet, and barely able to breathe.

"How did you get in here! Leave immediately!" she shouted, the order of a Queen, and she still obviously expected to be obeyed.

Instead, Kyrian stepped forward, and a blaze of blue fire shot from his hands. Alisia deflected it too quickly and laughed.

"Fools! Did you think avoiding the trap I set with Nevin and Tevin would save you?" She brushed aside another attack from Brian. Then she moved forward, kicking Derry and not gently, despite her bare feet. Vindictive woman. Petty.

Human.

Use humanness against her.

Derry suddenly understood what Wild One had tried to tell him. He had counted too much on fae powers and not enough on ingenuity. Derry didn't really know what the others were doing, though he heard a gasp of pain and feared it came from Shannon. He blocked that fear from his mind and concentrated on regaining control of his own body. Wished it very hard, though Derry knew using the power on himself was dangerous and difficult. Wasteful, perhaps, except Derry finally had some idea of what to do, and he couldn't act if he remained helpless at the Queen's feet. Derry was aware that the priest had made it to the door, that Brian said something and sent the man stumbling away. Good. Another who knew the truth.

Derry forced energy through his arms and moved -- and reached for her. His hand caught her leg, but it felt as though he had grasped fire.

Alisia screamed at Derry's touch, and power surged through her like another wave of fire coursing through him. She yanked herself free, stumbling back towards the bed, gasping and cursing in ways that were both unladylike and not very Queenly. Derry stumbled back to his feet, standing unsteadily before her. Shannon and Brian were both down. He hoped they lived and didn't dare allow even a hint of despair to touch him. Kyrian remained on his feet, looking determined, but worried. The fae had hit her with all the magic he could manage, and it hadn't slowed her down. Derry thought Alisia appeared as surprised by that as the fae looked worried.

Derry thought he might understand better, having captured a little of her power to use for himself. She was not aligned with life. The pure power Kyrian threw at her was what she destroyed for her own gain.

Derry needed to use her power against her.

"You were fools to try your puny strengths against me!" Alisia snarled as she turned to Derry and looked even less human. "I gave you no choice, did I, poor Derry? Either you would try to save Nevin and his useless, pretentious son, and die in my trap, or you come and face death more directly. Ah, no choice at all!"

Alisia lifted her hands and smiled. He wasn't going to get any more time, and he still didn't know what to do --

She began to whisper words, her hands moving as her eyes focused on him -- and then she shrieked for no reason that Derry could see she backed away, her eyes wide and her face pale --

"The others must be acting!" Kyrian warned, moving closer to Derry. "I guess we made a choice she never considered since the words' friends and cooperation' would mean nothing to her."

The statement enraged Alisa. She spun on Kyrian, and Derry knew she meant death for all of them now. They couldn't escape --

Derry threw himself at her again. As they went down, Derry realized he had made the right choice once again. He had pulled her down, and they rolled across the floor until he managed to pin her face against the rug --

Kyrian proved incapable of helping. When he caught a hand of her hair, he cried out in pain and jerked away. His fingers looked as though he had caught a handful of fire.

"Dark -- too dark and evil! I can't touch her. How can you bear it?"

"Still ... human enough." Derry gasped and pounded her head into the rug when she started to regain her strength. He thought Kyrian's touch had hurt her as well, but it wasn't something he wanted his friend to try again. "I need Shannon --"

"Yes!"

Kyrian leapt away so quickly that Derry knew Shannon must still be alive. The knowledge infused him with a new surge of power. He could hope that nothing had been lost yet --

A dozen heartbeats later, a shaking hand slipped over his own, and Shannon added his strength to Derry's. Alisia's sudden surge of fear and anger gave her strength, though. A flash of power tossed them both aside, burnt their hands, and scorched the carpet.

"Damn!" Shannon scrambled back to his feet and grabbed Derry by the arm. Derry glanced at the door and saw they had more trouble. Egan had come at a run. So did a few others of her allies.

Egan, Lord Cloisen, and Lady Jillian, two of the Palace Guards -- Derry thought he had lost the battle now that her allies had arrived. Then he realized that, except for Egan, the others stared at the Queen with shocked disbelief.

They hadn't known about the Queen's magic, and she was forming a ball of fire in her hands, ready to strike. She looked to the door and saw the new danger she faced with those witnesses and the news they could spread. Derry realized the implications in her rage as her hands lifted and she turned toward them --

"No!"

Derry threw himself between her and the people. Kyrian and Brian shouted in fear, and their magic surged around him. She had intended to kill seven -- or eight if Egan didn't move out of the way fast enough. This time the attack went far beyond pain or pure agony. The world didn't go black; it went red with fire. Every nerve blazed, and every sense became so acute that even touching the floor proved almost unbearable agony. Someone moved him -- gods, make him stop! And stop the people from yelling!

Derry understood that they needed to get him away from Alisia, but he didn't think he would survive it.

"God and Goddess, what did she do to him?" Lord

Cloisen demanded. Too loud, and the words felt like knives through his head, though it didn't hurt so much to move now.

"She tried to kill you," Shannon said, a hand on Derry's arm -- painful, but he wanted it even so.

"And he threw himself in front of that bolt of magic to save us," Cloisen said, his voice softer. "We saw. God and Goddess, what is she?"

"Witch," Brian whispered. He sounded shaky. "She's everything evil."

"You are fae," Lord Cloisen replied.

Derry felt a new wave of fear. He managed to sit up despite protests from Kyrian and Shannon. "Don't hurt Brian! Brian -- Kyrian -- go!"

"We won't hurt them," Lady Jillian promised. She pushed the hair back from her face and looked towards the door to the Queen's room. Derry knew they dared not leave Alisia there too long to recover, but he didn't know what more to do. "We may have been misled until now, but we're not blind Lord -- Prince Derry. The Queen used us. No more --"

"And you worry about her?" Egan said. "She always has been a stupid, blind cow."

Egan didn't look any different than he had a moment before, but now Derry could sense powers the prince had kept well hidden. The fire he brought to his fingers came effortlessly, and the smile on his fat face was anything but inane this time. "She has been useful, though. Everyone watches her. Mother thought she could hide the power she drained from the priests, but I knew what she did. I let her have the priests, you see. They were barely worth the time. I took the fae -- those two fae messengers were lovely while they lasted."

Egan's hand moved, and a whirlwind of fire engulfed one of the guards who had started to move. The man cried out briefly, and then there was nothing more than ash on the floor.

Egan smiled. "You don't know how good it is to finally let go. No more secrets, right cousin?"

Derry had stood. He felt Shannon's hand on his arm but paid no attention. Instead, he watched as Egan moved his hand again. The piggy little eyes were still the same, but now the power seemed to be bursting through the clothing. He'd hid it well.

Derry started to leap forward, but Egan waved his hand, and Derry slammed into the wall with enough force that he felt his elbow crack, though he had managed to bow his head away. His neck felt wrenched.

"I have so looked forward to meeting with you again, cousin," Egan said and smiled. His hand moved, and Derry felt his injured arm begin to twist -- but he didn't cry out. "So many years of dealing with you, everyone's favorite. You and Tevin and Roe. I'll be the one who wins this time."

Egan might not realize others had gone to free the King and Prince Heir. Derry was willing to keep him focused here --

The Queen stepped from her room, and she did not look at Egan with any love. She had thought she owned him, and the shock and rage in her face had turned her attention from them. Her hands trembled. She hadn't recovered, and if it had been only her, they might have won against her.

Derry didn't know what to do. He couldn't get close to Egan, who sent a wave of power against Shannon this time. Not to kill him; Egan wanted to play with them. He laughed when Shannon cried out, and Derry tried to move toward his friend.

Rage started to take Derry, but as he moved, Egan laughed and twisted Derry's injured arm again. The pain almost sent him back into unconsciousness.

Kyrian stepped forward. Egan's eyes brightened. Kyrian signaled Derry to be still, and the fae was so calm that it stilled Derry, and even Egan gave a frown of worry.

"I know what you are," Egan said, that same sneer he always wore still on his lips. He looked no better for having acquired the powers.

"I imagine so. However, you don't know what I can do." Kyrian lifted his hand and power swept out so quickly that it hit Egan before he could blink and sent him sprawling. Egan hit the floor with a yelp and a grunt like an enraged pig. It would have been amusing another time. "You cannot use fae powers against me, child. And as you took those powers from my friends, so I will take them from you."

"No!" Egan made it back to his knees and sent a wall of fire --

Kyrian brushed it aside, and for a moment, Derry thought Egan would be consumed. Egan gave a cry of fright as lace caught flame.

Alisia saved him. They should have moved against her, but no one had gotten past Egan yet, and he had looked like the real trouble. Now the Queen seemed to grab him up in an invisible cloak and dragged him across the floor, the fires dying.

"Damn!" Derry snarled.

Egan started to stand, and she caught his arm -- but it was not a motherly hold. Her other hand went to his forehead, and he made a sound of distress. Draining the power from him! Brian and Kyrian started towards her, but she growled words that sent them flying -- and a moment later, Egan collapsed, unmoving. Dead, Derry realized and looked back at the woman whose eyes blazed with power and anger.

Alisia had been found out. She could no longer rule through Egan, so she used him one last time for her own gain.

Derry had his back to the wall. The pain and backlash of her powers made him ill. He had trouble concentrating, and he was glad to see Kyrian and Brian on their feet. None of them moved quickly. Alisia took a step back to her doorway. Kyrian sent something against her -- a flash of light that she caught in her hand and laughed as it spread through her fingers.

"We can't use magic," Kyrian whispered. "She's made a transition; she can gain power from us."

"I noticed." Derry tried to gain some control over his own body. He didn't think he could move very far. How the hell could they stop her? They'd barely escaped with their lives so far.

Suddenly running seemed the wiser choice if they wanted to live. Derry felt -- something in the air --

Run!

"Down! Down to the main hall!" Derry ordered. He tried to move but fell back against the wall again. "Down where we have room and a little more time!"

Shannon caught hold and pulled Derry towards the stairs. Kyrian herded the others downward. No one questioned his decision, which wasn't as reassuring as he had hoped. Too late to change his mind. They were already halfway down the stairs, and he wasn't going to go up again.

The corridor outside the Queen's room erupted in a bright flame that melted stone where it touched. They probably couldn't have shielded everyone in time if they'd still been there. Good decision to move.

He had no idea what to do now.

Chapter Thirty-Five

The surviving guard moved ahead of them on the stairs, yelling orders to the few people below. Almost everyone had already run at the sight of the unnatural fire snaking its way down the stairs though it had sputtered and died before it reached the last steps. Derry didn't see even a servant within sight, and he wondered where the priest had gone.

Derry still had no clear idea of what to do. The rough trip down the three stairwells had sapped all his body's strength. His mind careened between need and agony until Kyrian did quick work of at least partly healing Derry's wounds.

"She wasted power on that last show," Kyrian offered quietly as they stopped in the room where Derry had been welcomed home. The benches, chairs, and tables were empty now, and Derry tried to imagine it with the king back at the High Table, music playing, and people laughing. That was his goal. "We gained a little time."

"What do we do?" Derry asked. He gasped as they settled him onto a chair. Shannon took hold of his shoulder, or he would have fallen.

"My powers will do nothing but strengthen her," Kyrian said with a shake of his head. "Alisia takes from life to feed the darkness within her. Fae powers can't stop her, only make her stronger."

"And the only powers we have are fae!" Shannon added as his fingers tightened, obviously worried. "We can't use them against her!"

Human.

"What would we do if we never went to the fae?" Derry asked.

"I don't know," Kyrian replied with a bemused look. "I've always been fae."

"Weapons," Brian asked, looking around the room.

"Weapons, yes! I need a dagger to go against her. Two to be safe," Derry said, looking around as well.

"Don't be a fool, Derry!" Shannon exclaimed. "You can't attack the Queen with only a dagger. You can barely move!"

"And besides, she must have some shield against human weapons," Kyrian added with a shake of his head. "I can't believe this woman would take a chance like that among her own. She knows she isn't loved."

"She does have one. I felt it when I had hold of her. Give me the daggers, because we don't have much time -- and she's going to come for me. At least give me a weapon, so I have a chance! Give me the daggers!"

One of the guards quickly obeyed. Lord Cloison, pale white and shaking, gave him the other weapon, though he looked uncertain about it.

"The rest of you go -- yes, you too, Shannon. Get back and form a second line of defense because I really don't think this plan has much chance."

"I'm staying," Shannon said with a shake of his head.

"No. Go! You are my weakness, Shannon, and she'll use you against me. Get back! All of you!"

Human power and fae persuasion sent everyone fleeing to the far side of the room. Shannon only went when Kyrian took hold of him. Derry took deep breaths while he watched the stairwell and waited. Calm. He called back what strength he could. He kept one dagger in his hand, and another inside his vest.

Alisia appeared on the long narrow staircase dressed in the guise of the Queen: red robe, golden crown, and jewels that sparkled everywhere. She came to dazzle them, and when she found only Derry, the woman growled in anger. Derry's decision to send the others away was another inspiration proved right. Anything that unsettled Alisa would help him.

Derry found himself clear-headed now. Although his body still ached, he could banish the knowledge of pain a little while longer.

"You've caused me considerable problems, Derry. Now there are so many others I'll have to kill and blame their deaths on you. People will revile your name before I'm done, and no fae will dare ever walk this land again!"

Alisia stopped hardly more than an arm's length away, and her hand lifted, light playing against her fingers and illuminating her face. Derry moved as quickly as he could as he shoved her backward with a force of his will and magic that came like a wind through the room. The others joined in that surge of magic, some with more than wind. The attack startled the Queen, but it wasn't enough to put her down. Derry hadn't expected it to, but he saw the rage grow in her face.

Derry threw himself out of the chair and to the floor. The chair splintered in her attack and sent slivers of wood everywhere. Derry felt a few hit him like little knives into his back and arm, but that wasn't any worse than the other injuries. He kept moving when part of the stone turned molten hot. Better. Alisia chased after him, thinking he tried to run away, afraid of her. The others threw their own attacks at her, drawing both her attention and making her waste more power against them. None of their attacks did more than brush against Alisia, and if she gained any magic from them, it was offset by the attacks she made in turn.

Each time the Queen used her magic, Derry tested out the feel of the shield around her. She had two spells; one blocked against the danger of solid weapons, and another worked against magic spells.

The spells were too specific and tried to stop one or the other. What about something that combined both at once? A shame all Derry had was two very normal daggers. He would have to improvise.

The others had come to help him, despite what he wanted, but that was all right. They distracted the Queen. Alisia had magic that was new to her still, and she was angry. It wasn't a good combination for her.

She turned towards Shannon -- and Derry leapt at her and slashed with the dagger, but the backlash nearly numbed his arm, and he dropped the weapon. Alisia laughed and turned her attention back to him again. Derry didn't have time to do what he needed --

And then new help arrived.

Alisia screamed in rage, and Derry looked up to see Nevin and Tevin entering the room at the far end with Roe and Leanora. A band of soldiers came with them, and more fae as well.

"No! I set a trap! No fae could get you free!"

"The fae only protected everyone from stray magic," Leanora said as she stepped forward. "Your fine son, Prince Roe, freed his father and brother. That's the problem with specific magic. It's too easy to circumvent."

And Leanora nodded to Derry. Maybe she knew what he intended. He pulled the second dagger and grabbed at every bit of magic he could and poured it into the blade. Alisia looked at him, frowning. He felt shaky with the loss of magic, but he forced himself up on uncooperative legs and leapt at her once more. Alisia looked annoyed as she waved a hand in dismissal.

The blade struck the fields with a flash of power before it penetrated and struck flesh with a glancing blow. Alisa froze in shock for one heartbeat and then screamed and hit back with more force -- pure magic, hardly directed at all. Derry grabbed all of it that he could and fed that magic into the blade as well. Then he drove the dagger toward her heart.

They tripped and went down, Derry landing atop of Alisia and shoving the dagger inward; it still felt like striking at a fire. Derry realized the other fae tried to shield him from the worst of her power, but the pain slipped over him -- and the screaming, screaming, howling wind --

"Derry! Stop using your power! Stop! She's gone!"

Shannon's voice finally called Derry back, and he found the red robe beneath him but not her body. The fae around him worked on healing wounds that should have killed him this time.

Only a robe. Blood.

"She -- escaped!" It hurt to speak. He wanted to rest, and there wouldn't be any. She would come for him again. She would destroy the land --

"No, Derry," Leanora whispered, her hand soft on his face, stilling him again. "She is gone. The power released in your battle consumed her body. Rest. Let us care for you."

Battle done.

Chapter Thirty-Six

Music played; a lovely tune that drifted through Derry's tangled thoughts and brought him peace. He slept better for the sound. There had been voices before, and questions he couldn't answer. The music soothed him. Far better than the words.

Then, sometime later, the lyre played a bright and beautiful tune while birds sang in harmony. Derry came awake to find himself resting in the soft grass, content to listen. The warm day lulled him back towards blissful sleep...

He remembered the battle at Tyleen.

Derry sat up, his heart pounding. His head ached, and that comforting sunlight of a moment before suddenly felt like daggers striking straight through this head. Derry's eyes blurred, and he gasped --

The music stopped, and a hand steadied him.

"Easy Derry," Shannon said. "Just rest for a while. I'll play more music."

Derry blinked and turned his head to look at Shannon. Changed -- very fae. He could sense it in the touch than in what he saw, though. Magic flowed through his friend, and Shannon had had time to get used to it.

Time.

"How long?" Derry whispered with a fluttering wave of his hand at the world around him.

"Seventeen days," Shannon answered as he caressed the lyre in his hand. He did not look bothered though the time startled Derry. "You gave us quite a scare, my friend. The fae kept you alive with magic, but even so, many feared that they'd never have a chance to thank you for what you did at the castle."

"Didn't matter." Finding even simple words seemed difficult as his mind danced between the battle and here. "She was ... my enemy first. What happened after we fought?"

"Are you certain you're up to hear the tale?" Shannon asked with a frown.

"Want to know. Please."

Shannon still frowned, but Derry sat up straighter and attempted to pull his wandering thoughts to here, wherever that might be. Grasslands. Near the forest. Shannon watched Derry carefully and finally smiled as Derry braced himself on one arm, hoping for the tale. The peace here soothed him. He couldn't feel any of the evil that had lurked in the world the last time he awoke.

"Your battle with Alisia ended the trouble, Derry. King Nevins's back in charge," Shannon said with a satisfied nod. "The nobles are appalled to learn that Queen Alisia dealt in dark magic and that she even used it against them. The priests have all condemned her. The common people are only relieved to have her gone, magic or not. If she and Egan had any true allies, besides the priest of Daria, they're silent now. The Daria priest fled, and the fae can't find him, so they think he's already left the country. Everyone is content enough with that answer."

"And the fae? How do the people of Lynashin feel about the fae after all of this madness?"

"We're keeping our distance as the King gets his people settled and accustomed to the idea that he's allied with the fae. So far, it hasn't seemed to matter much to them. Oh, and Roe has joined the fae -- and with his father's blessings. Roe rescued Nevin and Tevin since the fae would have been killed by Alisia's trap. The magic nearly killed him. The fae kept him alive for a second time, and that's why they didn't rush back up to help us. Roe didn't even have to say anything to his father about going to the fae. I saw how King Nevin watched Roe standing with Brian, and I think he understood very well what his son had done, and how much it had cost him. Nevin said he was free to go with them. It would have been harder for Roe to live in the castle after he had seen Alisia's evil firsthand while Nevin and Tevin remained in her trap -- asleep, mostly, though aware that things were not right."

"Roe has become fae?" Derry said, finally piecing together what Shannon said.

"Yes."

"Good. Roe never belonged in Tyleen." Derry stretched his legs and felt pain just below the knee. He reached for it with a grimace of dislike. "What about Egan?"

"Dead, we assume. Nothing in that hall survived Alisia's fire attack. Besides, he had likely already died at Alisia's touch -- though there was so much magic going on, there's no certainty. There was nothing but melted stone and ash afterward. Probably just as well, you know -- what would we do with him?"

Derry suddenly grinned. "We could have drained him of all his powers and sent him to The Isles. Queen Regent Olivia said I could turn to her in time of needs. She could doubtless have found some small island with a few sheep and chickens for Egan's companions. Maybe even a pig."

They both laughed. Birds sang. Two rabbits came out and watched with curiosity.

"I am glad to see you awake. Do you feel up to a trip to Tyleen? We're not far, and I have horses nearby."

"I thought the fae stayed clear of the place."

"King Nevin wants to see you as soon as you're well enough. To be honest, the man's worried sick about you. We're afraid he might act hastily towards others if he suspects them of complicity."

"You should have awakened me before now."

"We couldn't, and Leanora feared all the constant commotion at Tyleen made you worse. I've been out here with you for three days. I don't know if it helped you any, but I certainly feel better."

"Then let's go back," Derry said, though he liked being here in the wilds. Still too human, he supposed. "I want to see for myself that everything is all right. I want to go home to Tyleen and feel it this time."

Shannon nodded and picked up the lyre and a case.

"Beautiful instrument," Derry said, seeing it for the first time. The wood was inlaid with silver and gold, and jewels glittered in the sunlight. "I've never seen it before."

"A gift from Kyrian." Shannon smiled as his fingers brushed along the strings. The notes were pure and bright, and birds sang again at the sound. "He says he expects me to play at the Winter Solstice this year. Apparently, that's when the fae gather for a feast. I hope I'm up to the honor."

"You'll do well," Derry offered. The idea of Shannon performing again made the day feel better.

"Think you're ready to stand?"

"No, but let's try it anyway. Just don't expect me to walk."

"No, not at all," Shannon said and helped Derry to his feet. Derry found that he didn't feel as bad as expected. Muscles protested, and his leg ached, but neither felt overwhelming. In fact, after a couple deep breathes, he felt considerably better.

Shannon whistled, and two fae steeds appeared almost immediately. Derry recognized the one he had ridden to Kelkass.

"Maybe we should ride together," Shannon suggested looking Derry over. He brushed down some of Derry's hair -- a touch of magic that probably made him look more acceptable. "I don't think anyone who's been unconscious for a week should get up on a horse and ride off moments after he's awoken, magic or not."

"Yes, you're probably right. Falling off a horse now would be a bit anticlimactic after everything else we've gone through."

"And embarrassing," Shannon agreed. "The squirrels would laugh."

Derry grinned. He needed Shannon's help to get up on the horse, and gratefully leaned back as Shannon took the place behind. They rode away at a nice, sedate pace. Derry had never hoped they would both survive this madness. He had never expected to ride through Lynashin --

Free? Was he finally free of chains and duty?

The thought left him feeling oddly empty. Roe had already gone entirely to the fae. Shannon appeared closer to the fae than Derry, although he had been lingering at the edge of the fae world for months. He didn't want to go back to the world of humans with their dark cells and thoughtless cruelties --

Lost.

And he heard the bells.

In another moment, the fae gathered all around the horse, bright people in brighter colors, laughing and singing. Kyrian, Leanora, and Brian came close, Roe only a step behind.

"Ah, beloved!" Leanora greeted him. "How good to see

you well again!"

He blushed. Shannon laughed, knowing his reaction without even seeing it.

"We sensed that you were on the move," Kyrian explained. The usually taciturn fae looked ebullient as he put a hand on the horse's neck. "Since you are headed for Tyleen, perhaps we might keep you company?"

"You don't trust us to go among the humans?" Derry asked.

"I don't trust all of the humans," Kyrian admitted with a wave of his hand toward the distant city. "We don't know which ones might have been in league with the Queen. These are fanatics, Derry. Fanatics often continue to fight for a lost cause. We aren't going to lose either of you to them."

"So, you go to the castle with a guard," Roe said and smiled. Brian had followed close behind Roe and grinned with delight. Roe looked good, too -- though still far too thin.

"Or I travel with a few friends," Derry corrected. He seemed more at ease than his companions. They still expected trouble, and Derry felt only relief that they'd won the battle -- that final confrontation had taken place days in the past. Maybe other things had happened, and they had reason to be worried still.

They hadn't far to go. Derry and Shannon rode the horse while the other fae walked along beside them. The fae bells rang bright and clear, all down the hillside and even though the town. People watched in shock. No one moved to stop them or even make a sound of protest.

The unusual group made their way up the High King's Road and to the Gate of Tyleen castle, which opened for them without any disagreement. That might have been Killough's work since the man gave a shout of greeting from the wall, and Derry waved back. It had been the first amiable voice he'd heard since they came into the area of the humans. As they rode forward, Derry studied the soldiers on the walls, seeing too many frowning still.

Ah, but there were friendly faces as well. And they more than compensated for the others. Tevin raced down the stairs from the castle entrance and came running all the way to the horse. Derry heard sounds of surprise and dismay from the humans, but the crown prince didn't slow.

"God and Goddess Derry! You can't imagine how much we worried about you! Here, let me help you down. Father's on his way. He was just starting a council meeting."

"I didn't mean to interrupt the work."

"Don't worry. You know it's not his favorite pastime anyway." Tevin caught hold of his arm as he slid down from the horse. Servants and guards had finally caught up with the Prince Heir and only kept back a little from the fae. Some even smiled at Roe, so they must have gotten somewhat used to the idea of the fae being around. "We've worried about you for days."

"Better," Derry said though he did feel unsteady. Tevin and Shannon helped him walk past the humans. There was no real problem, except -- except that Derry suddenly realized he wasn't one of them. It didn't matter what they thought since this time he only visited here, and when he was done, he would be a wild boy again.

The realization cheered him so much that the fae bells came to him, a sound of both silver and gold, and bright as the day.

"Finally!" Leanora said behind him. He turned to look at her, delighted with the other fae bells that sang around them, mingling into a tune that com. "You finally made your choice. I admit this seems a strange time to accept the fae while you stand among the people you love and in the place you adore."

"I do love these people and this place," Derry admitted as he looked around. "But I was always wild, my love."

She stopped, wide-eyed, her face growing pink as she glanced at the humans.

Derry laughed. So did all the other fae, though the humans still looked worried. For Derry, this was another sign of change; he had accepted more than just becoming fae.

"Ah, you, Shannon, and Roe shall surely liven up our poor dull world," Kyrian said with an exaggerated sigh of boredom. "Perhaps we could entice a few more of your nobility over. That would certainly keep us busy."

"Ha!" King Nevin laughed as he entered the courtyard, rushing to the group. "You'll have your hands full with these three ruffians!"

"True enough," Kyrian agreed. He even gave this human King a very proper bow. "Look at all the trouble they've caused us already! A few short months in their company, and we're already cavorting with humans!"

King Nevin laughed loudly, and a few of the humans grinned, beginning to appreciate Kyrian's humor. Derry suspected there was, indeed, going to be a change in their world. He wanted to bring the fae and the humans closer together to make a better world in Lynashin. He wondered if he was up to the job. They could make a paradise of this land if both humans and fae could work together. Derry had proven it possible, and he thought, despite some of the worried looks they drew. He might yet win many of these people over.

Derry could try. Nothing better to do now that Alisia was gone --

And he suddenly heard her howl of anger -- Alisia, as clear as if she stood beside him, while a breeze blew hard through the courtyard. He looked around with a start, but the others only heard the wind. At least the humans, but the fae --

"Derry," Leonora whispered and took his arm. "Don't upset the humans."

"Not dead?" he said very softly. He desperately needed to know.

"Gone from this realm. Alisia's body was destroyed, and the magic she used, and you turned back on her, came from some other place. We sent that magic back, and it dragged some aspect of her with it. We don't think she can come back, but we don't know what has happened. We're working on it."

Kyrian and Shannon had entertained the crowd, covering their little discussion. Perhaps the people only saw Derry turn pale, and thought he needed her help. He and Leanora moved up the steps and into the castle, the fae falling in around them in a wall of protection.

The wind blew again, brushing through the building and bringing a chill with it.

"What do we do?" Derry asked.

"We'll watch. The Queen has been exiled to another place, and she can't reach us from there, except to howl in the wind."

"Exiled? Maybe that's appropriate after the hell she put me through. The fae can hear her?"

"Yes, when her voice rides the wind because it is pure magic. That's the best she can do. Now come, beloved. Let us visit with your friends for a while. And afterward, when the moon is high and the stars bright, I shall take you and Shannon home with me. We shall go to the wild places, and we'll have peace there."

Derry looked forward to that time, and however long the peace lasted.

Alisia did not intrude into their night again.

THE END

ABOUT THE AUTHOR:

Hello!

I am an eclectic and prolific author whose has published in several genres, including Young Adult Mystery, Urban Fantasy, Epic Fantasy, Science Fiction and works on the art of writing. While I started on the outer edges of traditional publication with sales to small press and magazines publishers, I have since moved most of my work to the Indie world and I am madly in love with the new world of publishing and the direct contact with readers.

I live in Nebraska with my husband, my cats, and a small but entirely useless dog.

Connect with Zette:

Web Site: http://lazette.net
Facebook: http://www.facebook.com/lazette.gifford
Joyously Prolific Blog: http://zette.blogspot.com/
Twitter: http://twitter.com/lazetteg

FIND WORKS BY

LAZETTE GIFFORD

ON

SMASHWORDS

BARNES & NOBLE

AMAZON

AMAZONKINDLE

LAZETTE.NET

www.ingramcontent.com/pod-product-compliance
Lightning Source LLC
Chambersburg PA
CBHW070901260626
47162CB00007B/2525